Y0-DKL-607

The Shooter

The Shooter

GREGORY G. VANHEE

Richardson, Steirman and Black
NEW YORK

Dedication

I will never be able to answer all the questions my children will ask regarding this book. But I would like to dedicate it to them, with all my love.

Kelly Leanne Vanhee	August 20, 1958–August 30, 1974
Shannon Marie Vanhee	October, 1959–
Erin Elizabeth Vanhee	September, 1961–
Wolf Gregory Vanhee	January, 1970–
Jason Eric Vanhee	August, 1971–
Damon Alexander Vanhee	August, 1981–
Mariah Skye Vanhee	February, 1988–

And to Jimmy Trask, one of The Few Good Men.

Gregory Vanhee
Seattle, Washington

The Shooter

GREGORY G. VANHEE

THE THREE CIA AGENTS crouched on the dusty ridge in North Korea. Two of them had been at the observation post for over two months. The third, a hard-bitten, taciturn Section Chief named Tinker, had been secretly helicoptered there during that June morning in 1954. He had come to see the man pass by on the twisting road across the rocky canyon below them. The man traveled that road every day, regular as the tick of a clock.

"It looks like you were right, Evans. How many days did you watch him?"

"Sixty-two. The Soundman has him on timed film for the past thirty-four days, just for confirmation. There are no variations. He visits his commanders, checks the troops and returns to his headquarters. And a hell of a lot of high brass return the favor. Busy road, both ways. It's getting hairy, I'll tell you. It's beginning to get harder to get close to him. More patrols."

"Bob?" Tinker motioned to the Soundman.

"Yeah, it's getting tougher. But I have miles of film on the guy. Him and his bogus Packard. You'd think they could build a car without copying it."

"The Communist system is a bogus system," Tinker said. "Ultimately, it will fail. We are going to assist in that process. The Agency says we kill him, before he rallies the troops and storms back across the 38th Parallel. He's planning it, and we must stop him."

Evans and Bob the Soundman looked at Tinker. Evans spoke first. "Those are orders? We have to go ahead and terminate this guy?"

"Of course we do, or I wouldn't have said so. The Director got it straight from the President. He explained the problem to me. This guy wants to restart the Korean War. He's got some big friends. They're listening to what he has to say. Our mission is to shut him up. This particular North Korean General needs to die. That is our mission, and we will carry it out."

"When?" Evans asked.

"No later than February first. We need more film, more details."

"Fine, Tinker," Bob the Soundman said. "Then what?"

"We assassinate him."

"Okay," Evans said, staring through the shimmering heat at Tinker. "Who does it?"

"I've decided we get our shooter from the Marine Corps. He shoots the General, and we send him back to regular duty, with our thanks."

"How do we find him?"

"No problem. We go to the Corps, spell it out, ask for help. In total secrecy, of course. Leave it to me. You just gather all the intelligence you can on this General in the bogus Packard. I'll locate the shooter."

"What if you don't?"

"I'll find him. He's around somewhere, waiting to give his all for his country. With good planning, the General is as good as dead. The Marine shooter will get him. I'm sure of it. If he doesn't survive the mission for some reason, well, those things happen. I'm the Section Chief on this. You leave it to me, like I said. Now, let's get out of here."

Evans and Bob the Soundman had a lot of questions. They didn't ask any of them.

Back in the United States, Daniel Gregory Wood entered the Marine Corps Recruit Depot at San Diego, California, for his first day at boot camp. He tried hard not to stare at the United States Marine Corps. The Marine Corps, in this instance, at least, was personified by three Drill Instructors, the stuff of John Wayne movies seen when he was younger. He now blamed those movies for his being at the Marine Corps Recruit Depot, San Diego, California, in the first place. Goddamn John Wayne.

Whether or not the Marine Corps was staring back at him, he could not be sure. Two of the three D.I.'s were wearing reflective aviator-type glasses. They could see out, he presumed, but he could not see in. The third, however, wore no glasses at all, in spite of the shattering California sun that wavered, bounced and slammed across the huge parade ground where the bus from the airport had unceremoniously deposited them. *His* eyes you could see, in spite of a salty-looking fatigue cap that nearly covered them. Incredible blue eyes. No warmth. Just that hard, almost nonblinking stare, like looking at eyes cut straight out of a damn Milk of Magnesia bottle. He was only about five feet eight inches tall and very slender. He was also the most terrifying human being Danny had ever seen. Starched, almost white fatigues, creased perfectly down the trouser leg, the arms, even the pockets. A buck Sergeant, ribbons four rows deep, battle stars all over them.

"Attenshunn!" said the Corporal with no eyes at the extreme left of the loosely grouped young men. They snapped to. Or rather, attempted to stand straight.

"Form four ranks!" the Corporal said. Or did he? Who the hell knew? "Goddamn you fucking people, form four ranks." Jesus, thought Danny, that whole command was one fucking word. "Now," bellowed the Corporal. That, by God, was a word.

3

"There are eighty-one of you. Can't you form four equal lines out of that?" The second no-eyes could talk in sentences but, as far as Danny could tell, the man sure couldn't divide eighty-one men into four equal ranks. As luck would have it, all bad, they almost did. Four ranks of twenty scared young boots formed a nice, tidy eighty-man platoon. Unfortunately, Danny was number eighty-one.

The parade ground was a full mile square, and the nearest place to run was at least a mile away. Without seeming to have moved, the Sergeant with the blue Milk of Magnesia eyes was standing directly in front of him, his face only inches away. Danny stood at what he thought must be attention, looking completely ridiculous in the blue suit his mother had insisted he wear, so he wouldn't look like a "ruffian." Oh, Jesus. The blue eyes were alive now.

"Are you some fucking kind of individualist, boot?" The voice was low, silky, but Danny was sure they could hear it in Chicago.

"No," answered Danny.

"No, what?" The same silky, soft voice.

"No, I'm not an individualist."

The smile vanished, replaced by a roar. "Sir!"

"No, Sir."

"And you ain't no 'I' either. When you people address me, or anything else that walks in this uniform, you call it 'Sir.' The correct way to answer my question is as follows:" Turning his wrath on all the recruits, the Sergeant said, "Sir, no Sir, Private..." Turning back to Danny, he asked, "What's your name?"

Danny did not hesitate. "Sir, Private Danny Wood, Sir."

A brief look of mild surprise, quickly suppressed, flashed across the Sergeant's face. "Private Danny Wood is not an individual, Sir. You fucking people got that?"

"Yes, Sir," came back the thunderous reply.

"I fucking doubt it." The silky voice again. "Wood, form on the front rank."

"Sir, yes, Sir." said Danny. God bless his weekends of drill in

4

the reserves at Sand Point in Seattle. Again, the mild look of surprise in the Sergeant's eyes. Danny took his place. The blue-eyed Sergeant strode quickly to the front of the now thoroughly cowed young men.

"I'll make this brief. You people think you're in the Marines. Well, you're not. You're not even human. You are boots. *Nothing* is lower than a boot. When you get out of this camp, then and only then, will you cease to be boots. It will be my extreme pleasure to have to teach you people to be Marines, although looking at you I would guess that to be an impossibility. But you'll do it, or you'll wish you were dead.

"I understand all you people are from Seattle. My ex-wife is from Seattle. As a matter of fact, she fucked Seattle. Every man in it. I don't like Seattle. I don't like you. As a matter of fact, I will personally strangle the first one of you that fucks up my platoon, of which you miserable excuses for manhood happen to be. The U. S. Marine Corps says you have to be fed. In your case, I can't see why. But, I follow orders. Corporal, take these people to chow. I'll see them later." With that, he spun on his heels, and strode away.

The two no-eyes formed on either side of the Recruit Platoon. One of the Corporals said, clearly, "You people heard what the Drill Instructor said. We gotta feed you. Foraaard march!" It sounded very much like "Fard lurch." Daniel Wood and his eighty fellow victims did exactly that.

The march to the mess hall, if you could call it that (what they served as food was certainly a mess, getting to it was most certainly not marching), took all of five minutes. At a dead run. One no-eyed Corporal, quickly realizing none of his charges knew their left foot from their right, dispensed with his unintelligible attempts at calling cadence, and simply screamed, "Run, you miserable assholes, run." They ran.

The same yellowish buildings flashed by, though, at a very fast run few of the young men noticed. They simply went "Left," or "Right," or "That way, goddamnit," which Danny thought was one hell of a precise command. So was "Stop, you

5

fucking idiots!" They stopped, but not without the rear ranks piling up and into the men in front.

Twenty yards or so ahead of them, in the center of a flat space of dirt that had not seen a blade of grass since the Indians had been driven out of California, stood a lone, one-story yellow building, number 1050. That was it. Food, chow or whatever lurked in that building, under Marine Corps Regulations, was called 1050. Danny Wood was famished, but he didn't know if he wanted a plate of 1050 or not.

The two no-eyed Corporals called them to attention. At least, it sounded like attention. Sweat was streaming down Danny's face. His suit clung to him, wilted and dirty. The two Corporals had run right along with the platoon, but their green fatigues still looked sharp, creased, not a tiny drop of sweat anywhere. Against their highly polished boots, not a whisper of dust showed. Maybe Marines didn't sweat. Come to think of it, John Wayne never did.

"Listen up, people. You will file in this building and chow down. You will file down the chow line, and take the tables at the rear of the building. Before you eat, you will remain standing in place at those tables until ordered to sit. You will have thirty minutes. You will not talk. You will not smoke in the mess hall. When you have finished, you will clean off the trays, stack them near the rear door and re-form behind this building. Do you people get that?"

"Sir, yes, Sir." The response was immediate.

"Wood, lead them in." Without hesitation, Danny started toward 1050. "Wood!"

Danny stopped cold. "Sir, yes, Sir." He had yet to see the Corporal's eyes, but he felt them boring into his back. The rest of the platoon stood frozen, silent.

"Goddamn you people, when you're given a fucking order, acknowledge it."

"Sir, yes, Sir," said Danny.

"Awright. Take 'em in, Wood."

"Sir, yes, Sir," answered Danny. This time, the Corporal was

6

silent, and Danny strode in what he hoped was the Marine Corps way to enter the chow hall/mess hall 1050.

The first thing Danny Wood saw as he approached the cafeteria-like service line was a huge sign, in Marine Corps crimson with Marine Corps gold lettering. It was at least twenty feet long and ten feet high. The message was simple: "Take what you want, but eat all you take." The words *eat all you take* were underlined. To Danny Wood, the sign was ominous.

The solution was simple. Quickly scanning what was available, he made his choice. It was not yet 9:00 A.M., so breakfast fare was it. In one huge tray, steaming hot, he saw gravy with occasional glimpses of red in it. Gravy and chipped beef. He'd had it before.

Next to it, scrambled eggs. Hot and steamy. Good. How could you go wrong on scrambled eggs? He thrust his tray forward. The mess-duty boot, almost bald, as were all the boots on mess duty, had hair only about one-fourth inch high, and only on the top of his head. The side of his head was clipped as short as could be done without a razor. One spoon of scrambled eggs landed thunk on his tray. Danny did not move. Thunk. Thunk. Three large scoops of scrambled eggs. Moving on, Danny took three pints of milk, one toast and one large, steel cup of boiling coffee. At the end of the line he picked up four small packets of sugar and marched with military precision to the rear table, setting his tray down and standing quietly at attention, a bit smug. How are you gonna go wrong with half a dozen eggs, a piece of toast, three pints of milk and coffee? Christ, by the time he got out of boot, they'd be on their knees to send him to officers' school, or pilot school, at least.

Finally, the last man in the platoon stood over his tray. They remained standing, timed perfectly for the steam to stop rising from Danny's tray. Cold food does not steam. It just lies there.

"Sit." The command came from somewhere behind them. Ravenous, the platoon obeyed this command at once, and as one. Quickly, Danny reached for his fork. After all, thirty min-

7

utes wasn't very long. Reaching for a fork is one thing, reaching for a fork, knife and spoon he had neglected to get was another. Panic hit him.

The two Drill Instructors, four tables in front of him, were slowly, methodically walking behind the men as they ate, saying nothing. Danny quickly opened a pint of milk and drank it straight down. Surprisingly, it was ice cold and delicious. Opening all four packets of sugar, he dumped them into the bowl-shaped steel cup of coffee, which was no longer steaming. Without thinking, he plunged a dusty finger into the coffee, stirring vigorously.

Jerking his finger out, he looked on helplessly as the D.I. pair moved so close he was staring directly at the bleached web belt of No-eyes, inspecting the table right in front of Danny. The man on his left bumped Danny's knee once, hard, then again, very hard. The man, about twenty, looked straight ahead, eating with his left hand. His right hand was under the table. He turned his face toward Danny. A Mexican, his olive skin set off fierce brown eyes and the most dazzling set of teeth Danny had ever seen. Looking straight into Danny's stricken face, he smiled, a slow, bright smile that started in the center of his face and traveled the full width and then up into his eyes. Banging Danny's knee once again, he winked, an obscene "fuck the Marine Corps" wink. Then, as if nothing at all had happened, he withdrew his right hand from under the table, placed a full set of silverware on Danny's tray, switched his fork from his left hand back to his right and resumed eating.

The eggs were powdered, and they were awful. Alternating sips of milk with powdered eggs, Danny thought about the Mexican youth sitting next to him. Directly behind Danny in line, he had obviously noticed that Danny had walked right by the silverware and to the trays. Danny could only guess where he had hidden the extra set. He finished quickly, rushing to leave with his new-found friend. Their verbal exchange was brief, neither young man seeming to look at the other as they slowly walked the fifty yards to where the platoon would again form. Danny whispered, "Thanks, man, saved my ass."

"It was nuthin', you miserable fuckin' idiot." On such things lifetime friendships are formed. When the platoon re-formed, Sonny Flores, Mexican sleight-of-hand artist, lined up right next to Daniel Wood.

No-eyes stood alone in front of the platoon, his companion apparently lingering over his coffee. "Smoking lamp is lit. When you finish your butts, field-strip 'em. Roll the paper in a ball and throw it away. Don't you people *ever* throw a cigarette away unless you strip that butt into shredded tobacco and a ball of paper that I couldn't find if it was lying like a virgin on black silk sheets. Rest. You got ten minutes."

Danny Wood, tall and slender, turned to Sonny Flores, short and stocky, who even in blue jeans and a T-shirt already *looked* like a Marine. Quietly, almost shyly, they shared two cigarettes. They field-stripped the butts. Grinning, the two young men hurled the tiny white paper balls into the southern California wind.

It was now 3:30 P.M., and they had stood at attention, alone in the exact center of the huge parade ground for over three hours, still in civilian clothes. After chow, the two Corporals had simply run them the two miles to the parade ground, lined them up neatly, called them to attention, or at least what looked like attention, and then they had just walked away. It had been a very weird thing. All around them, platoons of boots marched, some raggedly, out of step, their uniforms looking ill-fitting and sloppy. Occasionally two or three platoons would march by, briskly swinging their arms, their shining combat boots glistening in the hot sun, thudding hard and confidently into the hot, blacktop surface of the huge drill area. They didn't know it, but some of the fifty or more platoons drilling had been in camp for less than a week, and some would be out in less than a week. Whatever, the differences between each pla-toon were astonishing. Later, Danny would see those differ-ences in and about himself. But not now.

9

* * *

The boots gathered around the Corporal on the second floor of the receiving barracks. "Listen up, people," said No-eyes, "this is a bunk, not a bed. The Marine Corps bunk is made up of one mattress, one mattress cover, one sheet, one blanket, one pillow and one pillow cover. That's it. Now I'm gonna show you people how to make up this bunk. I'm gonna show you once, and you had better watch carefully, because any asshole who doesn't do it the Marine Corps way will make it over and over until he does."

Slowly, the Corporal first fitted the rough mattress cover over the thin mattress. Danny watched carefully as the sheet went on, tight hospital corners in the rear. Then the blanket, also tight hospital corners. The sheet was folded back exactly six inches. The pillow was then covered by the blanket. Then, the blanket was tightly packed under the mattress. The Corporal took a quarter from his pocket, flipped it in the air and smiled. On hitting the green Marine Corps blanket, it had bounced a full three inches into the air. "All right, people, pick a rack. When every rack is made, we go to chow, come back here, shower and hit the rack. Make 'em right, or sleep on the fuckin' deck."

Eighty men immediately scrambled to the nearest empty bunk. Sonny Flores did not move, but stood by the neatly made-up bunk. No-eyes said nothing, but viciously tore the bunk apart, hurling the mattress thirty feet down the row. "Go get it, fuckhead." Sonny got it.

Danny started on his bunk, right next to Sonny. Surprisingly, the room, for all the activity, was strangely quiet. An outsider peering through the windows would have thought he was looking at inmates in a prison.

In fifteen minutes, the job was done. The Corporal, far down the squad bay, started his inspection. At exactly the same time, bedding started to fly through the air, the quarter dancing up, down, up, down, as bed after bed was torn up. Finally, he got to the last bed, Danny's. Up went the quarter. Down went the quarter. Up went the quarter, a full two-inch bounce. No-eyes tensed, smiled and tore Danny's bunk to pieces. "Again, you assholes."

Each time now, a few bunks remained intact. Nine times Danny watched the quarter. Up. Down. Bounce. Rip. On the tenth time, Danny Wood's bunk was the last one to be inspected again. No bunk had been made better, yet none had been torn apart more. Up went the quarter. Down went the quarter. Thunk. No bounce. It lay on his bunk, accusingly. Tails. That figured.

"Fine, assholes. Just fine. You now know how the Marine Corps makes up bunks. Fall out downstairs, on the double. We are going to chow." Slowly, the Corporal picked up his quarter, which did *not* bounce on Danny's bunk. Slipping it in his pocket, No-eyes slowly took off his glasses. He did, in fact, have eyes. Blue. Carefully, he wiped the glasses with a spotless handkerchief, a slight smile on his face. "You gonna eat, sport?"

"Sir, yes, Sir."

"Then move it." Danny sprinted down the stairs, two at a time. Blue-eyes walked down slowly, flicking a tiny piece of dust off his boot. When he came out, he was once again No-eyes.

"All right, people. Straighten it out, and I'll take you to chow." They did. And he did. "Fard lurch." As the hot, weary young men marched off, Danny Wood smiled. What the Corporal said didn't *sound* like "Fard lurch." That's exactly what he *did* say. For some reason, Danny was no longer tired.

Danny Wood had slept that first night in boot camp as if drugged. Then, suddenly the overhead lights went on, all of them. Bright, glaring eyes stared down at the sleeping platoon, unblinking, unemotional, but somehow threatening. Danny's eyes snapped open. Quickly, he glanced at his watch. 3:45 A.M. A.M.? Jesus.

"All right, assholes, hit the fuckin' deck. Now." A steady stream of curses seemed to bounce off the walls, as Danny's body sprung up and out of his bunk. He was in bare feet, jockey shorts and T-shirt, his feet cold, yet he was sweating. No-eyes shouted order after order. How could anyone get them all? Finally, Danny's mind sorted them down to the basics. They had better get their miserable idiot assholes dressed and washed and down the stairs and into formation on the street in seven miserable fucking minutes. Basically, that was it. Danny and the others made it in six minutes, clutching their civilian gear, half-dressed, half-washed, half-assed, and scared shitless.

"Did you people make up your rack?" No-eyes didn't wait for an answer. "Get it done, you idiots." He had a voice like a 105mm cannon. The platoon scrambled back up the stairs, and Danny found himself alone. It was pitch dark, but the mirrored glasses reflected the lights pouring from the barracks. "Made yours up, huh, sport?" No-eyes' voice was quiet.

"Sir, yes, Sir," Danny answered.

No-eyes said nothing, just walked slowly back to the stairway as the platoon thundered back down the stairs in twos and threes. "Move, goddamnit!"

They were hot and flushed, breathing hard, as they formed ranks on Danny. Fear sure heats you up. Had they known it was forty-four degrees that early June morning, they might have been cold. Fifty degrees warmer that afternoon, they would be hot and not notice that, either. A scared boot's temperature goes neither up nor down. Cold mornings, hot days, no matter. Sweat. That's what Marine boots do best.

No-eyes, joined now by the other Corporal, called them to attention, then they both turned away and went up the stairs to the squad room. Danny wondered why they called a place a whole platoon slept in a squad room or squad bay. But repeatedly last night, No-eyes had referred to it that way. So, down to the last man in the platoon, their living quarters became the "squad bay." As soon as they got used to squad bay, No-eyes would change it to something else, accusing them of being "miserable fucking idiots," which, of course, they were.

The two Corporals came back. No-eyes said, "Still can't make up a decent rack." He did not yell. Just a simple statement of fact. "Stand at ease. Smoking lamp is lit."

The two Corporals lit up themselves and strolled around behind the platoon. No one talked. They had been told the difference between "at ease" and "rest." You relaxed in place "at ease," legs slightly parted. You did not talk. "Rest" allowed more freedom of movement, and talking was allowed. Quietly, the platoon smoked, and Danny discovered something. Smoking was never better than when you were *allowed* to smoke. It was as if, somehow, they were being rewarded. It was really a *good* cigarette. Danny watched the firefly glows of the platoon's smoking wink out one by one. Even in the dark, he knew each cigarette, when finished, was being carefully field-stripped. Nobody would find a trace of one when the sun came up.

"P'toon . . . ten . . . hut." The voice did not boom. It snapped and cracked like a whip. "Left hace." The platoon clumsily turned left. "Forhard . . . huh!" Not words, really, but somehow better than words.

Danny, leading the platoon, stepped out briskly. Behind him, the sound of 160 feet hitting the ground at different times jarred his ears. "Get in step," cracked the whip voice. Slowly, the voice began to count a left, right, left, right cadence. "I want to hear just one heel. Dig 'em in." The voice went on, cracking, sharp, constant. There could be no doubt. Sergeant W. R. Spradlin had them.

The two Corporals marched on either side of the platoon, silent. Sergeant Spradlin, sometimes walking backwards, slowing down, kept his cadence steady and sharp, even while moving quickly from the rear of the platoon back to the front. The footfall was still ragged, but better. "Column lef . . . Huh!" The whip cracked. Danny Wood pivoted precisely on "Huh," a sharp, exact left turn. Thank God for those six months of weekly reserve meetings. He alone in the platoon knew exactly when and how to execute a drill command. The Sergeant's voice was steady, still cracking out that crisp, precise cadence, switching from left, right, left, right to one, two, three, four, the one and three coming on the left foot, the two and four on the right. Danny slowed, marking time until the four ranks behind him were in line through the turn, then resumed his full pace. To his surprise, the Sergeant was now marching right alongside him, in perfect step, still barking out the rhythmic cadence. Danny marched straight ahead, but could feel the heat of the D.I.'s stare. He kept his eyes straight, and his back straighter. He also prayed the Sergeant would not hear his knees knock or his heart pound, because by God, Danny Wood could hear both.

They were approaching a huge, corrugated steel warehouse. As they drew abreast, the Sergeant snapped "Toon...Halt!" Danny slammed to a rigid stop. Behind him, rank after rank piled into each other, knocking Danny forward. "Straighten those ranks!" Quickly, surprisingly, the platoon did exactly that. "Look at you. You look like a fucking freeway accident. Put your right hand straight out 'til you touch the man's back in front of you. Dress it up." The commands now were full of sarcasm.

Finally, the platoon had satisfactorily lined up. Sergeant Spradlin moved to the platoon's right side. "P'toon right... Face!" Danny snapped to his right, took four steps forward and slammed to a halt. On the march, he had been on the left front. Now, he knew, after the command, "Right face," to step to the right front. Again, he felt the heat of the stare. The Sergeant walked slowly over to Danny. "Where did you learn that?"

"Sir, in the Marine Corps Reserve, Sir."

"Did you now. Well, this is not the Marine Corps Reserve. I give the orders. You move then and only then, got it?"

"Sir, yes, Sir."

"Good. What is your name?"

"Sir, Private Daniel Wood, Sir."

"Private Daniel Wood. All right, Danny. Do you like me?"

"Sir, yes, Sir."

"You're a liar, Wood. You hate me, right?"

Now, how the hell do you answer that? "Sir, no, Sir."

The soft voice now turned whip-like once again. "Goddamn you, Wood, I've got feelings, too. And I don't want you to fucking like me. Get down and give me fifty pushups and count 'em, dammit, out loud."

14

"Sir, yes, Sir!" And he did. Fifty. Out loud. The Sergeant was right. He hated him.

It was after the fifty pushups that Danny Wood learned about the alphabet. As the San Diego night slowly turned to early dawn, Sergeant Spradlin informed them the building they stood by would transform them from civilians to boots through the simple process of entering door number one and exiting door number two. Reading from a clipboard, he began, "Adams, Allen, Anders, Bradly, Cook . . ."

The alphabet. Oh, God, Danny thought, I'm gonna be last for the good stuff and last to the bad.

"Geller, Herbert, Herrisen . . ."

"Tupper, Turner . . ." Why didn't his mom marry Benny Angelini?

"Wood." Then again . . . "Wood! Goddamnit, follow the last man."

"Sir, yes, Sir." As Danny followed Fred Williams into the large doorway, he glanced behind him. The last man. No X. No Y. No Z.

Inside, Danny saw an eighty-man line, arms outstretched, rapidly disappearing under trousers, blouses (why the Marines called shirts blouses totally escaped him), jackets, socks, underwear. They looked to Danny like eighty individual Goodwill collection stations with legs. A burly, T-shirted Supply Sergeant growled at Danny, inquiring what size he wore in every category of Marine gear. Danny answered automatically, and the Sergeant stacked poker-chip-like tabs with the numbers Danny gave him stamped on them in the order they were given. "Okay, just go down this table. Stop at every Marine on the other side of the counter. Stick your arms straight out, and hold these chips in your left hand. They're in order, so don't drop 'em, or I'll fucking come down on you."

As he started down the long table-like counter, the stack of chips in his left hand went down. The stack of gear went up. Then it went up again. And again. He did not see the last three supply clerks. And because there was one wool sock in his

15

mouth, he didn't say anything either. Staggering under his load of gear, using a trouser leg like a periscope, he rejoined the platoon. Only it was disappearing back through door one. All that was left of it outside were eighty stacks of gear in four neat rows. They couldn't march, but they were neatly lined up. Danny set his down, front row right, and stood up.

"Back in there, Wood. What do you think you march in, bare feet?" It was No-eyes, bellowing as usual. Last one out door two, last back in door one. He had visions of an impatient platoon waiting for him to dress last, eat last, shit last. Oh, Christ, what was he doing here? He shouted, "Sir, yes, Sir," and sprinted back through door one.

This final trip was important. The Marines worried about only one part of a "boot's" anatomy. His feet. And, therefore, combat boots. He was carefully sized and fitted. They were heavy, tough leather, thick soled and thick heeled. The outside looked like sand-colored suede, and felt like it. As Danny stood up, booted, a Supply Sergeant threw his best dress civilian shoes into a large pile, after neatly tying the laces together. "Forget 'em, asshole. You ain't gonna need 'em for a long time. We give 'em to the poor. Now, get outta here. You're the last one. Always somebody doesn't get the word." Thump, thump, thump. Danny *marched* out door number two. On the way out, he was handed a heavy canvas seabag. "Get with it, you're holding up the whole platoon." That figured.

Outside, the platoon was furiously stuffing everything into their seabags. Danny was very fast. He finished last.

"Get 'em on your shoulders." Sergeant Spradlin again. The whip voice low, but still snapping. Looking at Danny, Spradlin said, "Wood, you're gonna have to change your fucking name, or move a hell of a lot faster."

"Sir, yes, Sir," said Danny, clumsily lifting the crammed seabag to his right shoulder. Goddamn alphabet. He was doomed.

"P'toon . . . 'Ten Hut!" Coming to anything remotely like attention with eighty pounds of gear on your shoulder seemed impossible. "Left . . . Face." That did it. A full third of the platoon turned left, as ordered. The other two-thirds, being miser-

16

able fucking idiots, turned right. Eighty pounds of seabag put twenty men flat on their miserable asses.

Sergeant Spradlin did not get mad. He did not scream. He simply said, "Forward . . . Huh!" And they did. By the time the wounded had re-formed and caught up with the marching seabags, Danny found himself roughly in the middle of the platoon. In some cases, anyway, being last in line had certain advantages. Danny Wood, last in line, had ducked.

The march of the seabags took approximately thirty minutes. Dawn had turned to clear daybreak, the sun low and shining straight into the platoon's eyes. Sergeant Spradlin's rhythmic cadence never stopped. "Heel, heel, heel, heel," switching to, "Left, right, left, right," switching again, "one, two, three, four," sprinkled with "Goddamn it, straighten up." The platoon did the best they could, burdened as they were. Still in their varied and multi-colored civilian clothes, one word suited them perfectly. Pathetic. Sergeant Spradlin kept telling them that too.

While standing at ease, Sergeant Spradlin addressed them, "The building you see in front of you will be your home for the next eleven weeks. It is composed of a squad bay, a shower room and a bathroom, hereafter to be referred to as 'the head.' It also contains the duty hut, or duty room. This area is for Drill Instructors *only.* You will show yourselves in that area only when ordered to do so."

Walking to the exact center of the formation, the Sergeant snapped, "P'toon . . . Ten HUH!" Well, that was easy enough. "Put those bags back on your shoulders." Oh, God, thought Danny, the alphabet. "Flores, Wood, get in there." Danny Wood and Sonny Flores ran like deer. Sprinting to the left door, they had already turned right and headed to the last rack in the line. Grinning, Danny accepted the top rack. Flores, throwing his sea bag on the bottom bunk, grinned back, wickedly. Slowly he raised his brown hand and pointed.

Their rack was located only ten feet from the duty hut. The door was clearly painted "Duty Hut, Restricted." But that wasn't what chilled Danny, and brought the grin from his bunkmate. The side of the duty hut facing the squad bay had windows, covered and closed now by venetian blinds. Ten feet... if Sergeant W. R. Spradlin chose to, he could *hear* and *see* everything.

As the platoon streamed in, first filling the racks on his side of the squad bay, then the racks directly opposite him against the far wall, Danny took little comfort that approximately ten other young men were as close to the duty hut as he and Sonny. For the first and last time in eleven weeks, his name, along with Sonny's, had been called without regard to alphabetical order. The rest of the platoon *was* ordered alphabetically. For obvious reasons, the smile on Sonny's face had been replaced by a "why me?" grimace. Danny was sure he was doomed.

When you look at the formal pictures of the *Graduating Marines Boot Camp Album,* you are struck by how rigid and straight the men stand. There are two very good reasons for this. The first is easy. Fear. The second, logical. Twenty-five minutes after receiving innoculations, your formal picture (in full dress uniform) is taken. Twenty-five minutes after being shelled by Navy Corpsmen, movement of your arms is physically impossible.

The United States Marine Corps thinks of everything in its untiring effort to make the young boot camp trainee's life more comfortable. To this end, they devised a very special dress uniform. Carrying their shirts, Danny and his platoon were marched off to the photographer. Here, Danny began to really appreciate Marine ingenuity. The dress uniform is a dress blue jacket with *sewn on buttons,* in the closed position, and a dress white cap. The back of the jacket is adjustable for closing, as is the back of the dress cap. The jacket is pulled on, in effect, by simply holding one's arms out. It is pulled on, tightened in the back, the cap stuck on a bald head and flash. Instant Marine. Asked to smile, you grimace. A grimace is good enough. Par-

18

ents will later, after graduation, ooh and aah over how wonderful you looked *after* boot training. You say nothing.

The next stop the platoon made was the Base Armory. Inside, Danny and the platoon were introduced to, and then issued, the main weapon of the United States Marines. The procedure was simple, the platoon went in single file, picking up their rifles in a fast-moving line, stopping only long enough to record the rifle serial number opposite each platoon member's name on a typewritten sheet. That was it. They then went outside, Sergeant Spradlin waiting for them, a serious look on his face. The serial number on Danny's rifle was 1406253. Spradlin, speaking in slow, measured tones, left no doubt as to the importance of the cosmoline-covered weapons they held awkwardly in their hands.

"I don't much like Drill Instructors who make a big deal about the main fighting weapon used by the large majority of all Marines. I prefer to think of the *Marine, himself,* as the main weapon of the Corps. However, you will treat your weapon with more care than you would a newborn infant. In voluntarily joining the Marine Corps, you have in effect, pledged to kill for your country. That greasy, cosmoline-covered piece of equipment you hold is the *main,* but not the only, instrument you may one day be called on to use to fulfill your pledge.

"Technically, it is a .30-caliber, clip-fed, gas-operated, semi-automatic rifle. It weighs nine-and-a-half pounds, without the bayonet. There is a *precise* way to care for this weapon. You will come to know it, and love it like no other thing, or no other human. *Never* call it a gun. It is a *rifle.* Never drop it. Any man in this platoon that drops that weapon will sleep on it for thirty days. I can assure you, you will never drop it again. It makes a very uncomfortable bed.

"In four weeks, you will go to the rifle range, where it is hoped, and expected, that *all* of you will qualify as Expert Rifleman. Until then, you will clean it *every* day. You will be taught the *Manual of Arms.* You will be completely familiar with *all* its working parts, so familiar that you will be required to take it apart and put it back together in three minutes, blindfolded.

"Now, you will notice the rifle slings are all open and loose. That is a precaution, necessary because I can't count on you assholes carrying your weapons unless they are slung. You can't be trusted to sling arms on command either, and I don't want barrels and sights banging into each other. Now, gently slip your right arm through the rifle sling, and settle it on your right shoulder, gripping the center of the sling approximately chest high to keep the weapon securely on your right shoulder. Do it."

An expert hunter, Danny swung the hefty, nine-and-a-half-pound rifle to his right shoulder. Sling arms. That's what it was called. He knew it, but doubted if too many in the platoon did. As the weapon dug into his shoulder, he pulled the sling in tight to the right side of his chest. Soon, all the platoon had their rifles slung over their right shoulders. It had been done quietly and without problems. Danny noticed the heavy smell of cosmoline, a grease-like preservative spread all over each weapon. Still, it was a good smell.

"Tonight, each and every weapon will be cleaned and inspected before anyone hits the rack. Right now, we'll bring the weapons back to the squad bay, and go to chow. After chow, you pick up cleaning gear, cartridge belts, and combat packs. Then, we'll go for a walk. P'toon...Ten...Huh! Forwaaard ...Huh!" The return to the squad bay was uneventful. Spradlin's steady cadence droned on. Their sloppy thumputy-thump boots thumputy-thumped along. Their shots hurt. The rifles got very heavy. They had been on base exactly thirty-six hours. Obviously, the hard part was over.

Sunday in boot camp. No shouted commands, no 4:45 reveille. A day set apart. Cleaning personal gear, bullshitting, no real *things* to do. The D.I.'s didn't bother you much, except to take you to chow. As Danny Wood shaved on this, his fifth Sunday in the Marine Corps, he grinned quietly back at himself in the mirror. He was still almost bald, with haircuts every week. But this week, they had not touched the top of his head, simply cutting high on the sides. He now had the beginning of a crew cut, very short but growing. He also looked very fit. Tanned deeply, more muscled, carrying 150 pounds. He'd never been that heavy.

As he shaved, he remembered the early morning march to chow, when miraculously, *it* had happened. One heel. One thunderous, clipped heel, the early morning sun glistening on spit-shined boots. Arms swinging in unison, the platoon had flashed by other, newer units, and Spradlin's even, steady cadence had stopped, and it had been a magic, special moment, a moment *shared* with Spradlin.

Except for turning commands, they had marched without his steadying voice for over a mile, the rhythmic hammering of their heels spanking onto the blacktop their only cadence. As it went on, it seemed to grow louder, as the platoon realized for the first time what *they* could do. When Spradlin noticed a half dozen other platoons standing at ease awaiting room in the mess hall, he gave the command, "Count cadence . . . Count!"

Eighty-one full-throated voices boomed out in thunderous unison, "One, two, three, four, one, two, three, four!"

He'd taken them right through the loosely gathered platoons, all standing at ease. "P'toon . . . HALT!" It could not have been more dramatic. Or more militarily perfect. Eighty-one men on *"halt"* had jarred to an earsplitting crash of one sound, the sound that only comes from four weeks of intensive, savage practice. The sound of the platoon's halt cracked and rolled across the early dawn. Half a mile away, Major General Clayton, Commander of MCRD, woke from a sound sleep, grinned, and went back to sleep.

Sergeant Spradlin did not order at ease. Ramrod straight, he stood close to them and barked, "P'toon . . . Parade . . . Huh!" Parade rest. It is not a comfortable position. The right leg slams away from the left, as both hands come together in the small of the back. Done properly, it is a thing of thunder and lightning. Platoon 175, Drill Instructor Sergeant W. R. Spradlin's "miserable fucking idiots," proved to be thunder and lightning. The

21

command barked. The response instant, a crashing, exotic display of pure discipline.

The other platoons could only gape, pitying those poor bastards in "175," cursed with that little martinet son-of-a-bitch Spradlin. The whole base knew they didn't make D.I.'s like him except in zoos. They were right. At that moment, on his command, Platoon 175 would have walked without question straight into hell. They hated him. But that didn't matter. They feared him. And that didn't matter, either. He was *their* Neanderthal, *their* throwback to the old Corps. They did not like him; but respect? Well, that was something else.

From that insignificant moment, Sergeant W. R. Spradlin knew he had the best platoon he had ever commanded. They didn't know how good the rest of the battalion was. What they were beginning to know was they would be Honor Platoon, or die in the attempt.

Sergeant Spradlin stared hard at his platoon. They did not stare back. To do so would be a breach of discipline. On the Sunday morning before the long march to three weeks at the rifle range, where they would attempt to qualify as Marine riflemen, there would be no breach of discipline. Eyes flashing, Spradlin snapped, "P'toon... Ten... Huh!" The thunder rolled again. "Rest. Smoking lamp is lit."

They were free to talk, to move around. Never before had W. R. Spradlin called "rest." A simple reward, but magnificently timed. Turning his back, Sergeant Spradlin lit a cigarette, as Platoon 175 began, tentatively at first, to speak aloud in formation. The other platoons stood at ease, quietly. Then, W. R. Spradlin joined his platoon, talking quietly, sharing their time, their thoughts, and expressing his confidence that they were capable, with an all out effort, of actually winning the three-week competition to begin the next day. He then told Cook, the platoon's Right Guide, to lead the platoon into the chow hall. They were to eat, and return as stragglers, not in formation. He trusted they would not violate his faith in them, but would return promptly, on their own, to the barracks. With that, he grinned wolfishly, field-stripped his cigarette, and simply walked away.

The other platoons saw it. They did not believe it. And finally, they had to. Platoon 175, under the nominal charge of a fellow boot, had been accorded the ultimate compliment a drill instructor can offer. Trust. It was a brief thing, they knew. Tomorrow it would be gone. They might never see it again. But this bright, sunny Sunday was the most magnificent day in Danny Wood's very young life.

The scratchy, mournful recording of the flag-lowering echoed and rippled across the giant training complex of Marine Corps Recruit Depot, San Diego, California. Advised to hit the rack early, most, if not all, of Platoon 175 had done so. The squad bay lights were out, except for the last bank near the door, where the usual "ten percent" were feverishly completing their field packs, checking gear, cleaning already spotless weapons. It was not quite dark on the late July night, and outside, small groups of men smoked their final cigarette of the day.

Sunday. Their fifth Sunday had been busy as hell. The next morning would send them off to the dreaded rifle range. Like smoke, Sonny's voice drifted up and over Danny's upper rack.

"You ready, patriot?"

"Yeah. You?"

"Hell, riding four-by-fours don't bother me."

"How you know we're ridin'?"

"Second Battalion rode. I saw them come back Friday."

"Oh?"

"Yeah. So sleep, Danny boy, for the morn comes rushing like a four-by-four." With that, Sonny Flores went instantly to sleep.

"You fucker, you can sleep while you march, eat, take a shit."

Sonny Flores did not answer. Danny Wood smiled to himself. They made a strange pair. Their friendship was solid and strong. The short, husky Mexican; the tall, slim German and French gringo. Danny, nervous, explosive, always at a high

23

peak or a desperate low. Sonny, steady, quiet, deadly as hell. Different as their personalities might be, they balanced each other perfectly. They stood slightly apart from the platoon. Not distant, just different. They were the best two boots in the platoon, and Sergeant Spradlin rode them unmercifully, pushing them harder and harder. Since the quickest way to draw attention, oddly enough, was to *excel*, the rest of the platoon kept that cordial, wary distance. It suited Danny just fine except for one thing. When Spradlin finally murdered him and Sonny, no one would see it.

At 1:00 A.M., Danny woke up. He had been asleep five hours and felt refreshed and strong. The squad bay was quiet, peaceful. Occasionally, faint light swept across the ceiling. It had taken him three weeks to discover that these were headlights, perversely nosing their way from the airport in San Diego, or the highways, or worst of all, that fucking Triple-X drive-in. The outside world. The civilian world. People actually driving cars after 8:00 P.M. Incredible. With growing trepidation, Danny thought about later that day, and remembered a few yesterdays.

The first four weeks, leading to this quiet, placid night, were primarily a frantic blur. There were, however, some standout memories. The Triple-X was one. Only two hundred yards separated the base fence, twenty feet high, from the adolescent haven for hot cars and carhops. One night, only two weeks into training, Spradlin had rousted them out of their racks at midnight, ordered them to dress and fall out, and taken them directly to that fence.

It had been a Friday night, warm and sultry. Except when needed, he had given no command on the way to the fence. Then he'd halted them, lined them up single file, noses almost touching the fence, its chain links strong and forbidding. Two hundred yards away were more convertibles and, God help them, more girls than Danny had ever seen.

"Stand at attention. You may look. You may move your eyes. Suffer, if you like. All that pussy. And just think, in only ten weeks you can chase it. Catch it, I doubt. But meanwhile, that's as close as any of you are going to get." Spradlin's voice was soft. Behind them, he said no more, the only sound being his Zippo lighter: click, scratch, snap.

Mesmerized, the platoon watched silken legs, thighs flashing in the garish lights of the drive-in. The sound of a lilting female voice drifted across the quiet, empty space between them, occasionally punctuated by the deep-throated growl of a powerful, unmuffled hot rod.

Only weeks before, all that they had watched had been theirs to enjoy. It was cruelty at its most subtle. Agony multiplied beyond all agony. In the hour they were there, they could hear the moans, feel the breasts, smell the musky odor of the *female*. Back seats. Beaches, blankets, easy lays. Any girl was an easy lay if you *imagined* her to be so. Sergeant Spradlin let them imagine, turned them around, and marched them away. When Danny climbed into his rack, he couldn't sleep. But he could remember, not so long ago.

The city had its share of clubs. The Seattle Yacht Club, the College Club, the Washington Athletic Club, the Rainier Club. The city's affluent belonged to one, all, or had applied to one and all. Danny Wood was riding a rickety elevator the one flight up to his "club."

The 211 club, though it had no official membership, was nevertheless just as clubbish as the others. Called the 211, simply because it was located at 211 Union Street, it was the place Danny Wood went to keep from being alone with Danny Wood. Thousands of people passed the green elevator door every day, paying it little or no attention. Those that did visit it might not understand it at all. But for Danny, it was home.

The club consisted of a well-lighted and busy cardroom, a restaurant and bar, and a dimly lit pool room, complete with old but superb tables resting on worn carpeting. The beer was cold, the food astonishingly plentiful and good, the card games hot. But it was the billiard room that drew Danny Wood, as it had since he was twelve. Now, at seventeen, he was one of the best all-around billiard players in the city.

25

Weekdays, the room was populated by a strange mix of doctors, stockbrokers, lawyers and lazy salesmen. Hovering around were the pimps, the pushers and the game players, drifting in and out in the manner of the streetwise, picking up a buck here and there, but mostly just taking up space.

In the evenings, the 211 fraternity became easy, relaxed and at home. The pimps played pool, visited often during the evening by their dazzling girls fresh from a turned trick. Pimps were notoriously poor pool players, and the visits were sometimes needed to replenish diminishing bankrolls.

The girls were hustled, but not very seriously. Danny was a favorite, and rolling his eyes skyward, he would turn his pockets inside out, claiming poverty. Always, the girls would chime, "Honey for you, I'll pay." The girls joked about it, but more than one, attracted by Danny's darkly handsome good looks and youth, had whispered serious propositions in his ear as they passed by. So far he had declined, much to the amusement of his friends.

One twenty-six year old, Anita, a dazzling blond with a spectacular figure, chased him constantly. Every time she came in, the crowd would chorus, "Hide the kid, hide the kid." He could never concentrate after that. Unknown to the other players, she frequently bankrolled his games, refusing to accept a percentage when he won. She made fifty dollars a trick, and a lot of it went to Danny. He never did understand why, but didn't turn it down either. Leery of close emotional ties, he let their relationship drift.

As Danny got off the elevator, his practiced eye took in everything. The stools at the small bar were all filled. The restaurant was busy also this early Saturday evening. Two young, pretty girls, about his age, sat at one of the booths, sipping Cokes.

Danny strolled into the semi-darkness of the billiard room, the only light coming through the draped windows and the individual lights over each table. The room was packed. Nodding hello, greeting friends, Danny spotted Lee playing nine ball with Johnny Temp.

26

Cadillac-driving, free-spending Johnny Temp, the wealthiest pimp in town, with seven girls working the late spring streets of Seattle. Dressed from head to shoes in powder blue, a straw hat perched on the back of his head, Johnny stared intently at the balls on the table. Lee Jordan, Danny's best friend, stood silently waiting for Johnny to shoot. The black man bent over, shot too hard, and watched bleakly as the ball rattled the pocket and stayed out.

"Easy money, Lee," Danny said, settling into a chair near the table.

"Candy, just plain candy."

"Shoot man. We're playing on my money." Johnny Temp was angry.

"You really want me to shoot that, Johnny-O?"

"You damn right. Shit, you might miss."

Grinning, the husky blond-headed youth stepped to the table, crouched, and gently knocked the yellow-and-white nine ball in. A wide grin on his face, Lee said, "How much is that, Johnny-O?"

"That's a 'C', man. I'm quitting while I'm behind." Peeling off a hundred dollar bill from a huge roll, Johnny Temp said, "See you, Danny. And later for you, Lee, much later." The hundred didn't mean a thing, and Johnny Temp strutted out toward the elevator.

"Bus fare," Lee said.

"Bus fare? Where's your short?"

"Blew a rod, man. My noble car is junk city. Do we need a car tonight?"

"Hey, Lee, I got a date, sort of. We're going to Vashon Island, man, and it's a goddamn long walk to Enid's house on the beach."

"How do you know? You never been there."

"She gave me directions. Anyway, we're going. She's got a chick lined up for you. Named Sally."

"May I remind you that the last time you got me a date she looked like a football player."

"This one's definitely not fat."

27

"Good," Lee said. "Let's go."

"She's skinny, though."

"Shit." Laughing, the two young men headed for the ferry dock.

"Hell, don't worry, Lee, maybe the goddamn ferry will sink, thus sparing you your appointed rounds."

"Jesus Christ," Lee said. But he was laughing when he said it.

Nancy Porter poured iced tea for the two young men sitting at her dining room table. Her once trim figure had gotten a bit too full, but she was still a very attractive forty-year old. She smiled easily, and talked too fast. Lee was gazing with frank admiration at her full breasts, barely concealed in her scoop-necked, sleeveless blouse. Well, it was nice to know she still had it, she thought, bending low and giving the blond youth a good look. They were such nice, clean cut looking boys.

"Thank you, Mrs. Porter. It was pretty hot walking out there."

"Why thanks, Danny. It's nice to be appreciated." Such a nice boy. "Have you known Enid long, Danny?"

"No, ma'am, only about a month. We met at a dance in Seattle."

"Well, she talks about you all the time. You've made quite an impression on her."

"A good one, I hope," Danny said.

Nancy Porter thought he was positively charming. "Yes, a good one. I'm only sorry I won't be here this evening so I can get to know you boys better."

The two boys looked knowingly at each other. "That is a shame, Mrs. Porter," Lee said. "Will you be back later?"

"No, I'm afraid not. I have an engagement in Seattle, and I won't be home until tomorrow. You fellows will just have to fend for yourselves. The last ferry tonight is at 12:45, so watch the time."

"We will, Mrs. Porter. We wouldn't want to miss the last ferry."

"Yeah," Lee said, "it's a long swim."

Laughing, Mrs. Porter went to the refrigerator and swung it open. "I may only have a daughter, but I know about you men. There's plenty of stuff in here for the hungriest. Enid is a good cook, for sixteen, so you four just help yourselves. The girls are down the beach somewhere. You'll just have to find them."

Danny smiled his most dazzling smile. "That won't be hard, Mrs. Porter. Enid looks a lot like you, so we'll just look for the prettiest girl on the beach."

Mrs. Porter gave Danny a slow smile. "You're sweet, Danny, you really are. No wonder Enid is so taken by you."

Gathering up her coat and purse, Mrs. Porter gave the two young men one more look. "Now, you behave yourselves. All of you. Okay?"

"Don't worry, Mrs. Porter. We'll be just fine," Lee said.

"Well then, like I said, there's food and soft drinks in the fridge, so you boys just help yourselves. Nobody visits the Porter ladies and goes away hungry."

Tossing the coat over one shoulder, Mrs. Porter winked once, and swivel-hipped her way out to her car. As she got in, her skirt hiked all the way up to her thighs, as the boys stood in the doorway and watched. For a moment, she sat that way, knowing full well she was putting on a show. Then, with a smile and a wave, the long expanse of nylon-clad leg disappeared, the door closed, and the car moved rapidly out of the curved driveway and headed toward the ferry dock.

"Jesus Christ," Lee said.

"Yeah, she's something all right," Danny replied.

"Did you see the look she gave you? Man, if she looked at me like that, I would have jumped right in the car with her."

"Yeah, but then what would you do?"

"I dunno," Lee admitted.

"Neither do I. She's too much for me."

Lee looked steadily at his friend. You never could tell about Danny. He joked all the time. Or did he?

"C'mon, Lee, finish your drink, and let's go find Enid and your skinny date."

"Okay."

"You got your watch?"

"Yeah."

"That's good. I don't want us to miss that ferry."

"You really gonna catch that ferry?" Lee asked.

"That depends."

"On what?"

"Who knows? Let's just play it by ear."

As they headed out the door and started down the beach to find the girls, Lee said, "I have a feeling we're not gonna make that ferry."

"Don't worry about it. They run in the morning, don't they?"

"Mama might come back early."

"Don't bet on it," Danny said.

Enid and Danny sat propped up on pillows near the fireplace, occasional sparks showering around them as the fire popped and roared.

"And I told Lee that Sally was skinny."

"Well, now he knows," Enid quipped.

Across the room, Sally Adams lay with her head in Lee's lap, one leg stretched flat, the other bent and slowly opening and closing, one arm around Lee's neck, the other crossed just below her breasts. The sound of a zipper drifted across the room, and Sally shifted lightly as Lee's hand disappeared deep into her bright pink shorts, as Sally's leg came to a stop resting against the back of the couch. Her blouse came open, and Danny could see her full breasts even in the darkened living room. Lee's free hand roamed over her breasts, the pink shorts moving slowly against his hand. Sally's breathing was rapid, shallow.

She had the longest legs Danny had ever seen. An excitable, nervous girl of seventeen, she'd been all over Lee the whole day. She was spectacularly pretty, with deep green eyes, and a pert, ready smile.

"Hey, Lee, we're gonna miss our ferry." The reply was muffled. "Okay. To hell with the ferry. But couldn't you at least go

30

in the bedroom? You're giving Enid ideas, I hope."

Sally extracted Lee's hand from her crotch, and without bothering to cover her breasts, slid sensuously up from the couch, pulling Lee after her. She kissed him long and deep, her hips grinding hard against him. Turning toward Danny and Enid, Sally waved, her breasts glistening in the soft firelight. Lee just stood there, until she pulled him after her down the hallway to the bedroom.

"He looks dazed," Danny mused.

"He hasn't seen anything yet. Poor Sally."

"Why poor Sally?"

"At school the boys call her Sally Suck."

"You're kidding."

"No, I'm not. I guess I'm the only girlfriend she has. She can't help it. She just can't get enough. She is really hung up on sex. She talks about it when she's not doing it. She told me she's sucked or screwed every boy in the senior class."

"Lucky Lee."

"Jealous?"

"With you here, the fire, the view of Seattle across the bay. Please, what else could I want?"

"Sally Suck."

"I like you better."

"Prove it, then." Enid's eyes were bright, her body tense. "But do it right."

Curious, Danny said, "What makes it right?"

"Make me climax. I never have. I've never gotten anything out of it."

It had never occurred to Danny that girls might not climax. Tenderly, he kissed her full breasts under the white sweatshirt. Slowly, his mouth trailed across her breasts, nipping gently at her extended nipples. He felt curiously detached, an observer more than a participant. Sitting up, he unzipped her white shorts and pulled them off, kissing her thighs as he did so. She'd put perfume on the inside of her thighs, and behind her knees. She literally tore off her sweatshirt, as Danny continued his slow, soft kisses across her thighs, gently kissing the curly

31

dark V of her crotch. He made no move to take off his clothes, but went on kissing her belly, her breasts, her legs, slowly bringing her to a wiggling, fever pitch of excitement.

She reached for his belt, but Danny shifted slightly away, continuing to kiss and stroke her body, still in that detached single-minded way. His own body was ready, but not over-ready. For the first conscious time of his young life, Danny was making intense, erotic love to a girl without thought of his own pleasure. From the back bedroom, Sally cried out loudly, once, twice, three times.

Enid was getting frantic with need. "Danny, honey, please . . . Danny?" But Danny just went on, his mouth insistent, his hands everywhere. Enid's body churned upward, and she began squeezing her breasts, pinching the nipples and moaning. "Danny, please, I need you in me. I'm so hot . . ."

Danny stood up, slipping his shirt off, looking down at Enid, her eyes bright with desire, her lush young body squirming, legs spread wide. Dropping his levis and shorts, Danny stepped free and watched Enid. He was erect and excited beyond anything he'd ever experienced.

"Danny, please . . ."

Still detached, Danny lay down and continued to kiss her, his mouth more insistent, his teeth nipping her thighs. Something signaled Danny, some inexplicable sureness that now was the right time. Rolling over on his back, he pulled Enid over his body and in one motion slid easily into her.

"Sit up, Enid. You do it."

Quickly, Enid scrambled up, her knees on either side of his body. Slowly, she rose and fell, pulling him deep inside her, rocking forward and back, as Danny held her breasts and watched her face intently. Her mouth hung slack, her breath came in loud gasps. "Oh. Oh. Danny, I'm coming . . . oh."

Squeezing her breast hard, Danny raised his hips high and stopped, as Enid's hips moved frantically against him, her hands clutching his thighs. Danny watched as her face contorted, a thin sheen of perspiration bathing her entire body. Her climax was massive, her whole body shuddering violently.

It seemed to go on forever, and then, exhausted, she fell forward across Danny's chest, her black hair damp and disheveled.

For a long time, she just lay there, unable to move, full breasts flattened against Danny's chest. Wonderingly, Danny softly stroked her back. So that's what it looked like. He had not climaxed, but Enid most certainly had. Enid lifted her head, softly kissing his eyes, his nose, her tongue darting into his mouth.

"God, that was wonderful. I love you, Danny Wood."

Danny felt a new pride, a new sense of maleness. It was funny. He hadn't climaxed, but it didn't matter. Still erect, still joined, he shifted a little, moving Enid to her side, one leg thrown across his thighs. Cradling her damp head on his shoulder, he patted her leg gently. In moments, the warm fire as a blanket, they fell asleep.

A few hours later, Danny woke up to the soft touch of Enid's nipples brushing across his face as she knelt by his side. Instantly awake, he pulled her down to him. Pulling him on top of her, she began to move insistently against him, her legs spread. Reaching down between them, she grabbed him roughly, and literally shoved him inside her, locking her legs over his.

"Now, it's your turn. I'm gonna fuck your head off." And she did, too.

Not one recruit slept dry for three days. Spradlin had said little, but made an enormous point. They, one and all, hated him beyond reason. On the other hand, frantic letters went out to girlfriends to cut the sexy stuff *out* of the letter from home.

At the opposite end of the base stood another fence, this fence separating Marine Boot Camp from Navy Boot Camp. Again they had been marched, again they had been lined up, to stare at Navy boots. Unlike themselves, on a Sunday, *visited* by girls, friends, parents. The Navy recruits spent a full hour taunting them. The girls (some of them, anyway) showing legs, breasts, smiles (smiles were the worst), all under the maternal eye of their Navy Chief Petty Officer instructor.

He made a solemn promise to march them back to that fence during the last week of boot camp, after which, he said with some venom, they could do as they chose, as he fully intended to absent himself from the immediate area for thirty minutes. The fence, he noted, was only six feet high.

"Dismissed."

They loved him. Momentarily. They *hated* the Navy. Permanently.

Two fences. Two objectives. Both accomplished. Actually, both "exercises" were straight out of the training manual for Drill Instructors. In later years, Danny Wood had time to reflect that he'd learned to hate the U. S. Navy, and have vivid wet dreams, all because of chain-link fences.

Consider the smile. Muscles work, the lips curl upward, teeth gleam and tiny wrinkles appear around the eyes.

The smile conveys so much. Simple amusement. Gratitude. Guilt. Hilarity barely suppressed. All of these things can be, and are, associated with this brain-activated muscle spasm. No one ever *thinks* about a smile. It's just done. Except that in the United States Marine Corps Boot Camp—it is thought of, but it had better be done when authorized, which is seldom. It is *not* authorized while standing at attention. Doing so is something akin to arson.

Danny's smile was provoked by Private James Kelly's fart. In perfect formation (for Platoon 175 in its third week), James Kelly's fart and Danny Wood's smile appeared simultaneously, one the result of the other. They also disappeared simultaneously. Obviously, from forty feet away, Sergeant Spradlin was deaf. Unfortunately, his eyesight was extraordinary, considering his back was to the platoon at the time.

"Wood, wipe that smile off your face."

What smile? thought Danny. "Sir, yes, Sir," shouted Danny.

When Sergeant Spradlin turned, his eyes triumphantly fell on Danny. With slow, hangman steps, he walked to Danny, stopping only inches from Danny's rigid eyes-ahead stance.

"Smile for me, Wood."

"Sir?"

"I said smile for me," roared the Drill Instructor.

Danny tried to smile.

"Private Wood, is *that* what you call a smile?" The best question possible is the one that has no correct answer. This was one of those questions.

"Don't answer that, Wood." Sergeant Spradlin now looked very pleased with himself. "That was the most anemic smile I have ever seen. You didn't even try. As a matter of fact, I would describe your facial expression as dead blank." Walking away from Danny, he faced the platoon.

"Private Wood has killed his smile. Burial services for the innocent victim, his smile, will be held behind the barracks at 1800 hours this date. Private Wood will bury his smile in six feet of good California earth, as befits something Private Wood once considered his friend. You are all ordered to attend. Formal dress is required. In this case, formal dress is sweat, to be drawn from two turns around the parade ground prior to burial services for Private Wood's smile. This formal dress is required by Private Wood only. Dismissed."

And so it was that at 1700 hours that day, Private Wood raced around the parade ground to acquire his "dress" uniform of sweat. At the prescribed time, 1800 hours, Danny and the full platoon were gathered on the sun-baked dirt, at the walk and recreation area behind the barracks.

Sergeant Spradlin walked out right on time, looking very serious. He had a shovel in one hand, a large, white piece of paper in the other. On it, in large block letters were the words "SMILE R.I.P."

"Dig."

For two hours, Danny hammered at the hard, clay-like earth, periodically checking its depth with a tape measure. When it was precisely six feet deep, Sergeant Spradlin carefully folded the white paper, and solemnly dropped it into the hole.

"Cover it."

Danny furiously began shoveling the loose dirt back into the hole. A cross made of two popsicle sticks taped together was placed on the spot. The shovel tamped the earth back as it had been. Danny Wood's "dead" smile had been laid to rest. Sergeant Spradlin called them to attention, ordered a salute to the now revered smile, and sent them to the squad bay to blessed sleep.

At two o'clock in the morning, the lights went on in the squad bay and the platoon, wide awake, cowered under the withering gaze of Sergeant Spradlin.

"Wood, front and center."

"Sir, yes, Sir," said Danny, coming to rigid attention in front of the D.I.

"Wood, are you absolutely sure that smile was *dead?*" Another, absolutely perfect, unanswerable question.

"Well, I'm not. For all we know, we buried the son-of-a-bitch alive. All you idiots outside. We're gonna dig it up and make sure." With this, he once again handed Danny a shovel.

In and down went the shovel, as Danny, clad only in his underwear, savagely attacked his "smile." Finally, out came the once white, now dirty, piece of paper. Carefully, Sergeant Spradlin, with the aid of a flashlight, scrutinized the paper, then carefully laid it down on the ground.

"Just as I thought. It's still alive. Hit it with your shovel and put it back in the hole."

It was now 3:00 A.M. For the briefest moment, Danny Wood considered hitting Sergeant Spradlin. He took the shovel and knocked the smile right off that paper's face.

"Sir, the motherfucker is definitely dead now, Sir!!"

"Well, don't leave the body there. Bury it. The rest of you idiots hit the sack."

Danny dropped the now thoroughly mutilated paper smile back down the hole and carefully, laboriously re-buried it. Slowly he walked back into the silent squad bay, and exhausted, crawled back into his bed. At precisely that moment, the lights went on.

"All right, you people, hit the deck. Big day today. Fall out for chow in fifteen minutes."

In the next four days, Danny would exhume and re-bury his smile seventeen times.

Now, in the predawn, fifth Sunday of Danny Wood's Marine Corps career, he remembered, *smiled* broadly and drifted off to sleep. In seven minutes the lights went on. His watch said 3:00 A.M.

"Sleep good?" Sonny asked.

"Like a baby."

"Semper fi-delis," Sonny said.

It was not yet fully light, the flat black of the massive parade ground yielding reluctantly to the oncoming dawn, the red glow slowly, persistently hammering at the chill darkness. Platoon 175 and fifteen other platoons were scheduled to go to the rifle range. They blanketed the dark asphalt, in full marching gear. Wearing seventy-pound packs and carrying their rifles, they stood in parade order, checking each other's pack straps. Sergeant Spradlin, going quietly among them, adjusted the packs high on the shoulders, distributing the weight evenly. They did not seem heavy. Many trucks stood like silent, sleeping pachyderms.

Sonny was right. They were going to ride. Their seabags contained the rest of their personal gear. Each item properly tagged, their gear had been loaded on four trucks earlier, and were already on their way. The packs they wore were full field packs. Bedrolls, C-rations, poncho covers, bayonet, cooking gear, the works. All a fighting Marine needed, including Danny's "smile burier" shovel, sat on their shoulders. Four trucks for each platoon. Fifteen platoons. A little over twelve hundred men. The full battalion, surprisingly, was very quiet, only the rattle of equipment breaking the evaporating night silence, as the sun rose in the eastern sky.

It was 4:50 A.M. The beginning of the day had been perfectly orchestrated. Dress, shave, eat, pack up, and here they stood, waiting to board the trucks for the thirty-plus mile trip up into the low hills outside San Diego. The D.I.'s had been strangely quiet, almost helpful. And, for the first time, Marine Corps *officers* moved among them. Danny had counted six, all Lieutenants. Actually, there were more. Major Axman, the Battalion Commander, had with him four Captains, and no less than sixteen second louies. The command to "mount up" came from the Major himself. Across the parade ground, the command was echoed by the underlings, all the way down to Spradlin. The Major, in a booming voice, bawled out, "Battalion! . . ." The four captains barked out, "Companies!" The Lieutenants, the loudest of all, snapped, "Platoons!" followed by the D.I.'s unintelligible gibberish (Spradlin's "P' . . . Toon . . . Ten-Huuh!"). Twelve hundred and forty-eight young men snapped to like a wave of Tinkertoy soldiers.

As the trucks, big brutish four-by-fours, started off, it was equally apparent that anyone who didn't grab that metal bench with both hands was going to fall flat on his ass. In a few moments, the trucks, booming along at convoy speed, were off the base, and driving through San Diego. The young men were boisterous and loud, and Sergeant Spradlin, smoking a cigarette, let them be. They whooped and hollered at anything female, Sonny almost falling out the back of the truck as a bright red convertible pulled up behind them with three beautiful California girls riding in it. For a while, the convertible stayed alongside and a bit to the rear, the bright sun, full now, showing tan thighs as the wind caught their skirts, revealing in order, one pink, one white, and one black pair of panties. As suddenly as it had appeared, the convertible was herded away by a jeep with two M.P.'s in it. Sonny cursed them, and announced solemnly that when he got out of boot camp, he intended to fuck his way through every panty color known to man.

For thirty minutes the trucks hammered on, giving the formerly cloistered young men a short, happy look at the civilized world: at women, aircraft workers, cabs, buses, ordinary everyday sights that became the stuff of a magic show to the young boots. Soon, the city dropped behind, the road grew empty and they settled back for the drive to the rifle range. They shouldn't have. At that moment, ominously, the trucks slowed down, slowed more and stopped.

"Stay here. Smoking lamp is lit." Spradlin jumped down from the truck, and disappeared. In five minutes, he was back. The tailgate was dropped.

"Everybody out."

The boots clanked and clattered down. A winding road lay ahead, as each truck emptied its living cargo.

"Wood, secure that tailgate."

Danny did so. One by one, the green trucks pulled out of line, made a U-turn, and roared back to the coffee and comforts of the motor pool. The First Battalion could only watch as the dust settled on an empty, no-truck road. Sergeant Spradlin gathered them around him.

"All right, hook up, sling your weapons. 1st and 2nd Squad, form on the left side, 3rd and 4th Squad on the right. Wood, you will act as my runner, and march with me in the center. If I have need of you, you will go up or down, as required. This is a route march. Fifty minutes marching. Ten off, fifty on, until we get there. NO ONE WILL DROP OUT. The strong help the weak. It is now 0800 hours. Lunch will be at 1200 hours. Dinner will be at the range. The chow hall at the range is run by the Navy. It's damn good chow. The Battalion Commander expects us to have chow in that Navy chow hall at 1730 hours this date. That will be a new record."

"Sir?" asked Sonny.

"What is it, Flores?"

"Sir, Private Flores wishes to know how far we have to go." He looked stricken.

"Well, by road, it's thirty miles. The way we are going it is precisely thirty-eight miles. Any questions?" Spradlin was exaggerating, but not by much.

Platoon 175 had no questions. Thirty-eight miles. In seven-

and-a-half hours. With seventy-pound packs. Uphill. Christ.

Walking beside Spradlin, Danny wondered if they would mark his grave. That at least explained why they all carried shovels.

As roads go, it was quite ordinary. Blacktop, winding, mostly upward, and really not too bad. Up front somewhere, somebody was setting one hell of a pace. Since it was route march, talking was permitted. Oddly enough, there was very little talking going on. A few bravado "piece of cake" remarks, and an occasional ribald remark about the ancestry of people who built roads like this one. The Battalion, at first, marched in step, out of habit, though on a march such as this it was not required. Very soon, the march in unison also stopped, as the young boots' faces became grimmer after each pounding step. A runner, a pale lanky blond sweating profusely, brought Spradlin an order on a clipboard. The D.I. read it, signed acknowledgement and handed it to Danny.

"Wood, get this reply up to the Major. He's probably at the head of the column. Move out."

Danny stared briefly at Spradlin, then at the pale blond youth. He looked exhausted, and he had come *down* hill.

"Sir, yes, Sir." Danny moved off quickly, holding his rifle at port arms, the clipboard snapped to his pack. The column stretched ahead as far as he could see, each twist in the road revealing more Marines, still stepping out briskly. The D.I.'s, spaced out every hundred yards or so, raised their arms simultaneously, fists clenched. On each side of the road, boots collapsed on the roadside, reaching for cigarettes and water from their canteens.

"Go easy, goddamnit. You people are carrying *one* canteen of water. You'll get no more." The speaker was Platoon 174's Samoan D.I., a Staff Sergeant. He seemed almost as wide as he was tall, with long arms and massive muscles. His commands on the drill field were rhythmic and strangely soft, yet with all platoons on the drill field at the same time, Danny could always pick out that unique cadence. Always, he knew where 174 was. He was said to be the best D.I. on the base, and the fairest.

Danny slowed down, stopping in the center of the road. Glancing at his watch, he jerked his canteen from its webbing. Unlike the others, he carried two. Spradlin had warned him about the extra weight. But Sergeant Spradlin also carried two. Danny figured his D.I. knew something he didn't. When Spradlin had seen the extra canteen on Danny, he started to say something, then stopped. It was then, Danny figured, that the "honor" of Battalion Runner had been his for the shoving. And Spradlin had shoved it, right between the two canteens, one hanging on each hip. 8:51. Nine minutes to rest, fifty into the march. Should he rest? No one would stop him, he was sure of that. Just another limp, green pile on the side of the road.

How in the hell had he gotten here? What was he doing in the Marine Corps, anyway? He could still be home if he'd been happy at home. But Danny wasn't happy living at home. His mother, still young and very attractive, led her own life, and meddled constantly in his. Only after days of pleading had she relented to his request to join a local Seattle Marine Reserve outfit in October of '53. Like all reserve units, it met only once a month.

Divorced, his parents couldn't be in the same room together without fighting. He rarely saw his father, but when he wanted to get away, to finally separate from his mother's control, his mother had unexpectedly suggested he ask his father to sign the release allowing him to join the regular Marines on a four-year hitch.

Danny had graduated from high school at sixteen, and had led an aimless life since then, playing pool and just hanging out. He had been a very good student, but had no desire to go to college. His father had signed for him without argument, much to his mother's surprise and displeasure. Danny understood it was just one more act in his parents' game of one-upmanship. But he jumped at the chance and here he was.

41

Whatever the reasons, he was a Marine recruit. The truth was, except for the occasional thought of 'why me?' he liked being a Marine very much, if he survived boot camp. At the moment, he had considerable doubt about that.

Danny tugged once on the canteen, replaced it in its webbed sheath, and started forward again. At once, hoots of derisive laughter exploded from both sides of the road, along with comments on the brown spot growing on his nose. Danny, very angry, stopped, reached for his bayonet and fixed it to his rifle. The hooting stopped. Grimly, Danny went on. At 8:56, nearly exhausted, Danny hit the head of the column and went directly to Major Axman, who stood in the center of the road, surrounded by four captains, the company commanders. Danny saluted, snapped to attention and extended the clipboard to the Major. The bayonet glinted in the bright morning sun. It was already eighty-five degrees.

"Sir, Private Daniel Wood, Battalion Runner, reporting to the Major as ordered, Sir."

The Major, tall and stern-looking, stared hard at Danny, then the bayonet. Slowly, he took the clipboard, read it and handed it to a short, equally stern-looking Captain.

"You mad at me, son?" He glanced again at the bayonet.

"Sir, no, Sir. The bayonet flops around when I move fast, Sir. I'm better balanced this way."

"Interesting. You do that on your own?"

"Sir, yes, Sir."

"Good thinking. That kind of thinking is what *I* get paid for. Sheath it."

"Sir, yes, Sir." Danny's left hand whipped across his body, disengaged the bayonet and resheathed it, all in one, blinding motion. The Major jumped, sort of a little hop, surprise in his eyes, if not on his face.

"Did you take ten, Private Wood?"

"Sir, no, Sir."

"Tough. Return to Spradlin. He *must* be your D.I." The Major still had not taken the clipboard from the Captain.

"Sir, are there any further instructions for the Drill Instructor, Sir?"

Again, the look of faint surprise. "Can you remember verbal instructions, Wood?"

"Sir, yes, Sir."

"Good. Tell Spradlin to cut up over this hill, directly behind me, and link up with the battalion at . . ." The Major glanced at his watch. "0950. Got that?"

"Sir, yes, Sir." Danny snapped a perfect salute. Boot or no, the Major was obliged by military law and courtesy to return it. Danny held his salute, rigid as granite. Slowly, ever so slowly, the Major's hand brushed his own field cap. Just like a real officer in an old World War II movie. Sloppy as hell. Danny dropped his salute, wheeled and raced down the hill.

Watching Danny's retreating back, the Major said, "Ain't he somethin'."

Danny's Company Commander, a young Captain, said quietly, "He's more than that, Sir. He's unbelievable. If that's an example of my platoon's people, I'll take any bets offered on which platoon takes honors on the range."

"No bets, Captain."

The Captain grinned widely, "A case of Scotch says '175' outshoots the whole battalion. All of it."

"*All* of it? All fifteen other platoons?"

"Yes, Sir."

"Fuck it. You're on," snapped the Major.

The young Captain of "A" Company, who knew a great deal about its platoons and particularly Spradlin's "175," grinned even wider. Turning to the other three Company Commanders, he said slowly, "How 'bout it? A case of Scotch. The Major accepted." He had them. Four cases on "175." If he lost, he'd have to forget about that off-base apartment, and the young blond dancer that went with it. Captain Steven Roucher, age twenty-eight, slowly began to wonder about fools and their money. He began planning on where to send Spradlin if "175" lost.

* * *

43

By 1600 hours that Monday, First Recruit Battalion and its sixteen platoons stood only four miles from Camp Mathiews' Edson Range. Edson Range was named after the famous leader of a unit of Marine Raiders whose combat exploits in World War II were legendary. Fifty-eight miles at full speed in combat were supposedly normal for the Raiders. But the First Battalion were not Edson's Raiders.

The temperature had risen to a steady one-hundred-and-five degrees. On a plateau, the range was clearly visible just ten short miles away. It might as well have been on the moon. In spite of Spradlin's and the other D.I.'s exhortations, the ambulances had been very busy. Heat prostration, thirst, the whole terrible, driving push to the range had cut their ranks by ten percent. No one had died and no one would. A few would be in Sick Bay at the range for days. Like the saying went, nobody asked you to join the Marines. You volunteered. Clearly, some should not have. This march showed the Drill Instructors who had that extra something, and who needed to learn it. Eventually, most would make it. Very few washed out medically.

From the plateau the range looked huge, and it was. Even ten miles away, it looked wild and ominous, but the distance to it looked even worse. A good blacktop road, mostly down hill. But the young Marines had the haunted look of P.O.W.'s. They were numb, finished. During the ten-minute break, Danny shared what was left of his second canteen, many of his comrades having done without water for two hours. Danny took the last full measure, swishing it around before swallowing it. Spradlin stood them up, pushing and pulling, putting them in standard platoon formation. They couldn't make it. There was just no way. They knew it. Why didn't he?

"All right. It's four miles or so to the main gate. That's only four times around the parade ground back at MCRD. We are going to make it, because I say so. *I'm* gonna make it. If you pussies are gonna let me go in alone, sit down. I'll go without you and send back the trucks. If you're coming, sling arms, right shoulder."

Platoon 175's discipline joined with its hatred of Sergeant

Spradlin. With grim purpose, they did as they were told. Slowly, the other platoons formed up. This was no longer a route march. If "175" was going to do it, they were all going to try. Spradlin stared intently at them for a long moment. Then he barked, "P'toon...ten...Huh!" As much as was physically possible, they did. "Forward...Huh!"

Slowly, raggedly, they started forward. Behind them, the other platoons jerkily moved forward too. Spradlin's cadence snapped at them. They responded as best they could, with no drill precision. Pain was all they felt. Still, Spradlin hammered out his cadence. At 1630 hours, the base looked closer. The pain, miraculously, began to subside. The booted feet slowly began to hit the pavement in unison. Backs straightened, arms began the steady, rhythmic movement of precise drill. Spradlin's cadence dropped lower, smoother and at 1640 hours, Platoon 175 thundered through the main gate of the rifle range, First Battalion streaming through behind it like the smooth wake of a fast-moving ship.

At precisely 1700 hours, Platoon 175 was called to a halt on a winding road, surrounded by hills. Four-man tents stretched out for a mile, in eight neat rows, four-inch-high wooden walkways running through the complex. Quickly, they were assigned tents, where, to their surprise, they found their seabags lying on racks, bedding ready, footlockers, and rifle racks for five rifles. The tent flaps were rolled up exactly three feet. At night, a simple tug on a line dropped them. The temperature this time of year varied from 32 degrees in the morning to as high as 105 degrees by late afternoon.

They were turned loose, and ordered to drop everything, wash up at the wash racks laid out every fifty yards and form on the road for chow. They had done well, they were told. Chow would be at 1800 hours, not 1730. No battalion had ever done better. They broke the all-time record by an incredible *thirty-nine minutes!* That fucking Major. He'd known all along chow would be at 1800. Six o'clock, not five-thirty. But bless that bastard Spradlin. By his threat to leave them behind, he'd brought "175" in first. They had the newest and best platoon tent area on base, only one mile from the chow hall. The last unit in, Platoon 170 from "B" Company, had over two miles to go. Water spouts stood like sentinels outside each tent, and Spradlin warned them sternly not to drink too much, since it was still ninety degrees. Everyone obeyed. They hated the bastard, but he'd got them here, all of them, and he'd got them here first. In a strange, quirky way, they were proud of him, *and* their new nickname, "Spradlin's Spartans."

For his part, Spradlin quietly showed his pride in them. He passed the word, through Cook, the Platoon Right Guide, that clean T-shirts, *without* dungaree tops, and clean trousers were permissible for chow. Those that were too tired to eat could hit the rack immediately. There were no requirements for the rest of the evening. Those wanting chow were to be on the road at 1755 hours. Spradlin himself would take them. "175" occupied the first twenty-two tents, eleven on each side of the wooden walkway, only one hundred yards from the road. At 1754 hours, clean T-shirts and clean trousers seeming to have eliminated the horrors of the march, all eighty-one members of "175" stood at ease on the blacktop road.

Spradlin wasted no time. Calling them to attention, he marched them, without cadence, to the Navy chow hall. He heard only one, thunderous boot. Cadence was not required. The chow hall was massive, the food plentiful and good. Steak, mashed potatoes, beans, rolls, milk, topped by coffee and apple pie. At 8:00 P.M., twelve hours and a million miles from anywhere, an exhausted bunch of Spartans, stuffed and clean, slept the sleep of winners, sweet and deep. One hour later, a bugler played a mournful taps. Platoon 175 heard not a note. Up to this point, this Monday had been the most stressful time of their young lives. It would get worse.

The first week at the range was strange, and to the eager boots, frustrating as hell. They did not go at once to the rifle range. They did not, in fact, unstack their rifles. The day after their arrival was used, at least in their eyes, in a fairly sensible way. Square away gear, clean weapons, set up housekeeping in the tents, wash clothes, and *eat!* The chow was truly great. If the seagoing Navy actually ate this well, they were all going to apply for sea duty. The explanation was simple, really. At MCRD, Marine boots cooked chow, under the professional supervision of Marine mess sergeants. In this lash-up, the Navy mess crew were all professional, career cooks. The food was no more plentiful than at MCRD, but it was cooked with style, and presented as *food*, not slop. The eggs were fresh, not powdered. *Two* meat choices. Good coffee. The Navy had a major medical facility here, and therefore ran the chow hall. There were even ashtrays on the tables, although the boots were forbidden to smoke in the mess hall. The average weight gain was seventeen pounds in three weeks.

Conversely, overweight boots *lost* an average of ninety percent overweight poundage, although they ate very well. The answer was simple. Intense, brutal physical and psychological stress, applied to its maximum. The food was good, but the work *never* let up. The boots rarely marched. They *ran*. Full speed, from lecture to lecture. Weapons lectures. The .30-caliber machine gun. The .50-caliber machine gun. The B.A.R. The .45-caliber 1911 Colt. But they did not *shoot* any of these weapons. They studied them. Held them. Tore them apart.

Two things dominated the first week. Swimming and something called "snapping in." For the uninitiated, "snapping in" is much like "let's pretend." The recruit is given a wooden rifle-like object, possessing only *sights* like a real rifle. Five hours a day, that first week, were devoted to "snapping in." This procedure, at least to a Marine idiot boot, made no sense whatsoever. Using this "toy" weapon, you were taught only the proper "sight picture" (what you were to see if the mighty Marine Corps actually allowed you to use a "real" weapon). You were also taught the "positions" required in order to fire your weapon. "Kneeling" position actually meant *sitting* on your right foot, bent at an absurd angle that could only result in permanently crippling you. "Sitting" was not quite so weird. You simply sat down, hurled both armpits over both knees,

47

locking your weapon securely into your shoulder and jaw. Then, you pointed your "toy," from whatever position ordered, at a one-inch target only ten feet away, and lining up the "sight picture" ("killee" balanced on top of "killer"'s front sight), you pulled the trigger, which satisfactorily enough, went "click," not "snap." After one week, each recruit had *killed* 30,000 one-inch pieces of paper, click by click, while "snapping in."

During this first week, those boots that could not swim were drowned. Well, not really drowned. Actually, the three weeks at the range taught you to swim, albeit in an unorthodox way. Good swimmers qualified quickly. Non-swimmers were simply thrown, over and over, into a beautiful Olympic-size pool, and pushed under by D.I.'s holding thirty-foot poles with boxing gloves on one end. When you went down the third time, you were *assured*, at least in your mind, that the thirty-foot pole would guarantee your *not* coming up again. Everyone learned to swim.

Week one was a running, snapping (clicking), jumping, splashing success. Platoon 175 placed first in the battalion. Eighty-nine percent of its people qualified. By week three, that figure would climb to one hundred percent. Friday of week one was great. Saturday, one week's worth of mail was received for Platoon 175. Those innocent green bags were full of home and mom and sex.

No-eyes called them out for that Saturday mail call. This was not unusual. He always gave out the mail. What was unusual happened as soon as they hit the blacktop, expectant and impatient for a full week of back mail. (A) He didn't have it, and (B), he marched them a few hundred yards off the road, and straight up the 552-foot hill called Little Agony. When they reached its flat top, he lined them up, called them to attention, ordered "about face," followed by "at ease." Two hundred yards away, as the crow flies, towered 878-foot Big Agony, its sides worn bare by well-stamped-down, wide pathways leading to its crest. Standing on its crest, battery-operated bullhorn

48

in hand, was Sergeant Spradlin, the full, green mail bag upright between two other D.I.'s. The distance, if you *were* a crow, was two hundred yards. Going down off Little Agony and up Big Agony, was easily three times that. The recruits began to hope for a no-mail day.

Mail call was always done alphabetically, so Danny watched as one after another of his comrades, called by the bullhorn, plunged down Little Agony, up to their mail and down again. They looked very tired when they got back. Somewhere in the G section, Danny was startled to hear "Wood, Daniel" across the valley between the two "Agonies." Danny sprinted down Little Agony and struggled up Big Agony.

"Sir, Private Wood reporting as ordered, Sir."

Spradlin just stared at him. "Wood, you got a big cock, or what?"

"Sir, Private Wood doesn't understand the Drill Instructor's question, Sir."

"It's simple. You got fourteen inches, or what?" The perfect question. No proper answer.

"Sir, Private Wood is quite ordinary, Sir."

"Ordinary?"

"Sir, yes, Sir."

"Twelve?"

"Sir, more like five, going on six, Sir."

"You tryin' to be funny, Wood?"

"Sir, no, Sir."

"Ten inches?"

"Sir, Private Wood only weighed four pounds at birth, Sir."

"It must have been all cock, Wood. Do you see what I have in my hand?"

Danny looked. "Sir, yes, Sir. The Drill Instructor has a stack of mail, Sir."

"Wrong."

"Sir?"

"The Drill Instructor has a stack of *your* mail, Wood. Fourteen pieces, to be exact. And one plain wrapped box of something."

"Sir, yes, Sir."

49

"Wood, do I look like a mailman?"

"Sir, yes, Sir."

"Take your fucking mail." With this comment, Sergeant Spradlin handed Danny *one* letter. Danny took it, but did not move.

"Well?"

"Sir, the Drill Instructor has more, Sir."

"Really? Well, you get your ass back to Little Agony. I'll call you."

"Sir, yes, Sir!" Danny roared down the hill, and back up to "L.A," as Little Agony was called.

"Wood, Daniel."

No . . . it couldn't be. Danny turned straight around and covered the ground again.

"That's two," said Spradlin. This time, the letter was yellow. Enid. I'll kill her. Danny raced back.

"Wood, Daniel."

Right.

"That's three." Pink again. Cindy.

"Wood, Daniel." Yellow. Enid *and* Sally. Back he went.

"Wood, Daniel." Blue. Printed return stick-on address. His mother.

It went on, then stopped, while the rest of the platoon got their mail. Danny had thirteen pieces so far. Finally, "Wood, Daniel." The last trip. He stumbled down, then crawled up. Totalled, he had run almost five miles, uphill.

"This goodie box finishes the mail call, Wood. Inform the Corporal mail call is over. And Wood, don't open that box until tomorrow. Tomorrow's Sunday, and since it's from Mama, I'm sure you'll want to share it with your Drill Instructors. Bring it to our tent at 1500 hours tomorrow."

Spradlin's smile was wide enough to swallow Little Agony whole. Normally, Saturday chow was a light meal, with Sunday's chicken a big feast. This Saturday, Danny Wood consumed four hamburgers, four milks, and a pound of french fries.

* * *

Danny took considerable ribbing about this "mountain climbing" from his tentmates. On the other hand, green was the color of their jibes. Envy, oh, such envy. All that fucking mail. His four-man tent, that Saturday night, had no less than fifteen of his platoon, waiting for the event. Danny Wood was going to *open* his mail, most of which had been drenched in perfume. Danny's supposed prowess with the female, never denied, made him somewhat of a celebrity, when combined with his miraculous ability to get into trouble with Spradlin.

"Open one, Danny."

"C'mon, Wood, you shithead, share the wealth."

"Goddamnit, my fucking mail is personal." Danny's voice did not match the pleased look on his face. He fully intended to share.

"Fuck personal," Sonny said.

Danny shuffled his mail like cards, selecting on purpose, the purple envelope. Jean Murray, the first, the best, the queen of raunch. "This, gentlemen, comes in multiples from Miss Jean Murray, of whom I have often spoken, with considerable panting, if you'll recall."

More whoops. Yes, they knew Jean Murray. Shouts of "open it," "do something."

Danny had a dramatic flair for describing his "ladies," as he called them. He was the only pornographic storyteller they'd ever met. With great solemnity, Danny opened the purple envelope. A picture fell out as he opened it, and only Danny's quick reflexes kept his hands from being crushed as everyone dived for it. The picture, like Jean herself, was spectacularly sexy. Sitting on her heels, on a bed, her long black hair held piled high on her head by her hands, wearing a daringly low-cut, breast-filled bra, and black panties. You could see more flesh on the beach. But not wearing silver high heels, mouth open, legs spread slightly, eyes blazing. She was definitely *not* your average seventeen-year-old girl. On the back, it said, "Come on home. We'll play golf. You bring the driver and ball/s, I'll be the hole/s. Love, Jean."

Solemnly, Danny handed it to Sonny. "Pass it around, but

remember, you tree swingers, I'll rip up the first idiot that
wrinkles or slobbers on it. I will, however, rent it out, two
packs of cigs a night."

One by one, quietly, the young boots stared at Jean Murray.
Danny may have been the youngest of them all, but never had
they seen anything quite like Jean. A new respect, almost awe,
quieted them down.

"Sonny, you think I should be charging something for all
this?"

"Dollar minimum, gents." Sonny was standing at his rack.
"One tiny dollar, and Private Idiot Wood will open yet another
of his treasures. One dollar."

He was immediately pounced on, threatened with castration
and charged with cruelty to animals, to wit, Platoon 175 and its
assembled members. The admission fee was quickly discarded.
Turned on, happy, they sat in a semicircle around Danny, and
respectfully waited for more.

The next two letters were from Enid, both containing photos.
Five photos in all, two of Enid in a white bathing suit, two of
Enid, same suit, same day, standing with Sally, in her usual hot
pink shorts and bra-less T-shirt. The fifth picture showed Enid's
mother, in a clinging black suit, same beach, same day, flanked
by Sally, her pink-and-blond confectionary look in sharp contrast to the darker beauty of the tinier Enid. Enid's mother
brought home another fact. Girls looked like girls, no matter.
Enid's mother, full, mature, voluptuous without being fat, was
a no-shit woman. Only Danny, among them all, noticed or
cared. Enid was pretty, leggy and sexy. She had proved to be a
very passionate sixteen-year-old. Now, after five weeks in boot,
she looked younger than ever. Danny Wood was changing and
he knew it. It was a vague, unexplainable thing, but it was
there, anyway. The letters were filled with home stuff, what the
girls did, the weather, just straight, sweet letters. Enid re-
minded Danny that she was dating nobody (underlined four
times) and that she was saving what she gave him the last time,
packed in a box. (This drew ribald laughter from all.)

The second letter mentioned that Sally and Lee had broken

52

up, and Lee had joined the Air Force. Reading silently, Danny read the request for "somebody nice and sexy" to write to Sally. Danny handed Sonny that page and Sally's picture. Sonny read it, looked at the picture and stuck both in his pocket. A year later, Sally became Mrs. Sonny Flores, by law and license. Twenty-five years later, they were still married. Sometimes, you just never knew.

The pictures, naturally enough, drew tremendous attention. By any standards, the girls were beautiful, and considerable envy was shown that *one* of them had *all* of these girls.

The next letter Danny did not read aloud. Written on flower-bordered stationery, it was far too personal and more passionate than Danny would share. Only Sonny read it later, with a wry "my goodness" his only comment. But Cindy Harrington had sent a picture. It was a simple, upper torso portrait, in a white cashmere sweater, professionally taken. Surprisingly, it got the rowdy group's absolute attention. First Jean, in her blatant sexuality, then Enid and Sally, sexy, coltish teenagers of a thousand wet dreams, everybody's cheerleader, everybody's "soch." It was Cindy who got them, her eyes a combination of innocence and lustful promise, the high swell of her full breasts straining at the white cashmere, topped by deep black, wavy hair ten inches below her shoulders. Danny Wood, from that day on, became the "what'll I do man," the wise seventeen-year-old who obviously knew *everything* about women. How else could he have *her?* How else could he have *them?* Nobody knew. But they were sure Danny did.

The rest of the letters were from his mother, his dad, and his uncle. Finally Danny took out a small, folded white sheet of paper. On it, it said, "I love you darling. We had this last night, and I thought of you." Danny opened it slowly, lovingly and then collapsed in laughter. Sonny picked it up. It was from Cindy, obviously.

"Gentlemen, the beautiful Cindy, whom you have seen but will never know, has sent our esteemed buddy, Danny Wood, actual strands of her most *private* self. Only Danny has tasted this, her most precious long-protected secret. It even still smells like it did, only four days ago, when, with love in her heart, she snipped these loving buds."

With great dignity, Private Sonny Flores held up six strands of *cooked spaghetti*, still covered in sauce, slimy, limp, gooey. Only by going out and under the tent flaps did Danny and Sonny escape with their lives. The spaghetti, alas, was lost in the dusty back rows of Camp Mathiews' Edson Range, and never seen again.

"Ten-Hut" Danny shouted as Sergeant Spradlin entered their tent. The boots snapped to immediate attention. It was eight Friday evening, and they had been cleaning and recleaning their weapons, going over and over their range notes taken during the five days of preliminary shooting.

"At ease," said Spradlin. "Go on, sit down. Tomorrow." He stopped, letting the word sink in. "Talk easy. You ready, or have we come up here for nothing?" No answer. "We have to outshoot '170.' That's all. Do that, and we'll take Battalion Honors for the range. Then Sunday, back to MCRD. Field Inspection Honors. Then Battalion Drill Honors. You people are this Battalion's Honor Platoon. I know it, even if you don't."

Danny Wood looked steadily at his Drill Instructor. Abruptly, Danny blurted out, "Piece of cake, Sir, just no sweat at all. You just tell them assholes markin' our targets that I can tell a bullet hole from a finger hole. I find any finger holes in my target, I'll kill the bastard that punched it in."

The tenseness melted away from the D.I., replaced by a slight smile. "I'll do that, Wood. I'll surely do that. Hit the rack soon. I want you fresh." He turned quickly, and left the tent.

The young men in the tent looked at Danny. "What was that about?" Sonny asked.

"Beats me," Danny answered. But it didn't.

For the first and only time in boot camp, Platoons 175, 174, and 173, comprising "A" Company, had chow together. Spradlin, typically, brought "175" to the chow hall last, but best. Wearing their shooting jackets, they marched like rolling

54

thunder to the chow hall, arriving at precisely 0800 hours. The three platoons had been allowed to sleep until 0700 hours this bright Saturday morning, rather than 0545. Qualification Day was special. So special, in fact, that "A" Company's Commander was there to share chow, and impress his D.I.'s that he had confidence in them, and their platoons. All of which failed to impress the young shooters. The broiled steaks, grapefruit, eggs, toast and coffee, the "shooter's breakfast," did impress them.

The chow hall was filled mostly with Navy personnel, including some WAVES. On this day, even the presence of women drew little notice. It was a strangely quiet group, even though for the first and only time, they had been allowed to talk and have a cigarette inside the mess hall. Morning chow, normally thirty minutes, was stretched to one hour. Passing Naval personnel, knowing this was a "shoot group," occasionally wished them luck. Though appreciative, the young boots were tense and strained, snapping at best buddies and coaching the "iffy" shooters. None of them really thought they would outshoot "170." But they were going to give it hell, anyway.

There were trucks ready in their area to take them to the range. Spradlin vetoed going by truck. The other platoons rode. "175" marched, and in the process, loosened up, singing the raunchy verses of their D.I.'s first line. By the time they got to the range, they were very loose indeed. The other platoons were a bit shocked to hear and see "Spradlin's Spartans," arms swinging, boots hammering the blacktop, as they swung onto the range. Incredibly, Platoon 175 were carrying their rifles with the bright morning sun flashing and gleaming off the cold steel of fixed bayonets.

"A" Company was on the line, five hundred yards from the targets. Ten rounds, slow fire. Two hundred thirty targets of the two hundred fifty firing positions were up, the line cleared and ready on left and right. Danny was on the extreme end, shooting at target #1. Eighteen Drill Instructors, twenty-five range officers, and "A" Company's own officers walked the concrete walkway directly behind the shooting line. The tension was thick and heavy, a dry metallic taste in the air that had no description, just a presence. Danny thought it was like being covered with a film of rust, and felt it on occasions for the rest of his life. Fifty-five seconds after permission to fire, Danny, sights adjusted according to the meticulous notes he had kept all week, touched the trigger, set the far-away black dot on top of his front sight, and squeezed. The rust vanished, the air lightened as two hundred twenty-nine 150-grain metal-jacketed slugs screamed out at almost the same time, followed by a funeral-like quiet. Target #1 was hauled down, followed almost immediately by the others. They quickly popped back up. White disks showing hits in the black, black disks spotting the outside white rings, and the occasional waving "Maggie's drawers," the red flag of a complete miss.

Danny Wood's target stayed down the longest, and finally popped up. The disk on the pole popped up black, reversed to white, and centered smack in the five ring. Smiling, Danny sent the next nine rounds, spaced approximately one minute apart, into a one-foot circle, for a perfect fifty points from five hundred yards. Standing, Danny cleared and checked his rifle, and stepped away from and behind the shooting line. Sonny finished right behind him, shooting at target #2.

Spradlin had skipped the alphabet system completely, letting friends shoot next to friends. Everybody helped everybody. Platoon 175 had one goal: smash the record. Sonny and Danny smoked quietly, saying nothing. Sergeant Spradlin joined them. The rifles continued their steady thunder. Platoon 175's assault was on in earnest.

Platoon 175 scored higher than their company mates at five hundred yards, but not as high as "170" had shot. There were no pep talks. Each boot dealt with his own problems. At three hundred yards, prior to shooting ten more rounds from a sitting position, Platoon 175 ran patches through their barrels. The others did not. "175" swept three hundred clean, dropping

"173" and "174" further back. Danny Wood, Sonny Flores and Paul Bradly led the way with perfect scores. Three hundred yards was considered the easiest, both from a comfort and distance standpoint. They now trailed "170" by only 1680 points. At two hundred yards, twenty rounds were fired, ten from a sitting position, ten kneeling. The firing order was up to the individual. Danny was very uncomfortable in the kneeling position, the awkward, "sit on your fucking foot" position as Sonny called it. It was "slow fire" in each. Danny put ten rounds in a fifty-cent-size hole in less than two minutes. Sitting, he used twelve minutes, and reduced the hole to a nickel. 100 points. Going to the one-hundred-yard range, Danny Wood had a perfect 200 score.

On the other side of the coin, twenty-two members of his platoon needed at least twenty points of the possible fifty available at one hundred yards, rapid fire. Much encouragement was given to these twenty-two men. Four 5's and six misses. Five 4's. Any kind of combination, and they were in. But Danny was not talked to. Nobody, not even Sonny, said a word to him. But they all knew. A possible 250. It had never been done, not by a boot. As Danny applied fresh lampblack under his eyes, he noticed the company's officers gathered directly behind shooting position #1. Spradlin was there, too. Danny was suddenly, very, very nervous. His hands shook, neatly coating his nose black, too. Spradlin separated himself from the officers and came to Danny. Forgetting "Sir," Danny asked, "How we doin'?"

"We'll get better. We need a thirty-six average for the platoon. Average."

Danny thought for a minute. "Can we do it?"

"You tell me."

Sonny Flores, grinning as usual, answered for Danny, "Piece o' cake, Sir."

Danny felt the tension leave him.

"No sweat, Sir. Just tell the guys to pretend that fresh new target that comes up is you."

Danny turned back toward the firing line. Sergeant W. R.

Spradlin, mouth open, could only watch Danny's retreating back.

This final part of qualifying, being rapid fire, timed, required each shooter to fire alone. The target dropped, was tabulated, and a paddle board with numbers run up to show the score. Danny, shooting #1 target, would actually shoot last. He and the other members of "175" watched "173," then "174" shoot. As "175" began, from position #81, cheers rang out as, one by one, the "iffy" shooters qualified. No one knew where they stood overall, only the official scorers and the D.I.'s were keeping careful tabulations. But the whole range knew "somebody in '175''s got a possible going." The "possible," meanwhile, was in a vacuum. He heard nothing, watched nothing. Sonny, only six feet away from him, slammed away, shooting a thirty-eight.

The Range Master's voice on the evenly spaced loudspeakers called #1 to the line. Danny walked quickly to the three-foot-square concrete shooter's pad, and waited for the timer's signal, the man with the stopwatch standing directly behind him. Go! The rifle, now a living, kicking thing, spat eight rounds out in what seemed to those watching to be too slow a time. Danny tapped the second clip against the butt, loaded, aimed and fired again. Was that one shot? No one could tell. But Danny could. Two jarring kicks, followed by a dead silence. The target went down. The timer declared nine seconds. A legal shoot. The score popped up. Fifty.

The "possible" was a reality. Danny was engulfed by his buddies. Platoon 175 had swept the range, smashing Platoon 170's record by one point. "Spradlin's Spartans" were Range, Battalion, and all-world Honor Platoon. Captain Steven Boucher, "A" Company Commander, was four cases of Scotch richer, the apartment and the blond dancer that went with it assured.

That evening, he sent one case of that Scotch to Sergeant W. R. Spradlin. The orders were explicit. This Scotch was contraband, illegal and otherwise contrary to Marine Corps regulations. The last line was particularly explicit, a direct order: "You and Platoon 175 are to destroy said contraband at once, in whatever way you deem fit." Late that evening, sitting on top of Big Agony, Platoon 175 carried out the Captain's explicit, direct order. They emptied the bottles and buried them.

"Spradlin's Spartans" were, simply put, the best damn platoon anyone had ever seen, anywhere. Four weeks later, no longer boots, but full-fledged Marines, "175" graduated, one hundred percent. Not one man washed out, for any reason. That was Friday. Orders and new duty stations would be issued Monday. In the meanwhile, and for the first time as Marines, they were given that most desirable of all things, shore liberty. Naturally, they were going to visit San Diego's culture centers. Sonny Flores grabbed an armload of friends. They went straight to Tijuana, Mexico.

Tijuana. T-Town. Tit-City. By any name, it is the grease on a new Marine's first slide into adventure. Its garish main streets beckon like a brightly painted hooker. And it is. T-Town is the ultimate hooker: For a price you can lose your virginity, your wallet, your mind or your health. The Marine Corps has invaded this dirty little city over and over, only to be thrown back across the border, in various stages of drunkenness, anger, frustration, and poverty.

This last day of September, another attack was to take place, led by the intrepid Mexican, Sonny Flores, followed eagerly, if not wisely, by Danny Wood, Paul Bradly and Private Eddy "Left Face" James. It was Friday, and until 0545 on Monday, they were free. And, at least temporarily, they had money. Three months' pay, one month wisely left on base. *They* weren't wise. Spradlin, as usual, knew best. Still, one hundred fifty dollars or so each ought to buy them the best-looking piece of ass in all of Mexico.

The Pink Flamingo Club was showing the four young men more than any of them had ever seen before. A stunning, raven-haired stripper, dancing on a four-way runway, was thrusting her pelvis in what seemed to be an effort to impale herself on Danny's nose. She was very young, very pretty and very good at her job. Her job was simple. Excite them. Lead them to the golden gate. Or so they thought.

As she gyrated only inches from their upturned faces, they were joined by four young, pretty girls. The girls immediately expressed their good fortune in finding four such good-looking men. The raven-haired dancer did something indescribable with her pelvis, squeezing her nipples and moaning.

"Jesus, she's gonna come," said Left Face. Danny watched, and agreed. At the same time, Paul and Sonny, caught up in it all, ordered drinks all around. Mixed for the boys, straight for the girls. Tea is usually served straight, and that is exactly what the four young women were drinking. The stripper lay down right in front of them, spreading her thighs wide, hips arched on five-inch silver heels. Flys were unzipped, hard-ons stroked (but not too much), breasts were exposed, touched, necks kissed. Another round of drinks. $20.80 again.

The stripper, sensing she was literally going to lose these idiot gringos, stood up and moved off to another group, this time sailors. Another round, another $20.80.

At the bar, men were placing silver dollars on edge, as a pretty young blond, standing on the bar in a tight, slit skirt, moved back and forth, squatting occasionally. The silver dollars vanished. Hell of a trick. The freshly minted Marines were, by now, really ripped. Each had drunk four ounces of cheap tequila. The girls had drunk four ounces of even cheaper tea.

"Let's go to my place." The blond sitting with Danny zipped up his fly. Danny looked steadily at her, not sure which of the two heads he saw was real.

"Yeah, let's go," agreed the redhead on Paul Bradly's lap, her tongue in his ear.

Sonny knew this was too good. "How much?"

The redhead spoke slow and cool, "We are not professionals. But, if you like, twenty dollars for all night would be nice. Just T-Town girls, with nice Marines." Pointing to a woman with a black medical bag in her hand, the redhead blandly said, "She's a nurse. She will check us. You don't worry about syph or none of that. Give her eighty dollars, she checks us and we go to my place."

She kissed Paul Bradly, almost swallowing his tongue, her hand rubbing her own breasts. On the bar, another silver dollar disappeared, and by magic, the stripper was once again about to masturbate to climax, one of her pointed heels resting on Left Face's shoulder. That did it. Eighty dollars appeared, and the nurse, advising the young men to wait ten minutes then follow, led the four giggling young women through some shoddy red-velvet curtains.

This time, the stripper *did* climax. The Marines were in heat. On the bar, ten silver dollars had been *stacked,* not on end. The blond, legs far apart, split skirt showing black garter belt and red hose, slowly knelt over the stack, hands on the bar. She bobbed once, wiggled slowly in a small circle, and triumphantly stood up. There was no place else they could be. Eddy "Left Face" James said, "I'll bet she can make change, too." They ordered one more round, and a stack of silver dollars for the blond. Thirty dollars. By now, who was counting? Gratefully, the blond sat, squirmed and simply flattened herself on the bar. Swinging her long legs off the bar, she stood over a wicker basket and deposited the receipts, one at a time.

Two rounds and thirty minutes later, the four young women and their "nurse" had still not returned through the shabby curtains. The young men, eighty dollars poorer, had decided to fetch their prize, the four "clean girls." They not-so-steadily went across the Flamingo, and right through the Flamingo, since the curtains went right out the back door. Reality is like water in the face. Sobered, frustrated and angry, they stormed out onto the street, and back through the front door.

Well, almost. The front door was a bit crowded. Five very big, very mean-looking Mexicans barred their way. "May we assist you, gringos?" "Gringos" came out like something you step in if you own a poodle and a small backyard.

Sonny spoke quietly. Danny restrained Left Face and Paul Bradly. Bradly, at six feet four inches, was flushed and angry.

"Perhaps you saw four lovely *señoritas* with us earlier. That is all we seek." Sonny's voice was low, restrained, and Danny knew it was taking all he had not to leap at the five Mexicans.

"Perhaps you are wrong, *señors*. We saw no women." Paul moved forward, and stopped at the click of the switchblade in the biggest Mexican's hand. "Are they worth dying for, Big One?" His voice was heavy with menace.

For a long moment, the Marines tried, through the fog of liquor, to gauge their chances. Danny did not like them. "No, they are not." Danny, though the youngest, was the nominal leader of the group. Quietly, they backed off, turned and walked away. The five Mexicans, laughing went back into the Flamingo bar. Ten seconds later, a flying wedge of green followed them at full speed. Their initial rush put all five Mexicans down, and cost the blond six silver dollars as Paul Bradly's forearm sent her ass first over and behind the bar. One silver dollar hung in mid-air, bounced on the bar and rolled right out the front door.

The big man with the knife came low and fast at Sonny, but ran head first into a bar stool and went down like a bull elephant. Danny and Paul picked the second one up by his head, turned him upside down and dropped him on it. The third man weaved slowly in front of Sonny, knife in hand. The knife the big man had been carrying before he attacked the bar stool was in Sonny's hand, held close to the body, left hand wrapped in a table cloth. The man moved forward, Sonny stepped inside, and slashed the man's knife hand, driving his knee into the man's groin in the process. The other two were gone. No one in the club moved.

The four Marines waited, breathing heavily. The big man on the floor got up to his hands and knees. Left Face calmly picked up a table and dropped it on his head. Sonny, still holding the knife, walked behind the bar, picked up the wicker basket of silver dollars and sprayed them with mixer. Shaking the basket as he went, he led the others out of the now half-wrecked Pink Flamingo. However she'd done it, the young blond had picked up, sucked up, or whatever, three hundred sixty-three silver dollars. Once outside, the victorious but slightly battered young men hailed a cab.

"Driver, take us to the best whorehouse in Mexico," Sonny said. The cab pulled away and out of town, the pink, thirty-foot-high Flamingo fading in the distance.

Much was said the next day as the four young men returned to MCRD. Paul Bradly said tall redheads were great, but then, to Paul Bradly, tall *redwoods* were great. Sonny Flores said, and no one doubted him, that he had come twice, but she had used the whole roll of toilet paper. Danny said his black-haired beauty was the best fuck he'd ever had. Danny Wood lied. The room, the roll of toilet paper, everything, had killed whatever sexual desire he might have had. Nancy, if that was her name, was a very wise lady. She had stripped him nude, pulled one clasp on her gown and pressed her own nude body to his. He had talked for four hours and finally fallen asleep on her breasts. Somehow, he felt more of a man, anyway. Given his pick of ninety women, he had correctly picked the one he needed most.

Friday had been Graduation Day. Monday, each new Marine received thirty days leave, followed by his first real set of orders. Some received orders to combat training, to be followed by leave time. Some were assigned to various schools across the country. And seven, including Daniel Wood, had previously cut orders cancelled literally as they boarded the buses to leave MCRD. They were told to remain at MCRD, Casual Company, pending the court martial of Corporal Browning for the alleged offense of striking one Private Allan Scourby, Platoon 175, thereby causing said Private Scourby to suffer permanent loss of hearing in one ear. Daniel Wood was supposed to have witnessed the incident. In fact, he had not, nor did he have any knowledge of it.

Danny Wood's orders, now cancelled, had been to take an immediate thirty-day leave and then to travel by air to Quantico Marine Base, Quantico, Virginia. There he was to begin Marine Radio and Intelligence School. His test scores had been high, he had requested the school—wanted it badly—and now it was to be denied him. The school was to begin in forty days, and last fourteen months. It was more than he had dreamed he might get. By missing it now, he would miss it forever.

Stung and furiously angry, Danny dropped his gear off and stormed to Battalion Headquarters. Major Axman was not sympathetic. Daniel G. Wood was a Marine. His orders had been changed for good reason. He could reapply for the school at a later date. For now, he would follow orders. Issued a green seven-day liberty pass, he was dismissed without further explanation. He knew nothing about the Scourby incident. Nevertheless, he was a witness, and could, *would* so testify in court. Meanwhile, he would be assigned to the Base Casual Company, with liberty every night guaranteed by his little green pass. Did Private Wood have anything further to ask? Private Wood did not. Most of Platoon 175 scattered to whatever their orders required. Danny Wood stayed. That simple change of orders would change his life and follow him grimly wherever he went.

Danny walked through the plush front doors of the El Cortez Hotel in San Diego. The first time he had seen the beautiful hotel, he'd been determined to spend one weekend alone with a local pretty, even if it cost him a month's pay. It would have. Instead, he was headed upstairs to see his father, his mother, and of all people, his mother's boyfriend, Dick. Oh, well, he liked Dick. If his mom and dad argued, he could count on Dick to get his mother out of there. As the elevator took him to the twelfth-floor suite, he realized he'd missed his parents very much. If that were true, why didn't he want to see them now? He was dressed in his tropical gabardine uniform, a light, soft tan, shoes spitshined, his hat cocked at just the right angle. Danny's parents both gushed in surprise when Danny entered their suite.

"My God, look what happened to him," his father said, his voice proud.

His mother hurtled into his arms saying, "They cut off your beautiful hair." The comments, made fifteen weeks after they had sent him off to San Diego in June, summed up neatly the differences between mother and father.

"It's a regulation haircut, Mom. A crewcut. I like it."

"Looks like you packed on some muscle, son."

"Yeah, Dad. Come in at 118, now I'm exactly 170 pounds. How 'bout that?"

His mother stepped back, holding him at arm's length. "Danny, you look, well, so different." There was a twinge of sadness in her voice. This tall, erect, powerfully built Marine had somehow stolen her son.

"What did you expect, Eva?" George Wood asked. "He's a Marine now. The little boy has flown the nest, and all for the better, from where I sit."

Dick Bradly had been around this before, and as Danny had hoped, walked forward and stuck out a big hand. At six two, and two hundred forty-five pounds, he had a massive upper torso, and dwarfed everyone in the room. "How are you, son? You look great." The words were sincere. Danny acknowledged the comment with a slight smile.

"Paul tells us you made Honor Platoon," his father said.

"Yeah, Dad, we did. Tough as hell, but we did."

"Tell us about it!" gushed his mother.

"You want a drink, son?" Dick asked. His mother looked shocked.

"Can I get a couple cold beers?"

"You got 'em," Dick said, calling room service. His mother glared at him. "Hell, honey, he's a man."

"He's only seventeen," his mother said defensively.

"Eighteen in a week," Danny said.

The beer came up almost instantly, a sixpack, icy cold. His dad took one, handed one to Danny, and they tipped bottles. "To my son, the Marine," said George Wood.

"To the Marines," Dick said, tipping his toward Danny. Saying nothing, Danny tipped his beer and tugged at it, looking at these three people who had once been a fair part of his life, and realizing, slowly, that they could never be part of his life again. As civilians, they simply didn't fit anymore.

"Go on, honey," his mother said. "Tell us about boot camp. Tell us about the rifle range. Paul says you shot a perfect score, and saved Honor Platoon for your outfit. Tell us everything."

George Wood tossed down his beer. "C'mon, Danny. You can tell us all about it over dinner. On us, whatever you want. We have reservations downstairs." Danny's father smiled wide and true at his son.

Oh, hell, why not? That's why they were here. Danny knew his perfect score had "finalized" the range win. He also knew the low shooters, the twenty young men who qualified very low, against much pressure, were more responsible for winning at the range than he was. Nevertheless, over the next four hours, Danny dutifully told them whatever they wanted to hear. Later, when he returned to base, he wondered if it had been worth $500 to listen to. Apparently, they thought it was. Since they were flying back to Seattle the next day, he hoped so. As he re-entered the base, he vowed when his leave finally came, to spend as little time as possible with his parents. The gulf that had sent him into the Marines was now wider than ever.

Two weeks after his platoon mates had gone on their way, Danny was called as a witness at Corporal Browning's Special Court Martial. He was asked perfunctorily what he had witnessed, to which he answered he had witnessed nothing at all. He was dismissed as a witness. Total time: three minutes on the stand. The trial had twelve prosecution witnesses, including the now partially deaf Private Scourby. It lasted two hours. The guilty verdict cost Corporal Browning his stripes and a ninety-day brig sentence.

On Monday, Danny boarded a bus in San Diego, enroute to Seattle and a long overdue thirty-day leave. His travel orders specified choice of flying or bus. Danny chose the bus home, and flying back, pocketing the difference and enduring the long, coast-length trip home. He saw very little on the bus trip back to Seattle. In his seabags were his new orders, effective after his leave ended. Danny had been reclassified to combat training at Camp Pendleton, California. He was to be one of the staples of the Marine Corps, the combat rifleman. There were to be no schools in his immediate future. Bitterly, Danny endured the bus ride in stony silence. Corporal Browning's trial had made him a prisoner of fate. In ninety days, Corporal Browning would resume his normal duties. For Danny Wood, nothing in his life would be normal again.

Danny Wood's homecoming went unnoticed, since he had sent no word as to the exact time and date, or even the method of travel. He did not want to be met by his mother, and simply not sending exact information was his only guarantee that she would not have a chance to orchestrate his thirty days back in Seattle.

Collecting his seabag, he went into the bus depot and to the men's room. Changing into winter greens, he shaved and got a shoeshine, tipping the elderly washroom attendant a lavish fifty cents, considering the base pay of a Marine private was only $83.20 per month. Abruptly, though he was within walking distance of his mother's apartment, Danny decided not to go there. Instead, he shouldered his seabag and walked the few blocks downtown to the Olympic Hotel, Seattle's largest and most expensive. It was impulsive, and for no particular reason, except a radical break from the rigidly oppressive discipline of the past months. These thirty days were his. He would damn well spend them the way he wanted. The desk clerk looked puzzled as Danny checked in, noting Danny's home address was less than a half mile from the hotel.

"Home on leave, son?"

Danny signed his name without answering. "My key, please." The desk man immediately handed Danny the key, popping the desk bell to summon the bellhop.

"Never mind. I'll find my way," Danny said, shouldering the heavy seabag. The bellhop looked relieved. That bag would have been a real bitch, and probably no tip, either. He was right on both counts.

The lush carpet made no sound as Danny approached the elevators, noting quickly that the operator, about twenty and blond, needed further investigation.

"Twelve, please," Danny said, flashing his most disarming smile and locking her eyes with his, having already determined her figure was sensational. She extended her right hand outward, in that curious move elevator operators use, as if they were going to catch the doors as they closed. She turned away, but not before Danny caught the deep, rose-colored flush that covered her cheeks when their eyes locked. Now, as the elevator moved up, the same flush appeared on the back of her neck. She had long legs, and the most compact ass Danny had ever seen. He had an immediate erection, and almost as if she sensed it, her back straightened, as if she were trying to make her lush curves disappear. It didn't work.

"This is twelve, Sir," she said, her voice cracking slightly on the word *this*. The doors swung open, the blond holding them, again with her right arm.

Danny glanced at his room key, then stared hard at the blond. She was worth staring at. "Ah...Miss, my room number is 1224. Which way is that?"

Again the flushed cheeks. "Down the hall to your left, Sir."

"Skip the 'Sir.' My name's Danny. What's yours?"

"Ellen." The name popped out on its own, and a slightly shocked look appeared on her face.

"When do you get off shift?"

"I just came on, at six. I don't get off until two."

"What then?"

"I go home, that's what then." This Marine sure had his nerve.

"Well, Ellen, if you change your mind about going home, I'll be having a late breakfast about then, or an early one, depending how you see it. I hate to eat alone. I'll see you then." Danny picked up his bag, smiled at her and said, "Room 1224. Just

68

knock. I'll be there." And he slipped out the door and down the hall.

Ellen closed the doors, then promptly opened them again, sticking her head out and calling out after him, "I won't be there, you know."

Danny just waved, and continued down the long hall. Room 1224 was a corner suite, with a view of Puget Sound that was breathtaking, even though as a native-born he had seen it all his life. After carefully unpacking his seabag, Danny glanced around the room. He had asked for a nice one, and 1224 was plush. The tiled bathroom was large, and well equipped. Danny stayed in the shower for a full twenty minutes, towelled himself dry and lay down on the large bed. He did not wake up until 9:00 P.M. Still no one in Seattle knew he was home.

Danny got up, and with a black turtleneck, black gabardine slacks and a short white mohair jacket he'd bought in San Diego, transformed himself into Danny Wood, civilian. He summoned the elevator three different times before the fourth elevator opened, and Ellen whatever-her-name-was said "going down" before she recognized him. "Well, that's quite a difference," she blurted.

"Better?" asked Danny.

"You look like two different people," she answered, as the elevator started down.

"You didn't answer my question," said Danny.

"It's just different," she replied.

The door swung open and Danny stepped out. "What's my room number?" asked Danny.

"I forgot," said Ellen, closing the doors in his face.

Lighting a Pall Mall, Danny flipped his key on the desk.

"Is your room satisfactory, sir?"

Danny thought about Ellen. "It's furnished beautifully."

The clerk beamed, and Danny crossed the lobby and headed home. Not to his mother's. Home. Danny headed straight for the 211 Club, his home away from home since he was twelve years old. It was to be different in a way he was not to fully understand. Now, it was just a pool room.

The 211 Club had not changed. Lou, the owner, was delighted to see him, telling him how great he looked, including the crew-cut hair. In June, when Danny had last been in the club, he'd been a skinny 118 pounds. Now, he was a hard-muscled 170. After much "howv'ya been" talk, Lou advised him the beer was on the house. Going to the cue locker, Danny inserted the tiny key and pulled the mahogany drawer out. There, in space 191, all three of his custom-made Chicago-built cues lay just as they had when he'd left. He noticed Lou had re-tipped his twenty-one-ounce three-cushion billiard cue. Pulling it out, he hefted it like an old friend, which in a way, it was.

Picking up a box of three balls from Lou, Danny walked back into the darkened interior of the club, threading his way through the players to his favorite table, as Lou obligingly removed its dust cover. He removed the lid from the box and tipped the two white and one red oversize ivory balls onto the perfect emerald-green covered table, watching with pleasure as they rolled straight and true.

As he chalked the stick, he looked intently around the room. The club was full of people he had known for years, mostly in their forties now. It was familiar ground, but somehow it, or he, had changed. Danny moved around the square green island, smoothly stroking the heavy balls, feeling the rustiness slowly melting away. His stroke was not what it once was, but he'd been the best. Even the long period of not playing had not changed that. He was a bit ragged, but still the best. Surprisingly, very few of the people he had known had said much to him. On the other hand, he had no particular need to talk to them either.

"Hello, Danny." It was Anita, the spectacular twenty-six-year-old blond who had so often bankrolled the high-stakes games he liked to play. She'd always seemed so much older. Now, he felt as adult as she.

"Hi, Neets, how are you? You look great."

70

Her wide blue eyes softened, and she smiled brightly. "Talk about looking great. Danny, you're beautiful. What did the Marines do to you?"

"Honey, they beat the shit out of me, that's what." Danny continued to practice, as Anita watched in open admiration.

"Danny?"

"What, sugar?" Danny answered.

"Are you busy later? I'm not. We've never made it, you know. I never could figure out why." Her flawless face was very serious.

Danny stopped shooting and walked over to her, holding her tightly at the shoulders. "Anita, to me, you've always been the best. You've bankrolled me, and been my friend for years. In my own way, I love you, but not in the way I would anyone else. We could make it, and I'd love it. But it might spoil what we have, whatever that is, and I don't want that to change. Do you?"

Anita leaned forward and kissed Danny, a long, slow, tender kiss. "You're right, Danny. I don't want to spoil it. I love you, too." There were tears in her eyes as she turned away and headed for the bar.

Danny continued his solitary play, drinking Lou's free beer and losing himself in the game. As he played, Danny noticed a husky, red-haired youth of about twenty watching him. After a short time, the red-haired man nonchalantly approached Danny and said, "You wanna play a game?"

Without looking up, Danny said, "What did you have in mind?"

"Oh, how 'bout fifteen points, five bucks and table time?"

"Okay. My name's Danny. What's yours?"

"Everybody just calls me Red. Funny, I come here every day and I never seen you."

Danny barked out to Lou to change the time card on the table. "How long you been comin' in here?"

"About two months. I'm from San Francisco."

"Well," Danny answered, "you haven't seen me because I haven't been around. Lag for break?"

"Suits me." The redhead called to Lou, asking for his best

billiard cue. Lou hurriedly brought it. Obviously, thought Danny, this dude has made a name at the 211. The two youths hunched over their white ball, and simultaneously lagged it across the table and off the end cushion. Slowly, the balls came back. Danny's ball stopped only one inch from the rail. Red's stopped flat and flush against it. "My break."

"So it is," Danny said, sitting down.

"Fifteen points a game, five and the time, right, sport?"

Sport. Wrong word. "That's the game," replied Danny, the word "sport" bouncing around in his head.

Red was very, very good. He made the almost automatic three-cushion break for his first point, and followed with a run of six, two of which were very tough. "Your shot, sport."

Danny shot and missed. Red ran four. Danny ran three, followed by Red's four and out for fifteen points, the game and five dollars.

"Again?" Red said, as Danny peeled off a five and handed it to him.

"Why not?"

"It's your money, sport."

Sport. Game two, three and four were much the same. The red-headed youth was cocky, shooting fast and loose, while Danny imperceptibly narrowed the gap in scoring.

"Tell you what, sport, I'll give you a chance to get that twenty back. Play for ten?"

"Why not?" Danny answered, as Anita came back toward the table, sitting down only a few feet away. Danny had $200 left in his bankroll. Five games later, at ten a game, that had been reduced to $150, and Danny had been beaten badly each time.

"Tough luck, sport, looks like it just ain't your night." Red sat down, tugging at his beer, his cue lying on the table. "You gonna quit, sport?"

"Maybe my luck will change," Danny replied, glancing at Anita. She crossed her legs, settled in her chair and nodded. "Okay, Red, let's shoot billiards. Shoot out. Five games. Best out of five, for a hundred."

Red leaped to his feet and picked up his cue. "You're on, sport."

Red won the first two, by three points and two points. "Easy money, huh?"

Anita stood up and moved to sit directly next to the table, her eyes smoldering. "Take him, Danny, he's a loser."

"Who asked you, chick?" Red demanded.

"Nobody, *sport*, just play the game." There was barely concealed fury in her voice.

"Well, looks like you got a rooting section of one. Won't help none. None at all."

Danny stared at his fingernails, not looking at the man, when he said, "I'm down seventy dollars and two games to zip. Let's make the bet two hundred and fifty."

The redhead grinned broadly. "It's your money."

And so it was, as Danny swept the next three games, winning each game by only one point.

"You were lucky."

"Yeah, well I need luck. You shoot a good stick," Danny replied, handing the two hundred and fifty dollars to Anita.

"What the hell is this? She your fucking banker, or what?"

"No, Red. It's just that big money makes me nervous. How about you?"

"Shit, I'll play you one twenty-five point game for whatever you want."

Danny stared hard at the red-haired youth. For a brief instant, he saw a flicker of apprehension in the man's eyes. "How much money do you have?" Danny asked.

"Enough."

"What's enough?"

Red's hand dived into his pocket, pulling out a wad of crumpled bills, counting it out on the emerald finish, angrily rolling the three balls out of his way. "I got five hundred and twenty dollars. That bother you?"

"Yeah. Bet the five hundred and keep the twenty for cab fare. Give it to the lady. She'll hold it for you."

"I wouldn't let her hold my cock, sport. You never know where her hands have been."

Anita remained impassive, not answering.

"No bet, then?" Danny asked.

"Sure, it's a bet. But I hold onto my bread. You ain't gonna get none of it anyway. Bet the five twenty." By now, twenty or so regulars, drawn to the action, circled the two players, including Lou the owner, and Johnny Temp, a regular victim of Danny's in the past.

"Lag for break," Danny said.

The two white balls went slowly down the table, and back. Red won the lag, and ran eight straight points. "How do you feel now?"

With a broad smile, Danny answered, "Fine. Just fine." And then, Danny Wood was back. Moving swiftly around the table, Danny ran seventeen consecutive points, the best billiard run of his life, the white balls chasing the three rails and the red ball as if by magic, the stroke clean and smooth. Red looked stunned.

"Shoot, punk." It came out a snarl, though the smile remained on Danny's face.

It was obvious his opponent was completely rattled as he stepped to the table. Somehow the man in black had changed. The whole atmosphere had changed. Beads of perspiration broke out on the redhead's forehead, as he bent over the table, running four and missing a very easy shot, making the score seventeen to twelve. He was not to shoot again. In a blur of perfection, Danny walked quickly from shot to shot, running eight straight, and out. "Now, give the lady five hundred and twenty dollars. We are through shooting billiards. Also, apologize, nice and loud, so I can hear it."

Johnny Temp laughed out loud. Lou looked very nervous. "Now, boys, there's no need..."

"Pay. And apologize. Right now."

"You hustled me!" Red said.

"I thought it was the other way around," Johnny Temp said, thoroughly enjoying the show.

Red furiously threw the fat wad of crumpled bills onto the table, some of them dropping to the worn carpet. Danny put down his cue, balancing lightly on the balls of his feet, hands held loose at his side. "Pile it up, punk. I'm only gonna ask you once."

The tall redhead rushed at Danny, cue stick in hand. As he swung it at Danny's head, Danny ducked inside the taller man, parried the blow with his left arm and, fingers stiff and pointed, thrust his right hand bayonet-like into the man's stomach. Red grunted in surprise and pain, gasping for breath, as Danny stepped around him, placed his foot behind Red's knee, and pushed, sending Red crashing to the floor, still doubled up in pain. "While you're down there, pick up my money."

Slowly, pain etched on his face, Red crawled around the floor, picking up the loose bills and, while still on his knees, reaching up to place them on the table. Finally, the table was covered with bills of all sizes, and feebly, Red stood up, clutching his stomach with one hand, his nose bleeding.

"Count it." Danny had never in his life been so sure, or so frightened, of what he felt. He'd wanted to kill the man.

Anita came to him, grasping his arms tightly. "That's enough, Danny. It's over. You have nothing to prove." She was startled by the coiled spring tension of his body. She sensed Danny wanted the man to say something, do something, so that he could strike again. It was not the Danny she knew. A sudden chill passed through his body as Danny relaxed, a smile without warmth on his face, his eyes cold and distant.

"Okay, Neets, it's over." Danny walked to the table and picked up the money, returning to Anita and handing her a wad of bills. "Two hundred and sixty dollars, honey, your share. And thanks."

Anita's eyes filled with hurt. "You never paid me before, Danny."

"Never was a long time ago, and time changes things. I'm changed." Kissing her lightly on the mouth, Danny turned abruptly away, the crowd parting to let him through as he went to the elevator and down to the street.

A few minutes later, Anita finally unclenched her hand, looked at the money and burst into tears. Danny had merely beaten Red, on the billiard table and physically. But he had left her forever. Her affection for Danny was a wishful illusion and he had stolen it away. Carefully, neatly, she stacked the bills in an ashtray, struck her gold lighter and watched her mirror image curl and twist into a glowing, smokey, gray heap. Times change.

The streets of Seattle on a November night have a color unseen anywhere else in the world. Raining or not, they shimmer basalt black, living streets that hold the city's seven hills in brilliant bondage. Those people unfamiliar with the city say, "Oh, yeah, Seattle, it rains there all the time." It doesn't, of course, but it bears the stigma nevertheless. A stigma that natives of the city promote, to keep outsiders out.

Danny Wood knew the streets as well as anyone, and better than most. His encounter with the red-haired hustler, coupled with some strange difference in himself and Anita, slowly washed away on the rainless streets. In walking these familiar streets, Danny touched his past, and peered tentatively at his future. Heading back to his hotel, he realized that he could see nothing clearly, past or future. He most certainly was no longer a boy. But it would take many more years than he knew to claim himself a man. When a boy child is born, he is issued a claim check on manhood, on what is expected, on what he will become or accomplish. Contrary to common male beliefs, rarely is that claim to manhood cashed in. The only time parental expectations are assured is during the term of pregnancy. Parental expectations after that are, at best, iffy. The price on parental expectations is high. For Danny Wood, it was too high. One day he would claim manhood and no one would notice.

The knock on room 1224's door came at 2:15 A.M. Danny, lying fully clothed on the bed, was not surprised. Some women you could read; some you couldn't. He had read Ellen with no difficulty. The tiny tap, tap on the door again. She was about to change her mind. Danny swung the door wide and there she stood, slim and blond and trimly dressed in a simple white turtleneck and dressy slacks, carrying her coat.

"I missed my bus." She made no attempt to enter the room.

"That's too bad," said Danny, doing his best to hide the pleasure he felt. It had been a long, long time.

"You said something about breakfast, or whatever. Does the offer still stand?"

Danny did not answer, simply grabbing his jacket and her arm at the same time. "Is the El Gaucho okay?"

She looked startled, and then her deep blue eyes widened in pleasurable anticipation. The El Gaucho was very expensive. At twenty-three, she'd never been there. It was famous for its "hunt breakfast," which began at 2:00 A.M. and went until 6:00 A.M. As she walked down the hall toward the elevators, she tucked her arm through Danny's. "The El Gaucho is fine. I'm famished."

The hunt was on.

The hunt breakfast, a marvelous mixture of steak, ham, a variety of fruits and cereals, plus a huge omelet, had been eaten with little conversation. Ellen had not exaggerated. She was famished. Danny had no idea where she'd put it all. He also had no way of knowing that her shift lunch consisted of one peanut butter sandwich and an orange. Ellen made very little money, and what she made went into well-made clothes and a well-stocked hope chest. At twenty-three, she was beginning to wonder if "hopeless" chest didn't better fit her situation.

Now, sipping coffee and leaning back into the plush, llama fur booth, she studied this brash young man who had treated her so nicely. Her mother had warned her since she was seventeen not to date servicemen. Until now, she hadn't; in fact, she had dated very little at all. She watched him closely, her luminous blue eyes bright with interest as he lit his cigarette, the Zippo clicking open and shut with only a slight flare of light. Reaching into her purse, she pulled out her own cigarettes, only to find the Zippo lit as soon as the cigarette touched her lips. The lighter cradled in his palm, his fingers touched her lower cheek as she accepted the light, her eyes looking straight into his. The touch, almost unnoticed, was a caress so intimate she trembled.

She had never been so drawn to anyone in her life. He made love to her with his eyes and with an air of intimacy that both excited and frightened her. He was smooth, but not too smooth, polished and poised, but somehow letting out bits and flashes of an intensity she had never seen. She was going to bed with him. She knew it. And so did he. Nice girls didn't do this sort of thing. Ellen Madden was a nice girl. She'd slept with two men in her whole life, both in high school, furtive, fumbling nothings in her mind. You loved a boy, and sooner or later, he said he loved you, and you just did it. Then the boy lost interest and went on to lie and lay another girl. For five years, nobody had even come close. She'd seen to that. Marriage first, or no go.

Now, she was more sexually aware than ever before. There was no logic to it, but there it was. These thoughts took only a minute to run through her mind. She flushed bright pink cheeks as she noticed the moistness magically dampening her panties. The embarrassment passed quickly. She felt thoroughly wicked, and she liked it.

"Danny, what's it like being a Marine?"

"It has its ups and downs."

With a throaty laugh, she answered, "That's supposed to be my line."

"It's basically the same. Every day, people tell you where they want to get off. They just tell me where to get off, and when."

She thought a moment, and said, "I gather you don't like being a Marine?"

"Wrong, sugar, I like it. I really do." The word *sugar* stroked her, its easy intimacy natural, not offensive.

"How long have you been in?"

Danny studied Ellen's face. Should he lie? "I just got out of boot camp. I was in the Reserves here in Seattle until June. I got

78

discharged from the Reserves and went regular, all the same day."

Ellen's blue eyes widened a bit. "Danny, how old are you?"

"Does it matter?"

"No, not really. I'm just curious."

"Well, if it doesn't matter, I'm eighteen. Just a baby."

The blue eyes widened even more. "God, I thought you were twenty-five, at least. I'm twenty-three!"

Danny smiled, his eyes intense and bright, almost black. "Don't apologize. I don't mind older women."

At first she had no idea what to think. Why, he was just a kid. But, seeing the amusement on his face, she could only laugh, slowly at first, and then loud and out of control. Embarrassed, she looked around the restaurant. Nobody was paying the slightest attention to her. "Some baby, Danny. I'll bet you say that to all the girls."

Now Danny laughed too. "Actually, I do say it to all the girls. Shall we go?"

"Where?"

"To bed."

The answer was quick and direct. "You take quite a lot for granted, don't you?" The words failed to hide her pleasure at *being* taken for granted.

"Not really. It just seemed like a good idea." Danny did not press the issue.

Ellen did. "I think you're right. Let's go to your room, and go to bed."

"What room?"

"1224. Down to your left, sir." Ellen's voice was gay and throaty. She'd never been so excited in her life.

"I told you you'd remember the room number."

"If I had not, we wouldn't be here now, would we?"

Danny brushed the back of her neck with his hands as he helped her on with her coat. She shivered at his touch, grabbed his hand and literally pulled him out the door and into the night.

Ten minutes later, the door to room 1224 shut behind them,

79

the click of the lock audible down the hall. The hall being empty, nobody heard it. Suddenly, Danny pulled Ellen to him.

Ellen Madden's back arched, her hips high and her feet flat on the bed, her head moving on the damp pillow, left, right, left, right. She was not experienced in bed. She had never climaxed. This lovemaking had been more than she had believed possible, more than her wildest fantasies. As soon as they had closed the door, Danny had stripped her nude, not bothering to turn out the lights. Proper girls turned out the light. He had then undressed quickly, and throwing back the covers, had simply pushed her down and taken her with such fury and passion, it had left her breathless and a little frightened. He had come almost at once, exploding inside her while holding his body high above her, the powerful muscles in his chest and arms knotted in a rippling, moving mass. Then it had been over. Two minutes, wham bam, before she could even react. He had rolled off her immediately, and walked into the bathroom. Disappointed, breathing heavily, she had the same feeling she'd experienced in high school. Frustrated and angry, she also worried instantly that this whole, fast, ridiculous episode would possibly get her pregnant. Damn him. Damn men. Damn eighteen-year-old boys with eyes that burned through you and made you what you *wanted* to be.

Then, incredibly, Danny had walked back to her, carrying a warm washcloth, a cigarette dangling from his mouth. Handing her the cigarette, he had gently spread her thighs, and with infinite tenderness, began to wipe her off, a soft smile on his face, bending occasionally to kiss her cheek, still flushed deep pink. The washcloth moved slowly over her, at once soothing her while at the same time bringing her ardently alive. Occasionally he would kiss her breasts, first one, then the other, springing her nipples erect with excitement. Using a small, dry towel, he gently wiped the perspiration from her forehead, taking the cigarette from her and, after one puff, snuffing it out in the ashtray next to the bed. Putting the washcloth and towel down, he lay down and pulled her to him. He was erect and hard against her stomach as he slowly stroked and kissed her everywhere. He'd had no intention of leaving her unsatisfied.

Talking to her, stroking her, he placed her hand on his cock, and she was shocked to find out how good it felt. She tried to remember if she had ever actually touched one before. He had clamped his mouth on her breast, sucking the nipple, softly, then harder, the pleasure almost pain. Without her realizing it, he had slipped under her, sitting her up, knees straddling his hips. Then, magically, he was inside her, big and deep, his hips still, his hands caressing her breasts, pinching her nipples. Her nipples strained toward his fingers. It wasn't pain, after all. It was indescribable pleasure. Her body was good, she knew, but now Danny was talking to her, telling her how beautiful she was, how perfect she was.

"What do I do?" She had no idea, as Danny remained perfectly still, big and tight inside her.

"Just move, Ellen. Just move. Feel me. Touch me. But don't worry about me. Don't think. Don't do anything but feel."

Slowly, she raised her hips, awkwardly, up and down, and his hands guided her, moving her hips in a slow, erotic circle. She felt filled, totally possessed, her blond hair wet, her whole body damp, the downy blond pubic hair matted with her own inner moisture. All the time, Danny talked to her, erotic words that had her hips driving down on him, impaled, lost, outside herself. Slowly, deep inside her, small explosions climbed, bumping over and into each other, her hips moving on their own, her head thrown back.

Suddenly Danny arched his hips high, pulling her down, and her first climax ever smashed through her body, as she froze still, locked hard and pulled down, Danny's cock high and deep in her. Her mouth opened, as spasms hit her like electric shocks. Vaguely she heard Danny saying "fuck it, fuck it, fuck it" over and over, an obscenity she hated that now seemed to be a word of infinite love. Even as she heard it, wave after wave of pleasure hit her again, until, legs weak, her body

81

sensitive everywhere, she collapsed forward onto Danny's chest, and burying her damp hair in his neck, wept softly as the pleasure slowed, stilled but remained with her.

Still joined to her, Danny slipped his left leg under her body, pulled her left leg over his right hip, and rolled her on her side, patting her gently, stroking her damp face, talking quietly. Exhausted, twitching with every movement, she felt him deep and hard, still in her. Under the soft blanket of his voice, she relaxed and fell asleep.

Staring at the ceiling, Danny, careful not to awaken her, reached for a Pall Mall, lit it and leaned back, pulling his upper body slightly away from Ellen, but still deep inside her. Slipping the sheet over her hips, he watched her damp, full breasts move, nipples still erect, as she shifted her head to his pillow, a contented sigh and even, steady breathing a sign she was happy and exhausted. Staring at the ceiling again, Danny smoked quietly, unsmiling. Inside her, he remained erect and hard. He did not sleep.

"Hi."

"Hi, yourself," Ellen replied, sleepily looking up at Danny's face as he sat nude on the side of the bed.

"How do you feel?"

"I don't know for sure." Ellen threw her arms around Danny's neck and pulled him down to her, putting his hands on her breasts, reaching down for him. "Danny, I love you."

Danny straightened up, still caressing her breasts. "Honey, you are not in love with me. Not yet. You're in love with what we have."

"It feels like love. I feel like love. It's okay if you don't. But I love you, and I know it."

Danny looked at her, his eyes soft, warming her without saying 'I love you.' "Go take a shower and get your body back here. Go on." His finger was suddenly in her, moving gently, insistently.

"I can't. Not if you keep that up. God, what are you doing to me?"

82

Danny withdrew his hand. "Not to you. With you. Us. Together. Go take a shower."

"Yes, Sir, Private Marine, Sir," said Ellen, bouncing out of bed. As she stood before him, completely naked, she was startled to discover she was not the least bit embarrassed.

"You have a perfect body, sugar." Danny, still sitting on the bed, pulled her to him, and kissed each breast, then trailed his mouth down the soft, firm belly to just below her navel, nipping her playfully.

She swivel-hipped her way to the bathroom, feeling wicked and womanly. While she showered, she tried to understand the change. But it didn't matter. She had been a twenty-three-year-old semi-virgin. Now, she was a woman. She loved Danny, and she'd make him love her, even if just a little bit. A little bit of Danny Wood was more than a whole lot of anybody else. As she towelled herself dry, she noticed her nipples erect, her thighs wet and musky.

Later, dressed for work, considering it was 8:00 P.M. and she was two hours late, she kisssed him passionately and jauntily walked down the hall and downstairs, explaining to the exasperated manager she'd been taking care of her sick mother all night, and was very sorry to be late. She looked beautiful, changed. The manager, a young man with a failing, cold marriage, melted in the face of the bright blue eyes and even brighter smile. For someone who'd been up all night, she looked surprisingly fresh. All was forgiven, he said. Her dazzling smile lit up the busy lobby and she walked toward the bank of elevators, her hips swinging provocatively, something he'd never seen before. Her breasts seemed larger, swaying slightly as she moved. She looked very, very different. Actually, her breasts were swaying beneath her sweater because her bra was in her purse. The sweater, brushing her nipples, made her breasts stand out, unencumbered. As she walked to the elevator, she was humming a tune.

"Going up." Her voice rang out cheerfully, as the elevator loaded, the doors closing her from his view.

It was 11:00 P.M. before he got it. Throughout the shift, every time the door to her elevator opened, he'd tried to place it. Triumphantly, it finally came. She'd been humming, of all things, "Oh, how I hate to get up in the morning." When he went home that night, he was humming it, too. His wife didn't speak to him for three days. Henry Armbruster did *not* hum. Obviously, he was up to something.

The two well-dressed young men had been in the Marine General's office for over two hours. The Marine General had listened with little enthusiasm. He had argued with considerable vehemence. The Korean War was over, period. The initial talks had begun on July 10, 1951, and broken down finally on October 8, 1952. In April, the 26th to be exact, 1953, they had resumed. The Peace Agreement, between the U.N. and North Korea, had been finalized on July 27, 1953. That was that, was it not?

How many Marines had died since July, 1953?

Not that many, replied the General. The First Marine Division was home, except for one regiment.

The earnest young men came to the point. How many dead Marines and other U. S. military people did he want? Fifty a day, one hundred, two hundred?

Exasperated, the General admitted that one was too many.

Fine, advised the well-dressed young men. We know the hard-assed bastard who is about to spill back across the border. A second Korean War. Did the General want that?

The General did not.

Well, neither did the President of the United States. This particular gook General needed to disappear. Somehow. Did the General have any suggestions?

The General did not. Did the well-dressed young men have any?

The answer was quick. Terminate him.

The General's eyes were hooded, withdrawn, as he lit a cigarette, characteristically blowing the smoke out of the right

84

corner of his mouth. The U. S. Marine Corps was not in the assassination business. The U. S. Government was not in the assassination business . . . were they?

The reply was straightforward. In World War II, Admiral Isoroku Yamamoto, Commander in Chief of the Imperial Japanese Fleet, had been assassinated.

The General replied, sarcastically, that Yamamoto had been shot down during wartime.

No, replied the earnest young men, he had been assassinated, by a complicated and daring long-range P–38 assault. The weapon made no difference. The order to kill Yamamoto had come directly from the White House.

Was this order from the White House?

It was.

Was it in writing?

It was not.

Would it be?

It would not.

How was it to be done, then?

The young men stood up. A major strike beyond the 38th Parallel was out of the question. What the General needed was one man. A very good shooter. Could the General find a very good shooter and get him in and out of Korea without anyone outside of this room knowing it?

The Commanding Officer of Camp Pendleton, California, a Medal-of-Honor winner, stood up. He would check it out. That was all.

The two young men walked toward the door. The youngest turned around. We will supply the details. Place. Time. Date. Find us a shooter. If the gook General wasn't dead by the end of January, '55, the Korean War could begin again. Did the General understand?

The General puffed his cigarette once, twice, then snuffed it out expertly with his thumb and forefinger. Who protects the shooter?

Smiles lit up the young men's faces. Hell, General, we do.

When it's over he can have anything the U. S. Government can provide. We tell you where. We tell you when. We get him there and we get him back. Forty-eight hours.

The General sat down. I'll find your shooter. But you buttoned-down assholes had better remember one thing. Not one dead Marine is worth fifty gook Generals. Did they understand?

Of course.

The man must volunteer, did they understand that?

Of course.

I'll see what I can do, then. Now get the fuck out of my office.

Of course. The two young men left as they had come, quietly, but bearing enormous power. The cream of America's Central Intelligence Agency. Legal hit men.

Inside his opulent office, the General reached for his private phone. He wanted a list of the top one hundred marksmen in, or coming to, the First Marine Division.

When?

Now, goddamnit. Were there any other questions?

No, Sir. No questions.

The General slammed the phone down, lighting another cigarette. College boys. All of them.

Danny Wood spent this thirty-day leave on a sexual binge. It was as if a whirlwind had taken the city. Enid, Jean, Ellen, and back again. Danny spent his time in bed, and playing pool, getting no sleep. The eager young bodies merged in his mind. Receptacles, something you just filled, without thinking about it. He told them all the same things, gave them all and more than they could handle, lied to them to make them happy. But they never touched him, not really. He resented them because they either did not know, or did not care. Like them, he needed to be *touched*.

Bob's Chili Parlor was a small hole-in-the-wall on Seattle's waterfront, distinguished by two things: its three-hundred-pound owner and the best damn chili-dog west of the Texas panhandle. It stayed open twenty-four hours every day, including Christmas, and was a stopover for Seattle's night people. Bums, pool hustlers, tired hookers and just plain lonely people were drawn to it by its garish, blinking neon sign and delicious smell.

Danny had been sitting at one end of the U-shaped counter, directly across from a dark-eyed brunette, very pretty, very quiet, wearing a light tan raincoat buttoned up to the throat, only the top button undone in spite of the warmth of the restaurant. Occasionally, she would glance at Danny, and then, pencil in hand, briskly sweep across a large artist's pad she had on the counter, alternately sketching, frowning and drinking coffee.

Danny was in dress winter-green uniform, and he was uncomfortably warm in the small room. He wondered why the hell she didn't take off her raincoat. She must be roasting. Bob swept around the counter, refilling the coffee cups. The brunette sipped hers, holding the cup in both hands, looking over the top of its steaming brim, and right at Danny.

"Do you always wear dark glasses?" Her voice was soft, hesitant, but without a trace of shyness. It was a logical enough question, considering it was 2:00 A.M., and raining like hell outside on this cold November night. Still, her directness startled him.

"Yes, I always wear dark glasses. Why?"

"Because I'd appreciate it if you would take them off for a while. I'm sketching you, and it's coming out all wrong because I can't see your eyes. Would you mind, please?" The voice was silky soft, the dark eyes wide and intense.

Slowly, Danny removed his dark glasses.

She stared at him thoughtfully. "You have nice eyes." She immediately put down her coffee, picked up her pencil and resumed sketching.

Danny didn't know what to think. "Do you always sketch perfect strangers?"

She looked up at him, a tiny fire dancing in the darkness

87

of her eyes. "I only sketch *perfect* strangers."

anny's reply was a meek, "Oh."

"Does it bother you?"

"I don't know. Should it?"

"Well, some people get angry, some don't. Are you the angry type?" All the time she spoke, the pencil darted and flashed across the pad, her long slender fingers occasionally wiping at it. She was shading the drawing, but Danny had no way of knowing.

"No, I'm not the angry type. What happens to the sketch when you're finished?"

"One of two things. I keep it, or I give it to you. Could you tilt your head a little to the right? I still can't get your eyes."

Automatically, Danny did as he was asked.

"Thank you."

Danny smiled. "Anything for the sake of art."

"Don't smile, please."

The smile vanished. This was one very pretty, very interesting lady. There was a sense of aggressiveness, a freewheeling "I'll get my way" attitude about her. He found her eyes, briefly, and locked his to hers. They were expressive, as if she knew something he didn't. Whatever it was, he was determined to find it.

"You're staring at me," she said.

"True. And you're sketching me. I can't draw or paint, but I'm doing my damnedest to read your face."

She went back to her sketch pad, not looking up. "So, how are you doing? Do you read me?"

Danny paused. "Actually no. I guess you'll let me know when the time for reading is through, right?"

She raised her face and looked at him with heated intensity. "Right."

"When?"

She looked up once more. "Like you said, I'll let you know."

"Well, do you like it?" She had walked around the counter and, introducing herself as Natalie, simply handed him the sketch.

"What am I supposed to see?"

"Yourself, as I see you." Her brown eyes flashed again, gone like lightning.

Danny studied the pencil sketch for a long time. Natalie sat quietly next to him, idly stirring her third cup of coffee. "Do I really look that mean?"

"Intense is the word."

Thoughtfully, Danny looked at the sketch. It was damn good, and she knew it. "What is my best feature?"

"You're not predictable. You're like mercury in a bottle. You react the way you're tipped."

"Am I being tipped?"

"My guess would be you tip only when you want to. Like me. That is why sketching you was unusual, exciting. You took those ridiculous shades off and I saw ten different men in your eyes. Your eyes were the hardest part to catch. I believe you're a very difficult man, when you choose to be."

"Is that art or psychology?"

"I majored in both."

"That figures." Danny glanced back at the sketch. They did not look like his eyes. He still thought she'd made him look meaner than hell.

"Don't try to figure me. Have you got a car?"

"Hell, I don't even have a license."

"That's okay. I do." She took the sketch pad from his hand, closed it and stood up. "What's your name?"

"Danny Wood."

"What happens now is I drive you home."

She took his hand, pulling him from the stool. "Never mind paying, Danny. I already have."

Danny was completely off guard. "What if I don't want to go home with you?"

She gave him a slow, amused look. "Of course you do."

She was right. Without hesitation, he let her lead him out the door and into the rain. A sleek Jaguar was parked at the curb.

"Get in. I never lock it."

"This is yours?"

"Of course not. If it was mine, I'd lock it. It belongs to a friend."

"Nice friend."

"He's a prick."

As Danny piled in the passenger side, he glimpsed a long flash of sleek, nylon-clad legs as her raincoat parted. "Nice."

"What?"

"Your legs."

As the car roared away from the curb, she glanced at him, smiled and went through the gears like a race driver. "My legs are not nice. They're great. You'll see."

As the car hurtled through the rainswept streets, Danny figured he probably would.

A deep, husky laugh erupted from her. "Do I scare you, Danny Wood?"

"You bet your ass," Danny answered.

The laugh again. "That's exactly what I'm betting. You should be scared."

Danny said nothing, just smoked quietly, while the Jag roared, splitting the driving rain. When the speedometer read eighty miles an hour, Danny glanced at her. Only a soft smile lit by the green dash lights showed. Fuck it. She could handle the car. In all probability, if she killed me, it wouldn't be by accident.

Natalie lived in a large home overlooking Puget Sound. "C'mon." She swung the door open, the overhead light once again showing a flash of long leg.

The rain smashed into him, wind driven and cold, as he pulled himself up and out of the low-slung car. She grabbed his hand and led him through a locked gate and around the back of the brick house. The key turned, the door swung open and she walked in. Danny just stood there, the rain running down his neck. A soft light switched on inside, and her voice floated out to him. "Well, ninny, are you coming in or not?"

It was a seven-mile walk back to town. He was not *that* big a ninny. He strode through the door, and it shut behind him.

The lower floor of the home was huge, and furnished almost entirely in black and white, including a checkerboard black and white rug. Across the room, Natalie, still wearing her raincoat, was bent over a large stone fireplace, already prepared to light. A long fireplace match flared.

"I love fireplaces. I couldn't live anywhere that didn't have one. Make us a drink, will you, hon. And either step on the black squares or take off your shoes."

A pair of dripping wet spike heels lay just inside the door. She must have switched as she came in, because she was still wearing spikes, bright red patent leather. Danny untied his shoes and dropped them next to hers.

"The bar's by the window. Scotch. No ice. I'm going to dry my hair. Make whatever you like. I'll be right back." She walked down a long hall, still wearing her raincoat, and turned into a door that was obviously a bathroom.

Danny, in his stocking feet, walked across the checkerboard rug that seemed to him to be a foot deep. A beautiful chess board stood near the fireplace. He picked up the king. It was white jade, and very heavy. White jade and black jade. The bar was black leather. He poured her Scotch freestyle, into an exquisite glass with the initial "A" cut into it. The drapes were open behind the bar, and the rain danced and bounced across a patio with white furniture and then ripped across the surface of a long swimming pool, eerily lit from underneath.

He closed the drapes, and after pouring himself three fingers of Johnny Walker Black, he turned back to the warmth of the fireplace. She'd come back into the room, and was sitting on the extended stone hearth, drying her hair with a towel, still wearing the raincoat.

"Your Scotch," Danny said, handing it to her.

An arm popped out from under the towel, to the glass, which disappeared under the towel, only to reappear empty. "Ah, that's so good. Make me another, please?"

Danny walked back to the bar and poured the glass full.

"You must be dying in that heavy coat. Take it off, why don't you. Play chess? You can learn a lot about people by how they play chess." As she sat next to the fire, her hair shone black, deep and rich. She'd set the elaborate chess board and its equally elaborate pieces on the hearth.

Danny said nothing, just taking off his dress-green coat. Loosening his tie, he walked over and sat across the board from her, switching it around so he had the black.

"I always play the black," Danny said, in as casual a voice as he possessed at that moment.

"That's good. I always make the first move."

For the life of him, Danny could not think of a thing to say. He just sat down, and they began to play. She played quietly, as if only the game mattered, still wearing the raincoat. She played an unorthodox, attacking game, seldom taking more than a minute to move. Danny watched in fascination as she gambled, retreated and gambled again. The fire was roaring, one side of her face brightened by it, the other shadowed. He decided she wasn't a beautiful girl. It was much more. His glass emptied as he studied a particularly aggressive move she had made. While he pondered what to do, she got up, filled his glass and put some records on. Dave Brubeck's piano slipped softly across the room, and she stroked the back of his neck as she handed him his drink and sat down.

"Do you like jazz?" she asked.

"Is there anything else?"

"Just one thing."

"What's that?"

"Steady panting."

"I beg your pardon?"

"Steady panting. I like the sound of steady panting. Don't you ever listen?"

Danny took a hard pull on his Scotch. "No, I don't think I have. But if it comes up, I'll listen for it."

"Oh, it will come up."

"Do you always talk like this?"

"Like what?"

"Whose move is it?"

"Why, Danny, it's been your move all night."

That did it. Danny quickly moved a piece, without thinking.

"Check," she said.

He moved again.

"Check."

Again.

"Check . . . and . . . mate."

He lit a cigarette, studied the board and looked at Natalie. "You play like a man."

"So do you." Slowly, she put a cigarette in her mouth and leaned forward. "May I have a light?"

Danny snapped the Zippo, holding it still lit near her face. "The 'A' on the glasses. What does it stand for?"

"Antonelli. Natalie Antonelli. I'm Italian."

The Zippo snapped shut. "I thought somehow if I knew what the 'A' stood for, I'd know more about you. It doesn't help."

"Try asking what you want to know."

"No. But I'll tell you what the 'A' could stand for."

"Okay. Tell me."

"Artist. Aggressive. Aggravating. Animal."

"Do you really think so?"

"Give me time. I'll think of more."

"That's the sweetest thing anyone ever said to me, Daniel Wood. Now can I paint you in the nude?"

Danny laughed softly. "All right. Why not? I suppose I should be flattered. Oh, bullshit, I am flattered. Where do we do it?"

"Right here. My paints and things are in the closet. Why don't you take off your shirt. We'll go on from there." She walked to the closet door, disappeared inside and popped out, arms loaded with paints, brushes and a fold-up easel.

"Freshen your drink, Daniel Wood?"

"I think that would help, yes."

"Done."

In a moment, she had given him a fresh drink, set up her easel and helped him off with his shirt and tie, folding them carefully over a chair. Her hands moved slowly across his deeply tanned chest. "You are beautiful, Daniel Wood. Now you just walk, or sit, or lie down. I'll use pencil first."

Danny said. "Are you going to wear that raincoat all night, even while you paint?"

"Of course not. I said I wanted to paint you in the nude." With a shrug of her shoulders, she unbuttoned the long coat and dropped it to the floor. She was wearing black nylons, a bright red and black bowed garter belt, her red high heels, and a smile.

"Now, Danny, remember. Just act natural. Don't be stiff and rigid. And enjoy your drink."

That was going to be difficult. As Natalie had shrugged off her raincoat, the fire behind her, firm breasts high and defiant, legs spread, the pencil poised to sketch, Daniel Wood had dropped his drink, glass and all, right in his lap.

"Well, don't just sit there, take off your pants."

Danny Wood did not know which shock hit him the hardest: the cold ice and Scotch that landed in his crotch, or the excitement of a raven-haired, lunatic woman.

"Here, let me." Sticking her pencil between her teeth, she crossed the room to the bar, grabbed a towel and walked to where he sat.

"I'll fix it." At least that's what he thought she said. With the pencil clamped in her teeth, he couldn't be sure. She knelt in front of him, and in one swift move with the towel removed the ice from his lap, and the pencil from her mouth.

"Haven't you ever seen a naked woman before?" She stood up.

"You're not naked."

"I know. Do you like it?" She turned away and walked back to the bar, dumped the ice and then crossed the room to the easel. She placed both hands on her hips, spread her legs and glared at him. "Well, do you?"

94

"I've never seen anything like you, ever. C'mere."

"No. I'm going to paint you. I just needed to feel beautiful. Now I do. Take off those wet pants. You'll catch cold."

Automatically, Danny stood up and slipped off his wet pants.

"The shorts, too."

Danny stared at Natalie.

"Daniel Wood, do you actually think a woman that walks the streets in a silk garter belt, spike heels and a raincoat could be anything but serious? Now take off your shorts."

Danny dropped his shorts on top of his pants.

"Oh my, what a big boy you are."

Danny had the biggest hard-on of his life. "Has it occurred to you that I may just bounce your ass on the floor and rape you silly?"

"You're not the type, Danny. We'll rape each other. Now will you sit, or lie down, or walk? I'm going to paint you."

Danny looked at her. "I'm supposed to look at you, while you look at me, dressed like you are, and try to act natural?"

He badly needed a drink. He walked to the bar and poured another Scotch. He should have been very drunk, but he wasn't. He turned back to Natalie. "Why don't you just put me where you want me?"

"Okay. Take that big pillow in the corner, and set it down right here, next to me. Then lie down. On your back, please."

He was less than five feet from her, and looking up at her as well. Never in his life had he wanted anyone more. She looked down at him with a soft smile, a real smile, a smile of pure pleasure.

"You're a beautiful man, Daniel Wood. Now lie still. Talk to me. It's going to be a beautiful painting. And a beautiful night."

Danny stared at her body, the long nylon-clad legs, the spike heels, the small but near perfect breasts, topped by that mass of black hair, and a mind like none he had ever encountered. His hard-on was insistent, throbbing. "I think you'd better talk to me, if you want that painting done."

"All right, Daniel Wood. I'll talk to you. Now lie still."

95

* * *

While Natalie painted, she talked, prodded by Danny's questions.

"Why the raincoat?"

"Why not? I know that all I have on underneath is what you see now. And what you see now has you turned on, and me painting you, and I'm turned on."

"You didn't answer my question."

"I answered it. You're not listening." The brush now flicked from palette to canvas, hung suspended, then swept over the canvas again.

"I'm all ears."

"Not quite, darling. Actually, Danny, I like fantasies. Think a minute. There I am, nude except for that coat, and no one knows it. I have wet dreams, only I'm wide awake. I rub my thighs together, touch myself, mind-fuck if you will. I can come that way. I already have, four times, since I saw you. It was delicious, and you didn't even know."

"Thanks a lot."

"Thank you. It takes a special person. It took you. You should be flattered." The brush flicked back to the canvas.

"You can do that, anytime, just with your mind?"

"No. Not anytime. You were a fantasy. So I came. Now you are here with me, and I intend to come, and come, and come."

"All the heat in this room is not from the fire," Danny replied.

"No, Private Daniel Wood. *We* are the heat. Can't you smell me? I can. That's heat. I'm so wet. I love it. You just keep that look on your face, Daniel Wood. It's going to be a beautiful painting."

"That look is not on my face."

"Sure it is. Besides, if I don't look at your face, I'll never finish this painting."

"Do you do this sort of thing often?"

"No. But I do it well."

"Have you ever been in love?"

"I have loved. In love? I don't think so. How about you?"

96

"No. I have never been in love."

"What are you afraid of?" The brush continued its easy strokes across the canvas.

"Who said I'm afraid?"

"You're afraid of *you*, Daniel. I doubt if a hell of a lot scares you. Your own feelings are what scare you. What you feel now scares you, doesn't it?" She shifted, spreading her legs wide, challenging him with her body as well as her words.

"Yeah. You scare me a little. You certainly haven't given me anywhere to hide."

"I don't want you to hide. I want you to turn loose. *Feel*, for christsake!"

"Come down here, damn you, and I'll feel whatever you want."

She grinned wickedly at him, putting the brush down and standing over him, touching and kneading her firm breasts. "I'm coming down, because my legs are shaking so bad I can't paint anyway. But I want you to let go. Don't touch me. Let me do it all."

"I want to touch you."

"I know. Later. Not now." She knelt by his side, bent over and thrust her mouth on him, her knees spread wide, the high heels going slightly off the rug as her mouth and tongue enveloped him.

Instinctively, he fought her, no matter his intense desire, his explosive need. "I can't come that way. I never have. I want to be in you."

She raised her head, looking at him with a quiet, sure beauty. "Yes, you can. You just won't let go. Watch my body. Watch my mouth. You are *in* me."

She put her right hand on his cock, thrust it deep into her mouth and ran her left hand across his chest, down between her spread thighs, and back across his chest, her smell musky and hot, her mouth tight and pulling him deeper. Watching her mouth, the erotic dance of her hand and hips, the garter belt and high heels starkly erotic, he exploded in her mouth, expecting her to gag. But she sucked harder, holding him, swallowing him, taking him in a way he'd never been taken before. It went on and on, as Danny let his body run wild. Incredibly to him, sucked dry and exhausted, he remained ramrod stiff. Quickly, she swung her legs over his body, and squatting on her high heels, her feet wide, her hands palm down on the floor, she impaled herself on him, moving up and down in a slow, circular motion.

"Watch me, Danny. Watch your cock go in me. Watch me come. Watch me. Now . . . touch my breasts . . . touch me . . ."

It was like no other time in his life. In spite of her, or because of her, he came again, as her inner muscles clenched his cock like tiny fists, her face wild and triumphant. Finally, wracked by her own series of tiny, rapid-fire climaxes, she bore down on him, shuddering, whimpering, her whole body shaking. Her breasts crushed against his chest, she lay flat on him, between his spread legs, her legs holding him tight inside her.

"See, Daniel, that's what *we* are. You let go. And it was so fucking good we're gonna do it some more."

Weakly, still deep in her, Danny patted her taut ass. "When do you figure I'll be able to move again?"

"Not for a while. Sleep." In one swift movement, she was up and off him, the rush of air cold on his wet thighs. She was back in a moment, tenderly washing his body with a warm wet towel, then vigorously drying it.

"Now rest a while. I'll paint." She got back up, without a word, and resumed her painting.

"Where did you learn to do that?"

"Popsicles. When I was thirteen, I practiced blow jobs with popsicles. I got very good at it."

"Popsicles melt."

"So did you, Daniel."

Fifteen hundred miles down the Pacific coast, the Commanding General of the First Marine Division sipped his 6:00 A.M. tea from an ornate, Russian-style glass encased in a pure gold holder, a gift from George S. Patton, the prick. Holding a hard piece of sugar in his mouth, also Russian-style, he sipped the steaming brew, and thoughtfully stared at the stack of green folders on his desk. Was his shooter in that pile of green, boldly stamped "secret" by some asshole who should know that was the best way not to keep anything secret? He picked one up, opened it, frowned. Adams, Richard A., Serial #1376243. Staff Sergeant. Okinawa. Chosin Reservoir. Silver Star. Sniper trained. Semi-psycho. Career Marine.

No. Wrong type. The college boys could never handle this one. The General was no fool. Damned if he'd waste a career Staff Sergeant. He closed the file, turned it over.

Number two. Baker, Darwin D. Darwin D.? He turned it over on top of Adams, Richard A. It wasn't the name. It was the picture. Clear, blue eyes. Iowa born. He sipped the tea again, placing the hard rock sugar on the gold tray. Oh, Darwin would do it. But he wouldn't like it. He needed a real shooter. Darwin did not have a shooter's eyes.

His intelligence chief looked at him from across the desk. The General said, "How many are here?"

"One hundred."

"One hundred. I need one shooter. One. You look at these?"

"I did."

"You pick 'em?"

"Yes, Sir."

"Then give me the top ten, and take the rest out of here."

"Whatever you say, General."

"You bet your ass, Colonel."

"We've been together too long, General. It's never our ass we bet."

"It is this time."

The Colonel stood up, the bulk of the folders under one arm. A small pile remained on the desk.

"Is he in there?"

"He's in there."

"You are dismissed, Colonel. You don't like tea, you don't smoke and you never get up at 5:00 A.M."

"General?"

"What?"

99

"We need someone who gets to bed at 5:00 A.M."

"Yeah. And one that can hit the deck at six. Of all the fucked-up ideas, this tops 'em."

"Yes, Sir."

"I thought I told you to get out of here."

"Sir, the man that goes to bed at five, and gets up at six?"

"Yes?"

"He's in one of those folders."

"He'd better be."

"Count on it, General."

At 9:40 A.M., Sergeant W. R. Spradlin reported as ordered to the First Marine Division's Commander. A chopper had picked him up at MCRD at 8:00 A.M.

The General looked at him coldly. Did the Sergeant like tea? The Sergeant did.

Did the Sergeant realize that Thursday was Thanksgiving? The Sergeant did.

"I have nothing to be thankful for at this moment. Would the Sergeant be interested in making the General thankful?"

The Sergeant did not reply.

"Tell me about this man." The General shoved an open green folder across his desk.

The Sergeant picked it up, glanced at the folder, closed it and put it down. What did the General wish to know?

What did Sergeant Spradlin know?

Sergeant Spradlin believed the young man in the picture was the best Marine, of any age, any time in service or any rank, that the Sergeant had ever known.

Did that include generals?

It did.

Is he a shooter?

He is.

Is he a killer?

He is more. He is a killer with brains. All Marines are killers. The Sergeant knew the difference. This was an individualist,

100

with a twist. He loved the Corps. It was doubtful that he loved anyone, or anything else. He was cool, and tough, and a maverick. But when ordered, he followed orders, explicitly, no matter whose ass or ego he kicked. He was brilliant, had been scheduled for intelligence. A shaft job had cost him that. He didn't like it. He also didn't complain. Begging the General's pardon, but this particular young Marine scared the living shit out of most anyone he met. If he stayed in the Corps, it was the Sergeant's judgment that he would, if he chose, one day be its Commandant.

"Is that it?"

"I believe so, Sir, unless the General has any specific questions?"

"Just one."

"Sir."

"Would you trust this man, all the way, no reservations, no problems? Would you trust him with your life?"

"I would."

"Thank you, Sergeant. The chopper will return you to MCRD. Have a pleasant holiday."

"And you, Sir."

A cold sweat broke out on W. R. Spradlin's neck as he offloaded the chopper in San Diego. At 1:15 that afternoon, he was advised he had been promoted to Technical Sergeant. Effective immediately.

At Camp Pendleton, California, the General stared intently at the face of number one of one hundred. The eyes stared back, quiet, waiting, aware. He took one last look at Private Daniel Gregory Wood, USMC, closed the folder and locked it in his safe.

At four that afternoon, the two earnest young men walked into his office, led there by his intelligence officer.

"General?"

"I have your shooter. He reports here in five days."

"From where?"

"He is presently on leave."

101

Danny spent the remaining days of his leave with Natalie. For the first time in his young life, he was completely fascinated by one woman. The easygoing but shallow younger women he had known before Natalie paled in comparison. Danny had always been more mature than his peers, and he was ready and eager for each new experience her quick mind and supple body presented to him.

Sexually, she shared more with him than he might have learned in a lifetime with anyone else. For Natalie, sex was an adventure, an exploration of limits. At twenty-six, she'd decided, after countless partners, that there were no limits. In Danny, she had a youthful, inexhaustible lover, without pretense and full of fire and energetic passion. They spent many hours of each day savoring each other. To their mutual delight, they were compatible in almost every way sexually, and the long quiet times after sex became a forum for open conversation and shared ideas.

Danny had never experienced the kind of quality time together that Natalie offered, and he responded to it like a thirsty man to water. She'd graduated from college with degrees in art and psychology. She played the piano, and painted professionally. She was well-read, and shared his passion for history and politics, a delightful plus that surprised them both. By their third day together, Danny had tried to explain what he felt for her, that he thought he was in love with her. She had put a stop to that at once, telling him what they had was not love, but better than love. She'd explained to him, in a nightlong conversation interrupted by fierce bouts of torrid lovemaking, that she would never love anyone exclusively. She would never marry. When he asked her if she wanted children, she told him that if she ever did, she would simply have one, with or without love or marriage. This was revolutionary talk in 1954, and Danny didn't understand it at all. But it only added to her mystique, and his fascination. For her part, Natalie had an almost equal regard for Danny. If what they had was not love, it suited them as close enough. They were both highly intelligent individuals, with strong ideas held to themselves. Together, they opened up and shared as much of body, soul and mind as was possible for either of them. It wasn't love, as Natalie said. It was better.

She lay next to him, her leg flung across his buttocks, her body glistening with perspiration. She could feel him running out of her, and she didn't care. She felt very close to him, and with Danny, she never felt the need to jump up and go to the bathroom. It was a special kind of sharing.

"When do you go back?"

"Sunday night. I have to report at 6:30 Monday." Danny, propped on his elbows, lit two cigarettes, handing one to her.

"You've seen too many movies, Daniel."

"It's continental, I'm told. I'm trying to impress you."

"Not necessary, sir. I'm already impressed, as you can plainly see." She pulled her legs up, placing her foot on his buttocks, wiggling her toes wickedly.

"Again?"

"Lord, no, Danny," in mock horror, she pulled her leg away and rolled to her stomach, smiling at him. He was always ready for her, and it gave her a sure, secret pleasure to know it.

"That's the problem with older women. They wear out," Danny said.

"Ha! Just wait a while, buster. We'll see who wears out." She leaned over and pecked him on the cheek, then pulled away, propping her head on one elbow and giving him her serious look.

"I don't want to see you again before you leave. I think you should spend some time with your mother. That gives you two days. Today was lovely, Thanksgiving dinner was lovely, your family was wonderful, if just a bit large. Tonight is going to be the best of all. But tonight ends it, for this trip." She studied his handsome face, waiting for the outburst of protest, the demands on her time, the possessiveness. It didn't happen.

"Okay. I think you're right. I've hardly seen Mom this month. I don't want to hurt her, and I think I have."

"That's it?" Natalie's eyes were wide with surprise.

103

"That's it. What did you expect me to say?"

"I don't know, but I'm pleased. I can fly down to Pendleton, or L.A., or wherever, whenever you need to see me, or vice versa. Would you like that?"

He looked at her with a steady, somber gaze, his hazel eyes fixed on hers.

"That would be expensive."

"I can afford it, Danny. I'm not exactly poor, you know."

"Then, yes, I would like it very much. But not too often. Let's keep it special."

Natalie looked back at him for a long time, reading him easily. He meant it. He had an amazing capacity to make her happy. She took his cigarette from his hand, and with hers, snuffed both out in the bedside ashtray. She put her face down on the pillow and spread her legs wide, rolling her slim hips and bunching the sheet in her hands. She turned her face back toward him, arching her hips. "Fuck me, Danny. Fuck me as hard and rough as you can."

Camp Pendleton was more than just up the coast from San Diego. The difference was incredible to Danny. He was now a Marine, not a boot, led by officers as well as NCO's. Fox Company was a real fighting unit in intensive training, six weeks worth, and he was enjoying it immensely, much to his surprise. Mixing freely with combat veterans, as well as young men fresh from MCRD, had finally let him be a Marine. As they were part of a replacement battalion, overseas duty was assured, although none had any idea where they might go.

Danny was close only to his fellow Special Action 1st Squad of Fox Company, the special action meaning snipers. The squad leader was a veteran buck Sergeant, and of the twelve-man squad, only Danny and Bob Richards had no stripes. The squad was the entire battalion's sniper unit. As such, they had a Quonset hut built for a platoon all to themselves. The rest of Fox Company regarded them as either having it made, or just plain weird. On the other hand, 1st Platoon, of which they were also members, had the best radio equipment, the best

104

weapons, the best officers and NCO's, because their primary mission was to support and, whenever possible, protect the sniper unit. First Platoon was, in effect, Fox Company's Honor Platoon. The company Commander, a massively built Captain, was tough, but fair. Danny's platoon leader, a very young Second Lieutenant, was small, compact and decisive.

Danny Wood, all thing considered, was content training under competent, tough Marines, high and deep in the hills of Camp Pendleton. He learned fast, and drew reserved, but honest, praise from NCO and officer alike. He was a good Marine. He was convinced he would remain a Marine for a long time. Perhaps, even a career man. He was quiet, but friendly, had no particular enemies and was learning the tools of his trade. The only thing that set him apart was his incredible shooting record. As training went on, he mastered more and more of the varied weapons available to the mud Marine, as the infantrymen referred to themselves. As a special action member, he was a cut above his mates, but not much.

The rain came straight down, heavy, cold, colder and wetter and, because this was southern California, totally out of place. Fox, Easy, and Dog Companies were dug in on the top of a steep hill, in a perimeter defense, engaged in what the Marine Corps termed a "night problem."

The three companies had been holding this position for two days, awaiting the attack from the "aggressor force," comprised of experienced Marines whose prime job was to scare the living hell out of the wet, miserable companies holding the perimeter. Live ammo was not used, but sudden attacks out of the dark swept the perimeter.

The war game umpires, battalion commanders, graded the young Marines on the hill who huddled under ponchos, sitting in four inches of water. Out of inky darkness came "aggressors," silent men who crept up to the two-man foxholes, rolling dummy hand grenades into them, the fizzling, popping fuses indicating two stupid, and supposedly dead, Marines. Sometimes rifles were jerked from their owner's hands and flung

105

down the rain-soaked hill, a particularly unnerving and humiliating experience, guaranteed to get your ass chewed, or worse. Losing your weapon to a silent, unseen enemy was bad enough, but the implication was deadly. Theoretically, some son-of-a-bitch had just cut your throat, infiltrated your lines, and could now move unchecked and silent from hole to hole, resulting in the loss of an entire squad, or even a platoon.

On the first night, the umpires had declared half of Dog Company, on the extreme left of Danny's Fox Company, wiped out in just this manner. The official tabulation was seventy percent casualties, all because one Marine position, on the point, had fallen asleep. The men responsible had lost their liberty cards for two weeks. The death and injury were not real. The punishment for falling asleep was serious, as was the offense.

Thus, on this second of two nights on the hill, a huge gap existed in the left flank. The night problem, to be studied in class after the field exercise, was going very badly. And all this with the General and his intelligence officer, Colonel Allen, ensconced in a trailer on the hill opposite Fox Company, directing the "aggressor" attack.

Danny Wood moved easily across the hill, toward Fox Company's CP, and popped in on his surprised company Commander, his squad leader at his side. Briefly, the Sergeant explained Danny's idea. The Captain listened quietly, nodded occasionally, then agreed.

Danny and his squad pulled back, leaving their section held thinly, and moved over the top of the hill, and down toward the aggressor force, an umpire with them. Bob Richards and Danny, accompanied by a .30-caliber machine gun crew, set themselves on the hillside directly below the observer trailer.

Lying down in a flat depression, they had a clear view of the gaping hole in Dog Company's position. Using his infra-red night scope, Danny soon picked up a full platoon in the driving rain, moving up the hill opposite him, toward the gap in D Company's line.

Danny turned to the major sitting next to him. "We're going to shoot now, Sir, with your permission."

106

"You don't need my permission. I simply judge whether your operation is effective or not. What is your estimate of their range to Dog Company's position?"

Danny peered through his spotter scope, the rain bearing down on its oilskin cover. "Six hundred yards, Major. I'm going to shoot. I will shoot the farthest man first, since they are advancing line abreast, and work back this way. Ready, Bob?"

"Ready, Danny. How do you want it spaced?"

"Thirty seconds."

With that, Danny pulled the bolt-action Springfield 1903 model .30-06 rifle to his shoulder, all fourteen pounds of it, and peered through the long infra-red night scope. The figures 600 yards away showed up as negatives of pictures when held to the light, white or gray against the dark night. The rifle cracked, the Major marked something on a covered pad.

Thirty seconds later, Bob Richards repeated the process. When the line was 200 yards from the crest, the muzzle flash of Danny's weapon, even with the extended flash hider, could probably be seen. Danny tapped the machine gunner next to him on the shoulder, set his sniper rifle down, and picked up his standard M–1, as did Richards.

At 100 yards, Danny opened up, and the machine gun ripped out across a now brilliantly lit hill. The pre-arranged parachute flares fired when Danny fired his M–1. The entire hill above Danny erupted in fire, with the advancing aggressor platoon caught in the blinding, fluorescent glare. In one minute a bright green flare arched skyward. The aggressor force was declared wiped out to a man. Danny and his team were credited with an unbelievable 80 kills of the 120-man force.

The General got the report, looked at it briefly and sipped his tea. The next day, Fox Company went down off the hill to warm beds and hot chow. Easy and Dog Company remained one more night. Nobody made much of it. After all, that's what special action units were for. It might have worked, it might not have worked. As it happened, it did. It was a good thing it had. Natalie was flying down from Seattle. Danny had no difficulty securing a two-day pass.

* * *

The General's only question to the umpire was simple, and to the point. When did Private Wood commence fire?

"Six hundred yards, Sir."

"Was it a kill?"

"Private Wood thought so."

"Did the Major?"

The Major had no doubt. Private Wood, according to his tabulations, unofficially, of course, had fired the sniper rifle thirty-one times. It was the Major's decision he had killed, again in theory, all thirty-one. Only when he was convinced he would be pinpointed had he opened up with conventional fire, under parachute star shells.

The General only nodded. The Major was dismissed.

The big DC–6 bounced once, reversed pitch on its four engines and settled into a long roll down the L.A. airport runway. On board, Natalie nervously checked her makeup for the third time, dropping a small jeweled compact into her purse as the plane swung around and taxied toward the terminal building. The plane came to a halt and in minutes Natalie, dressed in an eye-catching black wool jersey dress, was blasted by L.A.'s eighty-two-degree heat. When she'd left Seattle, it had been a typical January 4th day. Forty-two degrees and rain.

As she walked through the terminal, she checked her watch, 12:40 P.M. She had almost five hours to get to Long Beach, and the Buffum Hotel. When she had talked to Danny, he had asked her where she wanted him to meet her. She answered, "Where should I meet you?" And so she was bound for Long Beach, to "get something straight between us," as she'd put it.

Danny had laughed at that, but Natalie was here on very serious business. Lines must be drawn. Rules set. Natalie Antonelli was in danger of falling in love.

The L.A. cabbie looked very pleased when she ordered him to Long Beach. It was a hell of a fare, and she had the best legs he'd ever seen. When he pulled up in front of the Buffum

Hotel, she tipped him twenty dollars. As for the boyfriend she talked about non-stop, well... how could a buck-ass Marine have something like this? There was no justice.

Natalie checked into the hotel, only to discover that the Buffum was clearly home port to Danny, who apparently stayed in the same room as often as possible. She did some quick calculations and was surprised at her findings. And a little jealous, too. Danny had established himself as a regular weekend customer in less than six weeks. And why not? He didn't belong to her.

She had two hours until he arrived. She went shopping for some killer lingerie.

"I can't get this clasp undone."

"Just be patient, Daniel." Natalie pulled Danny free of his shorts.

"Patience has nothing to do with it. It's stuck."

"Rip if off." So much for patience, Natalie thought.

"You said it was brand new."

"Dammit all, rip it off. I'm going just slightly crazy here, Daniel."

Danny jerked so hard on the silken material Natalie toppled back onto the bed. Which worked out just fine.

"Danny, I want to talk to you."

"Okay." His mouth trailed across her breast and he tugged her nipple into his mouth. Sensation pulsed through her.

"Now listen, Daniel. You're in the Marines and things happen in the service. You'll go overseas. You'll go on liberty call. You'll meet women. All over the world. Some will be very exotic women. I don't want you to have some quirky idea about faithfulness, or any of that."

Danny's hand spread her legs apart, his fingers insistent and probing. She opened herself to him with a deep sigh as his mouth trailed down her belly and lower.

"Are you listening to me, Daniel?" she rasped.

He moved lower. "Of course I am."

109

"Well stop listening." She planted her feet and arched toward him.

"You know, I never said I wouldn't see anybody else. I suggested it."

"Same thing," Natalie said. "You want to be noble, to sacrifice, to make more of this . . . this, whatever it is. I intend to see other men, if I'm so inclined."

"Fine."

"Well, fine then."

"Sure."

"We agree?"

"Why not? You want to see other men, go ahead."

"And you, if you want to see other women, go ahead. We have no strings then, right?"

"Right."

"Danny?"

"What?"

"Move your fingers over a little. No, not there. To the left. Right there. That's a very special spot."

"That?"

"Yes, that. Oh, Jesus, yes . . ."

She kissed his face and his neck, tiny, intimate but nonsexual kisses. They had less than four hours until her return flight.

"Danny, there will be times, down here, when that wonderful body will need something, or that wonderful mind will need something, and I won't be here. I want you to know, it's okay if you are with someone else, if you need someone else. I don't believe in undying love, and all that. Sometimes people just need to be with people. I will, if the need is there. It doesn't change a thing I feel for you. We have what we have."

"And what, exactly, do we have?" Danny's eyes were deep and earnest. She wanted to give him a complete, reassuring, sensible reply. She couldn't.

"I don't know, Daniel. For the life of me, I don't know."

110

At 7:00 P.M. that Sunday, January 6th, the same cabbie picked her up to return her to L.A.

"Hi. I told 'em to dispatch me to pick you up, if you called today. Pretty clever, huh? How ya doin', legs?"

"Oh, go fuck yourself," Natalie said. It was a quiet ride, and an uneventful flight home.

Danny's summons to the base headquarters had come with little fanfare. Heading out on his usual two-man field exercise with Bob Richards, he'd been called aside by his platoon Sergeant, told to get into his class "A" dress-green uniform and to stand by. Not knowing what to expect, he had waited three hours, sitting or pacing back and forth in his squad's Quonset hut, smoking one cigarette after another. When a jeep finally arrived to pick him up, his platoon area was completely empty. His anxiety jumped even more as he walked toward the jeep and climbed aboard. The driver was a full Colonel, a hawk-faced, whip-thin man in sharply creased, near-white fatigues.

"Are you Private Wood?" The Colonel's voice was soft, with a clipped New England twang.

Danny had no way of knowing that by then the Colonel knew Danny's face as well as his own.

"Yes, Sir, I'm Private Wood." Danny had barely settled into the jeep when the Colonel jammed the accelerator to the floor, made a sharp U-turn, and roared out of the company area, almost ejecting Danny. As the jeep bucked and bounced onto the paved road, Danny felt the cold December air whip through his heavy dress greens, wondering how the Colonel stayed warm in just fatigues, and no coat.

As if reading Danny's mind, the Colonel said, "The cold doesn't bother me, son. It was damn hot on the Canal, and Iwo, too. I like cold weather."

Danny replied with a whisper, "Yes, Sir."

"My name is Colonel Allen. I'm Division Intelligence Officer. Whatever you hear or see today, you didn't hear or see it. Understood?"

"Yes, Sir, understood." Actually, Danny understood nothing

111

at all. The Colonel drove on, silent, expressionless. Not knowing what was going on, Danny was silent too. What the hell could a man ask a Colonel who'd already told him not to see or hear anything?

The headquarters building, two stories of ugliness, looked pretty much like any other yellow building on the sprawling base. That was Danny's impression when the Colonel jarred to a stop, motioning for Danny to follow him.

The interior of the building created a kind of culture shock. Officers of all grades came and went down the carpeted halls. Women Marines typed, bustled or seemed to be answering hundreds of phones. It was a beehive of activity, all done in a frantic but muted hush. Danny didn't know what he thought he might find in the headquarters building of two Marine divisions, but this was not it. It seemed like the executive offices of a bank, except these bankers wore a dizzying array of dress blues, greens, fatigues, and a brilliant array of bars and oak leaves, medals and hashmarks.

On the long walk down the hall, Danny tried unsuccessfully to count the officers, the women, the enlisted men. The building, almost a block long, was jammed to the walls with people. This plush building, with its picture-book Marines, was a vivid contrast to the drab, four-desk office of his company commander, tucked in a wet, drafty Quonset hut. Danny's company was only part of the legions. The Colonel turned sharply at the far end of the building, moving up a crimson carpeted stairway, taking the steps two at a time. Danny followed him the same way. On the second floor, there were fewer doors, and an eerie quiet.

Halfway down the hall, the Colonel stepped through a crimson-and gold-trimmed door, two stars over the entrance. Still hurrying, the Colonel turned sharply right and through the first of four doors, all open except the last. The Colonel slowed at the final door, the only door in the long hallway that was not open. He did not knock. The door opened to a small foyer, guarded by a severe-looking woman, wearing the twin bars of a

Captain, the chief secretary-sentinel sitting primly at a large desk covered with papers.

"Hello, Stuff, how's it going?" Captain Stufflebeam looked up from her work.

The severe face vanished in a dazzling, animated smile. "Hello, yourself, Colonel. All is well, so go right in."

The smile disappeared as she looked coldly at Danny. The best he could manage was a nervous, self-conscious twitch. He wanted desperately to get out of there. Nevertheless, he straightened his shoulders, and followed the Colonel through what was to be the last door.

The room Danny entered contained wide windows giving a panoramic view of the base. The entire room was covered with photos and war mementoes, with two 155mm cannon shells made into ashtrays. Two settees, crimson and gold, formed right angles in front of the desk. Two civilians, young, well-dressed, blank-faced, sat at one. Danny took in these details in a fraction of a second, his eyes jumping at once to the man behind the desk. He wore the same salty fatigues as the Colonel, two stars on each collar, a massive bank of ribbons on his left chest, dwarfed by the one blue, white-starred ribbon in his right breast, above the pocket. One small ribbon. The Medal of Honor.

"General, this is Private Wood." The Colonel guided Danny gently by the elbow, until Danny stood directly in front of the two stars, the white, short-clipped hair, the piercing brown eyes.

Danny overcame his nervousness, snapped to attention. "Sir, Private Wood reporting as ordered, Sir." His voice sounded like someone else had said it.

The General stood up, returned the salute, then said, "At ease." He walked around the desk, extending his hand.

The General's handshake was firm. "Sit down, Wood. Do you like tea? Colonel Allen, get Wood some tea." Looking steadily at Danny, he asked, "Or would you prefer something stronger?"

"No, Sir, General," Danny blurted. "Tea will be just fine."

The General looked pleased. "Well, then, tea it is. I drink the stuff all the time. Go on, sit down. You're among friends."

113

Maybe so, thought Danny, if there was any way a two-star Medal-of-Honor war hero could be the friend of a private, no-class, eighteen-year-old. Danny sat down, crossing his legs in a characteristic gesture of nervousness. A monkeywood table, with intricately carved legs of eagle talons holding down a world globe, was pulled over to Danny, and a golden samovar holder and hot tea were placed in front of him.

"I got that fancy set from George Patton. What do you think of him, Wood?"

Danny wasn't sure what answer was expected of him, if any. "I admired him, Sir. He would have made a damn fine Marine."

Colonel Allen sat down next to him. "The General thinks Patton was a pussy, Wood. I think all tankers are pussies."

Danny thoughtfully poured his tea, steaming hot, into the heavy glass set in the gold-handled holder. "I've met a few Marine tankers, Sir. I wouldn't say that to them. The ones I met looked mean enough to pick up their tanks and park 'em anywhere they wanted to." Danny was surprised at his own impertinence.

The General burst into laughter, as did Colonel Allen. "Well, Wood, apparently you feel no awe among high ranking officers. I like the way you stuck to your first thoughts."

"General, awe has nothing to do with it. I'm just scared witless, that's all."

The two officers laughed again. The civilians, who had yet to speak or move, just sat quietly, watching Danny. The General lit a Camel, leaning back in his chair, a high-backed black chair with two stars and the Marine insignia emblazoned on it.

"With all due respect, General, could you tell me what you want? If I have done something wrong, Sir, I'm unaware of what that something might be."

The General abruptly sat forward, eyes hooded under stark white eyebrows, his fingers weaving a trail of smoke as he moved. "You've done nothing wrong. Nothing at all. We have a job to do, and we think you're the man to do it."

114

The General's face had turned very serious. "Wood, how good do you shoot?"

"Sir?"

"I said, how good do you shoot?"

"Well, Sir, I guess I'm as good as any Marine. I'm training with a scout sniper unit now." Danny hesitated. "Of course, I'm sure the General knows what I'm doing." He remembered his shock at seeing Colonel Allen driving that jeep. Of course the General knew where he was, and what he did. Christ!

"Is there anybody better than you, in your outfit?"

"My partner, Sir, Bob Richards. Mostly he's my spotter, but he's one hell of a shot. We work well together."

"Fine. I'm sure you do. But is there anybody that can out-shoot you?"

"No." The answer surprised Danny. But he believed it.

"What would you say is your maximum range?"

"For a sure kill, maximum 800 to 1000 yards. Beyond that, I wouldn't be sure. I know the sniper equipment pretty well, and my platoon Sergeant had 80 confirmed kills in Korea. He works with us every day."

"Can you outshoot him?"

"I think so, Sir. So does he. It comes natural, General. I guess I was born with it."

"What is *it?*" The question came from Colonel Allen.

"Sir?"

"*What is IT?*"

"I'm not sure I understand the Colonel's question, sir."

The General said, "Sergeant Spradlin talked to me a few weeks back. He said you were a shooter. Actually, he said you were a killer. Are you?"

Danny was bewildered. What did they want? "Sir, I'm sorry, I just don't know what you want me to say. Sergeant Spradlin was a great D.I., Sir. His favorite theme was that all Marines are killers. Insofar as he meant that, I agree. All Marines are killers." Danny sat back in his chair. "Sir, may I smoke?"

"Go ahead. Colonel Allen doesn't smoke. Doesn't drink either. Wood, never trust a man with no vices."

The General's easy, small, buddy-buddy talk was getting to Danny, but he decided to let them say what they had to. He didn't intend to ask any more questions.

"Wood," said the General, "these two men have brought the Marine Corps an interesting field problem. You said your instructor had 80 confirmed kills in Korea, is that correct?"

"Yes, sir, that's what I understand."

"Well, how would you feel about going back to Korea, and getting us *one more confirmed kill?*"

Danny stared out the windows, idly watching a smartly dressed platoon marching briskly in the late afternoon sun. Slowly, he sipped his tea, the shock of the General's words bouncing in and out of his mind. Behind him, the other men sat in heavy silence.

Finally, Danny turned around, looking from man to man, his tea still clutched in his hand. "I'll go where I'm ordered. I hope that is a satisfactory answer."

Colonel Allen stood, and walked to a wall map holder, pulling it down. Danny could see it was a blown-up section of Korea. "That answer would be satisfactory, if this were an order. It is not. We are going to ask you to volunteer. What is said from here on out, what is done from here on out, is to be considered top secret, whether you volunteer or not. No one outside this room knows anything about it. No one will *ever* know anything about it. This order, if you can call it an order, comes to the Marine Corps from the very top. You may take that to mean anything you want. These men represent the United States Intelligence Agency. The CIA, if you will. As I said, the Corps has been asked to carry out this order. We are in turn asking you. You may, of course, refuse. There will be no publicity, no medals, no nothing. You must never leak one word, not now, not after the mission. Understood?"

"Do you believe in this mission, Colonel?"

"It's not up to me to make judgments. My job is to carry it out as best I can."

116

"Go on, Colonel," said the General, "tell him what you told me."

"Okay. Wood, I think it's flaky as hell, if you want to know."

"Well, you didn't say impossible. Maybe you'd better tell me who you want me to shoot. Confirmed, I think you said."

The General nodded toward the two well-dressed civilians, who slowly got up and walked to the map.

The dark-haired man spoke first. "Private Wood, the mission you are being asked to go on is vitally important to the security of the United States. We intend to fly you to Kimpo Airbase, outside Seoul, South Korea. From there, you will chopper in to here." The tall man pointed to a spot a short distance from Panmunjom. Actually, the spot, as Danny moved closer to the blow-up of the map, was *inside* North Korea. "When you arrive, you will intercept a convoy. In one vehicle is our man. This gook bastard wants to re-start the Korean War. We have hard intelligence on this. You're a shooter. You go in, shoot and get out."

The tall, blond-haired man picked it up from there, "The mission is scheduled to last seventy-eight hours. You'll leave on Sunday, January 16, and be back on Wednesday, January 19. Colonel Allen will detach you for special training at an on-base road. It has already been constructed to match the exact road in Korea where your man will be. He travels this road every day, in the same car, at exactly the same time. This is hard intelligence. You're the shooter. Your man will be there. Go in, shoot, come out, fly home. Seventy-eight hours. We've checked and re-checked everything. This man must be killed. If you accept this mission, that *must* be your foremost task. As I've said, everything has been checked, and re-checked. It's a piece of cake, son." The man who said this was all of twenty-six years old.

A slow smile came over Danny's face. "Then why don't *you* do it?"

The man looked confused, but quickly recovered. "I'm in planning, not operations."

"But what if your plan doesn't work?" Danny asked.

117

"You abort, that's all."

Danny looked at the General, who sat quietly, a cigarette dangling out of the corner of his mouth, eyes watchful. "No. If you fuck up, I don't abort. If he needs killing this bad, I shoot. *You* abort. It's my ass, begging your pardon, General, and if I get in there, the bastard's dead, or I am. I'm not particularly brave. But if you want me in there, I shoot. Or I don't go. On that basis, General, I volunteer, if you'll have me. Now may I have a stiff drink? I think you mentioned you had something."

"Ice?"

"No. Just fill the glass." He hesitated, then added, "Sir."

"Wood, you're crazy, you know that?"

"Yes, Sir, I believe you're right."

The General stood and walked to the bottle, poured three fingers' worth and turned toward the agents. "Well? Mr. Tinker? Mr. Evans? This is the Corps shooter. You have your volunteer. Now, do you want him, or not?"

Mr. Tinker, short and dark, and Mr. Evans, tall and blond, only nodded.

"Affirmative?" The General got another nod from Mr. Tinker and Mr. Evans. "Fine. But you remember something. You get this Marine in, and you get him out. And by God, you'd better not have fucked up your planning, because I don't want to lose this young man. I hope you understand what I'm saying."

Mr. Tinker and Mr. Evans said they understood perfectly. Everything was well planned. They guaranteed it. The only thing bad that would happen out there was going to happen to that crazy fucking Korean General. They shook Danny's hand, and made small talk about watching him train for the mission, where they would also explain further the logistics involved in what was not a piece of cake at all, but a harebrained mission, as far as Danny was concerned.

After they left, the General motioned Danny to his seat, and spoke curtly into his intercom. In a flash, the sexy Captain with the official-disapproving-secretary look was in the doorway, notebook in hand. "The Colonel, the Private, and I are hungry as hell. Steak and eggs all 'round, and make 'em hot. Wood, how do you like your eggs?"

"Over easy, Sir." The Captain gave Danny a pained look. Danny was feeling no pain on an empty stomach filled only with four ounces of straight bourbon.

"You can do this," the Colonel said. It was more a question than a statement.

Danny thought for a minute before answering. "Sir, while my mind is not up to the strategic or tactical value of this operation, I can definitely shoot the motherfucker. Sir."

"Let's drink to Private Danny Wood," the General said. And they did. It took two hours. They were toasting the Irish, cold beer, women and, over and over, the United States Marine Corps.

When Danny was returned to his unit, Colonel Allen said, "Good night, Private Wood, you poor bastard."

The poor bastard fell asleep in his clothes.

High on a lonely, windswept ridge in a remote section of Camp Pendleton, Danny Wood looked carefully through his telescopic sight. Across a ravine, a jeep was towing a plywood replica of the car the North Korean General would use on that road in Korea. Through the scope, it looked like an old Packard. He'd been told it was a Russian-made copy of a '48 Packard. He'd forgotten what it was called, since it didn't matter.

"Colonel, I'm going to shoot U.D.F."

The Colonel, nodding, knew that U.D.F. meant Unknown Distance Firing. Added to that was M.T.F., Moving Target Firing. The mission seemed planned well enough, but inexact distance, movement, wind, and probably poor visibility made for a difficult shot solution.

The jeep came to a sharp lefthand curve, and slowed to turn through it. The plywood car, mounted on a Packard chassis, followed the jeep around the turn, at eight miles per hour. After poring over photos of the actual road the car would travel, Tinker and Evans had determined that spot to be the most likely for the shoot, with the possibility that the car would then roll down the steep embankment and blow up. Assuming the car caught fire, the North Koreans would view this as an accident. There seemed to be a hell of a lot of assumptions in the mission plans.

When the "black box," as it was nicknamed, hit the spot in the turn, Danny could see clearly the painted-in head and back of his "general." He let out his breath, held it and squeezed the trigger. The .30-06 round, hand loaded to the limit for maximum velocity, screamed across the ravine.

"What do you estimate, Danny?"

"Seven hundred fifty yards, Colonel."

Tinker looked through a range finder removed from a destroyer. "Seven hundred eighty yards, Wood. Not bad for U.D.F., but not good enough."

The plywood car was backing up the hill, Evans looking ridiculous, jerking his body around in the jeep to keep from driving off the road.

"Evans, what do we have? Check it out." The Colonel was talking to the agent by two-way radio.

The jeep and the black box were now back on the level, 200 yards from the sharp curve. Evans scrambled out, and looked at the rear of the target. "Head shot. Dead center. That's twenty straight. Let's knock it off for the day."

"Okay, unhook the black box, and get over here. We'll do it again day after tomorrow."

Twenty minutes later, the four men were reunited, sitting in one of the two jeeps on the mission practice site. Evans and Tinker were ecstatic.

"Man, I never saw that kind of shooting. You're terrific, Wood, you really are."

"Yeah," chimed Tinker. "I agree. Twenty shots. Twenty hits. It's looking like we can knock off some of this practice."

"Well, Danny, you're the shooter. What do you think?"

"Colonel, I think the planning leaves a hell of a lot to be desired. We haven't really covered much. What if it's raining?

120

What if it's snowing, which I understand is fairly certain in Korea this time of year? We can't produce the snow, but I want to be sure to shoot in the rain, if it rains."

"Jesus Christ, Wood. Tinker and I planned everything." Evans was agitated. "But we sure as hell can't predict the weather, now can we?"

"Well, Mr. Evans, Mr. Tinker, you still have a considerable hole in your planning, as I see it."

Colonel Allen said, "Now, Danny, what do you mean, a considerable hole in planning?"

"Well, I am thinking of one particular possibility. What if he is *not* in the back seat? If he is not in the back seat, I have to shoot *before* the curve. And, a second possibility: he *is* in the back seat, but not alone. Two people, maybe three. Do I shoot them all? Is there a possible way to identify him for sure if he's not alone, or if he decides to sit up front, where I can only hit him before the curve?"

"Why can't you hit him in the curve if he's not in the back seat?" Tinker asked.

"Simple. In the curve I won't be able to see him, or anyone, in the front seat, except the driver. I could hit him, and *hope, assume, speculate,* that he *might* then roll the car off the road and down the bank."

"Okay, Wood, you've said your piece, now what do you propose?"

"Colonel?"

"Go ahead, Danny, say what you want. It's gonna be your ass hanging out in the cold."

"Okay. We will have to work at all possible shots, including up to four shots to take him and his bogus Packard off the road."

Evans jumped right in. "Four shots. It has to be one. Four shots will bring half the North Korean Army after your ass. This whole plan is based on speed, in, out, one shot."

"Colonel, with practice, I can get four shots off and on target, in five seconds. And where's the gas tank? If it faces me, I can put a round in it, too."

121

"That's ridiculous, Wood," Tinker said. "You have to trust us. He'll be there alone, in the back seat. We've been watching him for six months. Why would he change now?"

"Maybe you're right. But what if he does change the pattern? I say I practice for all possibilities."

"I agree," the Colonel said. "We shoot it all possible ways, then the mission *will* be properly laid out. We'll have twelve more sessions before mission departure. The General says I make it right, or abort it before it starts. Any objections, gentlemen?"

"It doesn't look like we can object, does it? Fuck it then, you want to blow up a bunch of plywood, okay. We'll have the figures painted in, the gas tank outlined in white, even though the car is black, and even though you won't be able to hit something you can't see." The two agents jumped into their jeep and roared off down the bumpy road.

"Stubborn, stupid civilian," the Colonel said.

"I'll tell the world," Danny replied.

"No, Private Wood, that is one thing you will not do."

"Sir?"

"Tell the world. You won't do that. Ever."

"Just a figure of speech, Sir, that's all."

"I don't care what it is. Don't say it again."

"Yes, Sir," Danny replied. The ride back to his unit passed in silence. Who would he tell, anyway? Nobody would believe it. Americans didn't do this sort of thing.

Colonel Allen sat in the General's office, idly swirling Scotch in a tall water glass.

"I never thought I would see the day," the General remarked, a look of wry amusement on his face.

"Sir?"

"The booze, Colonel, the booze. I've never seen you touch the stuff. But in the last few days, I've never seen you without it."

"New vice, General. Handy as hell, considering."

"Considering what?"

"This whole lousy operation. I'll tell you, Sir, I really like this kid, Wood."

The General's eyes narrowed. "Do you have doubts? It is not too late to stop."

"Doubts? Not about Wood. He's one sharp kid. If anyone can do it right, he can." Colonel Allen took a stiff belt of his Scotch.

"What doubts then? C'mon, Al, loosen up."

Again he hit the Scotch, hard, emptying and quickly refilling the water glass. "General, Wood is in this thing all the way. He's brought up a hell of a lot of smart, incisive questions. Tinker and Evans are having fits, but these questions make sense. He's not just the shooter, he's the planner too."

"Okay, Al, get to the point."

"Well, he asked me one hell of a hard question, General. I can't answer it. Maybe you can."

"Shoot."

"What if he gets killed on this thing?"

"He knows the risks. He volunteered."

"Right. What I don't know is whose body we ship home. What do we say? *How* did he die? *Where* did he die? General, I don't have an answer to that."

"I haven't even thought about it."

"Well, goddamnit, Tinker and Evans have. Auto accident. Sealed coffin, phony death certificate, everything nice and tidy. We just put that poor bastard in there, get his ass killed and send his folks a phony base-accident story and an empty coffin."

"What do you suggest?" The General's voice was very soft, but anger and sudden awareness showed in his eyes, his bushy white eyebrows seeming to bristle.

"Why don't we have a battalion of Marines at the landing zone? Accident. Just normal patrol. Maneuvers, hell, I don't care. Just want to know he's got every chance we can give him."

"Colonel Allen, that would constitute a provocative act, if the North Koreans wanted to take it that way."

"Yes, Sir."

123

"Tinker and Evans would veto it."

"That's correct, Sir."

"The order would have to be transmitted verbally. In secret. Without explanation."

"Right, Sir."

"You'll be a Pfc cleaning garbage cans if it goes wrong."

"Got my brush all ready."

"We'll be violating orders we don't have."

"Yes, Sir."

"Then let's do it." The General reached for the phone, asking for an overseas hookup, then put the phone back in its cradle. "Give me the map coordinates and the exact time, Al. I don't want to lose the whole fucking battalion, do I? But I have an idea. Two or three men should do."

"Yes, Sir. I wish to advise you that this conversation never took place."

The phone jangled, once, twice, three times. The General picked it up, holding his hand over the mouthpiece. "Fine, Al." The General leaned back, running his left hand through his short, white hair. "Max? How the hell are you? Listen, I have a favor to ask. What? Oh, yeah, the kids are fine. Now listen, Max."

In the dream, the rifle kicked, the silencer emitted a soft *puff* and the bullet dribbled out of the twenty-six-inch barrel, falling in slow motion to the ground, harming no one. What followed was the same, slow motion, terrible and true in its finality. The yellow men, larger than life, boiled up out of the flat, yellow earth, coming at him by the thousands. Again, the rifle, a fresh round smoothly, effortlessly chambered, kicked and puffed with reassurance, only once again to feebly expel its lethality, the bullet dropping like a small, dead bird, crafted from steel, yet impotent. The car moved on, unscathed, and the Asian horde crushed Danny in numbers uncounted.

Shooting straight up in his rack, wet with fear and terror, Danny would be temporarily free of his tormented sleep. But the dream went on, night after night, without fail, a malevolent, living thing, leaving him trembling and with a salty bitter taste clinging to him for hours. He told no one. In retrospect, perhaps he should have. The mission would have been scrubbed, his life changed for the better. It was not scrubbed. His life did, indeed, change.

The white convertible pulled slowly to the curb in front of the elegant Mexican restaurant in downtown Los Angeles. The driver shut off the engine. At the same time she reached for the vanity mirror on the visor, patting her luxuriant red hair, adding a slight touch of lipstick. She was quite pleased with what she saw. At twenty-seven, her face had the makeup-free complexion of a nineteen-year-old, green eyes wide and expressive, a pert nose topping a full, sensual mouth.

As she slid out of the car, her expensive white silk dress revealed slim, firm thighs, causing an appreciative whistle from a work crew standing around a tent-covered manhole. Smiling slightly, she sat that way a little longer than necessary, giving them a flash of red-gartered nylons as she slid free of the car, turning her back to the work crew, drawing yet another whistle. The wide, bright red belt accentuated her tiny waist and full hips. The casual way she swung her purse over her shoulder showed high, ripe breasts, seemingly straining against her bra, though they couldn't know she didn't wear one.

The final long, slow whistle came as she walked around the car, hips rolling slightly, taut buttocks revealed more than covered by the clinging silk. Slim ankles in bright red three-inch heels completed the picture. To the admiring workmen, she looked like a flashy, rich housewife, going to meet some lucky bastard for a fancy lunch.

The *maître d'* met her as she entered the restaurant, which was very busy on this warm January afternoon.

"My name is Rita Williams. I'm to join two gentlemen, Mr. Tracey and a Mr. Edwards. Are they here?"

Slightly dazzled, the *maître d'* escorted her to a rear table near a Spanish-style window.

Rita Williams sat down, crossing her sleek legs, eyeing the

two men opposite her. Lighting a cigarette, she ordered a Bloody Mary, and sat back in her chair, sliding her red purse down to the floor next to it.

"How are you, Rita?"

"Me? I'm just fine. And how are you, Mr. *Tracey?*"

Tinker and Evans looked at her with slow smiles. "How do you like the names, Rita?"

"Not very original, I'd say."

Evans looked at her very hard. "The names don't matter, really, do they, Rita." It was a statement, not a question.

"No, I suppose not. Now why don't you tell me what you want?"

"Shall we eat first?" Tinker asked.

"Hell, I might as well, but I can tell you right now I'm not interested in anything you two have to say."

With a knowing look, Evans said, "Twenty thousand dollars."

Rita looked startled, but quickly regained her composure. "Nice big round numbers. Anybody would think you wanted me to kill somebody, not fuck him."

Evans and Tinker said nothing.

"You're kidding!"

"Tell me, Rita, do we look like kidders?"

Nervously, she tossed down the Bloody Mary. "No. As a matter of fact, you don't." Reaching for her purse, she started to get up.

Evans grabbed her arm. "Sit down, Rita. We wouldn't like to find you in an alley somewhere, with your pretty face all scrambled, now would we?"

Rita Williams sat. "Order me another Bloody Mary. A double."

Tinker leaned back in his chair, a smile on his face. "That's better, Rita. You see, we have this thing going, and we may not need your help at all. But if we do, and you help us a bit, twenty big ones are yours, and you'll never see us again."

Rita glared defiantly at them. "You wouldn't dare. Not you."

"No, we wouldn't. But then, we wouldn't have to, would we?"

"What do you mean?"

"I mean we have a couple of miles of film of you and the people you've set up for us. That big-time hood ex-boyfriend of yours would just love to see it, just like he'd love to know where you live. We could arrange that."

A look of stark terror blanketed her face. "He'd kill me."

"Probably," Tinker said.

Evans handed her a manila folder. "There's twenty thousand cash in there, with instructions. Your man is in there. Read all you can about him, then burn everything. Except the money, of course." There was little humor in his laugh.

"You said you might not need me. What then?"

"Why, keep the money, and forget it. If we do need you, we'll call. Don't go running off now, Rita. If you don't hear from us by the twentieth, we won't need your assistance, and you're twenty thou' richer, and free as a bird. Plus, we'll burn the film prints. Not a bad deal, really."

"How do I know I can trust you?"

"You don't. Enjoy your lunch. We'll keep in touch." With that, Tinker and Evans, alias Mr. Tracey and Mr. Edwards, quietly got up and left her alone.

Hands trembling, Rita nervously lit a cigarette, even while one burned on in the ashtray, and opened the manila envelope. The cash, in two bundles of hundred-dollar bills, was there. So was a four-page, single-spaced, typed report on her mark. No name. Just a face. Tucking the money into her purse, she began to read, occasionally looking at the three-by-five picture. Christ, he looked so young. What could he possibly have done to bring Tinker and Evans down on him? Well, it didn't matter. She would do it, if she had to. What the hell, twenty thousand bought a lot of memory loss.

Danny, flanked by Tinker and Evans, walked across the flightline at El Toro Marine Air Base toward the silent military air transport service C–54, parked alone at the far end of the strip. It was a cold, dreary day, this January Sunday, and Danny was ostensibly on weekend liberty, with a one-man training mission scheduled to begin Monday and end Wednesday. It had been set up with great care, and no one in his outfit would be the wiser. Danny wasn't particularly worried since Colonel Allen had planned the exercise from start to false finish.

The three men, two in civilian clothes and Danny in winter greens, walked directly to the open ramp and into the aircraft. Another civilian quickly stepped forward, removing the ramp, while yet another reached out from inside the plane and pulled the outer door shut.

From the outside, the MATS C–54 looked like any other military transport plane. The inside was unlike anything Danny had ever seen. The entire crew, at least in the rear of the aircraft, were dressed in civilian clothes. All were wearing .45's on their hips; all were dressed in short-sleeved white shirts and dark pants. Along each side of the aircraft were plush blue and white seats, easily made into beds. A few cartons marked "Machinery, Jeep Parts" were stacked in the extreme rear cargo area, blocked off from the forward compartment by a floor-to-ceiling wall.

"Jeep parts?" asked Danny.

"Why do you ask?"

"Well, Tinker, this seems to be a pretty fancy lash-up to carry jeep parts."

Tinker laughed softly, "Hell, Wood, those are just empty boxes. Just part of the cover, that's all."

"And the crew?"

Tinker frowned. "Our people, Wood. Don't get too curious, okay?"

"Okay."

Danny's face showed his dissatisfaction with the answer, and Tinker tried quickly to dispel it. "Listen, Danny, you know how important this mission is. This crew doesn't even know why or where we are going. All they know is that it's a high priority flight to Korea."

"Is my gear on board?" Danny asked. "I want to check it out."

"There's plenty of time."

Danny's voice hardened. "I need to check it now, unless you want to fly back and replace it if there is anything wrong with it."

Tinker glared at Danny, then gave in. "Go ahead. Evans has it up front."

Without answering, Danny made his way forward, past two of the gun-toting civilians, and asked to see his gear.

Evans walked to the heavy box, hunched over it and twirled the dial, his back to Danny. "There you are."

Danny leaned over the box, staring at the neatly laid out camouflage uniform, the black-cased sniper rifle, the .45 Colt, combat knife and a wide variety of web belts and ammo pouches. He popped open the rifle case, bringing out the disassembled sixteen-pound weapon, its long barrel, stock, action and scope ready for quick assembly. Settling into one of the wide chairs, Danny quickly snapped the barrel into the stock, followed by the action and the bolt, screwing them together firmly with an Allen-head wrench. The long scope, a twenty-power wide-lensed monster, went on last. Danny picked up the fully assembled weapon, working the bolt smoothly, satisfying himself that, outwardly at least, it was the exact same weapon he had practiced with for weeks. Resting the barrel across the back of the seat, he aimed the weapon at the air control tower of El Toro Air Base. The plane was a full 1500 yards from the tower, but the figures behind the tinted glass were clearly visible.

"Don't shoot, Danny, we need those tower people to get off the ground."

Danny chuckled. "Those are Marines, Evans. I wouldn't shoot a Marine. Only Korean Generals." He didn't add civilians, but it was clear to Evans that he was thinking about it.

Danny put the rifle on the seat, and went back to the open

129

box. He broke the .45 down, put it back together, slipped a clip in and ran a round into the chamber, putting the weapon on safe.

"Not much you don't know about weapons, is there?"

"Nope. Not much. How about you?"

Evans looked at him. "Well, I can point the .45, but that's about all."

"Then why carry one? Somebody gonna storm the plane?" Danny slid the .45, still loaded, into its shoulder holster.

"Regulations, Danny. You know how they are."

Danny was reaching for the sheathed knife, pulling it out, testing the blade. Satisfied, he decided he would wear it in his boot, not on his belt.

"I know about regulations," Danny replied, as he stripped down the rifle and replaced it in the black case, the catch making a loud metallic snap as he closed it, "but I don't know a damn thing about yours. And I don't think I want to." Danny closed the box, hesitating before closing the combination lock. "Is this one of your regulations?"

Evans looked at him. "You want it unlocked?"

"Is there any reason it shouldn't be unlocked? We're on the plane, and I like to check my gear when I feel like it."

Evans did not hesitate, "You'd better lock it, Danny. We'll open it in plenty of time. Hell, we have eight thousand or so miles to fly, with two stops."

Danny said nothing, just snapped the lock closed. "Anything you say, Evans. You're running this show."

"Like I said, Danny, regulations."

Danny woke abruptly as the plane bounced lightly on the runway, its engines screaming in reverse pitch. Looking out the window, Danny could see in the distance a row of Quonset huts, two hangars, and not much more. "Hey, Tinker, where are we?"

"Re-fueling stop, Danny. It doesn't matter where we are."

"You mean I don't have a need to know."

"That's right. Sorry."

"I don't care anyway. God, I'm starved, Tinker. How long have I been asleep?"

"A long time. How about a steak sandwich, and a beer?"

"Sounds great, let's start with the beer."

"Feeling pretty salty, are you?"

"Never better, but I'm surprised I slept at all. I usually can't sleep on planes."

Tinker brought him a surprisingly cold beer, and a small capsule. "We gave you something to make you sleep. This is something to make sure you don't sleep."

Danny eyed the capsule warily. "I don't take pills, Tinker. I especially don't like being fed medication I don't know about."

"Listen, Danny, this is a thirty-four-hour trip. On this first leg, we wanted you to sleep. Including your time on the ground in Korea, you'll be awake for the next thirty or so hours. You'll need this little pill now, and another before you climb aboard that chopper. You know the schedule. Sixty-four hours air time round trip, nine hours in Korea. Take the pill. We know what we are doing. You can sleep on the way home, all the way. But until the mission is on its way back, we need to go over the mission completely. We need you awake."

Danny took the pill, and washed it down with the beer. "Okay, Tinker, I understand. But if you try this underhanded shit on me again, I'll cut your heart out."

"You don't much like me, do you, Danny?"

"No. But that makes no difference. I do need to trust you. If I can't, go shoot the Korean General yourself."

Tinker looked quietly at Danny. "I'll get you that steak. And don't worry. You're in good hands, and you can trust us completely. I mean it, Danny. We understand how you feel. All this sneaking around in the grass. Believe me, there's no other way."

While Danny's plane neared its destination, Rita Williams stared approvingly at herself in the full-length mirror of her bathroom. Just the right amount of makeup, a soft feather touch around the deep green eyes, a touch of powder on her

131

pointed nipples, a barely traceable scent of perfume, dabbed gently at her neck, behind her knees, and at her ankles. Completely naked, she checked carefully for any trace of a sag in her breasts. There was none. They were not large, but they were firm and in perfect proportion with her wasp-thin waist and long, elegant legs. Satisfied, she blew her image a kiss and walked into her bedroom to the closet, carefully selecting a sheer black gown which she tossed casually on her bed, while reaching for a matching garter belt, panties, and expensive black hose. Drawing on the black nylons, she pointed her foot directly at the floor-to-ceiling mirror opposite her huge bed, wiggling her toes as she slowly pulled the clinging fabric to her thigh, hooking it into her black garter belt, then repeating the process with the other leg. Standing straight, she bent over, smoothing her nylons, looking for imaginary runs. She made an elaborate, high-heeled walk around the bed to reach the lace panties, stepping into them with studied, careful sensuality, again looking at the mirrored wall. Lying on the bed, she stared at the ceiling mirror for a moment, then rolled onto her stomach, legs spread wide, slowly raising her hips up and down, and then in a slow, rolling circle. Abruptly she rolled over and off the bed, pulling the sheer see-through black robe over her body, and while staring once again at the mirrored wall, she stuck her tongue out and waggled her fingers in her ears, a childlike raspberry given by a stunning sexy female turned brat.

"The bitch. The dirty, rotten bitch."

"What's with you?" said the second man behind the two-way glass mirror. "She always does that. Christ, Ray, I'd think by now nothing she does would surprise you."

Ray was checking the camera, for the fifth, and completely unnecessary, time. "Yeah, I know. She does it all the time. But that doesn't help much. Goddamn, I want to fuck her so bad, someday I'm gonna just show up in this little love nest of ours and rape her ass off."

The other man, busy with a tiny recorder, looked at Ray reproachfully. "I wouldn't even think that, old buddy. She knows

132

how you feel, that's why she does it. Don't act like a kid. Just do your job."

"Some job, taking pictures of her fucking all those big wheels."

"You like taking her picture."

"That's true. I've got my own little private reel, all spliced together. Like tonight, that little show she put on. I'll keep that, too."

"Do Evans and Tinker know you have that?"

"Are you crazy? Hell, no. And don't you tell 'em, either."

"Don't threaten me, Ray." The Soundman's voice was low and ominous.

"That's not a threat. I'm just asking you to keep it to yourself."

"You got private, non-Agency film of her, I never heard about it."

"Okay. I never said it. But doesn't she bother you? I mean, look at her, for christsake!"

"I do, occasionally. Mostly I just make sure the mike is working and I'm getting it all down on tape. She's a looker, but she's a whore."

The doorbell rang, and Rita passed by the mirrored wall, patting her lush red hair. Ruefully, Ray checked the camera again, then turned it on. "Hell, man, I don't want to marry the bitch, I just want to fuck her." The tape began to turn, reel to reel.

"Shut up."

Ray looked at the Soundman, fiddling with his console and fitting his earphones carefully over his ears, not looking through the two-way mirror. "You know, Bob, you have no sense of humor."

"You got that right, Raymond. None at all."

The two men sat hunched in the dark, doing their work, as Rita answered the front door. Her soft voice reached the bedroom, "Good evening, Senator. You're a bit early."

Rita's mouth moved slowly up and down, the fat Senator's body straining upward to get more in her mouth, while she

133

skillfully played with his testicles, keeping her long hair away from her face as the camera whirred on, the tape rolling slowly, picking up the Senator's labored breathing and Rita's frantic but phoney moans and sighs. Without missing a stroke, she winked obscenely at the camera.

"Jesus, will you look at that?" Ray had a tremendous, throbbing erection.

"Yeah, I see it. She'd better ease up before she kills him. He's got a weird, raspy sound in his throat."

"Yeah, and look what she's got down her throat."

"Not much, if I'm any judge."

Rita suddenly stopped sucking, swinging her legs up and over the man. "Oh, no, baby, Rita gets hers, too."

The man rolled over her immediately, entering her with the skillful help of Rita's hands. Grossly overweight, the man plunged rapidly in and out, as Rita's legs stuck straight up in the air on each side of his heaving, sweaty body, her ass dancing in quick, jerky circles.

"Oh...oh...I'm coming...oh...Senator..." The big man plunged once, and went rigid, his climax clearly evident.

"Well, she did it again."

"What?" Ray asked. "She did what again?"

"She got him off when she wanted to."

"Oh, yeah. I never really noticed that before. She never really comes, does she?"

"I doubt it."

Rita's legs were now wrapped tightly around the man's back, her muscles tightening, milking the man dry, as he slumped, exhausted, on top of her. Deftly, she slipped out from under him, getting up and walking toward the bathroom, turning at the door to address the man, "Honestly, Senator, I should pay *you*."

The man, still sweaty, and looking old and fat, sat up on the black sheets. "Was it that good, Rita? Did I really make you come? I mean, I must have, you squirmed and hollered so much."

"Senator, I haven't got off like that in years. I'll just get us a

134

warm towel. After all, we have all night." The man gave her a weak smile.

In a moment she was back, still naked, wiping the man's body, now gone soft and flaccid. "I swear, Senator, you're terrific. I mean it. You should make porno movies, you know the kind."

The man laughed, "I've seen lots of those movies. I don't think I'm quite the right type."

"Why, Senator, I think you're the perfect type." She leaned over, putting her breasts near his mouth. "Go on, suck 'em. I love it when you suck 'em."

The Senator reached for her breasts like a greedy child, the sucking sound clear in the Soundman's earphones.

"Jesus Christ, look at her," said Ray.

The Soundman chuckled. "He oughta be in the movies. Goddamn . . . the movies."

Twenty minutes from landing, Tinker and Evans headed back to the rear compartment to alert Danny. The apparition standing in the aisle startled both of them. Booted, in camo fatigues, and wearing a .45 automatic in a shoulder holster, he was busily snatching a sheathed knife in and out of his boot with lightning speed. Satisfied, he straightened up, sat down and began to assemble the sniper rifle. Danny had streaked his face with charcoal, giving him a primitive, savage look, a warrior transported from the dark past.

"Twenty minutes, Danny. We'd like you to take another pill, if you don't mind."

Danny did not look up. "Okay. With a beer."

"Got one right here, Danny boy." Tinker handed Danny a white capsule, and a beer, and Danny dutifully took his pill, downing the beer in a hurry.

"What's the temperature on the ground, Tinker?"

"A nice cozy ten degrees. It will drop to about zero where we are going."

"Who is *we*?"

"You and me," Tinker said.

135

"I thought you were in plans, Tinker, not ops. When did you go operational?"

"Oh, I'm not going *all* the way in. Just to the landing zone. I'll wait for you, then fly back. Any problem in that?"

"No. Just don't get in my way."

Tinker laughed, "Don't worry. I won't be close enough to get in your way."

"How about you, Evans. You going too?"

"Nope. I'll wait at Kimpo. That's close enough for me."

One by one the four engines shut down, as the plane came to a complete stop. After a thirty-minute wait, Danny was again airborne, this time in a chopper, flown by a taciturn man who hadn't spoken a word to him during the entire flight to Korea. Tinker, sitting behind Danny in the chopper, said nothing, studying a map with a penlight.

"You lost, Tinker?"

"No, Danny. Just settle down. We'll get you there. Thirty-six minutes, that's all."

Considering how far they had come, Danny was surprised at how long thirty-six minutes seemed.

Danny had never been in a helicopter, and the ka-pok, ka-pok, ka-pok of the rotors was louder than he could have imagined. The machine dipped and climbed in the inky darkness, hugging the terrain like a mechanized grasshopper, seeming to leap from spot to spot, the drunken lurches making Danny nauseous and dizzy. The bitter cold outside blew through the machine from a hundred places, chilling him to the bone in spite of his cold weather parka and thermal underwear. Just when he was sure he was about to throw up, the chopper hovered, hummingbird-like, and then slowly settled to the snow-covered ground, the big rotor swishing through the air in a steady, even sound, then winding down to complete silence.

Danny had been gripping the rifle very hard, as if it were a lifeline had they crashed. While he had been sitting quietly in the chopper, his fingers had become stiff and cramped, and he felt foolish, and a bit guilty.

136

"Is this it?" he asked, surprised by how loud his voice was in the heavy stillness of the bitter cold Korean night.

"On the button, Danny. We've made dry runs many times. Your road is over that ridge about two miles."

Danny peered into the darkness, seeing nothing but the snow looking gray and dirty, the ridge invisible. "What ridge?"

"Wait until your eyes get accustomed to the dark. You'll be surprised what you can see. The ridge line is off to our left."

"Let's get out of this thing."

Danny worked at the awkward door handle, almost falling out as it suddenly opened, the raw cold like a slap in the face, quelling his nervous stomach, restoring his senses, a biting wind tearing at him as he jumped softly to the ground. The snow was about three inches deep, and crunched loudly as he walked to the rear of the chopper, the ridge he was to climb now visible even against the dark of the night sky.

"Marvelous place," Danny muttered.

Tinker jumped down and joined Danny, his face pinched against the cold. The copter's engine coughed once, twice, and began to howl. The blades started to turn, slowly, ponderously, then faster, and it slowly lifted off and climbed away, its rotor noise disappearing and softening, until in minutes, Danny couldn't hear it at all. Danny was struck immediately by a terrible loneliness. Bare rocks stood quiet sentinel duty, clearly visible, with scattered bushes and trees outlined against the snow. He wondered briefly how he had thought the night so dark.

Suddenly, Tinker exclaimed, "Danny! What the fuck?"

Danny saw them at the same time, and he clawed for his .45, diving behind a large rock, pulling Tinker after him, dragging him down, slipping on the snow, the sniper rifle slung over his shoulder suddenly a nuisance.

"Shut up, Tinker. Stay quiet," Danny whispered. He watched as three men came steadily up the hill toward them, plodding through the snow directly at their position.

"Jesus," breathed Tinker, "who the fuck are they?" His voice was low, the fear thick and real, almost a smell hanging over him.

137

Danny realized that the man was terrified. Danny ripped the rifle from his shoulder, slipping a round in the chamber, while slowly putting the .45 on the rock, within easy reach. Quickly he peered through the scope, settling on the man in the lead. The night scope pushed the dark away, illuminated the man, brought his face into sharp focus. The eagle on his helmet was clearly visible. Danny's face changed, the taut, tense muscles relaxing.

"What is it?"

Danny was standing up, holstering his .45, re-slinging the awkward rifle. "Tinker, you can breathe now. Here come the Marines."

"The Marines? What the hell . . . nobody's supposed to be here but you and me." The fearful voice had changed to one of anger and confusion. This was not part of the operation.

"Maybe not, but they're here nevertheless." Tinker watched as Danny stepped out from behind the rock, standing still, as the men drew near enough to be seen clearly.

Tinker cursed and sat on the rock, reaching with shaking hands for a cigarette, his mind racing. His plan was most likely shot to hell. He'd need Rita . . . goddamn!

"Colonel, what are you and your people doing here?" Tinker's voice was loud, angry.

The tall Southerner looked at Danny, the sniper rifle drawing a long, thoughtful stare. "We were advised you might be here. I've been asked to give you whatever support you may need."

"Who ordered you in here?" Tinker was furious.

The Colonel's gaze settled on Tinker. "Nobody ordered me, mister. I was asked. So here we are."

"Asked? By who?"

"That's none of your fuckin' business. We are here, and that's all you need to know. Now, Marine, what can we do for you?" He now returned his gaze to Danny, and his back to Tinker.

"Not anything I can think of, Colonel. You sure can't go where I'm going."

"I wasn't told where you are going, or why. I was only told to mention that Patton was a prick."

Danny now knew why this competent officer was here in this desolate spot. The General didn't like the set-up any more than Danny.

"Colonel, I think the best thing for you to do is withdraw immediately." Tinker's voice was flat and nasty.

"Mister . . . what is your name, anyway?"

"That doesn't matter. Getting back to wherever you came from does."

"Okay, fuck your name. I'm staying put, whether you like it or not." There was a distinct finality in his voice, the finality of a man used to giving orders, as well as obeying them.

The Colonel walked over to Danny, leaving Tinker standing frustrated and alone. "Well, son, I don't even know your name. Should I?"

"It might be better if you didn't, Sir."

"Fine. I got a TransPac call awhile back from Pendleton. We're here to help."

Danny smiled. "I figured that, Sir."

"Is that civilian supposed to go with you?"

"I guess so, but I didn't know it until he told me."

"Do you need him?"

"No, Sir, not for this I don't."

"Let me put it another way. Do you want him?"

"Frankly, Sir, no."

The Colonel stamped his feet, trying to ward off the cold. He looked absently at his watch. "How far from here are you going, and what time are you supposed to be there?"

"Two miles or so, Colonel, over that ridge. Daybreak."

The Colonel's eyes followed Danny's. "Over *that* ridge? Do you know where that will put you?"

Danny looked steadily at the Colonel, then answered, "Yes, Sir, I know exactly where that will take me. The chopper will be back at 0900 to pick me up. I'm sorry I can't tell you more than that."

139

"I understand that. No sweat. How about taking two of my men with you? They know this area real well."

Danny shifted the rifle on his shoulder, then grabbed the sling and eased it off, cradling it in his arms. "I don't know, Colonel. The security on this is unreal. I was not advised you would be here. I appreciate the offer, but I just don't know."

"*I* know. I was advised and ordered to assist you into the area, and back here to the L.Z. The General personally asked me to be sure your mission was successful. I have two top NCO's I'd like to guide you in, support you and help get you out. It's up to you. You can trust my people."

"The civilian won't like it, Sir. Not even a little bit."

"Fuck him."

"Yes, Sir. Truth be told, I'd be happy as hell to have a couple of Marines in there with me. But you must know, Sir, I'm going in there to shoot."

"My people, the two noncoms, have already been briefed. They will have nothing to say to anybody. I'll stay here with your civilian friend."

Danny did not reply. It seemed the whole mission would be compromised if anyone else was with him.

The Colonel lifted the responsibility from Danny's shoulders. "You will have to take my word for it. I've been ordered to assist you. The men were hand picked. I'm now ordering you, in the General's name, to accept our assistance."

"I gather that is a direct order, Sir."

"It is."

Danny checked his watch. 0100 hours. "Well, then, I guess we'd better shag ass, Colonel."

"That's the stuff. Go tell your civilian." The Colonel walked back to the waiting Marines.

The look on Tinker's face was one of stunned incredulity. "Listen, Wood, this is a secret mission. I'm going with you, and nobody else. Don't be a damn fool. You're going to blow this whole mission. Can't you see that?"

"I'm not going to blow anything, Tinker. But I'll tell you one thing, I trust the Marine Corps a hell of a lot more than I do

140

you." Danny's charcoal-streaked face was hard and implacable, and Tinker wilted under the finality he saw in Danny's eyes.

"All right. Do it your way. It's your funeral."

"No, Tinker, it's the gook's funeral. But I figure you had more than that planned, right?"

"I don't know what you are talking about, Danny."

"Well, maybe not. Maybe I don't know what I'm talking about. But whatever it is, forget it. I intend to carry out this mission, and then you're gonna take me back to sunny California, as planned."

Taken aback by the ferocity in Danny's voice, Tinker answered, "I have the feeling you figure I didn't intend for you to get back."

"That thought had crossed my mind."

"Hell, Danny, we're in this together, the Agency and you."

Danny's eyes narrowed. "I'm glad you feel that way, Tinker." The suspicion in his voice dropped like a curtain between the two men. "I'd hate to think different." Danny abruptly turned away, joining two heavily armed Marines, one carrying a Browning automatic rifle, the other a Thompson .45-caliber machine gun. Briefly, they checked Danny's map, then turned away and started toward the ridge.

He might just as well have been on another planet. The ridge was a white-cloaked ugly bump on the nose of an otherwise featureless moonscape. The wind . . . oh, goddamn the cold, slashing wind, sighing and moaning through the scrub trees and boulders. Danny glanced at the Sergeant. What was his name? Rodriguez, slipping and stumbling, carrying Danny's extra pack, a wide, out-of-place grin on his face, bathed in the too-bright, harsh light of the moon as it ducked in and out of the low, scuttling clouds.

The other sergeant spoke first. "Slippery as a wet pecker, Cap'n."

Atwood. Sergeant Atwood, Warm Springs, Arkansas. Or was it Georgia? Danny nearly went down, his boot caught in a tenacious bit of brush. "I'm no captain, Atwood. Just a big ass private."

The Southerner chuckled. "Sorry. I just couldn't imagine any Marine under the rank of cap'n would put himself in this place."

Danny laughed, warmed by the mere presence of these two able NCO's, Atwood carrying the B.A.R. and two web belts of extra ammo, a big, easygoing man who looked more like a Baptist minister than a Marine Master Sergeant. "Goddamn, I'm getting pretty warm, considering," Danny said.

Rodriguez glanced at him and said, "Keep your clothing loose, son, let your body breathe. When we get where you're going, then shut it up tight. Won't let that warm sweat turn to ice that way."

"Thanks a lot." Danny unzipped his heavy field jacket, flipping the hood off, his hair wet and cold as the wind rushed over him.

They were still climbing, crablike, switching back and forth, but always up. The ridge line looked no closer than it had when they'd started.

"Fuckin' ridge is growing right before your eyes," Danny snapped.

"Topped off, Cap'n," Atwood said. And so they were, standing now on the top of the ridge, the wind tearing at them, the moon brighter than ever, every detail of the far side sharp and clear, the road where it should be, a brown belt girdling the next ridge, stark and sharply defined.

"Okay. We have to go down now. I need to be closer."

Rodriguez shifted the Thompson from his right hand to his left and adjusted the straps of Danny's extra pack. "You know what's over there, son?"

"Yeah," answered Danny. "Unless I'm mistaken, that road's in North Korea."

"We gonna invade, or ask 'em to surrender?" Atwood asked.

Danny looked at his watch, the sweep second hand racing up from the left and rushing over and away, down the right side.

"Better button up right now, son, the cold will get at you going downhill."

Rodriguez. Bless him. He knew it wasn't the cold, but he'd

read it and let it go. Danny closed his field jacket, leaving the hood down. "I got 0345 hours. How about you two?"

The men checked quickly. "Concur, Cap'n. Where to?"

"Just follow me, Sergeant. It's Sherman's march to the sea."

Atwood and Rodriguez looked at each other, then at Danny. "Son," Rodriguez replied, "you just made us two scruggs feel considerably better about this operation. Lead on."

Cradling the heavy sniper rifle, Danny grinned at his two companions and dropped over the ridge, moving quickly. As they scrambled after him, the sniper rifle seemed to grow lighter. Somehow, it would be all right.

"Ya know, my grandfather got himself killed on a night just like this."

Danny looked at Atwood, startled. "How?"

"Well, you see, my grandaddy and my great-grandaddy were hunt'n grizzly bears back in Arkansas, and it was cold as a well digger's ass, just like it is here. Anyways, my great-grandaddy had to piss, and he didn't see my grandaddy a standin' just below him on this here ridge they were hunt'n. Had a grizzly all trapped in for the night, you see. Anyhow, my great-grandad hauls out his pecker, and lets go a yellow stream long as a coiled snake. Well, it freezes right off, soon as the air gets to it and hits my grandad on the back. That frozen piss hit him so hard it knocked him down that ridge, and he didn't stop rolling 'til he reached Kentucky. By then, he was proper done in, and that's the truth."

"Atwood, you know that's a lie," Rodriguez said.

"I wouldn't lie about my grandaddy."

"There ain't no grizzly bears in Arkansas. However, I do believe the piss killed him."

It had been like that, since they'd reached the place Danny had chosen to shoot. They had cleared a spot behind a natural bowl-shaped clump of rocks. Atwood had set up the B.A.R. with quick professionalism, setting ten extra clips where he could get at them, the weapon and its tripod invisible from the road, only the gun's snout poked between two rocks showing, and he'd covered all but the tip with dirt and snow. Rodriguez had unpacked Danny's spotter scope, setting its two-legged holder deep in the hard earth, but allowing the scope itself full three hundred sixty degree movement. Six grenades were laid out neatly, within easy reach of all three men, and he'd taped two extra clips back-to-back for the Thompson. Danny had taken the longest, readying himself carefully, first checking the weapon, then laying it carefully on the extra blanket carried in the pack, wrapping the rifle's bolt action in the blanket's folds, secure from the biting cold. He'd thoroughly checked the wind, which was blowing from his left to his right at about ten mph, much slower than it felt, quieter than it sounded.

Rodriguez had pulled the three quart-size thermos jugs from the pack, and they had settled back to wait, drinking the bourbon-laced coffee, its fiery warmth burning into their innards, quelling the cold, relieving the fear and tension. They had bantered back and forth, joking, laughing at each other's lies and tall tales. Needing to talk, Danny had exploded in a verbal, vivid life story, telling them about T-Town, the range at San Diego, everything, stopping short of explaining how he'd come to be here on this windswept hillside so far from home. The two older men had listened with fascination.

"Son, don't you think it's about time you let us in on what we're gonna do here?"

Danny, his hands around the stainless steel thermos cup, thought about his General. Yes, it was 0650, and they should know.

They had listened quietly, without comment, as Danny explained what he had come to do, how close to death he had brought them. He knew how insane it must sound. He felt that way himself. He felt badly about them being with him now, a painful guilt that if anything went wrong, and any number of things *could* go wrong, they would most likely die on this hill. Atwood's only comment had been, "Well, that sorta makes your pecker draw back on you, don't it?" Rodriguez had said nothing, a ho-hum grunt his only visible reaction. But all three

144

men were tense now, the jokes and small talk squelched by the harsh reality of what Danny had been sent to do. Now there was little to do but wait.

A few miles away, Danny's General was getting dressed, his mind lingering briefly on the pleasure of last night. The very young Chinese girl had been delicious, a pliant girl of exquisite beauty, who now stared at him from the padded mat on the floor, her almond eyes wide and fearful. Yes, power was better than drugs. Power had bent her to his will, power had kept her quiet, even as he brutally took her from the rear, her small hands clenched as his massive body enveloped her. Ah, young virginal girls, young boys—all the same, a hunger he satisified each day. Last night, it had been the girl, and tonight, if it pleased him, he would take her again, perhaps this time with the young Korean boy from the village. What was his name? No matter. He would come if summoned. Or, it might please him to give her to his aides. He trembled a little, looking at the girl, imagining her with three men at once. He would watch. He remembered the other time, in Shanghai, in 1937. That one had died, finally, her mouth open, without sound, the table leg covered with blood.

Part Japanese, part Korean, he had served in China during the war, running a labor battalion. That too, had been interesting. But nothing so much as now. He had a long way to go, but he was a very young General. Perhaps he was pushing his plan too hard. The Chinese were receptive, but one could never tell about the Chinese. No matter. He was a man of patience. He would bide his time. If not this year, or the next, perhaps five years. Yes, he could wait. The time would come.

He walked over to the girl on the mat, his penis huge and engorged. Grabbing her roughly by her silken black hair, wearing only his shirt and jacket, he forced her face toward his thighs, legs spread wide. Her mouth slid hotly over him, as he gave way to the sensations coursing through his body, radiating upward from the porcelain doll so greedily sucking him. She had learned well during the long, cold night. Perhaps he

145

would not share her. He would think on it. Oh, yes, he could wait. They would listen. They were listening now.

The noise from the long convoy of vehicles drifted faintly across the valley. Rodriguez heard it first, then Atwood. It was still near dark, with only the moonlight bathing their faces. Ghostly green apparitions appeared frozen against the side of the hill.

"They're on the way, son."

Danny shifted forward, straining to catch the sound, hearing only the wind. "I don't hear them. How far do you figure they are?"

"Two, three miles."

"How can you tell?"

"Son, I've been in the Corps for twelve years, and I've been in Korea since the Frozen Chosin. I got here first, and I'm still here. I can hear a vehicle start its engine two miles off."

Danny stared at Rodriguez in awe. This quiet man had served in World War II, and he'd taken part in the 1st Marine Division's epic retreat from the Chosin Reservoir, fighting through ten Chinese divisions over a frozen road, fifteen tortuous miles, bringing their dead and wounded strapped to their vehicles, under constant attack.

"How about you, Atwood?"

"I was there, too, Cap'n. It was hairy, I'll tell you. Bugles blowing, gooks coming out of the woodwork, us killing 'em left and every which way. The situation was fluid. I'll tell ya."

"Jesus," Danny said.

"Now, don't you worry about it. We aren't worried, are we, Rodo?"

Danny was flooded with genuine affection for these two men he'd known for such a short time. Spradlin had been right. You could drop a Marine anywhere in the world, mix him with any other Marines and you would have a team.

Now Danny could hear the convoy, suddenly clear and distinct, brushing aside the sound of the wind. "Sergeant Rodri-

146

guez, Sergeant Atwood, why don't we have another cup of the joy juice. We're gonna be pretty busy soon."

Solemnly, Sergeant Rodriguez filled the three cups, and the three men sat back to wait the few remaining minutes until the convoy reached the road, 700 yards away. There would be precious little time after that. Danny's General was on his way, punctual as always.

"How many is that?" Atwood's voice, as he lay flat on his stomach, the B.A.R. jammed into his shoulder, was muffled but steady.

"Sixteen. Including the two fucking T–34's. Tanks, for christsake." Rodriguez, using the spotter scope, was also hunched over, his breath rising like wispy traces of angel hair as he spoke in the bitter cold.

Danny sat between the two men, the rifle ready, its long, silencer-equipped barrel lying on the extra green blanket.

"I got the feeling our asses are in real trouble, Cap'n."

Rodriguez looked away from the scope, and straight at Atwood. "You worry too much, that's what you do. They can't see us."

Danny lit a cigarette and glanced at Rodriguez. "Stay on that scope, Sergeant. I think Atwood means this is one long train, and we need the caboose to come by before daybreak."

"You got it, Cap'n. By my watch, we have thirty minutes, then it's gonna get real easy to see. For us, and for them."

Rodriguez spoke softly, "Another tank. Three tanks, three half-tracks and fourteen goddamn trucks."

"What's the count, Rodriguez?"

"Twenty-two and still coming. What do you make of all this? I mean, this ain't what you expected."

"No, it's not. There must be a battalion, at least. I can't figure the tanks at all. To tell you the truth, I don't know what to think."

"Speaking of tanks, looka' that," Atwood exclaimed. Coming around the curve, clanking noisily, guns rocking, were four

147

giant Stalin tanks, forty-six-ton monsters, mounting long 122mm guns and two machine guns.

Inexplicably, the tanks stopped on the level stretch and just sat there, idling, their twin exhausts pouring a clearly visible plume of smoke into the wind, the smell drifting across the canyon, acrid and dangerous.

Danny checked his watch. Twenty minutes left, then the light would brush away the dark, leaving him naked and helpless.

Danny peered through his scope, settling the cross-hairs on the North Korean tank commander as he exited the lead tank, jumping nimbly to the ground, a cigarette dangling from one corner of his mouth. For a fleeting instant, Danny wanted to squeeze the trigger and shoot the insolent bastard. In the next instant, he was fighting himself desperately to keep from laughing out loud.

"What's going on, Cap'n?"

"Nothing, Atwood, nothing at all. He stopped the fucking column to take a piss." Danny thought he had never seen anything funnier. In fact, he was losing control of himself. The whole thing was just too much. All this way. It was too much to ask.

"Steady, son, the peckerheads are cranking up. They're leaving now. You just stay steady, you hear?"

Only then did he feel Rodriguez's hand on his shoulder, the voice perfectly pitched, the veteran Marine applying the reassurance to the green-ass Private. Danny mumbled, "I'll be okay."

When Danny regained control of himself, the two Sergeants were back at their posts, Atwood looking down the barrel of the B.A.R., as if nothing had happened. Rodriguez was at the spotting scope, but he was lighting a cigarette, sitting next to the scope, smoke curling slowly out of his nostrils. The wind had died down completely. The shot . . . good, it would be easier without the wind to worry about. There was only one thing wrong. There were fifteen minutes, perhaps twenty, before dawn. And the road was empty. The long column had passed. His General had not.

"Got 'em, son. About three clicks up the road, comin' real slow." Rodriguez's voice had jumped a pitch, as he swung the scope upward, the snow tumbling off his helmet and shoulders as he moved.

Three clicks. Three thousand yards and coming. The great, oppressive feeling of despondency and apprehension suddenly lifted magically from Danny's shoulders. The converted '03 Springfield, despite its weight, felt like a lightweight sporting rifle now. Hunched over the weapon, the butt jammed into his shoulder, Danny fed a gleaming cartridge from the magazine, watching with satisfaction as the polished brass slid like a golden phallus into the dark recess of the barrel. The safety made a barely audible click as Danny slipped it to the fire position. A curious, detached calm settled over the tiny rock fortress. In spite of everything, the shooter was in the right place, at the right time.

A little procession of vehicles moved slowly into view, sliding a little on the fresh snow, two small trucks about one hundred yards ahead of a black car. Danny studied them carefully through his scope. Not much. Two uniformed men in the blocky cab of each one, the rear covered in canvas.

"Can't be more than eight men in those, Cap'n," Atwood whispered, still lying flat on the ground, his cheek on the B.A.R.'s stock, his body nearly covered by the lazy snowfall.

Danny only grunted, his body and the rifle rigid, man as machine, machine as man. He followed the two trucks as they traversed the flat section of the road, finally disappearing around the curve, leaving the Packard-like car far behind, just entering the flat stretch.

They called it the sniper blanket. Concentration. The pure, singleminded purpose of the shooter. The barrel began to follow the black car, and Atwood and Rodriguez stared at it, transfixed as if by the slow movement of a cobra.

149

Rodriguez glanced at the road, the car's headlights picking up the snow as it fell softly through the yellow beams, a postcard of nature's beauty given a new and terrible menace, the snow causing the car to move at a snail's pace. He shivered involuntarily, the cold suddenly going to his very bones. This kid was gonna do it, he had no doubt. In all his years of combat, he'd never been around such cold, pure certainty. The barrel of Danny's rifle moved slowly, surely, from left to right.

"There's four of the bastards. Four." Danny's voice caused Rodriguez and Atwood to jump visibly, as it cracked through the stillness on the ridge.

With astonishing speed, though years later he would see it all in a kind of dreamy slow motion, he centered on the man in the front seat nearest him and squeezed the trigger, watching the man's visored cap flying into the air inside the car as his head exploded. The man in the rear reached for the shoulders of his dead comrade, as the driver spun the wheels in a fruitless effort to gain traction. The car began to slide dangerously close to the edge of the road, and the steep canyon below.

As the first expended brass cartridge settled hotly into the snow, Danny caught the shocked look of the man in the right rear seat. He seemed to peer straight at Danny, as if he could see through the wintry darkness. The gun recoiled again, its silencer a muffled punctuation mark as the second round hit the man just above the nose, hurling him violently backward. Again, the crazy jewel dancing through the air, the solid, deadly sound of a chambering round, a slight shift of Danny's shoulders.

The third man, in the back, had ducked down, could not be seen. He'd overcome his shock and dived to the floor of the rear seat. Danny knew that the man on the floor of the rear seat was the man he must kill. The car was creeping through the curve, only yards away from escape. The rifle shifted, stopped, as if sniffing the wind, and for a brief instant, the driver, struggling frantically to get the car through this deadly place, looked back over his left shoulder, the terror splashed on his face. The rifle bucked again, the little air dance was repeated, and Danny

150

could see no one in the shattered window where the driver had been, only glass smashed in a spider web pattern, the bullet hole becoming the spider, lurking, waiting.

Now the car began to roll backward, and the face he had sought, but had never before seen, appeared in the rear window. The face was calm, almost amused, no sign of fear, as the car continued to slide backward. The rifle seemed to remain motionless, a thing suddenly dead, or asleep, as Danny watched the slow grin spread across the man's face. What did he know? The rifle came back to life, and the face split apart, and went away, the smile gone, if it was a smile.

Slowly, the car rolled backward, the rear end dropping off the road, the long-hooded front end pointed suddenly straight up as it hung there. Then, with a grinding roar, it slid over completely, bounced crazily in the air, showing its naked underside, then it bounced again, and exploded in a fiery ball of steel and flesh and flame. It fell deeper and deeper into the canyon, 1500 feet below. It stopped, smaller now, bits and pieces scattered among the rocks, its fire flickering dully into the night sky. Danny's bolt flicked back, the sound loud in the deathly stillness on the ridge, the jewel-like empty case doing one final dance, tumbling over and over through the air and into the silence, seeking a place to rust.

Danny was suddenly very tired. The entire shooting sequence had taken less than one minute, but he felt arm weary and unable to move. The snow continued to fall, and any sign of the violent action on the road was rapidly disappearing under a peaceful coat of white as the dawn pulled the darkness from the land. He had done it, as he'd known he would, and now he sat shaking uncontrollably, only dimly aware of his surroundings.

"Drink this down, son." It was Rodriguez, arm extended, the steaming cup of coffee and booze like a small fire in the falling snow. Danny groped for it, and the rifle clattered off the rock ledge and into the snow.

"Let it lay, Cap'n. I'll take care of it." Atwood picked up the

151

sniper rifle, pulled the Allen-head wrench out of the extra pack and removed the bulky scope. "Heavy sumbitch," he muttered.

Danny sipped the scalding liquid, staring across the canyon at nothing, letting the booze warm and revive him, while Rodriguez and Atwood busied themselves with packs and extra gear, preparing to move off the ridge. Ready to go, they both jumped down behind the tiny rock wall on each side of Danny, poured themselves a drink and refilled Danny's.

"We'd better wait here a while, Cap'n. Them trucks should be back here soon, and I sure don't want my old ass caught out on the hill behind us when they do."

Danny only nodded, compliant now, willing to be led.

It didn't take long, the two squat trucks pulling into sight around the curve, and coming to a sliding halt on the flat stretch, disgorging sixteen soldiers in dark, quilted uniforms. One of the men walked to the edge of the road, stared down into the canyon, then called out in a voice loud enough to be heard clearly where the three Marines sat hidden in the rocks. The group of men huddled near the side of the road, then cautiously began a descent, slipping and falling as they went over the edge.

"Stupid bastards," Rodriguez growled. "It will take them two hours to get down there, and all day to get out, if they can get out in one day."

Atwood watched them, a toothpick switching back and forth from one corner of his mouth to the other. "Long way down to look at a coffin." The toothpick stopped, clenched in his teeth, and he smiled a satisfied smile.

Danny took one last, long look at the road, the two strange little troop carriers turning white with snow, mute and silent where only minutes ago he had wreaked such violence. He knew he was right. He'd never forget it. Without a word, he turned away and trudged up the hill, Rodriguez and Atwood a few yards behind him.

"Rodo," Atwood whispered, "the Cap'n there gonna be all right?"

"Yeah. He's gonna be all right. Don't worry. He's a tough kid." But even as he said it, he knew. The kid would never be the same. Not ever. None of them would.

As if on cue, the mission complete, the wind began its low, howling way across the ridge, driving the snow sideways, swirling in a violent fog of white that enveloped and finally swallowed the men. In minutes, there was no sign that any human being had been there at all.

As the big plane plowed steadily homeward, Danny sat in one of the large, blue chairs, a beer in his hand. He was dressed in greens, his tie loosely knotted, his collar open. Across from him, Tinker and Evans sat quietly, watching him.

"How do you feel, Danny?"

"I feel great. How long did you say I slept?"

"Sixteen hours," Tinker said. "We're on the last leg of the flight home. Couple of steaks coming up in a minute."

"Sounds great. Christ, I'm hungry."

"Tell me about the mission, Danny," Tinker said, handing Danny a lit cigarette and returning an elaborate gold cigarette case to his inside suit pocket.

"It went fine. Your General's dead."

"No complications?"

"Not unless you call an armored column a complication. Not unless you count four people in the car, not two." Danny's voice rose in anger. "You blew it. Your plan stunk, and if I hadn't had a couple of steady Marines to help me, your fucking General would still be alive."

"We will need those two men's names," Tinker said.

"What two men? If I wasn't there, neither was anybody else. Remember? None of this happened."

"You do know their names. And we must have them."

"No deal. Even if I knew them, which I don't."

"You know, Danny, I think we'll pass this by. It's not important, really." Evans sounded as if he believed what he was saying. Then he added, "Just the sincere thanks of ourselves, and

153

the government of the United States for a job brilliantly done, under what were obviously desperate conditions. Shake on it?"

Danny's anger left him as suddenly as it came. "What the hell." Smiling, he shook hands with each man.

Tinker smiled broadly, pumping Danny's hand one more time. "You've done everything asked of you. Go back and be a Marine. We'll pick on somebody else next time."

"Why does there have to be a next time?"

"Well, Danny, because that's the way the game is played. It's a cruel world. There will always be a next time."

With that, the two agents left Danny alone until the plane landed, and Colonel Allen picked him up to return him to Pendleton. As they watched the Marine car pull away, Tinker looked at Evans. "Well, I guess we know when the next time will be?"

Evans looked back at Tinker, frowning. "Do we have to do this?"

"Call Rita. I want that smart-ass motherfucker."

Evans knew by the tone of his partner's voice that there was nothing he could say. When they got into town from the air-base, he dialed Rita's phone number, all the time feeling this was a bad deal. When Rita's sultry voice answered, he just stared at the phone, saying nothing. Finally, after a long silence, he identified himself.

Mockingly, Rita said, "What's the matter, did your game go bad? Poor Baby. Now little Rita has to fix it."

Rita Williams slipped one leg up and out of her bubble bath, planting her foot firmly on the wide edge of the tub. Rocking it slowly back and forth, she scrutinized it carefully, deciding, though she needed no proof, that it was a fine leg indeed. Long, full in the thigh, tapering down to a slim calf, slimmer ankle, and one of her secret prides, a slim, elegant foot. She thought feet were very important. A lot of women had nice tits, a nice ass, good bodies, but her mother had told her... when was it? About ten? Yes. Her feet were *delicate*. Thinking about it

154

now, she could only smile. That particular foot had masturbated a prominent congressman into ecstasy, and a yes vote the Agency had needed. Slowly, she dropped her leg back into the very hot bath water, and it slid into the bubbles.

The tub in her penthouse apartment in L.A. was very large, and Rita, her head resting on a bath pillow, relaxed and let her body float, the heat pinkening her skin. She loved the heat. The hotter the better. After soaking in the tub, she would stand, and turning on the shower, let cold water slam into her. Most people wouldn't be able to handle the extremes, the searing heat of the bubble bath followed by an icy blast of shocking cold. But Rita Williams was decidedly not most people.

As she floated, she idly caressed her breasts with a sponge, watching as her nipples responded. Slowly, she swept the bath sponge downward, raising her hips slightly, moving the sponge back and forth across her pubic hair, cut and trimmed artfully and erotically into a perfect heart shape. How many men had gasped in surprise when they saw *that*? Tinker had. But that's all. He'd seen it on film, but he'd never touched her. She doubted if he could. Oh, she'd tried. But only once. What had he said? "I don't fuck what I own."

She doubted if he'd ever been fucked except by his fist. Jesus, what a cold-blooded dude he was. Of course, she was no different. How many men had been locked between those fine, slim legs? One hundred? Two? No matter. She'd never felt anything, except complete control. That was all she got out of sex. Sex was power; control was power. When to moan, squirm, squeal, oh yes, she knew when to do that. She'd watched the old ones, the fat ones, the cheating sons-of-bitches who wallowed on her like pigs. She'd watched their faces contort, come apart, dissolve, as her body and all its wonderful hidden muscles worked their magic. But they hadn't reached her. Not her. Not ever. That was power. Men were nothing. Only another woman could reach her, make *her* scream, beg, plead.

But Tinker and Evans didn't know anything about that, and a good thing, too. Let them use fear. Let them use money. She

155

would do most anything for either reason. But never let them get to her out of a known weakness. Actually, it was pleasure, and the world be damned. Women didn't paw her. Women didn't hit her, or ask to be hit. She was for sale. But not all of her. Not that secret part of her that needed gentleness, tenderness, even love, though she doubted she had ever felt that.

She'd been seventeen when Johnny Tessio found her. Only seven years ago? It seemed like fifty. Johnny Tessio, big-time New Orleans mobster, with his sugar tongue and fat wallet and black Cadillac and bodyguards. Poor Rita. Fresh out of Catholic school in Baton Rouge, gone to New Orleans to see the sights. Well, Tessio was a sight, she couldn't deny that. Tall, black-haired, with a wasp waist and broad shoulders. She'd walked into the Kozy Klub in the French Quarter, answering an ad for a hostess. In two weeks, she'd gone from cashier and hostess to bejeweled, expensively gowned mistress to Johnny Tessio, who seemed to own half the city.

At first it had been dazzling. He'd been attentive, granting her every wish, telling her he loved her. At seventeen, she'd believed every word. Of course, he'd had a wife, a forty-year-old crone who constantly nagged him, and he was going to leave her. The crone turned out to be tall and blond, the mother of four Tessio sons. Rita made the mistake of pushing Johnny about leaving his wife, and the true Sicilian had surfaced. He'd stared at her coldly, called his bodyguards in, and calmly poured himself a drink as she was raped repeatedly, once with the neck of an expensive champagne bottle.

Two days later, coming out of a drugged sleep, she awoke to find herself in a very expensive brothel. The madam, a cold, barren woman of about fifty, advised her that she would serve only customers sent by Tessio. For two years she'd never been allowed out by herself, although her life was still luxurious by most standards. Even Tessio came by once in a while, a bearer of trinkets and baubles and a hard-on that needed her "special" servicing.

In those two years, she'd learned every sexual trick in the book, and some that no book had yet described. She had also

156

developed first a hatred, then an utter contempt for men. She learned to give pleasure, but to deny herself pleasure. In bed she became a consummate actress, satisfying men but secretly cheating them at the same time. Except for the pleasure she shared with a few of the girls in the brothel who felt as she did, she recognized sex as a commodity.

Then, unexpectedly, Tinker had come into her life. He had simply appeared at the brothel, told her he was taking her with him and demanded that she go. She had laughed at this intense young man, and explained to him that she couldn't go anywhere, that Tessio would see to that. He'd given her a cold smile and left, saying he would take care of Tessio. Two weeks passed, and she forgot about him. Then, one hot August day, she and her brothel bodyguard had gone out to shop for some erotic nightgowns for the girls. A nondescript black sedan had pulled up to the curb as she and her bodyguard walked toward the shop. Tinker, and a man she now knew as Evans, simply got out, knocked her guard senseless and unceremoniously threw her into the back seat. After a two-month stay at a farm outside Arlington, Virginia, she'd been flown to California, with a new name, new place of birth, new age, everything she needed to escape Tessio.

But nothing had changed. She was still a whore. Tinker and Evans were pimps. Her clientele had changed, but not by much. Instead of hoods and drug dealers, she was used discreetly to blackmail, extort, or just entertain political crooks, policemen, judges, congressmen and high officials from all over the United States and beyond. Eased into it slowly and with great care, she was now a willing and valuable accomplice to whatever Tinker and Evans suggested. The money was good, and as long as she played her role, Tessio would never find her.

And now, tonight, the threat of Tessio clamped down on her hard. Tonight, for twenty thousand dollars and her freedom, she need only do one more thing for Mr. Tinker and Mr. Evans. Standing up, she turned on the shower, shivering as the icy cold water lashed at her supple body. Yes, just one more thing. All she had to do was murder that handsome young face she

157

had stared at for days, that face in the folder. No name. Just a brief biography, and a picture, and four pages of precise instructions on where to be, when to be there and how to do it.

Stepping out of her bath, she grabbed a huge towel and began to dry herself vigorously, as if to wipe away an unseen stain. Thoughtfully, she examined her conscience for a trace of remorse, a sign of regret. Looking at herself in the full-length bathroom mirror, she saw only a stunningly beautiful girl, a girl who stared back at her with sea-green eyes, eyes empty of conscience. The girl in the mirror was a long way from Baton Rouge, and she would do as she was told.

Corporal Downing, Fox Company, 4th Replacement Battalion, looked at the ringing phone in distaste. Goddamnit, as company clerk, he couldn't even eat lunch in peace. Still chewing on an apple, he angrily snatched the phone from its cradle and barked, "Fox Company, Corporal Downing."

The voice on the line was tentative, but cheerful. "Hello. Say, I wonder if I can find out if Private Wood is going on liberty today? Could you check that out for me?"

"Who's me, mac?" Corporal Downing was not happy.

"Well, you see, I'm his cousin, from Seattle, and I want to surprise him. He doesn't know I'm down here."

"You a civilian?"

"Why, yes, I am."

"Well, listen, mac, I don't even know a Private Wood, not personally, but I can have him call you back. Where can he reach you?"

"No, don't do that, Corporal . . . Downing, isn't it?"

"Yeah, Corporal Downing. And why don't I do that?"

"Well, you can understand, he doesn't know I'm down here. We're real close, and I'd really like to surprise him if I could. He's told me in letters that there's a shuttle bus from the base into Oceanside that hooks up with buses to San Diego or L.A. I figure if I knew he was going, I could surprise him in Oceanside."

Corporal Downing wanted to get back to his lunch. "Tell you

what, mac, I'll check the liberty list. You just hold on." He put the phone down, got up and crossed the room to the Captain's desk, picking up the clipboard that held the approved liberty for the day. It was a short list, because it was a Thursday. The weekend list was two pages long. He glanced at Thursday, January 20, 1955. Daniel G. Wood was one of only five names. He walked back to his desk, still munching on his apple. "You still there, mac?"

"Yes. I'm still here."

"Okay. Now listen. I'm not supposed to give out this dope, you see, so I don't even want to know your name, and you forget mine, will ya? I mean, I'll do it for the surprise and all, and that's the only reason. You got that, mac?"

"Yes, I understand, and I appreciate it very much."

"Yeah, well you're welcome. Private Wood is on the liberty list for today. Okay?"

"That's great," said the voice. "Now, just one more favor."

Out of the corner of his eye, Corporal Downing could see Fox Company's Commander coming down the hall toward the office. "Yeah, okay, but make it snappy, will ya?"

"What time would he be leaving the base area?"

"Hell, mac, that bus only leaves this hole weekdays at one time. 1630 hours. That's 4:30 to you." The Corporal slammed the phone back down, chucking his apple into the wastebasket. "Afternoon, Captain."

The Captain only nodded, going into his office and closing the door after him.

In a motel in L.A., Tinker grinned, and hung up the phone. "Nothing to it, nothing at all. Get you ass over to Rita's and tell her she's got a bus to catch."

Evans was out the door and in his car before he said anything. Then, sitting in the car, sweating, he pounded the steering wheel and said, "Son-of-a-bitch! Goddamn son-of-a-bitch!"

Danny's return to his company had caused not a ripple of surprise. He had been gone the better part of a week, but his one-men field mission, common enough as part of his training

159

as a scout-sniper had provided good cover. It was as if he'd been with his unit all the time. He had squared away his gear, and settled into the regular routine of the new barracks, an open, clean, three-story building. It was pretty swank compared to the damp Quonset huts his unit had been using during advanced combat training. There was to be little to do while his battalion waited to go overseas, except for the two weeks at Pickle Meadows for cold-weather training. Nobody seemed to know where they would go after that, the scuttlebutt including everywhere from Tokyo to Guam to Korea.

The only thing certain on this day was the battery of shots they received, administered once again by the Navy corpsmen. A series of five "overseas shots," as they were called, were administered to his company shortly before lunch, and few of the young men had chow that afternoon. No matter how many shots you received, the effect was always the same. After the needles had done their painful little dance across Danny's arms, he'd gone straight to the Captain's office and requested overnight liberty. A routine request from a man just off a field problem, it had been routinely granted. It was to be the last routine military matter in Danny's career as a Marine.

Rita leaned forward over her knee, deftly applying polish to her toenails, her slender fingers stroking on a bright Chinese red. Wearing only a towel fastened around her breasts, and one wrapped around her wet hair, turbanlike, she extended her right leg out in front of her, pointing her toes and slowly twisting her leg from side to side. "Tell me, Evans, do you like my legs?"

"I never paid much attention." Evans was sitting on a chair opposite Rita, who sat at an elaborate mirrored dressing table.

"C'mon, Evans, you really never noticed my legs?"

"Only on film, and then they were usually stuck straight up in the air."

Rita switched her attention to the other foot, the small brush moving in even, slow strokes of color over her big toe. "I don't think you like women, do you, Evans?"

160

"What the hell is that supposed to mean? That I like boys more?"

"Well, do you?"

"Rita, why don't you go fuck yourself? You pull this shit on me every time I'm around you."

"That's true. I do, and you love it."

Evans just sat there, not taking the bait.

"Tell me about the man in the picture."

"You read the bio. That's all you need to know."

Rita switched to another toe, concentrating on even, smooth strokes. "Yes, I read it. And it doesn't tell me very much. I usually know every little quirk about men you and Tinker set up for me. There's nothing quirky about this guy. I'm not gonna just fuck and film this kid. If you want this done, you'd better help me a little."

"Are you saying you are not going through with this?"

"No, I'm saying I've never gone this far before and I need a little help, that's all." She fixed her green eyes on his, looking somehow vulnerable and very innocent.

"His name is Danny Wood, and he is one tough kid, I'll tell you that. I'll also tell you this whole deal is Tinker's idea, not mine. I think it's stupid."

Still working on her foot, Rita said, "He must have done something real bad, because Tinker wants him in the worst way."

"You want to know what he did wrong? Nothing. He did exactly what he was supposed to do."

"Why do I have to do this?"

"Because he wasn't supposed to come back, except in a box."

"And now *I'm* the box you want to bury him in."

"That's it, sugar. That sweet little heart-shaped box of yours."

"Heart-shaped? You do pay attention!" Rita stood up, letting the towel drop from her body, facing Evans. Her tongue flicked across her lips, her eyes no longer innocent.

"You'd love it, Rita, if I just bounced out of this chair and fucked you." He stood up, pulling his shoulder holster in tight to his body.

161

"No, Evans, I wouldn't like it. But I know you would." Rita was rubbing her breasts, bringing her nipples to erect, pointed attention.

"Just do your job. Just take care of Daniel Wood. If you don't, Tinker will cut you up in little tiny pieces."

Evans stormed out the penthouse door, his hands shaking as he reached for the elevator button. Down the hall, he could still hear Rita's derisive laughter.

Rita stared long and hard at her image in the mirror. She had chosen her clothes carefully and she looked at herself with a practiced eye, finally deciding she had made the right choice. After dressing and undressing four times, she had picked soft black wool slacks, a white cashmere turtleneck and a matching white cashmere jacket that fell just short of her hips. Underneath the sweater, she wore no bra, a garter belt and black panties her only undergarments. The garter belt hooked into sheer black hose, her tiny feet tucked into a pair of strappy three-inch high heels of black and white patent leather. Her long, red hair was carefully brushed into silken waves dropping softly over her shoulders, the shiny copper color in contrast with her white turtleneck and jacket. She wore little makeup, just a slight blush on her cheeks, and a bright red lipstick that matched perfectly the red painted so carefully on her long nails. The same red on her toes, not visible now, but matched for what she knew would happen later.

Satisfied, she selected a large purse, its black and white checkerboard squares her careful match, this time with her spike heels. Slowly, she transferred everything she would take with her from a bright red purse into the empty black and white one she would carry. Everything a woman usually carried went into the purse: makeup, wallet, keys and even an extra pair of panties and hose. Sometimes they got ripped, and Rita Williams was a practical girl.

After filling the purse with all manner of feminine items, she grabbed the bag by its long shoulder strap and walked to the bed, dropping the purse on the bed next to a small package wrapped in brown paper. Swiftly she ripped the paper off, extracting three small vials of clear liquid, and three disposable hypodermic needles. Unzipping a compartment in the purse, she carefully put the vials and hypos inside, staring at them briefly before she jerked the zipper closed. Scooping up the paper, she walked to a dresser, pulled open a drawer and extracted the file folder with its picture of Daniel G. Wood staring at her, its neatly typed pages telling her nothing about the darkly handsome youth in the picture.

Briskly she walked to the bedroom fireplace and slowly, methodically began to tear the typed pages, the folder and the picture into small pieces, until they lay on the bare grate in a tiny pile. Holding a gold lighter to a cigarette, she puffed once, twice, then bent over and held the flame to the pile. It quickly burst into flames, and she watched quietly, one foot tapping on the rock hearth as the pile of paper dissolved in smoke and flames. The picture curled up into itself, the face dissolving into a pile of gray ash. Finally, she poked the ashes, scattering the pile across and under the grate.

Swinging the black and white purse over her shoulder, Rita headed for the door. Opening it, she hesitated a moment, then returned to her bedroom. She walked quickly to the nightstand near her bed, pulled open a drawer, and stared intently into it, trying to make up her mind. Finally she reached in, grabbing the dainty, pearl-handled .25 automatic and casually dropped in into her purse. The envelope containing her $20,000 followed the gun.

Satisfied, she closed the drawer and walked out of the penthouse, locking the door behind her. The elevator took her nonstop from the penthouse down to the parking area under the building. In minutes she guided the convertible away, headed south to San Diego, the top on so her hair would not be blown out of its carefully sculptured coiffure.

As the flashy car raced down the highway toward San Diego, where she would board a Greyhound to meet Danny Wood, two men let themselves into her penthouse apartment. By the time Rita parked her car near the bus station in San Diego, the two men had sanitized her apartment. Not a trace of her five-year occupancy remained. Before the two men left, the lock on the penthouse door had been changed. Within a week, a flashy twenty-year-old blond would be living there.

In San Diego, Rita Williams boarded the bus for Los Angeles, purchasing a round-trip ticket. As the bus pulled out of the terminal and headed back north along the same road she had just traveled, another man approached her parked car, unlocked it and drove it across town toward a body repair and paint shop. The glove compartment contents had been placed in the man's briefcase, the interior of the car completely wiped clean, sanitized just as the penthouse had been. The beautiful, pearl white convertible pulled up and into the body shop, its paint gleaming and flawless. The well-dressed man with the briefcase walked toward a man in paint-stained coveralls, the name "Ron's Paint & Body" sewn in red across the back.

"How much to paint this baby?"

"Paint it? What the hell is wrong with it now?"

"Nothing. Five coats of black lacquer."

"Hell, mister, painting this car would be . . ."

The well-dressed man with the briefcase gave the shop owner a hard, dark look. "Just paint it. How much?"

"Well, mister, I've got six or seven cars to do before I can get at this baby. How 'bout coming back in ten days or so?"

The man reached into his pocket, peeling off five one-hundred-dollar bills and jamming them into the coverall pocket with the name "Ron" sewn on it. "I'll need it Monday."

"But . . ."

"There's three hundred more in it if you have it ready by then."

That did it. "Hell, mister, for eight hundred I'll paint the damn thing pink with green polka dots."

A smile flickered across the man's face. "Monday at nine." The man flipped the keys to "Ron," turned around and walked out of the shop.

Ron studied the car. Christ, what a waste of money.

Outside, the man with the extra rolls of film of Rita Williams wondered what the hell he was going to do in San Diego until Monday. Four days. That would seem like a year. He hated San Diego. There was one thing. He did get to deliver the newly painted car to the blond in Denver. He was already planning to get extra film of her, too. He'd have quite a collection someday. He'd seen the young blond. Gorgeous, if you liked confectionary blonds with big baby-blue eyes. She was no Rita Williams, that was for sure. But who was?

As he walked into a darkened lounge, looking for some action, the bus bearing Rita Williams to her meeting with Danny Wood continued its way north. She had no idea everything she was or ever would be rested in her purse. Everything else was gone. What men could do to create Rita Williams, they could also undo.

Danny, like all the other passengers on the bus to Los Angeles, listened to the big man's conversation get louder and dirtier as he harangued the girl. It was impossible not to listen. The big man was very drunk, and it was obvious he didn't care what he said, or who heard him say it. The driver kept the bus moving, saying nothing to stop him. Danny was getting irritated.

"Will you please leave me alone?" The girl's voice was soft and plaintive, drifting forward to Danny, its tone a bit desperate and frightened.

If Danny could hear it, so could the bus driver. But if he heard it, he was obviously going to do nothing about it, the bus still on its steady course, the driver's eyes fixed on the road.

A soft, seductive perfume caught in Danny's nostrils, followed immediately by a touch of the girl's beautifully lacquered hand as it gently touched his left shoulder. Danny looked up into a face so beautiful his breath caught in his chest as he stared into the deepest green eyes he'd ever seen, eyes wide with genuine fear, the face framed in luxuriant waves of copper-colored hair.

"Excuse me, I hate to ask you this, but would it be okay if I sat here with you? That man won't leave me alone, and the

165

driver won't say a word to him. He's very drunk and he scares me. He's said some really awful things."

Danny took her all in, a quick glance showing a lush figure to go with the face, a beautiful young woman, who, oddly enough, was dressed in black and white, as he was. Danny stood up, taking the young woman by the elbow and steering her into the seat next to the window. He was quick to notice the black and white spike heels, the black and white purse, black fabric taut over her buttocks as she slid into the seat. In heels, she was only a couple of inches under six feet. Danny sat down next to her, saying nothing.

Her hand reached and gripped his thigh, the slim, crimson-tipped hand in beautiful contrast set against his black slacks. "Thank you." As quickly as she'd touched him, she withdrew her hand, gripping her purse with both hands. Then, setting it down beside her, she crossed her legs and held her hands, one atop the other, on her knee.

Danny could still feel the pressure and the warmth on his thigh and now, sitting next to her, the elusive scent of her perfume seemed to hover around him, a scent so subtle, yet so perfect, it claimed and reclaimed the air. "No thanks needed, miss. I haven't done anything."

"Oh, but you have. The damn driver should get another job."

"Well, that fellow is pretty big."

The redhead shuddered, her body making its own statement. "What if he comes up here?"

Danny turned to look at the girl, her eyes still showing fright. The look also told Danny she wasn't sure he could handle the man if he did continue his drunken verbal assault.

There was little time to wonder. At that moment, the man sat down in the seat directly in front of Danny and the girl, his massive shoulders filling the width of both seats, the bottle in his right hand held carelessly over the back of the seat, directly over Danny's leg. The man fixed Danny with a drunken stare.

The girl's hand rested once again on Danny's thigh, and she seemed to be trying to propel herself backward through her

166

seat. Danny returned the man's stare, his eyes flat and expressionless, showing the other man neither fear nor outrage.

The man's gaze remained briefly on Danny, then shifted to the girl. She looked down, her tongue flicking out over her lips nervously. "Why don't you just leave me alone?" The voice was tiny, pleading.

"Hell, I'm just gettin' started. I'll raise my offer. Five hundred bucks for all night. How about it?"

The slim hand gripped Danny's thigh, as she turned her head toward the window. Danny's voice came out low, his body tensing slightly. "The lady asked you to leave her alone. Why don't you do that? There's plenty of room in the back, and you can get as drunk as you want."

The big man shifted in his seat, giving Danny a slow smile. "Sonny, why don't you mind your own business?"

"I'm trying to, mister. But you're making it damn hard."

"Well now, that's a shame. Fact is, she's making my dick damn hard." With that, he reached out with his left hand and grabbed the girl by the breast, causing her to cry out in pain.

Danny exploded forward, his right hand flat and aimed at the man's nose, his left pinning the man's right arm, still holding the bottle, against the back of the seat. The heel of Danny's hand caught the man just over the mouth, the speed and power of the blow breaking the nose and hurling the huge upper torso backward, his right arm still pinned to the rear of the seat, clutching the bottle.

"Son-of-a-bitch. I'll . . ."

Danny grabbed the pinned right arm and stood straight up, twisting the big man's body sideways, the bottle clattering to the floor and rolling down the aisle toward the driver. Danny stepped out of his seat into the aisle, releasing the man completely, looking for an opening as the man struggled to get out of the confined area of the floor behind his seat. As he straightened up, Danny thrust his hands, fingers rigid, deep into the man's solar plexus.

The man looked at Danny, blood running from his nose. Before he could get clear of the seat, Danny cupped his palms and brought both hands together over the man's ears in a violent headslap, a popping sound that shattered the man's left eardrum. Stepping back, Danny gripped the seat across the aisle with both hands, and hurled his legs out, feet together, into the man's chest, sending him crashing into the window, his head bouncing off it violently. He began a slow-motion slide down and under the seat, his legs sticking into the aisle. He was out cold.

The bus had come to a stop. The driver walked back to where Danny stood and remarked, somewhat fearfully, "Is he dead? God, I've never seen anything like it."

Danny studied the man's feet, noticing the expensive shoes, polished to a high gloss. "No, but he ought to be. Now, let's finish your job."

"My job?"

"That's right. You should have put him off this bus. That's what we're going to do right now. Grab his feet."

They pulled the man down the aisle while the rest of the passengers, except for the redhead, stood and gaped. She sat calmly in her seat, her face serene and composed. As they reached the door, the man began to revive. Groaning, he staggered to his feet, only to be thrown out the door, landing on his back before rolling to his knees, his hands going to his ears.

Well, thought Danny, it could have been worse, mister. You could have been dead.

The driver needed no encouragement. In seconds, the bus was once more on its way. Danny had no way of knowing the best soundman in the business would never work his specialty again. The blows to his ears had deafened him.

Danny walked back to his seat, looking into those seemingly bottomless green eyes. "My name is Danny Wood. May I sit down?"

She nodded, the flash of her eyes electric. As he sat down, she slipped her arm through his, a possessive, but very natural thing to do. "Hello, Danny Wood. My name is Rita Williams."

Glancing down at her arm linked through his, Danny asked, "Where are you headed, in particular?"

168

With a happy sigh, Rita Williams slid very close to Danny. Without answering, she gave Danny a searching look. Just the right touch, she thought.

"I'm heading for Long Beach. How about dinner, if you'd like that? I know a nice place."

"Dinner. That's a nice way to start."

While shifting her hips and thighs, Rita Williams began to run her crimson nails across the black, curly hair on the back of his hand, pressing her lower body against his. Just like she'd planned. Perfect. Or was it?

She felt a long-forgotten warmth in her thighs, a happy feeling. God, he'd really handled Bob Chandler. Evans was right. This was one tough kid. Still, she'd do her job. No problem. Secretly, sweetly, she also let herself feel feminine, protected. He'd done that *for her*. Without expecting anything. If nothing else, for Rita Williams, that was a novel experience.

Rita Williams' planned destruction of Danny Wood was not going well. She was, in fact, being seduced, and liking it very much. Sitting outside on the upper deck of the Red Fox Restaurant on this unusually warm January evening in Long Beach, she sipped her Bloody Mary and wondered how she was going to complete her instructions.

Danny watched her with clear hazel eyes, as she dissolved into a mass of contradictory emotions. She was both perplexed and, much worse, excited. This quiet young man, drinking tequila and flashing an easy, sure maleness, was raising havoc with her resolve. She had picked him up without appearing to have done so. She had his undivided attention in one of his favorite haunts, a spot he obviously knew well and felt comfortable in. A few of the patrons had known him by name. She would undoubtedly get him alone somewhere. And that would be that. No more Danny Wood. Take the twenty thousand dollars and run, according to plan.

He lit her cigarette, his hand gently touching hers, his voice caressing her in a way so intimate she became physically weak. She began to accept that it was she, not Danny Wood, who had

169

no control over this night. This was no fat, cheating V.I.P. to be blackmailed and forgotten. No, this was something different. She would handle him. She had to. But how?

On their second drink, Rita leaned forward. "Tell me about yourself."

Danny answered, "There isn't a hell of a lot to tell."

"Try."

"Okay. I'm a Marine, stationed at Pendleton, like a lot of other Marines. I expect to go overseas soon. I'm eighteen, though nobody around here knows that. I was born in Seattle, and at the moment, I don't miss it at all. That's about it, really. Nothing special."

"I think you're very special." Her eyes widened slightly, just the right touch, she knew. Grown men had come unstuck looking into that gaze. This was just a boy. "And throwing giants off buses, is that something you do often?"

Danny laughed, his face animated and slightly embarrassed. "No, and I wouldn't like to try it again. The creep was big enough to take me apart."

Briefly Rita thought about the Agency soundman. The plan had been for him to hassle her, and then leave under the threat of violence. She doubted if he'd be working for a while. "But he didn't take you apart, did he? I've never seen anything like it. Why did you do it?"

Danny thought about why. "Hell, I don't know. I could stand his mouth, but when he reached out and grabbed you, and you screamed, I just wanted to stop him, that's all. I really didn't think about it. It was just reflex." But even as he said this, remembering, his eyes hardened, his face set, the boyishness was gone. He realized he'd tried to kill the man.

Watching his face, Rita pressed her thighs together, feeling the moist heat, her pulse quickening. Violence excited her. She shivered involuntarily, thinking about the bus, the terrible, thrilling quickness of it all.

"Are you cold?" Danny asked.

Slipping quickly to the business at hand, Rita answered, "No, Danny, I'm not cold. Not even a little bit. Tell me, what do

170

you do in the Marines? I mean, what's your job?"

Without hesitation, Danny answered, "I'm a sniper."

Perplexed, Rita asked, "Sniper, what does that mean?"

"That means I'm trained to sort of hide in the bushes with a fancy rifle and shoot some poor slob from so far away he never even hears what kills him." The last few days flashed across Danny's mind in stark detail, in spite of his efforts to forget them.

Even while pondering what it took to be a sniper, Rita Williams knew Danny Wood had it. And had done it. Startled, she realized he had to be much like her. Professional. Cold. He didn't look it. She was suddenly aware that Danny Wood was very dangerous. He'd bested Tinker and Evans. He'd thrown Bob Chandler off a bus in a bloody mess. And he warranted all her talents and twenty thousand dollars to get rid of him. They had all underestimated him. Now it was up to her. "Do you have a hotel where we can go?"

Sheepishly, Danny said, "I usually go to the Buffum Hotel. They keep a room for me, when they can. But payday is the first, and I can't afford it."

Reaching into her purse, Rita pulled one of the hundreds from the envelope Tinker had given her, and slid it across the table to Danny. "I can afford it. Get us a couple of bottles, and take me there."

Eyes flat, Danny said, "You don't owe me anything."

She was going to lose him. "No, I don't. I'm doing this for myself. I want to be with you. Don't cheapen it, please." Lowering her eyes, Rita looked away from Danny, seeming vulnerable and hurt. It was a great act, and she was good at it.

Danny reached out one hand, turning her chin toward him, a dark, visible sadness on his face, a look she'd hoped for, and now wished she hadn't put there. "I'm sorry, really. I want to be with you, too. I need to be with you, actually."

"Then don't look so sad about it. Just get the booze, and take me out of here. I'm going to powder my nose."

A dazzling smile lit up Danny's face. "It doesn't need powder."

171

"Listen, Danny Wood, when a lady says she needs to powder her nose, she needs to powder her nose. Now run along. Scotch for me. I'll meet you here in five minutes."

Not allowing him to reply, she quickly walked off the upper deck of the restaurant, heading toward the ladies' room at the end of a long hallway. Stopping at a phone just outside the door, she dialed a number quickly, tapping her nails on the wall as it rang four times. Tinker answered.

"The Buffum Hotel. Long Beach," Rita said.

"Any trouble?"

"No. Should there be?"

"I just wanted to know, Rita baby. He practically killed Bob. He can't hear a thing yet. Says his eardrums are busted. Hell of a thing for a soundman. You'd better get that kid, and get him good. You have the stuff, don't you?"

"Have I ever fucked up before, Tinker? He's only a kid. Quit worrying. I've got him around my little finger."

"Rita?"

"What."

"You had better use both hands, not just your little finger." The phone went dead.

Rita slammed it down and went to meet Danny. She saw him standing at the railing, looking into the street. Walking up to him, she slipped her arm through his, brushing her hip against him.

"Ready?"

Danny turned to look at her, his eyes bright. "I don't see any powder."

Rita laughed. "Powder room is a word that covers everything."

"Then let's go. We can walk. It's only four blocks."

Swinging her hips as she walked, clutching Danny's arm, she watched with pleasure the look of envy in the men's eyes as they walked through and out of the bar.

"You're really something, Rita. Whether you know it or not, you just made me a legend at the Red Fox bar. I'll be able to tell lies for years."

Rita stopped walking, and pressed her body hard against Danny's, her pelvis thrust against him. "Tell me, Danny, does that feel like a lie?"

"No."

"Good." Pulling away and tugging his arm, Rita walked on, her spike heels clicking as she walked. For a moment, she herself looked for the truth, but it wasn't there. She had her mark. That was the only truth that mattered.

The Buffum had only a small neon script in the window announcing that it was indeed a hotel. Located in nearly the exact center of downtown, it needed nothing else. Four stories high, it was a conservative, clean hotel. And those who knew it, used it often. Standing in the small foyer, just inside the door with its glass brick border filtering the lights from the street, Rita had a feeling Danny knew it quite well. The manager had a small apartment behind the desk. As he emerged, he smiled knowingly at Danny, and cast an appreciative glance at Rita while swivelling the register around for Danny. "Just your name will do, son."

A twinge of unexplainable jealousy tugged at Rita's mind.

"Thanks, Mr. Baker. Anybody in my room?"

"Nope. Thursday is kinda quiet, so you go right on up. Gonna be here long?"

Danny glanced at Rita. "Don't think so. But no calls or anything, okay? You never can tell."

Mr. Baker, taking a longer, head-to-toe look at Rita, only handed Danny a key and remarked, "Enjoy your stay." With that, he returned to his apartment, leaving the door open. From the sound of the TV, he was watching a wrestling match.

Danny turned to Rita, "I hope you don't mind walking. It's on the top floor, and there are no elevators."

"I don't mind. It's good for the legs." Grabbing Danny's hand she pulled him after her, leading the way up the carpeted stairs, rolling her hips provocatively as she walked ahead of him. As they reached the fourth floor, she asked, "Which way?"

173

"To your left, the last door at the end of the hall. It's a corner room, the best in the house. You'll like it."

As he fitted the key to the lock, she looked up at him and asked, "Tell me, did the rest of them like it?"

"The rest of who?"

"The other women."

Danny swung the door open, and pulled her in after him, taking her purse and tossing it on the bed, then taking her in his arms, his obvious erection hard and insistent against her thighs. "To tell you the truth, I never asked them."

Then quickly, with startling strength, he had crushed her to him, and tongue probing, kissed her full on the mouth.

Hookers don't kiss. Oh yes, they suck, they fuck, they do anything. But they don't kiss. Kissing indicates affection and anal, oral or upside down sex is rarely done with affection by a hooker. You pays your money, and you gets what you pays for. After her initial shock at this broken code, Rita Williams found herself responding with considerable feeling, her tongue darting in and out of Danny's mouth, her hips grinding frantically against his, her long-nailed fingers at his neck and shoulders, pulling him toward her. Her breath quickened like a teenager's, her thighs damp and musky under the tight wool slacks. Leaning back, her hips still pressed forward, she looked up at Danny, his eyes revealing naked, near frantic need. "My goodness," she exclaimed, "you're not Sir Galahad at all."

His hands, tightly clutching her buttocks, seemed to drop away as if bitten. "Sorry, I don't usually act this way."

Gently she put his hands back behind her, still joined to him by the forward thrust of her hips. "Don't be sorry. I'm flattered, really. And I like it."

Pulling his face down to hers, she kissed him again, this time moving her unconfined breasts against him, her mouth open, pulling his tongue into her mouth, as if to swallow him whole. Finally, she pulled back, looking around the darkened room. "Does this place have any lights?"

Danny hurriedly stepped around the room, switching on every light.

174

He was right. It was a nice room, with a big bed, two large, comfortable chairs, and a small fridge. Languidly, she followed him around, turning off all the lights except the one nearest the bed, then closing the venetian blinds that ran the length of one wall. She casually picked her purse up off the bed, putting it on a straight-back chair nestled into a small nook at an equally small writing desk. "Honey, I said we needed light, but not all of them. And you were right. It is a nice room. Is there any ice in that refrigerator?"

"Four trays, to be exact."

"Four? I think I'm getting jealous. That big bed's no virgin, is it?"

"No, it isn't. But then, neither am I."

"Well, I'm certainly relieved to hear that. Now, my young tiger, I'll mix the drinks, and you go take a shower. I think I need one to settle down. I'll be waiting for you, right here, when you get out." She shrugged off her short jacket, causing her breasts to leap and settle under her sweater, the nipples pointed and hard.

Danny looked at her with undisguised desire. "I don't think I can wait."

Rita walked over to him, and placed both his hands under her sweater, rubbing his hands roughly over her breasts. "Of course you can. Waiting is the best part. Well, almost the best part."

"Tell me, should I take a hot or cold shower?"

"It won't matter. I promise to make things as hot as I can when you're finished. Now, off with you. I'll mix those drinks."

Danny extricated himself from her grasp, and quickly, quietly, stripped completely naked, his erection full and hard.

"My, look at you."

"Are you sure you want me to take that shower?"

Bending down, still dressed, she drew the hard length of him into her mouth, once, twice, and then stood up. "I'm sure. But Danny, if you decide on a cold shower, keep the water off *that*."

Danny just grinned, still feeling the envelope of warmth on

175

his hard-on. "Don't worry. Hot or cold, it won't matter."

As he walked to the bathroom, Rita called out, "Danny?"

"Yes?"

"You're beautiful, do you know that? You really are. Bring it back to me."

Rita, ear cocked for the sound of the shower, made herself a drink, Scotch rocks, and then poured Danny three fingers of tequila over ice, discarding the water glass covers in the wastebasket near the bed. Then, sipping her Scotch, she removed Danny's wallet from his pocket, and began to go through it. Before examining its contents, she put three hundred-dollar bills, neatly folded, in the money pocket. Robbery would provide no motive. Slowly, she examined what Private Daniel Gregory Wood felt near enough to himself to carry.

Sipping her drink, Rita spread the photos from Danny's wallet fan-shaped on the bed. All girls. All very pretty. All very young. Seven in all. No pictures of family. None of mom and dad, nothing homey. Just the girls, like wanted pictures from the Old West, or perhaps trophies. In any event, he had obviously collected the bounty on each.

There was one picture of Danny and another Marine, both wearing camouflage outfits and carrying wicked-looking scoped rifles, taken against the wild backdrop of Camp Pendleton's hills. Danny had black charcoal smudges under his eyes, giving him a fierce, warrior look.

She glanced back at the girls, then back to Danny. She wondered if any of them had seen him like this. Not very likely. The Marine in the picture did not look like the boy taking a shower only a few feet away. A hoked-up picture for his grandchildren, who would never notice the danger, the pure menace in those eyes. Rita noticed it, and shivered involuntarily. She knew he had used that rifle, or one like it, and in so doing brought down the wrath of Tinker and Evans, and now she was here to clean up their mess.

The shower was still going, but she could no longer hear him singing. Hurriedly, she pulled out a small green liberty card

176

and his Marine I.D. card. The liberty card showed an expiration date of 21 January, 0545 hours. The picture, cold and lifeless, looked as if it had been taken in one of those coin-operated machines in Woolworths. It hardly looked like him at all. Nothing looked like him. He had many faces, many moods. He seemed to put them on and off, like masks. Which man, which boy, was she dealing with? The official picture, the childlike pose in full battle dress, the one she'd spent the past two hours with?

Only a tiny key was left in the wallet. She could only guess what it opened. A locker of some sort. She searched the key for numbers. There were none. She could not know it was the key to his private pool cue locker in Seattle, an innocent item that unaccountably bothered her. It might be dangerous to her, she couldn't be sure. Replacing the pictures and I.D. cards, she removed the key and slipped it into her purse. Tinker would be pleased. The locker key might open a door somewhere that could nail them all. Tinker would know. He'd track down the lock, and open it. End of mystery.

In the bathroom, the shower had stopped. Quickly, she slipped the wallet back in his pants pocket. The left pocket, the one most men carried their wallet in. Danny carried his in his right pocket. She hadn't noticed. Rita Williams was getting careless.

Rita was on the bed, still dressed, her head and shoulders propped up on the pillows when Danny emerged from the bathroom, a cloud of steam trailing after him, a towel wrapped around his waist.

"I see you decided on a hot shower."

Reaching for his glass of tequila, Danny replied, "And I see you decided not to leave."

"Not me. Wild horses couldn't drag me away."

"You've still got your clothes on. I feel awkward as hell. I must look like a man who just stepped into the street direct from a Turkish bath."

Rita stared at him, eyes bright and intense. "I wanted to wait,

177

so you could watch me. Tell me, Daniel, are you a watcher, or a doer?"

Danny just chuckled, lighting a cigarette.

"Which one?"

"Both, I like to watch what I do."

In one sinuous motion, Rita was up and off the bed, gently pushing Danny down to where she had lain, the bed still warm from her body, the elusive perfume hanging in the air. "Okay. I like to be watched."

Unbuttoning her tight slacks, she shifted her hips slightly, letting the slacks fall to the floor, then daintily stepped free of them. The garter belt and nylons stayed on as she stepped free of the tiny panties, dropping them on the floor next to her slacks, still wearing her heels and sweater. "How am I doing so far?"

She spread her legs wide, hands on her hips, her breath quickening as it always did when she knew she was on camera.

"So far, terrific. Why don't you come get this glass and refill it? I think I'm gonna need it."

With an exaggerated hip roll, Rita walked to the bed, raising one leg and placing her knee only inches from Danny's face.

"Who does your hair?" Danny asked, staring intently at her heart-shaped pubic hair.

Rita lost all sexiness, dissolving into laughter. "I do. Give me your glass." Again, as she walked away from the bed, she let her hips roll, knowing that from the rear it was highly unlikely that Daniel Gregory Wood had ever seen anything quite like her perfect ass flowing into her gartered and stockinged legs, tucked into tiny, spiky heels.

Danny, propped on one elbow, watched as Rita strolled back to the bed, handed him his fresh drink and in one fluid motion pulled the turtleneck up and over her head, shaking her hair back into place as she stood there. As she watched him sip his drink, she placed her knee back on the bed, and in one swift movement snatched the towel from his body.

"Look what I found," she said, her hand closing tightly on

his cock, pulling it straight up and moving her hand up and down on it.

"My God, you're awfully big."

"Not really, I'm just awfully horny."

"So am I. Should we start the way I'm dressed? It makes me feel sexy."

Even as he looked at Rita's flawless body, so near he could smell it, Danny thought of Natalie, painting him, loving him, devouring him. "No, why don't you take everything off. You look too good to have anything on between your body and mine."

Rita was surprised, but quickly hid it. Every other man had flipped out when she'd been dressed like this. Wordlessly, she sat down, and with elaborate, slow movements removed her heels and stripped the nylons from her sleek legs, removing the garter belt last, dropping everything into a loose pile on the floor. Completely naked, she padded barefoot back to the bed, reaching out and taking Danny's glass, only to have him pull it back and drain it.

"Now?" she asked.

"Yes. Now." He reached a tanned, muscled arm out and around her hips, and pulled her roughly down on the bed, tangling his hands in her hair and pulling her mouth down on his. She suddenly felt tiny and vulnerable, and without consent, her supple body began to move against his. With shocking quickness he was deep inside her, and she forgot completely what she was in Long Beach to do. Lying on top of him, his cock deep and hard inside of her, her body raced away and left her mind betrayed.

At 10:00 P.M. on the last normal day of his life, Danny Wood watched as Rita Williams slipped into her strappy heels, and strutted around the hotel room, doing bumps and grinds to imaginary music, a drink in one hand, a cigarette in the other.

"Don't you ever wear out?" Standing at the foot of the bed, she rolled her hips provocatively, her eyes unnaturally bright.

179

She'd been taking Benzedrine all night, and she was flying high.

"Don't let 'em fool you, kid, those young chicks of yours. It won't wear out, and you can't hurt it." Watching her, Danny couldn't help it. His erection was back, insistent, throbbing. For pure, undiluted wildness, he'd never before encountered anyone like her.

"Oh...I get some more! Goodie. Now listen, Danny Wood, this is for me, so you just lay there, and don't move." Snuffing the cigarette, she set her drink on the floor and scrambled onto the bed, grabbing him and holding herself high, straddling his hips.

"Rita, I've never..."

"Well, I have. You'll love it, but I'll love it more."

"I'll hurt you, won't I? I mean..."

"Shut up! Now don't move. Promise me."

Slowly, steadily, she lowered herself, and then, with a sharp cry, she dropped straight down. Amazed, Danny did as he was asked, his body still as she moved slowly up and down, joined but not touching him. Her palms flat on the bed next to her spike heeled feet, she asked him to touch her nipples, then pinch, then to pinch harder, her torso twisting wildly, until his young mind finally caught on. She was purging herself of something. Suddenly angry, he twisted her hair in his left hand, and slapped her nipples hard, left, right, left right, his arm arcing back and forth between them.

Her knees spread wider than he thought possible, and he was bigger and deeper than he thought possible, when she shook her hair from his grasp and bit down hard on his hand, drawing blood. Jamming her pelvis tight on him, she pulled back, their bodies still joined, drawing him up and on her, cursing and scratching, turning the room into a blurred vision of sex bordering on hate, smothered in sensation and beyond.

For a brief instant he thought she was doing battle, not making love. Then it was there, in her beautiful, contorted face. She looked as if she were...trying to kill him. The look disappeared from view as she leaned forward and bit him, tiny nip-

180

ping bites on his shoulder, her body forming a perfect V, toes pointed, her back arched high off the bed. With a terrible, body-wracking shudder, she locked her heels behind his neck, gasped "Oh, my God!" and passed out cold, her body suddenly and limply falling away from his.

The shower beat down on Danny's back, full blast, as he soaped Rita's breasts, almost invisible in the steam-filled bathroom.

"Oh, that feels good."

"Aren't they sore?"

"Yes, but I don't care."

They switched places in the small tub, and she gently soaped the vivid welts she'd left on his back and hips. "I just went crazy. Do the scratches hurt much? Turn around," she commanded. As Danny turned, she went down on her knees, the water drenching her long red hair, her mouth hot on him again. "Dead soldier," she commented.

"Dead Marine."

Rita stood up, laughing softly, putting her arms around him, still thrusting her pelvis and breasts at him like weapons. And, indeed, that's what she was. A weapon. She threw her head back, her startling green eyes looking deep into his.

Danny said, "Let's get out of this shower, before we drown, or shrink. By now George has stocked the box with cold beer, and cleaned the room."

Alarm showed in Rita's eyes, and just as quickly vanished. A tidy room didn't fit her plans at all. "What? You must be kidding."

"Nope. I called down before we came in here."

Danny picked off a towel and stepped from the bath into the bedroom. He was right. George had been there.

Rita poked her head out of the bathroom, one breast upright and pointing from the door. "Hon, be an angel and hand me my purse, will you? I want to get beautiful for you."

Danny studied her a moment. Even with her hair straight and dripping water on the floor, there was no doubt that she was a great beauty. Wrapped in a big bath towel, Danny picked up her black-and-white-checked handbag, and as an afterthought, the matching spike heels.

She gave him a smile. "We'll do it slow and sweet this time, Danny. No bites. Well, maybe."

Rita ducked back into the bathroom, and popped the door shut behind her. The purse was heavy. Going to the mirror, she vigorously brushed her wet hair, then even more vigorously, began to dry it, all the time thinking, how do you kill a man? Opening the heavy purse, she ignored the small .25-caliber automatic pistol, the twenty thousand dollars, and the small glass ampules. Instead, she reached for her makeup. At that moment, it was the only lethal weapon she was experienced with.

In Rita Williams' sanitized Los Angeles apartment, Tinker paced back and forth in the bedroom, his fifth double Scotch in his hands, as Evans, sprawled on Rita's former bed, watched with nervous amusement.

"What time is it?" Tinker snapped, his Browning 9mm pistol swinging in his shoulder holster as he threw his head back and emptied the glass of Scotch in one gulp.

Evans didn't bother to look at his watch. "It's about five minutes later than it was the last time you asked me."

Pouring another double from Rita's well-stocked bar, Tinker glanced down at his partner. "Well, what time was it then? And by the way, you look pretty fuckin' ridiculous on that bed. You like staring up at that whorehouse mirror?"

Evans took the jibe without comment, but he was involuntarily staring up at the mirrored ceiling above the bed. Absently, he wondered how many victories Rita had chalked up on this bed. How many men, how many miles of film, the cameras grinding from all four mirrored walls around and above where he now lay.

"It is exactly 10:00 P.M.," said Evans.

"She ought to be finished by now," grumbled Tinker.

"I doubt it. She's probably having the time of her life. I

182

wonder what she's like with no cameras, no Agency, just one man."

"What do you mean?"

"Well, if the kid fucks like he shoots, she's gonna take her time."

"She doesn't have any time."

Evans looked carefully at Tinker. He looked ugly, mean, drunk. "Relax, Tink. She'll do it. But you know how she is. This thing is more than we've ever asked her to do. She's probably nervous. Hell, let her fuck the kid to death, what do you care?"

"Yeah, what the hell, what does it matter? Nobody's ever gonna see her again anyway. You sure Bob's there?"

"I'm sure. He can't hear so good, but he's there. After what Danny did to him on that bus, he wants Rita's ass almost as bad as you do."

"Good."

"Ease up," Evans said, sliding off the bed and heading toward the bar. "You know, Tink, Rita Williams has been damn valuable to us in the past. She's still got those fabulous looks, that fabulous body. That Denver blond, Christ, we'll have to train her for months, if she can be trained. Besides, she's just a pretty, greedy little kid. Face it. There just isn't anybody quite like Rita."

"I can't let her loose, and you know it. Not after this. Not ever. She'd hold us by the balls with it. We'd wind up working for her. For christsake, use your head."

"But killing her. That's just more heat. The kid's bad enough. I don't understand that at all. I mean . . ."

Tinker exploded, shocking Evans into silence. "The kid goes, Rita goes and that's it!"

Quietly, Evans asked, "Did the Agency order this? That's all I want to know."

A sly smile spread across Tinker's face, "Jesus Christ, Evans, be serious. You don't think I'd pull this without Agency clearance?"

"No. I don't think you would." But Evans thought that was exactly what Tinker was doing. He couldn't be sure. But if it went wrong, in any way, there would be the worst kind of mess. Sipping bourbon, Evans measured what he knew about Rita, and what he felt about Daniel Wood. It should be easy. But . . . he pushed thoughts of failure from his mind.

"What time is it?"

Evans looked once more at his watch. "Ten-thirty."

Tinker resumed his pacing, muttering, "It won't be long now. Then Rita. Then this little episode is a wrap."

As Evans watched, Tinker lit a cigarette, his hands shaking.

In the bathroom, Rita sat on the edge of the tub, staring at the three glass ampules of pure morphine, and the throwaway syringes. Goddamn, she was scared. She would never get Danny with the needle. Grabbing two of the ampules, she broke them into a piece of tissue, and carefully poured the crystalline particles into the bottle of beer she'd carried with her. Tinker had said the ampules contained enough pure stuff to kill anyone. Her plan now was simple. She'd get him to drink two ampules, which she was positive would, at the very least, knock him out. Then, inject the third and last ampule.

But she'd have to work fast, and get out fast. She walked back into the bedroom, staring down intently at Danny, naked and apparently asleep. God, what a beautiful man. Walking over to the bed, she sat down heavily, and Danny's eyes snapped open, wary and hard, his body tense.

"Hey, ease up. It's me, sleepy head. And you said you weren't the rollover type. I brought you another cold beer."

Danny's eyes softened, and a slow smile began at the corners of his mouth. Uncoiling, he sat up, reaching for the beer.

Trying to keep the smile on her face, her arm trembling, she extended the lethal drink to Danny, who took it and pulled her to him, all in one motion, kissing her long and softly on the mouth. Involuntarily, she shuddered.

"Hey, are you cold?"

"You just affect me that way. Now go on, drink your beer."

184

Danny tipped the bottle straight back and drank it. "God, that was a bitter son-of-a-bitch! Grab me another, will you?"

Quickly, she brought two fresh bottles, handing one to him, keeping the other for herself.

"That's much better," Danny exclaimed.

It had never occurred to Rita that morphine crystals might have a taste, particularly when mixed with cold beer. Sitting tensely on the edge of the bed, she sipped her beer, and watched Danny carefully. He was talking about how goddamn good he felt, how it was one fine fucking world and something about how she was the most beautiful thing in the world.

Then, abruptly, he shakily handed her his half-finished beer and lay back down on the bed, languorous and relaxed, saying, "Jesus, I'm tired." He closed his eyes, and seemed to be asleep.

She waited. Five minutes passed. Ten. Fifteen. He had not moved. Leaning over him, she gently tugged back one eyelid. A tiny, unseeing pinpoint of a pupil stared up, looking at nothing. She felt for his pulse. It was very rapid, too fast to count, then, under her fingers, it became very slow and feeble. His respiration was slow and shallow. He seemed completely unconscious. She shook him again, then slapped his face very hard. He did not respond. His muscles were flaccid, completely relaxed.

Rushing into the bathroom, she snatched the third ampule from her purse. Placing the ampule down on the edge of the sink, she dug frantically into her purse for the syringe, tearing off the paper with her teeth and spitting it into the bottom of her purse. Reaching back to the sink, she watched in horror as her hand slapped the ampule off the sink edge and against the steel bottom stopper of the sink, where it shattered and vanished in the swiftly running hot water. Motionless, she watched for what seemed hours, but was in reality only a split second, as her hand, on its own, dived to retrieve the shattered, tiny glass capsule that would guarantee Daniel Gregory Wood's death.

She walked slowly back into the bedroom. Calm now, she bent to touch his chest. It was cold and damp. Checking carefully, she detected no pulse, no heartbeat. Two had been enough. She wouldn't have needed the third. Relaxed even though she'd popped another handful of Benzedrine and washed them down with a beer, she set about the job of cleaning the hotel room. There would be no trace of Rita Williams, just a hint of unidentifiable perfume left to haunt the room. Just a dead, overdosed Marine—a tragic accident.

At two in the morning, once again smartly dressed, her work finished, the twenty thousand safely tucked away in her purse, Rita closed the door to Danny's morgue, and walked down the stairs and past the desk of good old George. She checked the register. Just Danny's name. No problem. She was free.

Feeling more alive, more sexually vibrant than at any time in her life, she walked out of the Buffum Hotel, slung her purse over her right shoulder, and, hips swinging, walked toward the bus depot. The first time hadn't been all that tough. She'd have to tell Tinker and Evans all about it. Shock the hell out of them. Fucking a man you didn't know was easy. There had been plenty of them. Blackmail was easy. Tough titty for the poor slobs she'd ensnared in that web. But killing a man . . . that was thrilling. They would not have to ask her next time. She would volunteer. Nothing approached what she felt at this minute.

Savoring the memory, she strutted down the dark, early morning streets of Long Beach. She paid no notice as the beat-up '49 Ford pulled away from the curb and slowly, purposefully, stalked her. The street lights were mirrored in the driver's aviator-type glasses, the bulk of the driver nearly filling the front seat, blocking from view the small Asian male sitting directly behind the driver. The Ford's beat-up exterior hid a finely tuned, quiet engine. Its custom exhausts were almost soundless. Rita, lost in thought, heard nothing as it slowed at the curb beside her. The short, wiry Asian, dressed in black slacks and black turtleneck, was a brief shadow flicking out of the rear seat and snatching her without a sound from the streets and into the car, which pulled away and disappeared into the night.

Meanwhile, in the quiet room on the top floor of the Buffum Hotel, Danny Wood groaned softly, tried to sit up and fell back.

There is a saying among the elite scout snipers of the United States Marine Corps. Close. But a miss might just as well be a mile. Rita had missed.

The beat-up Ford pulled into the underground garage below Rita Williams' penthouse apartment, sliding smoothly to a stop next to Tinker's Agency Cadillac. The Soundman got out, and spoke to the apprehensive woman for the first time since he pulled her from the brightly lit streets of Long Beach, an event witnessed by no one.

"Welcome home, Rita." There was no hint of welcome in his voice.

Meekly, Rita let herself be yanked from the car by the wiry Asian, sensing the power in his small hands as he gripped her by one wrist, a silent, human handcuff. "Bob, tell him to ease up on me, will you? He's damn near crushing my arm."

The Soundman, who would be a soundman no more, only grinned and opened the doors to the penthouse elevator, silently motioning to the man in black. Rita was wrenched violently and propelled into the elevator with an effortless movement by the Asian. She crashed into the elevator wall and bumped her head, almost falling. He had finally let go of her wrist, and she rubbed it gently as he watched her, his eyes without emotion, his body at the same time at ease, yet taut with controlled energy.

The bulky Agency man closed the elevator door, lit a cigarette and punched the "up" button. As the elevator began its slow rise, Bob said, "Rita, this is Chin. He's from out of town." With a laugh that chilled her to the bone, he opened the door after the elevator stopped. "C'mon, cunt, Tinker and Evans would like a few words with you."

As she entered her apartment, cold terror struck her. It was her apartment, but everything belonging to her had been removed. The rugs were changed, and new paintings hung on the walls. Only as she was led into her bedroom did she see anything familiar. The mirrored walls, the canopied bed, everything in this room remained as before. She couldn't have

187

known, nor did she realize that the bedroom remained unchanged only because the lighting and camera equipment hidden behind the two-way glass were deemed too expensive to alter.

Evans was lying on the bed, cleaning a .45 with his handkerchief. Tinker, obviously drunk, tipped his whiskey glass at her, his shoulder holster swaying like a tree in the wind as he raised his arm. Her mind racing for a reasonable explanation, she could only think that in the years she had worked with Tinker, she had never seen him drunk, had never seen him without a jacket. Somehow, those two facts only served to increase her terror. Desperately, she fought to remain calm, to take whatever it was in stride.

Drunk as he was, the flat, steel eyes bore into hers and increased her terror. Something was wrong.

"So tell me all about it," Tinker said, emptying the contents of her purse on the bed. Struggling to regain her composure, Rita pulled away from Chin and walked alone to the bar. Pouring herself four fingers of Scotch, she tossed it straight down, the fiery warmth melting away some of the cold fear that gripped her stomach and made her want to retch. She turned to face Tinker, her face animated, smiling, beautiful.

"No problem, Tinker. I like it, as a matter of fact. Anytime."

Tinker picked something shiny from the bed. "What's this?" Tinker was holding the tiny key she had taken from Danny's wallet, the innocent key to a billiard locker some 1500 miles up the coast. Nothing more.

"I don't know. I just figured it might be important. You know, a bank box key, something like that. I thought you might want it."

"Did I ask you to take anything?"

"No, I just thought..."

"Shut the fuck up, Rita. You never think." Tinker's eyes were pools of fury. "Strip."

Rita quickly began to remove her clothes. As she did, she

188

noticed Tinker held two wrapped syringes in his hands, and the empty wrapping from the other.

"Why did you use only one?"

Quickly, Rita answered, "He was asleep. I only needed one."

Tinker's eyes narrowed. "Shouldn't lie, Rita my girl. One ampule. One needle. That's how it works. That's what you were supposed to do. Why didn't you?"

Down to heels and panties, Rita made a quick decision to tell the truth. After all, Danny Wood was dead, she knew that. As Tinker and the other men listened, the night's events tumbled from Rita, speaking very fast.

"Well, it sounds like you did it."

"I told you I did." A bit of defiance crept back into her voice, pushing away at the pall of fear.

"All of your clothes, baby. Shoes too."

When she stood naked, her clothes in a pile at her feet, Bob walked over and picked them up, placing them in an oversize canvas bag. Tinker was tossing the little pearl-handled .25 automatic in the air, catching it and throwing it back up like a child's brightly decorated ball. Rita, stark naked, padded barefoot to the bar. Hell, they'd certainly seen her naked before. On the other hand, this, this was something different. This was *naked*.

"Where did you get this little gem?"

"I bought it. Some gun shop down in Peco. I've had it about three years."

"Why?"

"Shit, Tinker, I don't remember, really. Just a whim. I didn't use my own name, and I wore a short black wig. My own mother wouldn't have known it was me." A strange combination of sweat and gooseflesh caused her to shiver, though the room was warm.

"Rita, you never had a mother." The gun went up in the air once again, was caught and then thrown to Bob. It too disappeared into the canvas bag.

"How long before you figure somebody will find our dead hero?"

189

"Three, maybe four days. He's got, or had connections down there, at the Buffum. The old guy that runs the place even came in and cleaned up the room while we were in the shower, for christsake."

"You figure nobody will bother him until he starts to stink up the place, is that right?"

Rita grimaced, remembering how much pleasure the kid had given her. Tinker picked up on her expression almost at once. He no longer seemed drunk. Evans, not looking at her, just went on wiping his pistol, avoiding her gaze.

"Pretty good, was he?" Tinker's leering eyes bore into Rita's. He was enjoying this.

Again, she shuddered involuntarily. "You know me. This is just a job. I don't feel any of them. And I never have."

Tinker's eyes narrowed. "Yeah, but Danny Wood, the way I see it, was different. I think he got to you. You did a messy job." Tinker tossed the brown envelope, heavy with nearly twenty thousand dollars in cash, over to Evans, who wordlessly tucked it into his pocket, giving Rita a sad, resigned smile, accompanied by a slight shrug of his shoulders.

"That's mine, Tinker. I just killed a man for it." Her fear momentarily gone, Rita stood, fists clenched, slim legs spread, and glared angrily at Tinker. She watched as the black and white checkered purse flew across the room to Bob Chandler, and like everything else, went into the canvas bag. Ominously, Bob shut it tightly. Except for the money, all she had was beyond her reach in the canvas bag, bound for . . . where?

"Like I said, it was messy. Not up to Agency standards."

Rita couldn't help it. In angry frustration, she forgot her fear, and stormed naked across the room, only inches from Tinker's face. "Agency standards my little ass. If you'd got the bastard in the first place, I wouldn't have had to clear up *your* mess!"

Tinker's eyes blazed up, and he hit her a backhand slap that sent her sprawling, opening a slight cut on her lip, the warm taste of her own blood in her mouth. As she struggled to her knees, she found herself staring down the barrel of Tinker's 9mm, held only inches from her face.

"Tinker! Goddamnit, don't be a fool." Evans' voice rang out in the stillness of the room. "Listen to me." His voice was low and soothing, but urgent. The Browning waved in front of Rita's face, snakelike, the muzzle a dark hole growing larger as she stared at it.

"You pull that trigger and every cop in L.A. will be all over this building in a few minutes. Put it away." The gun wavered, still cocked, only a quarter pound of finger pressure away from blowing Rita's pretty face into a bloody mess.

"Put it away." The gun lifted slightly, then disappeared from Rita's vision. An audible sigh of relief swept over Rita, as she slowly, awkwardly stood up, her knees shaking, her face pale and tight with fear.

"I'm sorry, Tinker. Jesus. For a minute there, I thought..."

Tinker turned away from her, shrugging his arms into his suit coat. He said only one word. "Chin?"

Unleashed, darkness swept across the room.

The Los Angeles County Medical Examiner had never seen anything like this. As he conducted the post mortem, he talked calmly into the overhead mike that dangled from the ceiling to catch everything he saw in detail, for the record. She had been beautiful once, of that he was sure. Her nails still held a flawless manicure, as did her toes. Her hair was a rich, natural red, the pubic hair matching in color, trimmed and shaped carefully into a heart. Beyond the bright lights over the table he could hear the gasps from the homicide detectives as he spoke in his usual detached, professional way, a jeweler's voice examining a precious stone.

Each bone, every bone, had been broken, one at a time. Her pelvis was split, but, as he intoned, not with any blunt instrument or sharp knife he could imagine. If he didn't know better, and here he paused, all of the terrible work had been done by someone's bare hands. The finger tips had been burned, as had the palms and the bottom of the feet. Burned smooth. No prints. The facial bones had also been smashed. Shredded was a better word.

But there was one thing he was sure of. She had felt none of the atrocities done to her. She had died from a single swift blow to the back of the neck, which had, from the sheer brutal force of it, severed her spinal column from the outside. He had no idea how that could be done.

The homicide detectives, led by a squat, stoop-shouldered Lieutenant with an unlit stub of cigar jammed in his mouth, had been silent. Now, the cigar shifted, and the tired-looking, rumpled lieutenant, with only seven months left on thirty years' retirement, asked quietly. "Well?"

The pathologist turned away from the alabaster flesh spread like a lumpy rag on the stainless steel table, stripping off his rubber gloves. His hands were steady as he lit a Camel and eyed the detectives, their faces perplexed, anxious, waiting for the words that would answer, or at least provide a basis, for their investigation. "Okay, gents, this is it, as I see it. Somebody, a very powerful somebody, simply took this woman in his hands and destroyed her."

"With what?" asked the rumpled Lieutenant.

"As I said, with his hands. No blunt instrument. No cuts, hardly a bruise."

"Jesus, how big would he have to be?"

"Pretty damn big, I suppose. No maniac did this, though one might think so. From what I've seen, he knows as much as I do about human physiology."

"Can we trace her?"

"My guess is she was supposed to be found, that's why she was just dumped in a bay. No weights, no nothing. Whoever did this, however it was done, I venture to say you will get no positive I.D. on this Jane Doe. I also doubt a missing person claim exists anywhere. This lady did not come to the big city from grandma's house."

The Lieutenant lit up his stub of cigar, the smoke enveloping his face. It was a very cheap cigar, and one of the young officers began to cough. "Okay, Doc, what we got her is a D.O.A. female, all busted up, no prints, no face, no identifying scars, nothing. Is that it?"

"Basically, yes."

"'Kay. How long has she been dead?"

"There is no way I can tell you. I just don't know. Whoever, or whatever did this made sure of that."

"What! How the hell did they do that?"

"Well, Lieutenant, as far as I can see, they hung her up somewhere in a freezer. Then, sometime, they let her thaw out, dumped her in the bay, and here she is. Theoretically, she could have been dead fifty years."

"I'm supposed to write that on my time of death? Zero to fifty years?"

"I'm sorry, Lieutenant. Like I said, I've never seen anything like it. Except, perhaps, in medical school, on cadavers, frozen and thawed just for dissecting. In essence, that's precisely what we have here."

The Lieutenant took one last look at his "homicide," and decided he had better things to do than figure this one out. He assigned the case to a couple of hot shot young detectives, telling them, "Listen, no newspaper stuff, you understand? Who'd believe it, anyway?"

And so ended Rita Williams, buried, finally, compliments of the County of Los Angeles. In the end, what she was mattered only to Rita Williams. She was unlucky.

Danny stood in the shower, letting the icy water play across his neck and down his back, his head tipped forward, watching the water roll off his legs and down the shiny drain. His body remained heavy and awkward to him. His mind grew sharper as the water beat steadily down on him. After thirty motionless minutes, the water began to feel cold for the first time, and he was suddenly chilled. Shaking, teeth chattering, he stepped out of the shower and grabbed a large, white towel. Back in the bedroom, he poured himself a quick shot of tequila, waiting as it burned its hot path through his system, then quickly poured another. He lit a cigarette, plopped down on the lone chair and tried to piece together what had happened to him.

Whatever had happened, it all began with Rita. According to

193

the radio announcer, it was Saturday. How could that be? Even drunk, he could not have slept two days. He padded barefoot to the small desk chair where his clothes remained neatly folded, just as he remembered. He reached for his wallet. He carried his wallet over his right hip. It was now over his left. The small key that opened his pool cue locker in Seattle was missing. The pictures he carried were in the wrong order. Danny was a meticulous man, and felt there was a place and order for everything. The three one-hundred-dollar bills Rita had placed in his wallet clinched it. For whatever reason, she had wanted no apparent signs of robbery. Danny jammed one of the hundreds into his left front pocket, and folded the other two neatly between his liberty pass and the other pictures.

Okay. She had gone through the wallet, taken his key and mixed up his photos. Then she had slipped in the crisp hundreds and placed the wallet in a pocket he never used. Wallets were much like women's purses. Personal. Most men would know if their wallet had been tampered with. There seemed to be only one reason she'd been so careless. It wouldn't matter. Nobody would know, because Danny would be dead.

With a chilling awareness, Danny realized Rita Williams had tried to kill him, and for whatever reason, believed she had killed him. The enormity of his predicament washed over him, and he sat down heavily on the rumpled bed. What had Tinker said on the plane? *Well, Danny, because that's the way the game is played. It's a cruel world. There will always be a next time.*

It had not occurred to him then what Tinker had meant by the remark. Everything men like Tinker and Evans did was part of the "game." And now, he realized, killing him seemed to be the central part of their plan. He was right. He'd felt it on the way into the cold, still landscape of Korea. The unspoken part of his mission had been to not come back. So the game *had* gone on and they would soon find out Rita had failed. He was sure they would keep after him.

Hurriedly, he shaved, dressed and left the room as it was. In the tiny downstairs lobby, he stopped at the desk, and rang the

194

clerk's bell. In a moment, the manager came out from his small apartment. He did not appear to be surprised to see Danny alive.

"Mr. Baker, do I owe you any money?"

Mr. Baker's smile faded, replaced by a puzzled frown. "Hell, no, Danny. You're all paid up. Don't you remember? Your lady friend left me one hundred dollars. I'd say that more than covers it, wouldn't you?"

"Yeah. Guess it does. Did she say anything to you?"

"We didn't talk, son. Just the money left with a note not to bother you 'til you came down. Course, I was gonna come up tonight. Gett'n a little worried, to tell the truth. You don't look so good, son. You awright?"

"Just too much redhead," Danny said, thinking what poor old Mr. Baker would have gone through if Rita had tried just a little bit harder.

"Yeah, she was a real looker, that one, if you don't mind me saying so. You gonna see her again?" the manager asked.

"I don't think so. To tell you the truth, she wasn't nearly as good as she looked."

With that, Danny stepped out into the Saturday-night streets of Long Beach, leaving the Buffum Hotel behind him.

Mr. Baker shuffled back to his rear apartment, scratching his head, murmuring, "Goddamn, she looked pretty good to me."

Tinker leaned into the car window, a look of stark disbelief on his face, his skin chalky white, the corners of his mouth twitching as he spoke.

"He's not there. The goddamn kid is not in there." Tinker's eyes were wide with agitation, his hands shaking as he straightened up to light a cigarette, trying to regain his self-control. Jerking the Ford's rear door open, he climbed wearily into the seat, loosening his tie, his handsome face beaded with sweat, even though the day was cool.

"The bitch. The dirty, rotten little whore. Goddamn her!"

Evans turned in the front seat to look back at Tinker. "Tink, you'd better calm down. What do you mean? Who's not there?"

195

"Danny Wood. The fucking body." Tinker's voice cracked, his hands nervously brushing through his hair. "Don't you understand? He's not dead. We've got to find him. Where would he go? Back to Pendleton? Where could he go? Shit, he must have it all doped out. He must know we tried to kill his ass. Goddamn everything to hell."

Finally, Evans understood. Rita had failed. Suddenly dizzy, he rested his forehead on the top of the seat, struggling to understand. Danny was alive, and if Danny was alive, they were in serious trouble. From the very beginning he'd known it was a bad deal all around. Now, there would be considerable hell to pay.

Talk would change nothing now. Danny Wood was the target. Again. What could be said? A small cell of the Intelligence Branch of the United States Government was committed to murder for the pleasure of it.

In Long Beach on that bright Monday in January, Danny Wood bought a five-inch Italian-made switchblade at a pawn shop, breaking the first of the three hundreds Rita had unwittingly donated to his escape fund, and headed for the bus station. Arriving purposely only minutes before the bus left for Los Angeles, he slipped out of the station only an hour before Bob, the Soundman, walked in, bought a paper and sat down. He would stay there a week, waiting and watching for Danny. By the time he gave it up as a bad job, Danny was in San Francisco, having stayed quietly in a small hotel in L.A. for six days before moving on, still unsure of where to go, of what he should do. He had no way of knowing that before he left San Francisco, he would kill a man.

In San Francisco, Rita's attempt on Danny's life remained vividly fresh in his mind, and he was not yet sure of when he was safe, or when in danger. While sitting in a bar, he was experiencing the same uncertainties he'd felt on the mission in Korea while waiting for his target to appear on the Godforsaken, snowy road. At least then he'd been in the company of two experienced Marines. Largely because of them, the job had been completed. Too bad they weren't with him now. He was on his own, and that was that.

The door to the bar opened, and two M.P.'s walked in, one a Marine, the other a world-weary Navy chief. For the briefest moment, Danny felt panic, and he nearly bolted between the two M.P.'s and out the door. Lighting a cigarette, Danny casually ordered another beer. The Marine and the other M.P. moved toward the back of the lounge and its crowded dance floor.

The two M.P.'s completed their swing through the lounge and dance area, came back toward and then by Danny without so much as a glance his way. The tenseness left him as he watched the backs of the M.P.'s disappear through the door. He would have to remember that normal occurrences were of no danger to him. It was unlikely that Tinker and Evans could enlist the aid of the Military to locate him.

More bored than worried, Danny left the bar and headed up the street on Market. Corchran's was just off the street, up two dilapidated flights of stairs. It was a legendary pool room, a big money house, and mecca for hustlers and the hustled. Danny had played pool at the 211 Club in Seattle with players who mentioned casually that they had just come up from San Francisco, telling wonderful tales of big money games they'd been involved in at Corchran's. Danny had never been there, so he believed it only when the player beat him, which few players from Seattle could do.

A pool room, any pool room, was familiar ground. He bounded up the stairs two at a time. After entering, he leaned casually against a Coke machine, and watched the action. The play was generally skilled, but reputation or not, Corchran's did not appear to be much different to Danny than the 211 Club back home. Five dollars on nine ball, some twenty-dollar straight pool, five-dollar three-cushion billiards. It was a quiet night, and if Danny had anything right now, it was time. He picked up a set of billiard balls from the counterman. For thirty minutes, Danny forgot everything, losing himself in practice, reveling in the way his stroke came quickly back to him, even

197

on an unfamiliar table and using a house cue instead of his customized cues back home in their locker in Seattle, the locker key now resting in Tinker's pocket, a silent shiny enigma.

Danny knew nothing about his locker key, or where it was, and he would not have cared. Playing three-cushion billiards had always been like a calming drug to Danny. He loved it, pure and simple. It was also the perfect way for him to finance his flight from Tinker and his men.

Danny adapted very quickly to the pace of San Francisco's night people, hustlers and players of all manner of games. Unlike conservative Seattle, San Francisco never closed down, day or night. For Danny, unsure if not afraid, the people he met in pool rooms and restaurants were ideal cover as he melted easily into a hodgepodge of young men and women that slept wherever they happened to be and asked no questions in the process. He quickly established a reputation as a pool player of some merit, and drew big money games with local players, most of them mistaking his youth for inexperience, much to their chagrin and financial loss. The days melted into each other and Danny began to feel more comfortable with the city and his ability to survive on his own.

But while he established a wary pattern of activities, coupled with hiding himself away in public libraries or hole-in-the-wall bars, he did nothing to solve his primary problem. To escape Tinker and his men. To stay alive. Familiarity with his surroundings was comforting, but it was at best a cosmetic security. The truth was, he was staying in San Francisco because he had no idea what to do.

Tinker did not use the Agency apparatus available to him to search for Danny. Since all he was doing was outside the Agency, without sanction or approval, he was in effect a rogue agent leading a rogue operation. Denied the network of official information, he fell back on the spy's oldest techniques, a feet-on-the-pavement, eyes-open search of Los Angeles. Taking Chin with him while sending Evans north to San Francisco, he left Bob in Long Beach, where much was learned about

Danny's liberty habits and what he liked to do there. The agents shared what they learned by telephone.

During the long training sessions before the Korean mission, they had spent a great deal of time with Danny Wood. They knew what he liked. They knew about his family. They knew a great deal more than Danny suspected. They had the equivalent of a hundred-hour interrogation to guide them to their quarry. Yet they couldn't find him, for all their efforts.

Frustrated and angry, Tinker decided to gather his team together and head for Seattle. But when Evans made his regular daily call to Tinker on the twentieth day of the search, he told Tinker not to bother going to Seattle. At that moment, in San Francisco, Evans was watching Danny Wood eat a bowl of chili. Evans' persistence had succeeded. Tinker told Evans to stay with Danny every second. He and his fellow agents would be in San Francisco within twenty-four hours. They would join Evans, and it would be over. Evans gave Tinker a phone number at a Nob Hill hotel, and asked him to wait for his call. It was going to be easy.

The next night, Evans spotted Danny as he came out of his hotel and into the crowded streets of an early rain in San Francisco, a cold, steady rain that made the brightly lit entranceway glisten. For a brief second, Evans was sure Danny had seen him, as he looked up and down the street, the head cocked with the expectant air of the hunted.

Adjusting the outside rearview mirror, Evans followed Danny's retreating image in its rain-streaked reflection. When Danny had walked a block without looking back, Evans quickly exited the car, and began to follow. At that moment, Danny suddenly sprinted across the street, and was now on the same side as Evans. Evans immediately stopped walking, peering into a tobacco shop window, lighting a cigarette, not looking down the block at his prey.

When he next looked up, Danny was not there. The busy street had swallowed him. Panicked, Evans began to walk very fast down Powell Street, passing a cable car going up. Hurrying, he did not see the figure in the white coat step lightly off the car about two hundred feet behind him. The figure looked very much like a Marine on patrol.

And so it was that the agents and Danny pulled inexorably together, knowing little of what the individual participants were doing, or precisely where they were. Tinker and his morose, hard-of-hearing soundman, trailed by the silent Chin, were looking for Evans, in the hope of finding Danny. Evans, after shadowing Danny for the better part of two days, had lost the track. Only Danny, the object of so much attention, knew where he was, as well as where Evans was. Knowing where Evans was, however, solved nothing for Danny.

After eluding Evans on the cable car, he had followed Evans' futile efforts to resume the hunt, thus becoming the hunter himself. After an hour, Evans slipped into a Chinese restaurant to get out of the rain, bewildered by Danny's wizard-like disappearance, never realizing that Danny was following him. For a long time, Danny hesitated outside the brightly lit restaurant. Finally he walked through the doors, caught sight of Evans sitting alone in a booth and slid into the seat opposite him. "Looking for me?"

Evans, startled, dropped his tea, the small, sturdy cup ending up in his lap, scalding his thigh. He recovered quickly, an alchemist's trick of turning naked surprise into studied nonchalance. "Hello, Daniel. Where've ya been, kid?"

Danny looked steadily at Evans, his face impassive, while under his shirt his heart thudded against his ribs so rapidly he thought Evans could hear it. A beautiful waitress in a black and gold gown slit to the thigh stopped at the booth to bring him a menu and a steaming pot of green tea. "Take your time, sweetie," she said, giving him a wide, slow smile but shattering her image as an oriental dragon lady, with a pure Boston accent that caused him to smile back at her.

"Thanks. It will be awhile. Meantime, I'd like a Millers if you don't mind."

"Sure, sweetie. Back in a jiff."

Waiting for his beer, Danny studied Evans openly, until the Agency man looked away, struggling to light a cigarette with damp matches. Picking up a candle in a bright red bowl, Danny extended it to Evans, who glanced over the top of it as he puffed.

Evans was smoking odd, black-papered filter cigarettes, and his hand shook a little as he drew the smoke deep into his lungs. He looked unkempt and tired.

"What do you hear from Rita, Evans? She left before saying goodbye." Danny was surprised at how steady his voice was.

"I don't know any Rita, Danny, so I haven't heard from her."

"Really? Let me tell you about her, Evans. An incredible girl. Red hair. Heart-shaped pussy she could do tricks with you wouldn't believe. Picked me up on a bus from Pendleton, went to a hotel with me, fucked me nearly to death. Are you sure you don't know her, Evans? Could it be you forgot her, although I don't know how that could happen. She's a real hard girl to forget, that one. One-hundred-dollar underwear, and a purse full of hundreds. Paid for everything through Sunday. I left the hotel on Saturday, only I wasn't supposed to leave at all, was I? Somehow she blew it. How did she do that, Evans?"

"I don't know what you're talking about, Danny. I don't know any Rita. For that matter, I don't know any redheads." The boyish grin didn't quite come off.

"That's bullshit, Evans." Danny's voice had risen, and he received a disapproving glance from a matronly couple across the wide aisle. "Okay, so you don't know Rita. Then what brings you to San Francisco, and why are you following me?"

Sipping tea, Evans tried his most disarming look. "I heard you were AWOL. I just thought I'd try to find you, see if the Agency could be of help. Tinker's due in tonight, too. What the hell's going on? The General's worried, Danny. He asked us to locate you, help you get back. He can't sit on this much longer."

"Sit on what, Evans?"

"Well, kid, the Marine Corps doesn't know much of what's going on with you, so they are holding off on any charges until we get back to them. I can tell you, Danny, it's taken the full resources of the Agency to locate you. Now, we'd just like to get you back. I'm here to help you in any way I can."

The waitress brought their meal, steamy hot and aromatic. Danny loved Chinese food, and dug his fork into the fried rice.

Danny ignored Evans, eating quietly, enjoying his food, putting it away as if he hadn't eaten in a long time. Finally, he stopped, reaching for his beer, lighting a cigarette and pushing the food aside. Evans had barely touched his.

"Evans, I'm going to tell you why I think you are here. I did a job for you, a job I don't believe was supposed to include me getting back."

"Danny, I don't . . ."

"Shut up, and listen. I don't have any idea why I fell out of favor on this deal. But I obviously did. Complete success was not on the agenda, was it?" Without waiting for a reply, Danny rushed on, everything very clear in his mind. "The original deal was Agency approved. A perfect mission. Tinker decided, by himself and for whatever reason, that I needed to be dead. I don't know how you people pulled it off, but you knew I would be on that bus. The big guy, the drunk, wasn't drunk at all. Rita slid in right on cue, I bit on that lovely bait, and everything was just right to take me out. But, somehow, some way I don't quite understand, she either couldn't finish it, or thought she had. And if I'm alive, I figure that poor, sexy, little bitch has paid a big price for a missed shot.

"Now Rita blows it, and you go to pick up the body, and it's not there. I think you're already in too deep. You still have to finish it. So here you are. Tinker too. Thanks, Evans, I wouldn't have known that part. Well, I'll tell you what I'll do, Evans. I'll make it easy for you. Pay the check. I'll be in the alley right outside. Don't make me wait for you."

Without another word, Danny got up and walked out, turning into an alley next to the restaurant, vanishing into its darkness. Frightened, exhilarated, he meant to stop running. If he was followed again, he'd decided he had no options left.

The alley behind the restaurant was very narrow, only wide enough for a medium-sized truck to travel. As Danny walked carefully into the darkness, the light from the next street began to penetrate, gradually brightening enough for him to see clearly. In this fifty feet of near total blackness, Danny could not be seen, but he could see anyone coming into the alley from either direction. A hundred hours of night problems at Pendleton had given him above average senses for functioning in darkness, training him to use it to his own advantage. A recessed doorway revealed its contours to him after he had stood, pressed against a brick wall, for five minutes. It was a fire exit, with no handles or door knobs for entrance from the alley. Stepping into its shallow welcome, he was invisible even to headlights until they were right on top of him. Cars and foot traffic moved across both alley entrances; the late night crowd happily pursuing fleshy pleasures.

It hit him then, the very real, almost certain fact that he might die in this foul, damp, narrow cesspool. He might have to kill, or be murdered if he did not. Daniel Wood had no idea what to do. How would he prevent a man, armed and purposeful, from shooting him and walking away, leaving the police to find the victim of a random street crime? The terrible injustice of it all rose in his throat, and with the bile, an implacable hatred, a fierce anger rolled over him. Rigorously trained to kill in combat, and in every sense a combat veteran after the ridge in Korea, killing again seemed shockingly easy to him. The only light in the alley was the reflection from the street that caught the long thin blade of the stiletto as Danny punched the button and it snicked open, locked and lethal. Since he'd bought it in Los Angeles, he'd carried it taped inside his waistband. Now, it felt like an extension of his hand, and his psyche.

Tinker was driving past the alley when he saw Evans, walking rapidly, swing around the corner of a Chinese restaurant and disappear into the darkness. Already past the alley entrance, Tinker was stuck in traffic and could not follow in the car, could not park the car. He elected to go around the block. In the time it took him to do that, about five minutes, violent death would shriek from the darkness.

Evans stepped out of the brightly lit street and into the dark ages. Pulling the 9mm Browning from its shoulder holster freed him from whatever twinge of conscience he might have felt. Danny had become a vast arbiter of Evans' life—a life already complicated by other men telling him what to do. Danny was a drug in Tinker's system, and until it was purged, Evans would continue to suffer under Tinker's capricious swings of mood. Danny needed killing.

Evans followed his own outstretched arm down the alley, his step slow and deliberate, the snout of the gun catching occasional light and reflecting dully, flickers of menace cloaked in throat-constricting fear walking the shadows with him. Hugging the wall as he moved into the deepening blackness, he tried to hear the dark.

"Hey, Daniel, are you there, Daniel? It's only me, Buddy Boy. C'mon, kid, we need to talk." Evans stood completely still, holding his breath, his gun hand sweeping the alley ahead of him, his finger tense on the trigger, only a light touch away.

Danny couldn't see Evans, but he visibly jumped at the sound of his voice. Stupid thing to do. Evans would have a gun, of course. There would be no talking. If Danny answered, Danny died. Danny pressed back into the shadowy doorway, willing himself to remain still. A pebble skipped down the alley toward him, rolling to a stop just out of his sight. Evans was on the move again.

The sound of the pebble caused Evans to press himself hard against the wall, arm outstretched, gun pointed straight down the alley. He did not move for a long time. A woman's throaty laughter drifted down the alley from the far street. Reaching into his jacket, he pulled out a black cylinder, snapping it onto the Browning. Now, the gun would go *phftt*.

Danny heard the metallic sound clearly as the silencer was snapped onto Evans' gun. While he couldn't identify the sound, he now knew almost exactly where Evans was in relation to the doorway: across the alley, twenty five feet or so to come. He would have to move before Evans was abreast of him. Silently, he slid into a crouch.

"Daniel, do you hear me? C'mon, Buddy Boy, step out where I can see you."

204

Fifteen feet.

"Hey, Daniel." Evans was whispering now. "Let's talk, kid. What have you got to lose?"

Ten feet.

Evans continued to move forward, on the balls of his feet. The light was brighter about twenty feet further on.

The forearm clamped hard around his neck. He felt the violent bodyslam and rebounded off the wall, the gun waving crazily in the air as he tried to shoot backward. He felt himself lifted by the throat back on his heels, heard the phftt...phftt ...Felt the recoil. A scream of pain choked off in his throat as a silver flash passed by his shoulder and ripped through his hand, then ripped up through the webbing between his fingers. The gun was gone, clattering across the alley, the tendons to hold it sliced and shredded. The forearm pressure threatened to crush the life from his body. What was the judo move? Think! Then the arm was gone and he snapped his head forward, lunging across the knife blade as it slipped across his throat from right to left, and there was a bright pain, and the cool rain on his chest.

Evans lay on his back, not moving, his eyes open and wide, his mouth a silent "O," a dark wet stream pumping rhythmically from his severed artery. While he would remember every action of this terrible night, Danny moved now without thinking, pulling off Evans' coat, stripping the shoulder holster from his body and slipping it on, retrieving the gun, unsnapping the silencer and putting it into his own pocket along with the extra clip. He removed Evans' wallet, and stuck it in his coat.

He stood up, looked at Evans, and then, impulsively, bent down to the dying man. Evans was trying to say something, gasping soundlessly, eyes terrified with what he knew. Danny strained to hear, the words passing Evans' lips as the light of his eyes brightened, flickered, and went out... "Run... Run..."

On his second pass around the block, Tinker swung the car into the alley and cruised slowly into its darkness, switching

205

the car's headlights off, slowing to a crawl as he neared the spot where Evans' body lay draped in blackness. The car bumped over Evans' legs without Tinker ever seeing him.

"Oh, shit!" said Tinker, switching on the car's lights and throwing it into reverse at the same time. The car bumped once again, the lights picking up the sprawled body.

"Wood?" Bob asked, his eyes wide with expectation.

"No, that's not Wood," Tinker said, switching off the car's lights and plunging the alley back into darkness. He grabbed a flashlight from the glove compartment as he slid out of the seat. Bob and Chin exited the back seat and moved down the alley with Tinker, all three men with guns drawn.

"Jesus Christ," Bob said. "We ran right over him. Look at the tire marks across his legs!"

"The kid cut his throat. What the hell are we dealing with here?"

Tinker's question found no answers as Chin moved silently forward, his body a muscular dam holding back the light as he swung Evans effortlessly over his shoulder.

As the men returned to the car, the rain came back, gusting up and down the alley.

For a long while the car was motionless, only the soft purr of its engine and the rhythmic swish of its wipers disturbing the quiet. Then, it sped down the alley and into the flow of street traffic. Back in the alley, a drunk crawled out of a dumpster, weaving his way toward the street, not sure of what he'd seen.

Danny walked the streets of the city for an hour. Oblivious to the rain and wind, his clothing soaked through, he ignored the pointed remarks of the male hustlers who stood sentry in the dry doorways and shop fronts along Market Street, too lost in his own terror-filled mind to even get angry.

He had no idea what to do, or where to go. It seemed an obvious fact he had to leave San Francisco. He felt an over-whelming need to go to Seattle, to see Natalie, to feel and touch things real and positive. Tinker would certainly know this, but

206

it didn't matter. On home ground, his city, he would deal with whatever came.

He was chilled to the bone. Common sense finally drove him out of the rain and into an all-night cafeteria on Market, near the bus depot. He bought a steamy pot of tea, and moved to a table in the rear, with a clear view of the cafeteria and the rain-swept streets outside. He removed his soaked jacket, hung it over a chair and poured his tea, lacing it heavily with sugar. Reaching for a cigarette, he was shocked to notice he was wearing a leather shoulder holster, with Evans' gun swinging lightly under his arm, the weight unnoticed, the hammer still cocked after Evans' two wild shots in the alley. Quickly, Danny stripped the gun and holster from his body, slipping it carefully under his wet jacket on the chair next to him.

When had he taken the gun? He struggled to remember, but could not. The Browning's extra clip and silencer protruded from his jacket pocket, and he hurriedly jammed them deeper into the coat, causing a wallet to fall out of the other pocket. Bending to pick it up, he could not recall taking it either. Dropping the wallet on the table before him, he lit a cigarette and sat a long time without touching it. A group of ballet students wearing practice tights poured through the front of the cafeteria, chattering back and forth, congregating at tables near Danny, their happy laughter and gaiety a welcome intrusion.

Opening the wallet, Danny was struck by a rush of confused emotion as Evans stared solemnly at him from his Agency I.D. card. Evans, Richard Albert. Age 26, height 5'11", weight 165, brown eyes, brown hair. Ordinary vital statistics of a not very ordinary man, a special agent for the Central Intelligence Agency. "Well, tough luck, you rogue son-of-a-bitch," Danny thought, glad that it was Evans dead in the alley, and not the other way around. Danny admitted to himself he had a clear conscience about slitting the man's throat. He would most certainly be dead if he hadn't, and Evans would be going through *his* wallet.

Danny went through the items in the wallet and found nothing special, except a lease receipt for an L.A. apartment for three months, $6500. Must be one hell of an apartment. He also found over sixteen hundred dollars. Why did Evans carry so much cash? Whatever the reason, Danny now had enough money to go most anywhere he chose. The wallet contained only one snapshot, a picture taken in an unidentified foreign city, probably in Asia, a close-up of Evans and another man, arms around each other, smiling happily in front of an orange temple. Danny struck his lighter and dropped the photo into an ashtray. He watched it burn. He felt nothing at all.

After finding Evans' corpse, Tinker left Bob and Chin in the city, and headed out of San Francisco, going north along the coast. At 2:00 A.M., while rain and wind lashed at him, he buried Evans in the deep ravine of a wooded hillside above the ocean. He had carried the body almost two miles through thick, soaked underbrush. Back in San Francisco, he wired the Agency that Evans had been sent back to the Orient. A Chinese Communist agent was said to be in a defecting mood. Evans' task would be to first locate him, and then assist him. It would be a very dangerous one-man job. High stakes, high risk. The Director, when he read this missive, was not unduly surprised, or worried. He didn't like Evans. Never had. His fervent prayer was that somebody would slit his throat in some dark alley in Hong Kong or Singapore or wherever the unstable son-of-a-bitch wound up.

The youngest of four children, and the only boy, Tinker had been doted on as a child, raised by a mother whose love for him bordered on the obsessive. He'd been four years old before he'd had his first haircut. His father had watched with grim satisfaction as his long golden curls were shorn by his thirteen-year-old sister, his mother crying audibly behind her closed bedroom door. Later that evening, his parents had a screaming argument, punctuated by the slamming of the front door. His father had angrily left the house.

His older sister had stood in the hallway, arms folded disapprovingly. He left his room and crawled into his parents' wide bed. He pressed his face against his mother's ample breasts while she pulled his small body against hers, naked under a thin nightgown. As the years passed and his parents grew farther apart, Tinker continued to crawl into his mother's bed for comfort that changed into something dark and secretive. His father began to absent himself from the home for days at a time, and the teenager began to experience orgasm under the swift, knowing fingers and ministrations of his mother as he clutched her in the darkness, feeding on a sad, pathetic love that had gone beyond all bounds.

In a time when incest was a word of such terrible import that its mere mention could paralyze whole families with silent denial, Tinker's increasingly torrid relationship with his mother was an accepted but never mentioned fact by his older sisters. Incredibly, his father, who should have been the first to know, died of a heart attack on Tinker's fourteenth birthday without ever acknowledging the twisted passion that filled his house. His father's death at thirty-six triggered a crushing rejection of the boy by his mother, who, overcome by guilt, refused to be alone with her son at any time, making her bed off limits to him at a time when he was bewildered by grief and loneliness.

A savior in the person of his uncle, a vigorous, decent man, entered the home and began to provide male leadership and love for the first time in Tinker's life. He sent Tinker's sisters off to a private school and threw his energies into "saving" the boy from himself. He largely succeeded.

Tinker responded to his uncle's genuine concern and affection. He began to excel in school, even re-establishing a normal relationship with his mother, who appeared to be awakening from a terrible dream. Even so, as an adult, Tinker could form friendships only with people who in one way or another were as twisted as he was. An honor student at the University of California, he sought employment with the Government, and was accepted by the postwar CIA.

He immediately drew the attention of his superiors by his willingness to do the dirtiest jobs, revelling in the freedom it gave him to let his peculiarities run free and untrammeled. In the cold war atmosphere of the fifties, his hard, anything-goes attitude became a tremendous asset, cloaking his more bizarre behavior in a cloud of expediency, the prevailing excuse for intelligence operative of all nations. Marked as a comer by some, distrusted by others, misunderstood by all, he rose quickly to command a tightly knit group of spies selected by him personally for their loyalty to Tinker and a prevailing attitude of ends justifying the means.

On the surface, Tinker was a near-perfect example of the well-educated, hard-charging American patriot from a good home, a man who had overcome the tragedy of the unexpected death of his father at an early age. Even under the most intense scrutiny that he was subjected to when he applied for the Agency job, not a trace of scandal reared its ugly head. He appeared to be a Rockwellesque example of America and apple pie. He was in fact a sadistic agent in a near-Godlike position to abuse power.

With the assignment of the Korea mission, he stepped across even the blackest line permitted by the Agency, into a twilight world where he wrote the laws and made all the judgments.

"Okay. So what do we know?" Tinker had a tense, impatient look about him, and Bob the Soundman got right to the point.

"Well, we have lots of addresses. We have his mother's. His dad lives in Moses Lake, in eastern Washington. All his other relatives live in Seattle. They are listed in the phone book. If he heads to Seattle..."

"He'll go to Seattle," Tinker snapped.

"Okay. He has no shortage of places to stay. He's lived there all his life. I don't know how we can watch twenty relatives, do you?"

Tinker chewed thoughtfully on a fingernail, a sure sign of irritation. "He won't go to just any relative."

Bob's massive shoulders set, then relaxed."He will go to a friend, probably a woman friend. He will see his mother, like the dutiful son he is. He will probably go where he's comfortable, old haunts, that kind of stuff. Not too difficult, as I see it. Local pool rooms. Local bars. I don't know. But we'll find him."

"And then?" This question from Chin. Tinker left the question unanswered.

Danny hitched his way north to Seattle. It took him two days and four rides, the last two by long-haul truck. The drivers were content to drive and leave him to his thoughts. The two-day trip served him well. By the time he got to Seattle, he had banished his fears, and decided on his course of action. He would run no more. Tinker and his friends would surely come after him, probably within days. There would be no help from anyone. The authorities, any authorities, were out of the question. Fine. He would kill them here, in his home town. He didn't care what happened to him after that.

Danny stepped off the big rig in the heart of downtown Seattle, thanking the silver-haired driver for the ride and the companionship on the trip from Portland. Gripping his small travel bag, he watched the semi roll down the street, bound for its final destination in Canada.

With a bouncy, light step, he headed for the 211 Club, for a drink, a game and a hot shave in the owner's private bath.

One block away, Tinker, Bob and Chin exited a cab, grabbed their bags from the trunk and headed into the Olympic Hotel.

Danny stopped in his tracks, as if catching a scent. His head tilted into the steady, wintry Seattle rain. Shaking his head and grinning to himself, he resumed his walk to the 211. For christsake, now he thought he could smell the guy.

It was raining, it was very cold, it was windy, but it was Seattle, and the warmth of home ground wrapped Danny in the arms of things familiar. Compared to L.A. and San Francisco, the city had a flavor best described as bland. Tight and secure, Seattle sat on its seven hills, bounded on all sides by water, a city of beautiful vistas. The rest of the United States had little or no knowledge of the city, or even just where it was. It had been raunchy and raucous in the past, during the gold rush days, and during wartime, when its streets and waterfront teemed with servicemen and camp followers of all kinds. But between the social upheavals, it went back to its sleepy, conservative gray color, resisting culture, or expansion, or just about any sign of progress. It had few hookers, or at least their presence was muted. Cruising homosexuals found it a dreary hunting ground, and fled the city for greener pastures. Seattle in the fifties was a decade or more behind its California neighbor, and preferred it that way. It was a shockingly beautiful city, pristine and untouched, eager for a suitable suitor, but unaware of how to initiate a courtship. And so it remained, tucked up in the northwest corner of the map, undiscovered by the movers and shakers of the world. You could get laid in Seattle. You could get drugs in Seattle. You could get killed in Seattle. But it wasn't easy.

Ellen Madden paid little attention to the three men as they entered the elevator at the Olympic Hotel. Just more baggage to haul. "Watch your step, please."

Bob, standing behind her, cast admiring glances at Ellen's trim body and blond hair, arching his eyebrows at Tinker, who frowned back at him as the elevator made its way to the tenth floor.

In his best salesman's voice Tinker said, "Miss, ah, excuse me, but do you know where the nearest billiard room might be?"

"211 Union Street, sir. That's just two blocks over and down toward the bay."

"That's what I call service, miss," said Bob, his eyes fixed on the rounded swell of her buttocks. "What do you think, Tinker, does Danny Wood shoot pool there?" In front of him, Ellen Madden's body flexed and stiffened, and the car shot five feet past their floor before she steadied it and settled it evenly at the tenth floor, opening the doors with a jerky motion, her eyes bright.

"This is ten, gentlemen," she said in a low, timid voice.

For a moment, Tinker studied her face, then stepped out into the hall before turning back to look at her again. "Which way, miss?"

"Down the hall to the right, on the end."

The doors closed, almost catching the Soundman's foot as he ambled out.

"That girl knows Danny Wood."

"Oh, for christsake, Tinker, what are you talking about? What makes you think she knows Danny Wood?"

"I don't know, but did you see her react when you said his name?"

"C'mon, Tinker, so she missed the floor a little. So what?"

Tinker stood silent for a moment, then grabbed his bags and headed down the hall. Bob followed him toward the room, thinking Tinker was really losing his head. Danny Wood was a ladies' man, for sure, but he didn't know *every* woman, did he?

As Danny waited for the self-operated elevator to bring him slowly up the two stories to the 211 Club, the phone rang at the desk upstairs. Lou, the owner, was accustomed to answering the phone for the many players in the room, and likened it to taking messages for children at home. The 211 was like that, a home to many of its habitués. Lou was writing down the message when Danny walked up to the counter, a wide grin on his face.

"Hi, Lou, long time no see."

"Hi, kid. How ya been? Got a message for you."

"For me? Don't think so, Lou. I just got here."

"Maybe, but it's your message anyway."

Danny took the message, written on pink paper printed with "While You Were Out" across the top. It was simple and straightforward. "Danny. Three men staying at the Olympic want to play pool at the 211. They wonder if you play pool there. Are you back, or what? Love, Ellen."

"Lou, you haven't seen me since Thanksgiving. You got that? Thanksgiving."

213

"Sure, Danny, but wha..." Danny was out and down to the street before Lou could finish.

Danny walked hurriedly through the quiet downtown streets of Seattle, heading for his mother's apartment. Normally, he would shy away from any place where he might be observed without his knowing it, but this time he knew exactly where Tinker and his friends were, at least for the moment. As he walked, he briefly considered busting in on Tinker, gun in hand, and ending it in one blazing confrontation. He liked the finality of it. He rejected the idea because he just didn't think it would work. He would do it the Marine Corps way. Planning. Stealth. Maximum violence. Seattle was a combat zone, and that would be his approach.

"Hey, son, where do you get girls in this town?" Bob the Soundman said, extending a twenty to the bell captain.

"What kind of girl, sir?"

"Girls. Pussy. Skin stretchers. What kind of girls have you got?"

"Hundred-dollar girls, sir."

"A hundred. Hell, I don't want to marry one, I just want to rent one for a while."

"I'll see what I can find, sir," the man said, sliding out the hotel door with a low bow full of contempt that was totally lost on Bob the Soundman.

"I want you to check out the pool room, Bob."

"Tonight? Well, fuck it tonight. You want it checked before tomorrow, you check it."

Tinker, not wanting to irritate the big man, let it drop. "Okay, tomorrow, but first thing. I'm tired tonight myself, now that I think about it."

"I didn't say I was tired. I said I'd go tomorrow."

"Okay. You made your point," Tinker said. Let him have his little victory.

"What I'm gonna do is fuck some happy little whore 'til she begs me to stop, then I'm gonna fuck her some more. I've heard tales about what it takes for you to get it up, Tink. You have to beat on 'em just a little, don't you? Something about your mama, or like that, right?"

Before Bob could move, Tinker was out of the chair and at his side, the muzzle of his automatic stuck under Bob's chin, pushing his head back brutally, his breath hot on Bob's cheek.

"Go on, you stupid bastard. Say some more. Go ahead. But you'll never hear it because your one good ear will have a new hole in it. C'mon Bob, mouth off some more." The gun pressed up into Bob's neck, buried in the soft flesh, making him gag as he tried to stay on his feet, only to fall backward onto the floor with a resounding crash.

Tinker was on him in an instant, this time resting the gun gently between Bob's eyes, barely touching him as he knelt on the floor over Bob, his body shaking with rage.

Suddenly, Tinker's face changed, and he stood up, pulling Bob up off the floor as he jammed the gun back into his waistband, in the small of his back. Bob had not even known it was there. Tinker had taken to carrying two guns, one in a holster, one hidden away.

Rubbing his neck, Bob slumped into a chair and glared at Tinker, who laughed loudly, but said nothing. In the other chair, Chin, who had not moved, closed his eyes and went to sleep. It was a neat trick, and he did it all the time.

Although Danny had a key and it was his home, Danny knocked at his mother's apartment door. Tinker was right. Danny was a dutiful son. When his mother opened the door, she simply stood there, mouth agape, speechless for the first time in his memory.

"Hi, Mom. Can I come in?"

His mother stepped aside, and he brushed past her, down the hallway and into the living room. His mother's boyfriend, a captain in the sheriff's department, was sitting in his favorite chair, the nightly paper in his hand. He was in uniform, and Danny was momentarily startled. Dick put him at ease, standing, his hand outstretched. Danny took it.

"Hello, son. We hear you've got some trouble."

"Some trouble. Is that what we're to call this, some trouble? Danny, what the hell is going on?" His mother came around to face him, arms folded across her ample chest, an age old sign of real anger that he'd seen since he was a baby.

"The Marine Corps has called us, Daniel. They have wired us. Your commanding officer called me personally. According to him, you've been gone since the twenty-first of January. Absent without leave. He says if you don't come back, they will charge you with desertion. You've been gone from your base for almost two months."

Danny looked at his mother, at her face all screwed up in righteous indignation, and very nearly broke out laughing. It was as if he'd come home late from a dance, or left his room messy. She still thought of him as her little boy. Well, this time, he could explain nothing. He loved his mother. He lied to her.

"It's a long story, Mom. I'm AWOL, but I'm going back. I promise you, I will. I am not deserting the Corps. I just have some personal problems right now. I'll settle with the Corps as soon as I can. That's all I can tell you right now."

"Well, that's not enough."

"It will have to be, Mom. I'm not here to make deals. I'm here to show you I'm all right. I'm here to ask you not to worry, and not to interfere. And no matter who asks you, you haven't seen me."

His mother studied his face, and whatever she saw, it softened and then alarmed her. She dropped her folded arms to her sides, and then walked to him, drawing him to her. She was very tiny, even in high heels, and she stared searchingly into his eyes, looking for mother's answers to a mother's questions. "This is serious, isn't it, Daniel?"

"Pretty serious. I can handle it."

"Will you be staying here, with me?"

"No, Mom. I can't stay here. I don't want you to have to cover for me. Or Dick, either."

"I'm not a cop in your mother's house, Danny. I'm not going to interfere, if that worries you."

216

"Thanks, Dick, I appreciate that. But I'm only here so Mom knows I'm okay. Now she knows."

"Where will you stay, Daniel?"

"Hell, Mom, this is my town, remember? I can stay almost anyplace."

"Yes, I seem to remember exactly that. You're a hellish kid on your mother." She wasn't angry when she said it, and Danny knew she'd decided to let him handle things himself.

"Will you stay for dinner, at least?"

"I can't, Mom. I'll take a raincheck."

"Will you call me, if you need help?"

"You know I will, Mom." It was only a little lie. After he left, his mother went into his bedroom and shut the door behind her. She was in there a very long time.

"Natalie?" For a moment the other end of the phone line was silent.

"Daniel? Where are you?"

"Here, in Seattle. I'm at Vito's, on Madison."

"Are you on leave?"

"Not exactly, no."

"Oh . . . well, then, should I come and get you?"

"That would be nice. Shall I order a drink, or wait outside?"

"Wait twenty minutes, then order me a drink. It will take me that long to get undressed to pick you up. Bye, love."

Natalie swept into Vito's bar, spotted Danny over at a corner table, hurried to him, then stood at the table and looked him over. She was wearing a white trenchcoat, buttoned to the throat.

She looked more beautiful than ever to Danny. She had an amazing capacity to make him happy.

"How do I look?" asked Danny."

"You don't seem damaged in any way. Are you?"

"Not much."

She leaned over and kissed him full on the mouth, her

tongue darting across his, her lips soft and open. She pulled away and took the seat across from him at the small table.

"Does that mean you're glad to see me, Natalie?"

She gave him a dazzling smile, all teeth and happiness. "Yes, I'm glad to see you. Now where is my drink? By the way, you look about a hundred years old. Did you know that?"

A little later she said, "Daniel, we've had two drinks, we have discussed the weather, and much other nonsense, and you've asked what I'm wearing under my raincoat. Not much, to answer that one. I'm wearing what I wore the night we met. Now, having put all this aside, don't you think you'd better tell me what's going on here?" Natalie took Danny's hands in hers. In the dim light of the bar, her face was serene and calm.

"Natalie, this is not easy to tell. It's a pretty ugly story. To be honest, I'm afraid you'll just get up and walk out of here after you know what I've done."

Natalie's gaze remained steady, and she squeezed his hands in hers. "No, I'll not walk out of here, whatever it is. My goodness, it can't be all that bad."

"Yes, it can. I'm AWOL from the Marines. I've killed two men, one on a mission in North Korea, and one only days ago, in San Francisco. And it's not over. Three men are here today, in Seattle, and they want to kill me. The worst part of it all is I've come to you for help."

Natalie let go of his hands and tossed her drink down in a gulp. "Daniel, that's the best part. I'm glad you came to me. I have very strong feelings for you, in case that fact has escaped you. Order us another drink, please. You talk, I will listen. Then, we'll decide what must be done."

When the fresh drinks arrived, Danny began to talk. He spoke non-stop for forty minutes.

Natalie listened, fascinated, as Danny walked her back in time, the details sharp in his mind, now pouring from him. She saw the mission training, and experienced the terror of the mission itself, as well as the obvious pride and satisfaction he felt in having accomplished it. Jealousy tugged at her as he recounted how he had been set up by the beautiful agent on the

218

bus to Long Beach, but she could understand it. She was obviously skilled, and Danny had been embracing life after his close brush with death on the mission. Still, Danny spoke of her in great detail, and Natalie was surprised to find the details hurt, even though the woman had meant to kill him, and nearly succeeded.

His narrative rolled on, unbelievable details she knew to be the absolute truth. She could feel herself in isolation with Danny in the L.A. hotel room as he told of his fear and indecision as to what to do, then traveled to San Francisco as he explained his methods of survival and escape until Evans had somehow found him.

Fear for him rose in her heart as he talked of the terrible happening in the alley, in terms so graphic she could not watch his face as he spoke in a quiet, almost expressionless voice. In spite of herself, tears rolled down her cheeks, and she quickly wiped them away before he saw them.

She knew she must protect him from further harm, whatever the cost. And she knew the cost might be very high.

"Oh, Daniel, darling, I'm so sorry." It was all she could think of to say.

"Yes, so am I. I need some forgiving in there somewhere, don't I?"

"Rita?"

"Yes, Rita."

"I understand that better than anything else I've heard. And I forgive you, if I must, if it will make you feel better."

"It does."

"Well then, forget her. What I can't understand is how anything like this could possibly happen here, in this country. We are a nation of rules, of laws. How can this little group run amok like this without anyone knowing it?"

"Natalie, I have spent countless hours trying to answer that question. There was a zany moment, in that hotel room in L.A., that I was going to call the President of the United States and ask him if he had any idea what his government was doing. Luckily, that bit of weirdness on my part passed. I have

219

no answer. I don't understand any of it. Hell, I can't tell anyone but you about this. Who would believe me? They'd straight-jacket me. Like you said, this country is a nation of laws. Apparently, all laws do not apply to all people. Some are not accountable, somehow. You are. I am. But Tinker and his people apparently are not."

"Well, are you threatened by the Marines, the Government of the United States or just Tinker and his men?"

"I really have no idea. At the moment, I feel threatened by everybody. I've got to get my head straight, make some decisions and act on them. These men are experienced professionals. I must find some way to deal with them."

"And you will, Daniel. But right now, let's go home. I know what you need right now. World affairs come later. I have a much more important affair in mind. Come along. The car's right outside."

"Are you sure, Natalie?"

"Of course I am. Where else can you go? That's why you called me, isn't it? You've shared the whole thing with me. What did you expect me to say?"

"I don't know."

"Yes, you did. Now, let's go home."

The Jaguar sat out in the rain, its sleek hood glistening under the lights.

"I'll drive, Natalie."

"Not this time, Daniel. I'm in a very big hurry."

It was like their first night together, as she raced the car through the dowtown streets, the green dashlights falling across her legs as she unbuttoned her coat, revealing the gartered hose and panties she'd worn that night.

"See what I'm wearing, Daniel? Do you remember? Oh, God, I remember!"

The car rocketed along the wet streets, inviting policemen. Somehow, they managed not to get stopped. Danny watched Natalie drive, her breath quickening as she glanced at him, her free hand stroking his leg, grabbing at his belt. "Undo that."

"Now?"

220

"Yes. Undo it. This excites me. This whole thing. Am I very wicked? Yes, of course I am. Danny, undo your belt."

When her fingers found him, she began to stroke him, her hands rough and insistent, stopping only to shift gears as they climbed the steep, twisting road to her house. She pulled the Jag's nose up to the garage door, shut off the engine and turned to him, her hand going inside his shorts, her mouth on his as she twisted around in the bucket seat, pulling at her panties as she struggled to get them off.

"Natalie, let's go in the house. There's no room in this car." Danny's words were muffled as he tried to speak around Natalie's darting tongue.

"No. Here, now. Oh, Jesus, I'm on fire. Put your finger in me. Touch my breasts. Oh, Danny, hurry." She was trying to pull her body from her seat and across the gear shift console.

"Honey, there's no room . . ."

She thrust her breasts at him, her breathing ragged and gasping, pulling his hand between her thighs as she tried to pull herself above him. She was soaking wet and ready. "Yes, there is room. I'm tiny. Help me, Danny. Oh, it's all so hot."

And he was finally caught up in her intense need, and somehow she was positioned above his lap, scraping her knees, and she gripped him and pulled him deep into her in one fierce motion.

"See, I'm really tiny. Oh, but you're not, you're so big . . . Oh, Danny, help me . . ." It was almost impossible to move, and it was the best it had ever been for both of them.

Bob the Soundman sat quietly in the 211 Club, positioned so that he could see the elevator door from the semi-darkness of the billiard room, which was lighted only by lamps directly over the tables. The place was busy for a Saturday afternoon, he thought, with all but one of the tables occupied. Bob had never played the game, not once, but even to his inexperienced eye, the players seemed to be pretty good. Strangely, he liked the atmosphere, the male clubiness of the room, the soft click of the balls punctuated by an occasional obscenity or good-natured laughter. Everybody seemed to know everybody else, a sort of hustler's fraternity, because he was quick to note nearly every game in the house had a wager going. It was not all that obvious, but money would be placed down by one player, while the apparent winner strolled by and picked it up, adding to the stash in his pocket, usually without comment. It was a stylistic ritual, carefully choreographed by each player, every-thing very cool, very hip. Bob was fascinated, and for a while forgot why he was there, just concentrating on the mini-dramas taking place all over the room.

And then a foxy blond in a tight skirt and bobby sox headed across the large room like a torpedo heading straight for a ship. His distraction was complete. She stopped directly in front of him, one hand on her full hips, the other holding a cigarette like a spear she was about to throw at him. He'd thought at first she was a teenager, but up close he could see she was close to thirty. The spear moved toward him, stopping just in front of his face. "Got a light for a bored lady?" Holding the cigarette still, poised in the air, she moved her head down to snare it with her mouth, an effective movement that placed her face only inches from his as she bent over. "Well?"

Bob fumbled awkwardly in his suit pocket, catching, then losing his lighter while she smiled down at him, her green eyes still amused, still locked on his. Finally, freeing his hand, he brought the lighter up to her face so fast she jerked back, then moved slowly forward to accept the proffered light, before standing straight again. Cupping one elbow in her hand, she puffed slowly and deeply, the tip of the cigarette flashing bright orange in the gloom.

"Thank you."

"You're very welcome, miss." A trace of fresh washed hair and the scent of White Shoulders hung in the air around Bob's head. He drank in her full figure, packed so completely into a matching green sweater and skirt, the skirt so tight he would have seen her panty line, only there wasn't one.

"You're new." It was a statement of fact, requiring no answer.

"I just got to Seattle yesterday. I'm here for a sales convention."

"Oh, really? What do you sell?" She had not moved since he'd lit her cigarette. In fact, he could not get up unless she did.

"Farm equipment, tractors, that kind of stuff."

"Sounds interesting."

"Only if you're a farmer." Bob was intrigued by this woman, dressed like a high school student playing hooky from school.

"I was raised on a farm, but I'm a city girl now. Buy me a drink, and you can tell me all about your tractor." She extended one hand, and he took it, allowing himself to be gently hauled from his chair and led into the bar area. Walking behind her, he marveled at her walk, a hip-swinging roll that etched her buttocks clearly through the tight wool skirt. His mouth went very dry with desire.

She led him to a rear booth and slid in, the skirt bunching up tightly over her thighs as she sat. She pulled him down next to her, the warmth of her leg pressed to his as she moved close to him. "Beer for me, please. They don't serve hard liquor here." Her hand came to rest on his thigh, moving very slowly back and forth while she looked into his face.

"My name is Anita, and you just saved me from a very dull day."

"Mine's Bob, and I'm glad to be of service."

"Good, now we're properly introduced. Tell me about your tractor." Her fingers moved insistently on his thigh, inches away from what was becoming a raging erection.

Of the surviving members of Tinker's team, Bob the Soundman was the most conventional. He actually did know a lot about tractors, and most other things found on a farm, having grown to manhood on a farm in central Iowa. Bob, Jr., the oldest of five children, had pitched in at an early age, helping to make his father one of the richest land owners in Iowa, with four thousand acres that were bountiful in the extreme.

Over six feet tall at thirteen, he'd discovered sex and science all in the same year, and he'd begun to leave the farm mentally and emotionally years before he actually did. In high school, he'd been every father's dream boy, excelling in baseball, basketball and particularly football, where his size and ferocity had plastered his letterman's jacket with countless awards, dutifully sewn on by his adoring mother.

But his most active sport was sex, and he pursued it single-mindedly. Back seats, haystacks, hallways and dancehalls—Bob, Jr. planted his seed wherever and whenever he could. A handsome, big-man-on-campus type, he turned high school lust into an art, breaking hymens and hearts everywhere he went. Of course, there were the inevitable complications, and twice his rich father, with a "that's my boy" pat on the back, paid very handsomely for abortions, available even in 1940 if you had the money, even in Iowa.

If sex was young Bob's favorite sport, science and photography became his all-consuming passion, an obsession fueled by his entry into the Army after Pearl Harbor. Assigned to an early Army intelligence unit, he spent the war in Europe, refining listening devices and boldly jumping behind the German lines with sophisticated camera gear, providing invaluable information for the allies' advancing armies until the end of the war.

When the war ended, he remained in Europe for two more years, and was finally recruited by the CIA, who valued a man with his technical skills and proven ability, as well as his brilliant record of bravery above and beyond the call. Flattered, Bob was discharged from the Army and reentered the service of his country, thrilled with the unlimited funds and scientific and technical expertise put at his disposal by the Agency.

Already possessing more experience than anyone else in the Agency, he became the guru of clandestine surveillance, the chief monitor of agents abroad. His wiretapping skills grew to legendary proportions, exceeded only by his photographic scanning of everything from car interiors on dark nights to dark rooms on bright days. Clearly, he was a rising star, and as a star he was heavily recruited to head the surveillance section of another rising star. Tinker sought him out. Like the parent Agency, Tinker told his associates who the bad guys were, and they followed without question, a brilliant, unorthodox team led by a fanatic.

Bob's allegiance was curious, because Bob was a loner, interested primarily in fooling with new and more exotic equipment, expanding his ideas and seeing them practiced Agency-wide, a big picture man tied to a small caesar going his own way. There really was little mystery to it, however. Tinker needed Bob the Soundman, and he flattered him and provided him with the best equipment, the top jobs available and all the women he could possess.

Gradually, Bob had come to know most of Tinker's vices, and he learned to ignore them, while at the same time easing himself into practicing what Tinker preached. Eventually, he became that most dangerous combination, a technician without a conscience, never letting the morality of an operation get in the way of his performance. He carried out his duties without emotion, accepting without question whatever assignment came his way.

"I thought you were gonna die on me, the way you were breathing. You make one hell of a lot of noise when you screw, you know that?"

"No, I didn't know that, but it just means I'm enjoying myself." Bob the Soundman knew that was not quite the truth. For a moment there, just before he came, his heart had begun to thump wildly out of sync, scaring the hell out of him, and now he was covered with a clammy sheen of sweat, not entirely brought about by sexual passion. Anita had been wild and enthusiastic, but it had never occurred to him at the time, and his irregular heartbeat had made him an observer, not a participant. For Bob the Soundman, it was the worst thing that could happen to him, to get laid and miss out on the best part.

"In a little while, we'll do that again, and I'll be better this time."

"I didn't say it was not good, I said it was noisy."

"Oh? Well, then, tell me, was it good?"

"It was terrific. You're a lot nicer than some of the guys I meet in the 211," said Anita, rubbing his neck and shoulder as he sat up in bed.

"Do you get a lot of business out of there?" asked Bob, always alert to a possible recruit.

"Not much, I guess, because I don't have a pimp. I work alone, and I stay out of trouble that way. I had a pimp once, but he beat me up, so I got out of that situation, down in L.A. So, for the last five years, I've worked up here in Seattle. It's a good place to work, really, because there's not all that much competition, if you're any good."

"You're plenty good, Anita, and believe me, I know."

"I believe you." Anita reached around Bob and stroked his thigh, finally grasping him lightly with her fingers, stroking him back to life, his flaccid penis rising through the circle of her fingers.

"Ah, that's good, baby . . . tell me, do you know a lot of people down there?" Bob's breathing was getting loud again.

"Down where?" Her fingers grew insistent, her tongue flicking over his shoulders, her thighs opening to him.

"At the 211 Club." Bob turned her around, and without preliminaries, pushed her over on her back and entered her, getting what he needed to pay for.

"Did you ever meet a guy named Danny Wood down at the 211? Back in Iowa, we hear he's the best player in town."

"Yes, I know a guy named Danny Wood. He's an old friend of mine, a guy I used to bankroll once in a while."

Fighting to conceal his interest and his surprise at this astonishing piece of good luck, Bob the Soundman turned on the charm, nuzzling Anita's neck and stroking her body as a lover might.

"Well, hey, that's good to hear, Anita. I'd really like to see him play, if you could help me find him. I'm only going to be here for a few days, so I figured I probably wouldn't get to play him."

226

"You'd play Danny? I thought you said you didn't play at all?"

"I lied. You know how it is, one guy trying to hustle another." Bob the Soundman was using his sincere, 4-H voice.

"Danny's gone into the Marines. About the end of last summer I guess. Besides, he'd found a steady girlfriend when he was home on leave at Thanksgiving time. He sure didn't have much time for his old friends."

Bob picked up on the new tone in Anita's voice, the tone and flavor of love lost, love missed.

"You were sweet on him?"

"Yes, but he could have cared less. Hell, I bankrolled him lots of times. The last time I saw him, I practically begged him to take me to bed, but he turned me down flat. I'll never forget that, as long as I live. A goddamn kid, that's all he is, and he turns down the best piece of ass he'd ever find. Damn, that really hurt me."

Bob continued to stroke her.

"You say he found another girl, and not you? Jesus, Anita, I feel sorry for the guy. He must be a real loser, that one."

"He got hustled by some Italian bitch. What was her name? Natalie. Natalie Antonelli, a spoiled little rich painter, about thirty-five I figured, though he only introduced her to me once when they were out on the street shopping or something. I don't even think she's very pretty, but I guess she has a nice figure and all, if you like them skinny like that."

"What kind of painter?"

"Portraits and stuff like that."

"Do you know where she lives?" He had stopped being solicitous and loving, and was now hurrying to get dressed, slapping whatever money he had on the dresser without counting it. It would have been cheaper if he had, because he was paying a fifty-dollar whore two hundred and sixty dollars.

"Wait a minute, Bobby. How would I know where she lives, and why would I care? Why do you care?"

"It's a long story, Anita, and I would only lie to you. You

don't know where she lives, that's fine. But you're sure of the name?"

"Yes, I'm sure of the name. C'mon, sweetie, what has playing pool with Danny got to do with his girlfriend? I told you, Danny's away in the Marines."

Bob the Soundman was dressed and ready to go out the door, but he stopped and turned back to Anita, the good-old-boy attitude gone.

"Danny's here in Seattle, or coming here, Anita. When he does, I'll let you know where to find his body. If you see him before he dies, tell him I said that. By the way, you got a pussy like a desert. Big, empty and dry. You really ought to get out of this business, don't you think?"

In spite of everything that had gone wrong in all of Tinker's plans up to now, he still felt good about cleaning up the loose ends, as he referred to Danny in his conversations with Bob and Chin. Rita had fucked up, and had now disappeared into the anonymity of a county burial in Los Angeles, an event he now spoke of as a positive development for the Agency, describing her as a liability he'd needed to get rid of anyway. That he had first subjected her to a terrifying inquest, forcing her to stand naked and defenseless before him while attempting to answer his questions in a manner that might save her life, bothered him not at all. He felt the same contempt for her after her death that he had while she lived, and by the simple expedient of sanitizing her apartment and replacing her with the young blond-haired recruit due in from Denver, Rita became a non-person in his eyes.

Evans' death should have been different; should have provoked a sympathetic response if not outright grief, but the response had been merely reflexive. Give the Agency something, a cryptic message without information, and once again, get rid of the body, cover the tracks, clean up the spilled blood.

Sitting alone in his hotel suite, staring out the window at the rainswept streets of Seattle, he realized and accepted the fact that this operation had taken on a completely personal cast for him; a life of its own that he intended to let run its course until Danny too was dead. For the first time in his life, Tinker felt he could do anything he wanted to do, and it would come out all right. He was enjoying himself immensely.

"I have a positive contact."
"From the 211 Club?"
"Indirectly, yes."
"Okay. Who do you have?"
"Danny's girlfriend."
"What's her name?"
"Natalie Antonelli."
"What do we have on her?"
"Nothing yet. Just the name."
"Then you'd better get busy, don't you think? Keep it loose. I don't want her spooked."
"I'm not a goddamn amateur, Tinker."
"Just don't push her, do you understand?"
Bob the Soundman hung up on Tinker without saying goodbye.

Natalie Antonelli's phone number and address were in the Seattle phone directory. Bob the Soundman found it without difficulty.

On that same evening, Chin was a mile south and culturally centuries away, strolling the damp sidewalks of Seattle's Chinatown. Chin did not feel at home in Chinatown, because he was not Chinese, but Burmese, and he would find very few countrymen in Seattle, if he'd been looking. But he wasn't looking for countrymen, or Danny Wood, or anyone else. Chin was looking for opium. The "white clouds" would free his mind, for just a little while.

Chin was born in Shanghai in 1925, the son of a rich Burmese trader and a White Russian mother who had fled Russia to join the large White Russian colony living in exile in Shanghai. Arriving penniless from Paris in 1921, she had been promptly dumped by the German gun runner she'd accompanied to Shanghai from France. Chin's father headed the list of the most corrupt international traders in the world, and he collected the White Russian noblewoman the same way he collected any other merchandise. He bought her.

Human beings in China were handled that way, if they were without resources, but the Countess Krupskaya was not without resources, and to the amazement of all who knew him, Chin's father fell in love with the haughty member of Russia's cast-off royalty, and he married her.

Chin's mother then became one of the richest foreigners in China, and set about to get even richer, placing her only son in a succession of exclusive schools. Caught up in money and politics, living and playing in a man's world, she failed to notice her son's descent into the decadent world of pleasure and hedonism available to the very rich in Asia. Half Burmese, half White Russian, living in China and traveling the world when the mood sent him on his way, Chin belonged to no world but his own, a wealthy half-caste heavily influenced by his mother, a bitter counter-revolutionary, blinded by mother love to his excesses.

Chin, more by accident than design, became a sort of international hired gun, a fanatic student of the martial arts practices, living on the edge of death all over the world, seeking release from himself in mindless violence for causes he did not share and money he did not need. His dark presence was felt in Europe, in Africa, and particularly Asia and India, where he struck blows against colonialism without personal political involvement. Violence for the sake of violence was Chin's only political philosophy, and it was this credo that led him to work with two American agents in Indo-China in 1952, where Tinker found him, and recognized a kindred spirit.

Since that time, he had worked under contract for the CIA only once, and had satisfactorily concluded that contract by killing a Soviet agent and his German mistress in West Berlin by cutting their throats with the Soviet agent's own razor.

Consequently, when Danny was returned from Korea, unharmed, Evans had called on Chin and secured his services for Tinker, promising nothing more than plenty of work. For Chin, that had been enough.

It did not take long to find what he sought, and Chin was soon in a basement den under an alleyway, watching a man of indeterminate age prepare his pipe, the black tar turning to liquid, the smoke deep in his lungs, the world far away as he traveled the ancient road to a better place. He laid his head on the wooden pillow, and flew the hard bench, up, up, to the white clouds.

Danny remained at Natalie's for a week, making no effort to go out. He spent long hours listening to music and staring into the fireplace, silent and apart. Natalie painted, read and generally left him to his thought processes. It had been raining steadily the entire week, and he would sit in a chair overlooking the garden, watching the rain ripple across the surface of the swimming pool. Except for their lovemaking, which they indulged in frequently and at any hour, he hardly acknowledged her presence. Natalie was a patient and understanding woman, and she was content just to be with him, and to know he was safe. The week was strangely domestic for them both. In many ways, it was the best time they had shared, yet it resolved nothing, and it couldn't last.

In the same week, Tinker set his men to work to find Danny. Bob the Soundman haunted the 211 Club, while Tinker checked and rechecked relatives and any other friends of Danny he could locate. It was very slow, and completely unprofitable.

Chin proved to be unreliable, and spent his days in Chinatown, working out at a martial arts studio. He was a hired killer. The detail work did not concern him.

After Bob the Soundman acquired Natalie's name and address, Tinker made three cab trips, rolling slowly by the house.

The closest he could get was the bottom of her driveway, over a hundred feet from the front door. As far as he could tell, no one was home. The Jaguar was in the garage.

The fourth time he went out, he drove a borrowed Treasury Department car. Danny and a dark-haired woman stood on the front porch. Danny was changing the porch light. Tinker hurried back to town.

Knowing where Danny was hiding was important, but Tinker thought that knowing whom he was with was more important. Through the girl, he might make Danny do exactly as he was told. He would deliver them a message, and Danny would come to him.

When he got back downtown, he returned the Treasury car and took a cab back to his hotel. He ordered dinner in his room and then sat on the bed. He pulled out a leather dispatch case, opened it and dumped everything he knew about Danny Wood onto the blanket. Notes, addresses, family, maps, more information about one man than he had ever gathered before. From this jumble of material, he intended to trap Danny Wood with ease.

Tinker clapped his hands together, and set to work. This was his element. He was a skilled planner, only this time he was going to execute the plan as well. He labored over the paperwork for hours, making phone calls, studying local area maps, arranging, cajoling, fixing, covering up.

He needed a car and a key from the FBI. The Treasury car was available. Would that do? Fine. The key was no problem. Was this an op of some kind? No, nothing like that. Did he need any local help? None. It was basically vacation stuff. He was assigned a radio call signal, just in case.

When Bob and Chin returned together late that night, his planning was complete. They would kill Danny Wood without ruffling a single official feather. He explained the operation to the men carefully, noting he had built in changes for any circumstance. The main objective was to get Danny to one particular spot.

* * *

232

Natalie opened her eyes and rolled over in bed, reaching for Danny. He wasn't with her. Sleepily, she pulled on a robe and headed toward the living room, the smell of fresh coffee and frying bacon wafting from the kitchen. Danny stood at the stove, coffee cup in hand, stirring the bacon with a fork.

"Hello, sleepyhead. It's about time you got up."

"What time is it?"

"Eleven thirty."

"Sleepyhead? We went to bed at nine, but as I recall, we were still up, and I do mean up, until 4:00 A.M. I should still be in bed."

"Busy day today," Danny said.

"Oh? How busy?"

"Very busy. Sit down, and I'll fry you some eggs."

"Oh, Daniel, spare me that. You sit down, and I'll make the eggs." She kissed him lightly on the mouth and relieved him of his kitchen duties. He sipped his coffee, watching her prepare breakfast.

"You have the greatest legs in the world, Nats. Just incredible."

"What do you have, x-ray vision? I'm wearing a robe. You can't see my legs."

"Photographic memory."

"I see. Well, after breakfast, I'd like to have you rub those legs. I need a massage and you are so good at it. To improve your memory, of course."

"Not this morning, Natalie."

"No more foolish small talk, Danny? Today's it, isn't it? You've decided what you are going to do."

"I'm going after them, one at a time if possible. All together if I can't help it. But I'm not going to wait for them anymore. I've gotten little clues from some friends on the phone. They are about to make a move of some kind. I'm going to move first. Just basic Marine Corps combat doctrine. I don't know why the hell I've been so passive."

Natalie turned to look at him. "You haven't been passive, Daniel. You've been girding your loins, so to speak. Killing men is not a natural thing for you. You had to justify it first. You took as long as you needed, and now you've decided, as I knew you would. Of course, now that you've done that, I'm absolutely terrified for you." She turned back to her cooking, her back straight. She did not want to cry.

"I didn't want to decide, Natalie. I just wanted to stay here, in your house, in your arms, and maybe the bad guys would go away. But inside, I knew all along what I had to do."

"I understand, Daniel." She walked to his chair and laid his breakfast on the table. She joined him, sipping coffee, smoking her first morning cigarette, the one she always enjoyed the most, that somehow tasted awful this morning. He ate quickly and silently, finally pushing his empty plate away.

"What do they call the place during battle where the Generals are?"

"The Command Headquarters, I guess."

"Okay. This house is your Command Headquarters. You go and do what you must. I'll be right here, all the time. If you need me, just knock on the old Command Headquarters door."

He got up from the table, pulled Evans' shoulder holster off a kitchen peg where it had hung for a week and put it on. Natalie watched him slip on his coat, biting her lip so she wouldn't try to stop him. He bent to her and kissed her on each cheek, then each eye, then softly on her mouth.

"See you later, General," Danny said.

"So long, Marine."

She heard the garage doors open, and then the roar of the Jaguar as it coughed to life. She sat at the table until she heard it back out of the driveway. She ran to the front door and flung it open, calling his name. She caught a brief glimpse of the Jag as it left the driveway and headed down the hill. Then he was gone.

Danny sat in Natalie's Jaguar, parked discreetly up the block from the Olympic Hotel, with a clear view of its main entrance. A cold, wind-driven rain drummed across the canvas roof, blotting out the quiet thunk of the windshield wipers as he watched the hotel, the engine running smoothly.

In the past few days, odd bits of information had convinced him they were hot on his trail. Calls to his mother at home. Inquiries at the 211 Club. They were putting out the word, and it wouldn't take long before they located him. He couldn't just sit and wait any longer. It was time to force the issue.

He pulled Evans' Browning from its shoulder harness, checked the clip, popped it back into the butt, leaving it cocked, safety on. He jammed the gun back into the holster, and lit a cigarette. Not much of a plan here. Just go upstairs and blow them away in their rooms. If he was right, the last place they would expect him would be at their front door.

He reached forward and shut off the ignition and snuffed his cigarette in the tiny ashtray. As he pushed the door open, the streetlights went on, a losing fight against the late afternoon March storm. He struggled free of the car and turned to cross the street, pulling his jacket collar up around his neck.

Rush-hour traffic streamed past him as he waited to cross, eyes fixed on the hotel entrance. Tinker and a wiry Oriental stood at the cab stand, huddled under an ineffectual umbrella. A gaudily dressed hotel doorman had his arm raised, a whistle in his mouth.

Danny did not hesitate. He dived back into the Jaguar, starting the engine as he slammed the door behind him. Close. He watched intently as a yellow cab rolled to a stop. The Oriental got in and Tinker turned away and hurried back into the hotel. He couldn't believe his good fortune. If the traffic had been lighter, he would have walked right into their arms.

The cab pulled away from the hotel. Danny made an instantaneous decision. In half a block, the Jaguar's nose was tucked behind the cab, weaving through the rainswept streets, headed for Chinatown. Danny's heart raced, his pulse accelerating. But it was a good feeling. His mind was clear, his senses sharp. One on one. Fair enough.

As Danny trailed Chin, Tinker made a phone call in the hotel lobby. He spoke for a minute, hunched over the phone, one hand over his free ear. When he stepped back, a smile spread across his face. She was home, and she'd told Danny's "father" that Danny was out, and wouldn't be back for a few hours. Would he call back? Stupid bitch. Danny's "father" would make this call in person. He hurried back out to the cab stand. There was only one Agency car available in Seattle, and he didn't have it.

Danny rolled to a stop only fifty feet from the cab as it pulled to the curb. The Oriental exited and hurried across the sidewalk and up the stairs into a martial arts studio. Danny didn't like that at all. He shut down the engine, lit a cigarette and waited. In an hour it would be dark.

In the large, high-ceilinged training room, Chin was moving with practiced ease through a series of complicated warm-up exercises, standing in front of a floor-to-ceiling mirror. Naked except for a jockstrap, his skin was covered with a fine sweat, his compact body tightly muscled and sculpted, without imperfections. He had pursued this regimen since his time in the monastery, a dam against all the sins he exposed his body to with drugs and other worldly pursuits. As he moved into more vigorous action, lightning-fast strikes with his hands split the air, so rapid they seemed to be one movement, when in fact they were multiple assaults designed to blast an opponent into submission. Occasionally, he would leap into the air, his legs delivering devastating kicks as he whirled and spun about the room, his body in perpetual motion.

There are many practitioners of martial arts in the world, drawn to it by its spiritual resource as well as its physical benefits. Chin did not practice the normal arts, but he did practice the martial arts most conducive to killing and maiming. He approached his calling with a reverence spawned by the darkest demons of his soul. Possessed by them, he was driven to serve the darker side of man. Chin took enormous pleasure in his ability to break a little, or break a lot, to apply minimum pressure or snap a bone like a dry twig. He had crushed Rita's bones with hardly a bruise, while Tinker had watched it all, his eyes bright and excited, the maniacal foreman of a master craftsman at work.

Chin understood men like Tinker, and he felt utter contempt for them. Men who could not handle their own problems were lower than dogs, in his estimation, but he would do their work for them, because it gave him pleasure and substance. For Chin, other people's deaths were his way of life.

As he grew even more frenzied, whirling and seeming to fly about the room, he began to concentrate his mind on killing Danny Wood. Tinker wanted to watch, and that was acceptable. But he, Chin, must first prepare his soul, for killing was a business not to be taken lightly. It would be easy, of course, but preparation was paramount to a proper exhibit of his talents. Whirling and spinning, arms and legs ripping the air with an audible snapping sound, Chin pursued his demons in solitary, frightening preparation.

Danny picked up Chin's trail as soon as he exited the stairs and began walking along the busy early evening streets of Chinatown. Shops and restaurants rapidly filled with customers, and overworked cooks labored non-stop to keep up with the demand, and on the restaurant floors, waitresses carried trays full of steaming dishes to the district's ravenous visitors. Out on the streets, the smells of this activity wafted through the night air and mixed with garbage in the alleys and carbon monoxide from the cars patrolling the streets in search of a place to park, the whole blending to give the area an exotic, truly oriental feel. As he moved closer to Chin, Danny felt for a moment he was someplace else, not in the geographical heart of a major U. S. city. It could have been Bangkok, or Singapore, or Shanghai.

Two blocks ahead, the crowd thinned, the streets were nearly deserted and Danny saw a lone cab, its bright yellow "vacant" sign a beacon in the night, as Chin picked up his pace and headed for it. Off to the left, a large, darkened vacant lot, with what appeared to be the start of construction on a new building, caught Danny's eye, and moved him to act. Stepping up directly behind Chin, he jammed the Browning 9mm muzzle into Chin's neck, gripping him by the shoulder with his free hand. Chin came to a sudden halt, and Danny could feel the energy coursing through the man's diminutive but powerful body.

"Don't even think of it, you son-of-a-bitch! Just move to the left until I say stop."

Chin responded to Danny's whispered threat by doing exactly as he was told, walking with a measured pace into the darkened construction site with Danny only a few feet behind him, gun cocked and ready to fire.

As the pair moved away from the street Danny directed Chin through the skeletal framework and masonry of what seemed to be a two-story building in progress, stepping over stacks of wood and steel into the even darker interior of the work, completely shielded from the busy community. Even the sound of autos faded and died, and as the two men neared the center of the unfinished building, they were as completely alone as possible, isolated from the public eyes and ears only a hundred yards distant.

"Stop, and turn around. Slowly now." Danny stood back from Chin as the man followed his orders, opening a space of about ten feet between them. Chin, dressed as usual in head-to-toe black, was barely visible in the near total darkness.

"Ah. Daniel Wood. We have been looking for you."

"Well, here I am, mister."

"Do you intend to use that gun?" Chin had not seemed to move, but he was now closer than he had been. Danny did not notice, even as Chin closed the space between them.

"I'm thinking about it."

"Ah. Indecision. An occidental mistake."

Chin launched his body, feet first, across the narrowed gap between them. Danny attempted to move to the side, but was struck a thunderous kick to the ribs and knocked to his knees, still clutching the gun. Chin's hand rocketed through the night air, catching his wrist and sending the gun clattering away into the darkness. Danny spun away, the pain an audible, radiant wave, numbing his arm. Enraged, he spun around, trying to see which way Chin had run. But Chin had not run at all, and was standing quietly only a few feet away, a broad flash of teeth revealing his smile in the darkness.

"You are not very good at this, are you, Marine?"

Chin's hand snapped forward, catching Danny in the throat, dropping him to his knees once again. Danny held his neck, struggling for breath, choking and spitting up blood. Chin seemed to float around him, and the man's hands and feet came from all directions, inflicting terrible pain as Chin grunted exultantly with each strike. Danny struggled to his feet, only to receive multiple shocks to his ribs, hearing them crack as he vomited into the dirt and fell to his hands and knees, his mind a red haze of pain and helplessness. He felt his cheek rip open as Chin worked on his face and head before delivering tremendous blows to Danny's kidneys, which put him flat on his stomach.

Rolling over in the dirt, he lay frozen with pain as Chin delivered a series of vicious kicks, before he bent down and picked Danny up by the coat collar, handling him as if he were a child. Danny struggled to get loose, but Chin's grip was relentless as Danny pulled at his hands, keeping on his feet with a willpower born of desperate fear. His groin exploded in pain as Chin drove his knee upward with terrible force, letting Danny fall to the ground, doubled in pain he could no longer localize.

His voice contemptuous and shrill, Chin said, "You bore me, my friend. How do you feel? Ah . . . I know how you feel, really I do. The pain is very great, is it not? I am very good at this, I know. You should have shot me, my friend. I was yours to shoot. Surely, Tinker would not have hesitated. Now, get up. Do you wish to die on the ground like that? I will wait." Chin backed away a few feet and stared down at Danny.

With enormous effort, goaded by Chin's tone and his own hatred, Danny struggled to his feet, his body terribly beaten, but his spirit indomitable. Blood trickled from his mouth. He took a half step toward Chin as pain shot through his rib cage. Chin heard the switchblade snick open, but it was too late. Chin moved forward, stopped, and then his face contorted with pain, the corner of his lip jerking up in a jagged slash

239

toward his cheek, his eyes bulging. For a brief instant, he was motionless, then, arms flailing, he dropped dead at Danny's feet, the knife buried in his chest.

It took Danny a full hour to gather the strength to leave the construction site. Though Danny had been terribly beaten, Chin had nevertheless spared him from lethal injury before the sudden knife attack had killed him and he fell in a heap at Danny's feet. Weary and in considerable pain, Danny checked Chin's pockets. Nothing. As it turned out, he thought, he could hardly ask for a better resolution to the problem Chin presented. A Chinaman, in Chinatown, attacked while sleeping in a construction site because he was a transient.

Danny walked slowly back to the car, glad he was alive but feeling new pain messages with each step. Jesus, the guy had really had him. He would have to be more careful. No more mistakes. But who had made the mistake here? Chin never saw the knife that killed him. Danny settled painfully into the Jaguar's cramped seat, and started the motor.

He would go home to Natalie for some repairs. He was on a roll, and the odds were getting better. He did not see the black sedan parked just two cars behind him. The Soundman had come to pick up Chin after his workout. He'd found Danny instead.

While Danny had waited in the rain for Chin, Tinker had halted his cab a few blocks from Natalie's house and started up the hill on foot, head down against the rain. It was a good setup, he could see. Single road, long driveway, her house at the top of the drive, isolated. He walked up the curving driveway until he stood on the small porch, the porch light seeming to be the only light on in the large house.

He made no check of the grounds, simply ringing the doorbell like any old friend. And, like an old friend, Natalie had flung open the door, wearing a black satin robe over a lacy red gown, a broad smile on her face.

"Danny, what did you . . . ?"

The smile vanished instantly as she tried to slam the door,

but Tinker had banged into it, sending her sprawling back into the room and onto the soft black and white checked carpet, the lights off but the roaring fireplace across the room casting a warm glow across her startled face. Tinker closed the door behind him, and moved to where Natalie lay, her gown up around her thighs, long legs gleaming ivory in the firelight, one shoulder of the robe pushed down, the black robe in sharp contrast to the red gown and the white of her skin. Even though she was terribly frightened, she pulled the robe back to her shoulder and across her legs, tucking her feet under her, high heeled slippers clicking together as she raised herself to a sitting position. Only inches from her face, Tinker's gun waved, and Natalie stared into the barrel, quelling her fear and trying desparately to think clearly.

"Who else is here?"

"No one is here, and I know who you are."

"Do you? Then you know what I'm after. Get up. Sit on the couch, by the fire, and don't do anything stupid."

Natalie got to her feet and moved to the couch, conscious of the way she looked in the low-cut gown, pulling the thin robe across her breasts as she sat down. She looked at Tinker. He'd put the gun in a shoulder holster, and tossed his wet raincoat across a chair.

"Take the robe off. You look better in red."

"Why? I don't think I . . ."

He moved to her very quickly, lashing her face with his open palm, sending her sprawling across the cushions. "Don't ask why. Just do it!"

As she sat up, he slapped her again. She pulled the black robe off, her face stinging from his blows. The red nightgown, slit high on the sides, fell away from her legs. She tried to cover her thighs, but it was useless. She hadn't bought it because it was modest. She wore nothing underneath its sheer wisp of material, with only tiny spaghetti straps at the shoulder. She felt more than naked.

Tinker walked to the bar and made himself a drink, ignoring Natalie as he made a quick check of the rooms. Natalie did not attempt to get away, even when he checked the bedrooms at the end of the long hallway, assuring himself they were alone in the house. He walked back to where she sat, and pulling a stuffed chair directly across from her, settled into it and lit a cigarette. He loosened his tie and sipped his drink, studying her body.

The minutes dragged on in silence, and Natalie, growing ever more terrified, finally blurted, "What are you going to do?"

"I'm here to leave a message for your boyfriend, Natalie. I've been chasing him for a long time, and I figure this is the best way to get his attention."

"I don't know when he will be back. He could walk in that door right now." If Danny just walked in . . . her eyes telegraphed her fear.

"That's right, honey. If the kid walks in, he's dead. But I don't want it to be that way. I have other plans. I want him to come to me when I'm ready for him. When I leave here, he'll do just what I expect him to."

"Why will he do that?" Even as she asked, Natalie thought she knew.

"Stand up," Tinker said, dropping his cigarette into his drink and setting it down next to him. Natalie hesitated, and Tinker jerked his gun from its holster and pointed it at her head. Trembling, she did as she was told, arms at her sides. Tinker lowered the gun, and hooked its barrel under one of the straps of her gown, pulling it from her shoulder, then repeating the process with the other strap. Natalie instinctively pulled her hands across her chest, stopping its descent, holding the flimsy material at her breasts.

Tinker settled back into his chair, eyes boring into hers, the gun pointed at her belly. She couldn't meet his gaze, and looked away, drawing her legs together, knowing what was coming. A feeling of total despair and helplessness washed over her, and she began to cry.

"Are you going to make this difficult for me? Because if you are, I wouldn't mind." She felt the gun muzzle move slowly up

242

her naked thigh, then shift, moving between her legs, its cold length against her pubic mound, prodding and pushing at her until she sat back down in retreat.

"Please . . . please don't." Natalie looked back at Tinker, tears streaming down her face, her hands still holding her gown across her chest, her knees held together tightly in defense.

"We can do this easy, or we can do this the hard way. Either way, I'm going to leave Danny a message I know he'll respond to." Tinker pushed his chair back and stood up, still holding the gun. He began to strip off his clothing. He left his shoes and socks on. Natalie could not take her eyes off him. She thought she was going to be sick to her stomach.

Tinker moved to her, until he stood very close, his flaccid penis at direct eye level to her. She felt the gun muzzle at her throat. It was very cold, and she could not hold her head level as he tilted her face upward with a slow pressure.

"Touch it."

"No . . . I . . ."

"Touch it. With both hands." The gun dug into her neck. Her resistance collapsed. She was going to be raped, or she was going to be killed. She was certain. She decided to do the one to prevent the other. She willed herself to do as she was told.

Natalie reached forward and touched him, as her gown fell free, exposing her breasts, the nipples hard with fear. He reached out with his free hand and stroked her breasts, pinching and pulling her nipples, interpreting their response as sexual arousal. Numbly, she stroked him to hardness. He seemed detached, far away, only his hardness in her hands a real connection to what she was doing. His hips moved toward her, his hand on the back of her head, twisted in her long hair, guiding her. Her mouth closed over him, the gun at her neck an extension of what he was doing, pushing into her throat as he thrust at her. For a moment she sucked at him, hearing his breathing go ragged above her. He grew larger in her mouth as she slid over him, gagging her until she set an easy pace, and the gun fell away as he tensed, spreading his legs, the weapon tossed to the couch beside her.

Natalie couldn't do it. Shame and hatred washed over her, and she pulled her mouth free and launched herself at him, clawing at his face as the weight of her body carried both of them over the back of his chair and onto the floor on the other side.

Tinker landed violently on his back, Natalie on top of him. She scrambled onto his stomach, her long nails raking his face and chest as she pummeled him, cursing and shouting at him in rage and humiliation. Momentarily out of wind, he had eight deep scratches on his face before he arched under her and threw her off. She came to her feet like a cat, and quiet now, rushed at him again, trying to grab his throat, wanting to kill him. He lashed at her with his hands, surprised at her strength and ferocity, before he closed his fist and crashed it into her face, knocking her to the floor. As she struggled to get up, he pounced on her, straddling her slim hips, and began to slap her with the backs of his hands, cutting her mouth.

She tried to shield her face, but he kept hitting her, slapping her breasts, until she couldn't tell where the blows were coming from. Had his fists been closed, he might have killed her. But she was his message to Danny, and he wanted her to live.

Finally arm weary, he pulled back and rolled her onto her stomach, spreading her legs wide and pulling her to her knees, her head hanging down between her arms as she wept, all resistance gone. He positioned himself behind her, his hand probing, opening her, and then he rammed into her, pulling her hips toward him.

The pain of his thrust was immediate and terrible, and Natalie bit her lip to keep from screaming. She held herself still, not moving, as he pounded at her, the flesh of her hips pinched in his fists as he pulled her toward him. Finally, he stiffened, and cried out his release as he flooded into her, the cold heat of his semen signaling the end of her pain.

He pulled away, and left her on the floor. The only thing she felt as she lay there was an overwhelming sense of relief that she was still alive. She watched him as he picked up his clothes and walked down the hall to the bathroom. Subjugated, she made no attempt to run. She wanted very much to give Danny Tinker's message. She already thought of Tinker as a dead man.

Natalie pulled herself up into a sitting position, her torn nightgown puddled at her waist. Inexplicably, she was still wearing one high heeled slipper. Tinker sat at the bar, fully dressed, his tie neatly knotted, the gun swinging free under his arm. Except for the vivid red scratches on his face, he looked exactly as he had when he'd arrived. She could not remember when that had been. Minutes? Hours? There was blood on her breasts from her nose bleed. She could taste fresh blood from her cut lips. There were welts on her breasts and stomach.

"May I go to the bathroom?"

"Why not? It's your house," Tinker said.

Natalie struggled to her feet, kicking off the slipper and stepping free of the tattered nightgown, padding barefoot down the hallway without a glance at Tinker.

Gently, she washed away the blood and doctored the cuts as best she could. Her face was puffed on the right cheek, and she applied a bandage to the cut on her eye, which was rapidly turning black. He'd done that with his fist. She took a brief, cool shower, and brushed her hair as she dried. She looked at herself in the mirror, then slipped into a terry cloth robe and went back to the living room, somehow sure that Tinker was done with his violence. The message was there for Danny to see. She was very calm, though a doctor would have called it shock.

She went back to the couch and sat down, pulling her legs up under her, covering them with her robe.

"What do you drink, Natalie?" Tinker asked in a matter-of-fact tone.

"Scotch. And a cigarette."

Tinker made her drink, and gathered up a fresh ashtray and her cigarettes and lighter, setting them down on the cushion next to her. They both acted as if nothing had happened. Natalie felt nothing at all.

"I've written my instructions on a piece of paper. Just give it

245

to Danny when he gets here. Tell him I said not to be late."

"Oh, Danny will be there, I'm sure. I doubt if I could talk him out of it after he sees what you did to me. Not that I will try."

"Why not?"

"Because I want him to kill you."

Tinker chuckled. "Fair enough, but it won't happen. That kid has fucked me over for a long time. This is the end of the line for him."

"Why have you done this? Why do you want to hurt him? He did exactly what you asked of him."

"All but one thing. He came back from Korea. That wasn't part of the plan. Then, things just escalated, and now it's a very personal thing with me."

"Because he killed Evans?"

"No. Before that. It was always personal, since the day he got back."

"Danny's going to kill you, Tinker. Now get out of my house."

A dark shadow crossed Tinker's face, but he said nothing. He simply tossed down his drink, put on his raincoat and walked out, closing the door softly behind him.

Natalie got up and walked to the fireplace, adding a log, then she stripped off her robe and spread it in front of the fire. She lay down and closed her eyes. She wanted Danny to get the message, exactly as Tinker had left it. She would still be there when he came home.

Bob the Soundman kept his distance as he snaked through the early evening traffic behind Danny. He had no idea where Danny was heading, but he was determined to stay with him. Chin would have to fend for himself after his workout. If the opportunity presented itself, Bob intended to kill Danny. Tinker's plan, like all the ones before it, was too convoluted for the Soundman.

The Agency Cadillac was built like a tank. The Jaguar Danny drove through the wet streets ahead of him was very fast, but

246

very light. It wouldn't take much to knock him right off the road. The Cadillac accelerated, closing the gap between the two cars. He followed the Jaguar tenaciously as it sped along the western edge of the bay. In the distance, the Soundman could see the flash of a lighthouse on a point of land stuck out into the water.

Abruptly, the Jag increased speed and swung to the left and up a winding road. Cautiously, the Soundman followed, the heavy car sluicing dangerously as it pulled up the narrow road behind Danny, whose tail lights appeared and disappeared as the Jaguar climbed nimbly up the crest of the hill before pulling quickly into a winding driveway and stopping. As Bob slowly passed the driveway, he caught one final glance of the Jag's tail lights before they went out as Danny shut down the engine. Home to Natalie.

Okay, Bob the Soundman would wait. He pulled the Cadillac farther up the road, where it crested before heading back down the other side. After a quick reconnaissance, he backed the Cadillac into a gated driveway. From there, he could look directly onto the rear of the Jaguar. He lit a cigarette, and settled down to wait. Danny, according to Tinker's plan, was due on Squak Mountain at dawn. The Soundman meant to see that he didn't make it. It would be payback time for his ruined hearing. It was over twenty miles to the mountain. Plenty of miles to blast that Jag and Danny Wood right off the highway. He couldn't wait to see the look on Tinker's face when he told him.

At about the time that Danny entered the house and Bob the Soundman settled in to wait for him, Tinker arrived in the sleepy little town of Issaquah, Washington, about sixteen miles east of Seattle. Issaquah was a one-trick pony of a town, off the main drag, and content to be that way. A farming and dairy community, with one main street and not much else, it suited Tinker's purpose to a tee. Out of the way, yet heavily used for sports and recreation in the summer, it was nearly empty this time of the year.

Squak Mountain, just outside of town, had a steel-gated road that led to the county sheriff and State Patrol radio towers at its summit. Alongside their radio technician shacks was another, more secret radio installation, containing the FBI and U. S. Treasury Department radio equipment and tower for this region. During Danny's training at Camp Pendleton before the mission, he had mentioned Squak Mountain as one of his earliest hunting spots, a place he had learned to shoot. He'd even mentioned a spot on the mountain road nearly identical to the road in Korea where the mission took place.

Tinker had no trouble getting the keys to the gate blocking the road. The FBI agent in charge asked no questions, just handed him the key, warning him to watch for snow in the higher elevations. He wasn't going high up, only about halfway, by the map the agent gave him, to a road very much like another road. There, he and Bob and Chin would eliminate Danny Wood.

Savoring the drama of it, Tinker walked into a restaurant, the only one open at 8:00 P.M., and ordered a steak. It was surprisingly good, for a one-trick pony of a town. After dinner, he would check into a local motel until 5:00 A.M. when Bob and Chin would join him. They expected Danny to appear on the mountain at 7:30 A.M. He was sure Danny would get the message.

Danny stood over Natalie's nude figure, the light from the fireplace casting flickering shadows across her pale, satiny skin. She looked up at him with wide, grave eyes, her face puffy and red, her lip swollen. The scratches on her breasts and belly were angry red splashes on a soft canvas framed in her white terrycloth robe. Her right eye was circled in a greenish-black, raccoon-like mask.

"Natalie?"

"Tinker was here, to leave you a message. He raped me, Danny. There's an envelope on the bar, with instructions." Natalie sat up, legs curled under her, and lit a cigarette. She extended an empty glass toward him, her eyes cool and dark as she studied his face.

"Fill this, please. I'm trying to get drunk, but it's not working."

Danny stood as if rooted to the floor.

"Danny, please?"

Danny took the empty glass and stumbled to the bar, splashing Scotch into the glass and adding ice without thinking. "How did he get in?"

"I let him in, Danny. I thought it was you. And I'm not used to being afraid to answer my door at five o'clock in the afternoon. Perhaps I should have let him kill me. Yes, that's it. I should..."

Danny rushed to her, spilling the drink as he set it down, and closed her in his arms as she rose and threw her arms around his neck, finally crying, finally letting go. Sobs shook her body as she clung to him, her face buried against his wet jacket.

The storm of emotion passed as quickly as it came, and she pulled back, looking up into his eyes. "Kill him for me, Danny. Kill him for me."

Danny's eyes turned nearly black.

"I'll be back in a minute, hon. I feel dirty." Natalie picked up her drink, and headed for the bathroom. Danny went back to the bar, and ripped open the envelope Tinker had left him.

A Forest Service map dropped out. It was a map of Squak Mountain. Folded inside were two glossy photographs of Rita Williams. In one, she was vividly alive. In the other, she was even more graphically dead. Hands shaking, Danny poured himself a drink, and read the one sheet of typewritten text. It was unsigned.

Danny:

If you are reading this, you have seen the messenger. As you can see by the enclosed pictures, it could have been much worse. And it will be, if you don't show up in the morning at 0730. I have marked the spot on the road I want you to stop. We'll be there. You had better be, or I'll be

249

back to visit your little lady again. The gate will be opened at 0700. Come alone. My best to Natalie. She is a great piece of ass.

Danny studied the two pictures. In one, Rita was straddling a male body, head thrown back, red hair flying. It was a pose he remembered well. She was surrounded by mirrored walls, and there were images of Rita Williams from all angles. In the second picture, she was a lumpy rag of battered flesh, lying on the same bed, the same multiple images assaulting his senses. One thing was clear. Tinker was insane.

He sipped at his drink, staring at the two pictures, unable or unwilling to look away.

Natalie had been in the shower for nearly a half hour, and still she felt unclean as she worked the soap into her skin for the fifth time, trying and failing to wash away her nightmare. She had visible bruises on her thighs, neck and breasts, her ankles and knees had slight cuts, and she had the overall feeling of having been struck by a car. In a few hours, more bruises would appear, but the bruises she was scrubbing so vigorously were not physical, and the mental bruises would never scrub off.

She had douched twice, very thoroughly, and then she had sat on the edge of the tub and carefully shaved off her pubic hair, leaving only a tiny oval patch, which she had then scoured with her sweetest rose-scented soap, the soap Danny loved. She'd stood up and let the hot water wash across her thighs, until the sensitive skin had reddened under the needle-like spray, and she'd stepped back, looking down, expecting to feel clean, to feel whole. So far, it hadn't worked.

After a final rinse, Natalie stepped from the tub and onto the cool tile of the bathroom floor, wrapping herself in a huge bath towel, then quickly opening it, dropping it to the floor as she stood in front of the mirrored wall, searching for her body through the heavy steam that dampened the black tiled walls and clouded the glass. The overhead fan whirred softly, sucking the steam from the room. The blower hummed as it drew the haze from the mirror, gradually revealing her body from the feet upward as the image grew bright and clear, the mist rolling up and off the glass.

She was startled at how pink she was, forgetting that she had baked and pounded her flesh for over an hour. She looked the same. The few cuts and bruises had not changed her.

Okay, I've been raped, and I've been terrorized, and it was none of my doing. What now, Natalie, she thought? I mustn't blame Danny. I mustn't blame myself.

Natalie smiled at her image, and squared her shoulders, telling herself everything would be all right... it was over. It's time to think ahead. She sat down at the vanity, still nude, and selected a polish for her toenails. Painting her toenails had always made her feel good, had always made her feel beautiful, young, gay.

Lost in thought, Danny was unaware Natalie had rejoined him in the living room until her hand appeared over his shoulder and reached for Tinker's note. She had it before he could stop her.

"Natalie, you don't want to . . ."

Her face never changed as she read the note, the pictures and map held in her other hand. Slowly, she brought the pictures close, studying them. "This is the woman that tried to kill you, isn't it?"

"Yes."

"He's crazy, you know. He's absolutely crazy."

"Yes, I suppose he must be."

She raised her eyes to his, and gave a kind of startled little jump and dropped the pictures to the floor. "Danny. What happened to you?" For the first time, she noticed his battered face. In the aftershock of her rape she had, naturally enough, been primarily concerned with herself. Chin had done a very workmanlike job.

"Tinker had someone try to kill me. Of course, I was going to kill him at the time. I was overmatched. The guy was some kind of martial arts expert, but he never saw the knife. My drill instructor told me once that American fighting men wouldn't use knives. He was wrong."

Gently, she traced the deep cut on his cheek with her fingertips, then just as gently, she kissed his battered face with tiny, featherlike kisses, and drew him to her, her arms around his waist. He let out a harsh breath, and stiffened in the circle of her arms. She pulled away. "Danny?"

"Honey, I think Tinker's killer bruised some ribs, that's all. Not too bad, considering what he might have done."

Danny drew her to him. "I'm going to be fine, Natalie. My bones will heal. I'm a lot more worried about whether you will heal."

"I'll heal, Danny. Nobody's going to point at me when I go down the street. I'll deal with it." She hesitated, then went on. "Are you going to be there, Danny? Are you going to do as he says?"

"I'm going to be there." He tipped her face upward, looking into her eyes, his face set in stone. "But I'm going to do it my way, not his."

"Are you afraid?"

"No. I'm not afraid."

"Good. Now, take off all your clothes. I want to fix your hurts, and then I want you to lay down and just hold me, okay?"

"We don't have much time. I want to leave here about midnight."

"Midnight? But he doesn't want you there until 7:30 A.M."

"Yes, I know he does. That's why I'm leaving at midnight."

"If he gets away, will he come back for me?"

"He won't get away, Natalie."

She looked at his face, noticing the dark passion in his eyes, wilting under his intensity. "No, I guess he won't, after all," she said.

Natalie shifted down, drawing Danny up into her, settling gently on top of his thighs, moving very slowly, filled with love for him. Carefully, she moved up and down, her hands flat on each side of him, palms pressed to the rug, careful not to hurt him. It had begun very naturally, the cuddling and talking, the drinks, the touching growing more urgent, until he'd pulled her over him. And now, she felt her climax rush at her with shocking quickness, and his hips, lifting her slim body off the floor, brought her to shuddering, blessed relief.

Later, closed in his arms, she told Danny for the first time that she loved him. He told her that he loved her too. Then he explained to her exactly how he intended to kill Tinker and whoever was with him.

Bob the Soundman was nodding off to sleep in the Agency Cadillac when the Jaguar roared to life below him, its tail lights amber beacons in the dark. Instantly awake, he glanced at his watch. 12:10 A.M. Wood was on the road again. As the Jaguar backed out of the driveway and headed down the winding road, the Soundman slipped after him, headlights off, until Danny swung out along the beach road, heading back toward downtown Seattle. As Bob turned onto the road, he switched his headlights on and closed the gap between the two cars. But there was plenty of time, and Bob was in no hurry. He switched on the windshield wiper. It had begun to rain again. The Jag was getting hard to see.

As Danny drove through the industrial area of the city's waterfront, he noticed the black car behind him for the first time. He made two detours, doing complete round trips of waterfront blocks. The car stayed with him, but did not close the distance. He swung over and parked the Jag directly under a street lamp. The car behind him slowed to a stop, still keeping its distance. Whoever it was, he wanted Danny to know he was there.

Danny raced away from the Caddy. He went through the Jag's gears smoothly as he made quick turns and diced his way around the waterfront streets he'd played on as a kid. When he finally finished his evasive tactics and headed up Madison Street toward his mother's apartment, it was 1:15 A.M. He looked in the rearview mirror as he swung up on the fourth-floor rooftop parking lot. The Cadillac was gone. He'd lost him. Bob the Soundman could not outmaneuver a Jaguar on the city streets. He gambled that Danny was going to his mother's apartment on the hilltop above the waterfront. If he was wrong, he would head out to Squak Mountain to meet Tinker. He went straight up one of Seattle's steepest hills, and parked the Caddie. In ten minutes, Danny roared around the corner and onto the roof of The Nettleton Apartments. Bob the Soundman had been right.

Danny let himself into his mother's apartment. Six months and a hundred nightmares ago, it had been his home. He walked silently down the narrow hallway, past his mother's bedroom door. It was shut tight. In the dimly lit living room, he could see Dick's uniform hung neatly over a chair. He'd walked past that locked bedroom door many times before. Some things never change. Well, Dick was a hell of a guy, and that was good for his mom. He spent quite a bit of time on Squak Mountain. He'd taken Danny up there when Danny was twelve years old. The key ring on the uniform had a key to the Squak Mountain road gate. It took Danny less than ten seconds to remove it.

Danny stepped into his old bedroom. His mother had left it unchanged since the day he'd left for boot camp. On his dresser, and taped to his mirror, was a catalogue of adolescent and teenage love. Jean, Enid, Sally, Becky and Rose. Pretty young women he had lusted after and, on occasion, caught. A thrill a minute. There had been back seat gropes that seemed now to be from another life, so far removed from the present it was difficult for him to grasp their very existence. His high school letterman's sweater was draped over a chair, exactly as he had left it. One tennis shoe lay upside down under his dresser, the other on the corner of his bed. His bookcase was full to overflowing with history and war books. An empty Coke bottle clung precariously to the edge of the windowsill. It was a high school boy's room, awaiting the boy's return. But the boy was gone forever.

Danny changed his clothes, putting on his favorite wool

hunting shirt and a pair of jeans. He kicked his dress shoes off, and replaced them with his best hunting boots and wool socks. He hung his clothes carefully in the closet, something he would not have done in the past. He slipped Evans' 9mm Browning back on over his shirt, and put on his black wool hunting coat. He opened the bottom drawer of his dresser, removed a full cartridge belt and hooked it around his waist, dropping a handful of loose .30-06 shells into his pocket for good measure. He hung his binoculars around his neck, careful to leave the lens covers on. The last thing he picked up was an expensive, hand-tooled leather gun case. Inside was a custom built Springfield 1903 .30-06. Silently, Danny let himself out of the apartment, and headed to the Jag.

Back in the apartment, his mother hadn't heard a thing. Lying beside her, Dick rolled over and closed his eyes. He'd heard his keys rattle. He'd heard his keys rattle many times in the past. Squak Mountain was a great place to take girls. His policeman's mind told him to check it out. His boyfriend's mind told him to forget it. He went back to sleep.

It was 2:15 A.M. when Danny poked the Jaguar's long snout down the ramp and headed east on Madison, on his way to Squak Mountain and Tinker. It was 2:15 and 20 seconds when he picked up the headlights of the shiny black Cadillac in his rearview mirror. It was raining harder than ever. The Marine driving the Jag did not panic. He removed Evans' 9mm from its holster, and set it down in the bucket seat next to him. You can't hunt an animal who knows where you are.

Danny entered the tunnel that leads to the Lake Washington Floating Bridge at 45 miles per hour. Halfway across the longest floating bridge in the world, he was going 120 miles per hour. The Agency Cadillac was less than ten yards behind him.

Danny exited the bridge and began to cross Mercer Island at close to 140 miles per hour. The Cadillac ripped along behind him, steady as a rock. The Jag was getting fussy in the driving rain. Danny dropped his speed to 120. The Caddie pulled out and screamed past him, narrowly missing the Jag's long front end before slowing and dropping back. Point made. The Caddie could run with the Jag all night long.

At the east end of Mercer Island lies the East Channel Bridge, a short, quarter-mile span. The Jag and the Caddie crossed it side by side. Danny looked across the two feet between the vehicles as they raced. The Soundman waved at him, a cigar clenched in his teeth. Danny now remembered him vividly. But it was going to be very difficult to throw him off this bus.

The Caddie nudged closer to the Jag, occasionally bumping the lighter car, until finally, the Jag fishtailed down the highway, doing a complete spin before righting itself miraculously and heading east, still at 120 miles per hour. The Soundman pounded the Caddie's steering wheel in sheer delight. The rain beat down harder than ever.

Ten miles west of Issaquah, the Jag went into a sideways slide, skidding down the highway at 100 miles per hour. When Danny finally got it stopped, he was headed west, as the Caddie roared by him, still headed east. Danny rocketed the Jag westward, toward Seattle. By the time the Caddie had turned around, two miles separated the cars. Bob the Soundman got it together and headed west after Danny. As he sped along, he was startled to see the Jag parked at the side of the road, the door open. He slammed on the brakes, pumping quickly to keep the heavy car in the center of the roadway. He rushed past the parked Jaguar at 80 miles per hour, sliding 400 yards before righting the car and turning back east, flicking on his high beams. Danny Wood was standing in the middle of the road, hands at his side. Toro...eh...Toro! Danny stepped nimbly out of the way as the Caddie flashed by and slowed, turning to make another run.

The Caddie picked up speed, closing the gap rapidly as the high beams picked Danny from the surrounding gloom. The Soundman bit through his cigar as he aimed the Caddie's snout at the rain-soaked apparition in he middle of the highway. Then Danny extended his arms, and a winking light went on milliseconds before the Caddie's windshield shattered into

Bob's face and lap. The Cadillac slid sideways as it went past Danny, its tires clutching at the road. Bob the Soundman let out a high pitched scream as he came abreast of Danny and saw the gun wink again before four 120-grain hollow-point bullets stitched across his neck and separated his head from his body. The car slid off the highway and bounced over and over down a steep embankment before exploding in a crackling fireball. The fireball grew smaller and more fragmented as it rocketed into a stand of fir trees 400 yards down the highway and 100 yards down the embankment. They would never find his head.

At 3:45 A.M. Danny rolled slowly past the Squak Mountain Motel in Issaquah, Washington, headed for the locked gate that led to the mountain itself. Tinker, sound asleep, was the last surviving member of his section. A commanding officer without a command.

The Jaguar bumped along the graveled back road, its lights cutting through the murky night and falling across the gate that barred the way to Squak Mountain. Danny stopped the car and walked to the heavy lock that held the three-inch chain closure. The key was difficult to turn, but he finally heard the metallic click of the bolt as it slid back, and he swung the huge steel and timber gate out of his way. After driving through, he relocked the gate and started the Jag up the steep but well-maintained road. Ahead of him, a small herd of deer, standing in the middle of the road, froze in his lights before bounding away.

A year ago, the sighting would have thrilled him. Tonight, they hardly rated a second glance. As he climbed higher, the driving rain turned to sleet and by the time he neared the place on the map Tinker had chosen, it was pure, windblown snow, one of winter's last stabs at the foothills of the Cascade Mountains.

Danny pulled the car off the road, and drove it into a thick stand of trees. He shut it down, lit a cigarette and sat there. He searched his mind and heart for justification for what he intended to do. He was on Squak Mountain to commit murder. For almost two months, Tinker and his men had been trying to

257

kill him. The body count stood at four. Natalie's ordeal was even worse than death in Danny's mind.

Danny began to check over his gear. At 5:30 A.M., he headed up the hill. Behind him, the Jaguar turned white with snow and disappeared.

Tinker was on his second cup of coffee in the same café where he'd eaten the night before, having stowed away a huge bacon-and-egg breakfast. The café closed early at night because it opened at 4:00 A.M., and it was jammed with early rising locals already into their day's work. He was getting very impatient with Bob and Chin, and finally went out to his borrowed Treasury Department car and called the dispatcher, asking if there were any messages for T-One. The dispatcher had no idea who he was, but replied that there were no messages. Could he be reached if there were? Tinker shut off the mike without answering. He was operating in a domestic area that had rules, and he was presently far outside both rules and the Agency charter. He went back into the café for his third cup of coffee.

Danny walked steadily through the falling snow, with only the squeaky crunch of his boots marking his progress. Even though it was still dark at six-thirty, the hills and ridges stood out bleach-white amid the trees, and the road far below him was clearly visible. He finally stopped at a cluster of huge boulders, and estimated he was about 600 yards above the Jaguar, maybe 700 to the flat stretch of road Tinker had chosen. He brushed the snow from the boulder tops, and began to unpack his gear. Thirty feet away, a doe watched him with liquid brown eyes. Danny watched her dark shadow as she hurtled through the underbrush at top speed, marveling at her escape from what she thought was danger.

At six-forty, Tinker backed the Treasury car away from the café and headed toward the mountain. He was agitated. Bob and Chin were no-shows, and he could only handle this two ways. Go alone, or go away.

Going away was out of the question. At seven, he rolled up

to the gate and went through, leaving it open for Danny. When he arrived at the selected spot, he parked the car, turning its nose down in the middle of the road. He got out, leaving the headlights on, and walked to the rear of the car. He opened the trunk and extracted a Thompson .45-caliber sub-machine gun from a case. He left the trunk open and returned to the front seat, switching the lights off, but letting the engine idle, to keep the wipers working on the snowy windshield. In twenty minutes, he wouldn't need the headlights.

Danny watched the sedan climb the hill, level off and then turn around before parking. He watched as a man exited, went to the trunk, then returned to the front seat, leaving the engine running. He couldn't tell how many men were in the car, even with binoculars. He glanced upward, into the lightening sky and the falling snow. Twenty minutes, if that . . .

It was a gray day, but it was finally day. Tinker checked his watch. Eight-forty. No Bob. No Chin. And now, bitterly, no Danny Wood. The gutless bastard. Well, it would be interesting to see what Natalie would do with three men. He was looking forward to it. Tinker opened the door and stepped from the car, removing his hat and running his hand through his hair, the Thompson dangling loosely in his other hand. He bent down and shut off the wipers. The snow had stopped falling. All around him the green, forested hills of Squak Mountain wore a mantle of peaceful white, fresh and serene. He lit a cigarette, idly thinking this particular view would make a hell of a Christmas card.

To Danny, the road looked exactly like Korea. It was an eerie feeling as he centered his binoculars on the dark gray car, surprised to see that it contained only one man. Pointed down and away from him, he couldn't identify who it was in the early morning light. The snow stopped abruptly, and the man got out of the car, removing his hat and scratching his head. The car's exhaust trailed blue-gray smoke into the still morning air. Danny dropped his binoculars and picked up the custom .30-06, snugging it to his cheek and adjusting the 3-to-9 power

259

scope to its highest magnification. He centered the crosshairs on the face as the man turned to look up the hill behind him, walking slowly to the rear of the car. Tinker's face filled the scope. Danny slipped the safety forward to the fire position, hunching over the rifle. It was Korea, and his General had come down the road.

Tinker was not a hunter, and he was not woods-trained. He looked straight at Danny, but saw nothing.

Danny's finger tightened on the trigger. He centered the crosshairs of the scope on Tinker's forehead. Tinker's face dissolved and he saw Natalie's battered face and bruised body, Tinker over her, hurting her. He shifted the gun downward, stopped, and squeezed the trigger.

Tinker heard the roar of the gun after he was hurled against the rear of the car, his kneecap gone and his leg twisted under him where he lay. He scrambled frantically to get behind the car, dragging his useless leg under him, rolling over in the snow to escape what he had not yet realized to be the end. In terrible pain, he used the stock of the Thompson as a crutch to get around the car.

Danny ejected the shell, chambered another, centered the scope and fired again. The roar in the mountain stillness was deafening as unburned powder flashed from the long barrel.

The slug from the second shot tore through the butt stock of the Thompson, blowing it in half, dropping Tinker like a stone to the ground. Blood trailed behind him as he crawled on his belly to the far side of the car. He pulled his .45 from its holster and peered up the hill from behind the rear tire, shifting his body, sticking the gun out in front of him. The pain was streaming red into his gray flannel pants from the knee down.

Danny shifted slightly, watching Tinker's frantic struggle behind the rear tire. He moved a few feet to the right, in full view. He chambered the third round. He could hear and see the .45 as Tinker fired wildly at him. He might just as well have tried to kill Danny with a bowling ball. The rifle recoiled again. Danny sat down and flicked the bolt open, chambering another round.

Tinker had fired six times at Danny, who was standing in a black coat, stark against the white of the snow. Before Tinker could fire a seventh time, a slug tore through his hand, traveled down his forearm and exited just behind the elbow. His gun slid down the road, out of reach. All around the rear of the car, the snow was flecked a rich crimson.

Tinker was screaming now, a steady stream of curses and incoherent babble. The words drifted up the hill. "Wood, I'll kill you. Do you hear me? I'll kill you."

Danny got back up and moved along the hill for 100 yards. He took his binoculars and adjusted them until he found Tinker, clearly visible on the now exposed right side of the car. He trained them on Tinker's face, and was shocked to see a man shot to pieces, but still trying to kill him. Tinker's face was dark with hatred. He clutched a hide-away type revolver in his good hand.

"Danny, I'm all shot up. I have no gun, you know that. Don't let me bleed to death. Come down here, kid. You can't let me die!"

Danny centered the scope on the good wrist and squeezed the trigger.

The impact flung Tinker's hand against the side of the car, sending the gun over the car's roof and into the bloody snow on the other side. Danny walked back to his original spot and gathered up his gear, heading down toward Tinker, the rifle slung over his shoulder. Evans' 9mm swung loosely in his right hand.

Tinker saw Danny as he jumped lightly down onto the road a hundred yards away. The pain vanished, and Tinker began to pull himself up the road even as his strength flowed into the snow. He felt light and comfortable, one yard at a time. As Danny drew nearer, Tinker thought he must have moved a long way. He looked back. His shattered leg was still under the rear bumper of the car. He turned his face away and laid it on the cold snow, looking off into the distance at his Christmas card. The booted feet came into his view just as things grew hazy and dim, black dots behind a sea of red in a space behind his eyes he had never known about. A blue pain slipped softly over his body, and he was cold in a way he'd never been, and the boots walked away, their clean leather smell wonderful and familiar, and then silence rushed at him . . .

Danny stopped by his mother's apartment on his way back to Natalie's. He changed his clothes, leaving everything in his room as it had been. He'd considered burying his rifle somewhere on the mountain, but he decided against it. It would bear no evidence against him, since none of this had ever happened, if he remained silent. There would doubtless be an internal CIA investigation of the agents' deaths, but Danny was now sure Tinker's efforts to kill him were without the Agency's approval or knowledge. He felt safe from further harm. Those few people aware of the Korean mission would do nothing, could say nothing.

With Tinker's death, Danny's mission was over. Only the Marine Corps, which had him listed as absent without leave as of January 21st, could prosecute him. He would go back and deal with that. But he would never reveal a single fact about the Korean mission, or its aftermath. It occurred to him that with a sworn statement, he could provide the information that might topple the present Government of the United States, impeach its President, and destroy the careers of countless Government officials. He could do this except for one hard fact. He believed that killing the Korean General had been the right thing to do.

He left his mother a short note and walked away.

Natalie burst out of the front door as Danny pulled himself free of the Jag, hurling herself into his arms and nearly knocking him off his feet. She was crying and laughing at the same time, her body pressed to his, her hair soft and sweet-smelling against his face, both of them oblivious to the rain as it pelted down on them. "I love you, Danny. Oh, Danny, I love you so!" Her words lifted the weight of the last sixty-seven days, and made him whole again.

Natalie lay in the circle of Danny's arms, her leg tossed over his thighs, her ragged breathing returning to normal after the most intense lovemaking she'd ever experienced, all tied up in shared danger and removed threats and a new-found, deep love that she joyously acknowledged. But Natalie Antonelli was a very perceptive young woman, and she also realized that if this was a beginning, it was also an end.

"What was it like?"

"What was what like?"

"Killing Tinker. Did you feel bad about it?"

"No, I didn't feel bad. I hated him."

"He thought hating him would get you killed, you know."

"Well, he was wrong, wasn't he?" Danny said.

"Yes." Natalie thought about what it must have been like, and shuddered.

"I have to go back to the Marine Corps."

"I know you do, Danny. When do you think you should go?"

"Right away. In the morning."

"All right, if you must. What will happen when you go back?"

"I'm not sure. I guess they will court martial me. But it doesn't matter. They have to, you know. They don't have any idea about all of this, and I can't tell them. I'm just an AWOL Marine. I have to pay for that."

"It's so unfair." Natalie sat up in bed, looking down at him with fierce, sweetly loving eyes. "You should get a medal, not a court martial."

"For what? For killing five men? I don't think they make medals for that. I'm alive. You're alive. That's enough for me, all things considered."

Danny stared at her, his eyes dark and grave, the saddest eyes she'd ever seen. She lay back down, her hands going over his body, her mouth on his throat. "We have so little time."

As Danny and Natalie arrived at the airport the following morning, a small group of men and official cars were grouped in a semi-circle around a gray Treasury Department car on

Squak Mountain. They were viewing what was no doubt a murder. The body, frozen solid in the snow, had been shot to pieces. None of the hits had been fatal. Cumulatively, they had bled him to death.

"Is he one of yours?" asked the FBI Agent.

"Yes, he's one of ours," answered the Western Regional Section Chief of the CIA.

"What do you make of it?"

"Can't say much, of course. I'm sure you understand. We lost another Agent on the highway just down the road yesterday. We believe they were connected."

"What the hell was he doing up here?" The FBI man looked rumpled and upset.

"We believe he met a Russian defector here, or what he thought would be a defector. As I said, we can't say much. We will handle it, of course."

"Well, sure, we understand that. But we'll have to put out something."

"We think we can still nail the defector. We've lost two brave agents. It's personal, you see. And, of course, national security is involved."

"We understand that. Jesus, that was one mean Russian."

"Well, it's what we're up against. The cold war isn't so cold after all."

"If you need us, just call. We'll assist you in any way we can." The FBI man looked very sincere.

"I'll do that. Thank you." The CIA Chief watched the stiffened body of the Agent he now knew as Tinker being loaded into a hearse. His assistant came up to him and both men watched as the gray hearse pulled down Squak Mountain.

"What defector are you talking about, sir?"

"I haven't the slightest idea, John. I don't even know this man, or the other one. But I had to say something, didn't I?" Michael Jordan was sure of only one thing. One hell of a lot of shit was going to need sweeping under the rug.

* * *

264

Danny walked up to the main gate of Camp Pendleton at four o'clock in the afternoon, wearing civilian clothes.

"My name is Private Daniel Gregory Wood. I was with Fox Company, First Replacement Battalion. I'm AWOL, and reporting in."

The MP at the gate, a Corporal, gave Danny a slow look and exited the tiny guard shack. "C'mon, buddy, you just sit in here. I'll call the Provost. How long you been gone?"

"Sixty-eight days."

"Whoo! Sixty-eight days. You're a real bad ass, ain't you?"